東野圭吾

白銀ジャック

実業之日本社

実業之日本社文庫

ランチタイム

1

目覚まし時計代わりにセットした携帯電話のアラームで、倉田玲司は眠りから覚めた。部屋に備え付けの時計は、何日か前に壊れたままだ。

固いシングルベッドから身体を起こし、閉じられたカーテンのほうを向いた。隙間から陽光が差し込んでくるには、まだ少し早い時間だ。

倉田はベッドに座ったままで耳をすませた。聞こえてくる音は何もない。その静けさが、カーテンの向こうに広がっている光景を想像させた。眠りにつく前、細かく固い粉雪が窓ガラスに当たっていたのを彼は覚えている。

倉田は窓に近づき、カーテンを開けた。ガラスには、びっしりと水滴がついていた。傍らに置いてある雑巾で拭いた。

彼の部屋からはホテルの駐車場が見える。駐車場を囲むように白樺の木が植えられている。それらの枝には真新しい雪が載っていて、淡い照明を浴び、きらきらと光っていた。停められた車の屋根に積もった雪の厚みは、優に五十センチ以上はありそうだ。

倉田は思わず拳を固めていた。これでおそらく積雪は二メートル近くになったはずだ。年明け前にここまで積もったのは久しぶりのことだった。シーズンに入ったばかりの頃は雪不足で心配したが、これならば年末年始に訪れる来場者を失望させることはない。

着替えを済ませ、管理事務所に向かった。事務所はホテルの一階にある。倉田の部屋とは廊下で繋がっている。

事務所に行くと、すでに津野雅夫と辰巳豊の姿があった。どちらも濃紺のスタッフジャンパーを羽織っている。二人は早くも会議机の上で図面を広げていた。倉田に気づき、おはようございます、と揃って声をかけてきた。

「おはよう。二人とも早いね」倉田は手を擦り合わせながら応じた。ストーブに火をつけたばかりらしく、室内はまだかなり冷え込んでいる。「雪、どんな具合？」

「ファミリーコースで、昨日から一気に六十センチほど増えてます。三十分早めに作業にかかろうと思います」辰巳が答えた。彼にはゲレンデ整備主任の肩書きがついている。スキーヤーやスノーボーダーたちが快適に滑れるよう、ゲレンデのコンディションを整えるのが彼の仕事だ。

倉田は頷いた後、津野に目を移した。津野は索道部主任だ。

「今日から、ほぼ全部のリフトを動かすことになってたと思うけど、係員は大丈夫だね」

「大丈夫です。昨日から四人を待機させてますし、今日から新たに四人が来てくれることになっています。全員、気心の知れた連中ですから、戸惑うこともないでしょう」

「整備もばっちり？」

「もちろん」津野は胸を張った。

「オーケー。じゃあ、パトロールの連中に見て回ってもらって、雪崩の心配がないようだったら、その方向で進めてくれ」

わかりました、と辰巳と津野は声を揃えて答えた。

それから約二時間後、中央クワッドリフトを皮切りに、新月高原スキー場のリフトが次々と動き始めた。ホテルの宿泊客は、手つかずの雪面にファーストトラックを刻もうと、スキー板やスノーボードを抱えて足早に出ていく。すぐ目の前にゲレンデが広がっているというのが、新月高原ホテルの最大の売りだ。

倉田は防寒コートを羽織り、ゴンドラに乗った。ゴンドラは八人乗りで、全長三三五〇メートルを十分少々で上ることができる。山頂駅からは、コースがいくつかに分

かれており、スキーヤーやスノーボーダーたちは自分の技量や好みに合わせて、様々なコースバリエーションを楽しめる。もちろん、途中にはいくつもリフトがあり、気に入ったコースだけを選んで滑ることも可能だ。

ゴンドラの窓に顔を近づけ、ゲレンデを見下ろした。カラフルなウェアに身を包んだスキーヤーやスノーボーダーたちが、思い思いに楽しんでいる様子を眺めるのは、彼にとって最高の楽しみだった。索道の管理は気遣いが多いし、気象の変化には右往左往させられ通しだが、来場者たちの嬉しそうな顔を見ると、苦労した甲斐があると思える。

倉田が広世観光株式会社に就職したのは二十年前だ。会社はその少し前からスキー場経営に乗り出していた。その代表格が、このスキー場だ。元々は、いくつかの町村が別個に運営していたのだが、それをまとめて買い取り、新月高原スキー場としてリニューアルオープンさせたのだ。経営しているのは新月高原ホテルアンドリゾート株式会社で、広世観光の百パーセント子会社だ。

入社して五年目に、倉田はその会社への出向を命じられた。しかも配属されたのは、ホテル事業本部ではなく、リフトやゴンドラの運行を行う索道事業本部だった。以来、シーズンに入る直前の十一月から五月のゴールデンウィークまで、毎年ここで生活し

ている。おかげで四十歳を越えたというのに、結婚するチャンスに恵まれなかった。

索道部マネージャーに抜擢されたのは六年前だ。社長、索道技術管理者という肩書きも同時についた。リフトやゴンドラを安全に運行する上で、索道事業本部長に次いで責任のあるポストだ。もちろんリフトやゴンドラのことだけを考えていればいいわけではない。ゲレンデ全体が安全で快適なものに保たれるよう管理するのも、彼の重要な仕事だった。

今の生活がいつまで続くのか、彼自身にもわからなかった。いずれは別の職場に移る時が来るだろうと予想はしている。その日が来るまで、どうか大きな事故は起きないでくれと願っていた。

「ちょっとお尋ねしますが」

不意に男性から声をかけられ、倉田は我に返った。彼の向かい側には、男女のスキーヤーが座っている。ゴーグルを付けているので人相はわからないが、年配だということは全体の雰囲気から感じ取れた。二人とも、リュックサックを背負っていた。倉田の防寒服にスキー場のロゴが入っているからだろう。

「スキー場の方ですか」男性が尋ねてきた。

「そうですが、何か」倉田は微笑みかけた。彼はゴーグルを付けていないので、表情

が相手にははっきりとわかるはずだ。

「北月エリアというのは、どこにあるんですか」

倉田は当惑した。あまり訊かれたくないことだった。だが答えないわけにはいかない。

「山頂から、さらに少し登って、北側に進んだところにあるんです」

「登るというのは、歩いてですか」

「そうです」

男性は首を捻り、隣の女性のほうを向いた。「そんなところ、あったかな」

女性は、さあ、というように首を傾げている。

「今シーズンはまだ通れるようにはなってないんです」倉田はいった。

「ははあ、そうなんですか。それは何か理由があるんですか」

「ええまあ、安全上のことです。それで整備が遅れてまして」

「安全確認がされてないということですか」

「そういうことです。御迷惑をおかけして、申し訳ございません」倉田は頭を下げた。

「そうなんですか。それは残念。ほかにゲレンデがあると聞いて、せっかくだから妻と二人で滑ってみたいと思ったんですがね」

「こちらに比べると、かなり狭いんです。滑り降りた後、こちら側に戻ってくるのも少し大変でして」

ああ、と声を漏らしたのは女性のほうだ。

「それなら行かないほうがいいんじゃない？　戻ってこれなかったら大変」

「いくら何でも、戻ってこれないということはないだろう。どっちにしろ、まだ安全確認がされてないんじゃ仕方がない」男性はいった。

すみません、と倉田は改めて詫びた。

ゴンドラが山頂駅に到着した。老夫婦に続いて、倉田も降りた。係員の若者が彼に気づき、「お疲れ様です」と挨拶してきた。

「御苦労様。変わったことはないね」

「問題なしです」

倉田は頷き、出口に向かった。すぐ前を先程の夫妻が歩いている。二人が担いでいるスキーのビンディングを見て、おやと思った。テレマークスキー用のものだったからだ。

男性が、別のエリアに関心を持っていた理由がわかった。テレマークスキーは、ふつうのアルペンスキーと違い、ブーツの踵がスキー板から離れるようになっている。

距離競技で使われるクロスカントリースキーと同じだ。当然滑り方もアルペンスキーとは全く違い、それなりに難しいのだが、雪上を歩く際には非常に都合がいい。したがってリフトがない場所へも積極的に入っていけるという強みがある。男性は、その強みを生かして、未踏の地へも行ってみたいと思ったのだろう。

山頂駅の外では、大勢のスキーヤーやスノーボーダーたちがそれぞれの板を装着していた。スキーヤーは立ったままで簡単に装着できるが、スノーボーダーたちの殆どは座り込んでいる。スノーボーダーが増え始めた頃は、邪魔だという苦情がスキーヤーから多く寄せられた。それでスノーボードの装着場所を設けてトラブルを避けるようにしていたのだが、今では敢えて装着場所を指定していない。何も表示されていなくても、スノーボーダーたちは自主的に隅に寄って装着するようになったからだ。比較的新しいスポーツだけに、ルールが定着するのには時間が必要だったということだろう。

とはいえ、トラブルが全くなくなったわけではない。古くからの常連客の多くが、未だにスノーボードを目の敵にしている。なぜ解禁にしたのかと倉田たちに詰め寄ってくることも少なくない。

本来スキー場はスキーヤーたちのものだ。彼等が楽しめることを前提に造られてい

る。そんなところへ一枚板に横乗りして滑る若者たちが押しかけてきたら、旧来のスキーヤーたちが面白いはずがない。スノーボードは、スキーヤーたちが予測できない動きをする。加えて、ゲレンデでのルールに無頓着（むとんちゃく）な若者たちは、どこででも平気で座り込む。スキーヤーたちから不満の声が上がるのも無理はないのだ。

新月高原スキー場がスノーボードを解禁にしたのは十年前だ。スキー客からの反発は予想していた。それでも踏みきったのは、解禁によるスキー客の減少と、スノーボード客の来場数とを天秤（てんびん）にかけた末のことだった。

その決断が正しかったのかどうか、じつは倉田にはよくわからなかった。スノーボードを解禁にしたことで、来場者が増えたのはたしかだ。もしそうしていなければ、それから十年も営業を続けてこられなかったかもしれない。

しかし一時的な延命措置に過ぎなかったのではないか、という疑問もあった。スノーボードのブームは、期待していた以上には大きくならず、また長続きもしなかった。

新月高原スキー場の来場者数は、ここ数年、ずっと右肩下がりだ。

ゴンドラで一緒だった老夫婦の姿が目に留まった。二人はスキー板の装着を終えると、慣れた様子で滑り始めた。ターンをする時に片方の膝（ひざ）をつく、テレマーク特有のテクニックには、かなりの年季が入っているように見えた。ほかのスキーヤーはもち

ろんのことスノーボーダーたちでさえ、一瞬目を奪われているようだ。

あんなふうに年配になってからも夫婦で楽しむ客が増えれば、スキー場の経営も少

しは楽になるのだろうな——二人の優雅な滑りを見つめながら倉田は思った。

2

焦げ茶色の影が、木の間を縫うように動いていた。目立たない色のウェアを着てい

るのは、たまたまではないだろう。

待ち伏せに気づいたらしく、焦げ茶色の影は急に方向を変えた。速度を落とす気配

はない。そのまま逃げきれると思っているらしい。

根津昇平はストックを使い、アルペンスキーのようにスタートした。斜面を下り

ながらスケーティングし、加速していく。

迷彩柄のウェアを着たスキーヤーが、ロープをくぐって滑走禁止区域から飛び出し

てきた。なかなかの腕前だ。履いているのは、どうやら幅広系のカービングスキーら

しい。昨夜から降った新雪を楽しもうと乗り込んできたのだろう。

根津は滑りながらホイッスルを口にくわえた。相手の背後につき、思い切り吹いた。

彼自身が顔をしかめたくなるほど甲高い音が出る。

周囲の客が、驚いて止まり始めた。彼等に注意を促すのも笛を吹く目的の一つだ。前方のスキーヤーは、まだ観念しない。パトロールごときに追いつかれてたまるかと意地を見せているのかもしれない。

相手のほんの一瞬のロスをつき、根津は隣に並んだ。その横顔に向かって、もう一度大きく笛を鳴らした。

ゴーグルを付けた相手の顔が歪んだ。げんなりしたように減速し、やがては止まった。

「うるせえなあ。わかったよ」吐き捨てるようにいった。二十代前半の若者のようだ。

若者は顎を上げた。

「何がわかったんだ？　自分が馬鹿だってことか？」

「客にそういう言い方していいのかよ」

「ルールを守らない奴は客じゃない」根津は右手を出した。「リフト券は没収だ。そういうきまりだからな。リフト券売り場に、そういう張り紙が出てただろ」

「そんなもの、持ってねえよ。回数券でゴンドラに乗ったんだ」

「じゃあ、回数券を渡してもらおう」

「ない。全部使った」

「嘘つけ」

「ほんとだよ。下まで降りたら帰る。それで文句ねえだろ」

「俺はおまえのことを覚えてるからな。今度やったら承知しないぞ」

「もう二度と来ねえよ、こんなとこ」

ふん、と鼻を鳴らし、若者はスタートした。一刻も早く根津の視界から消えたかっ
たのか、すぐそばの斜面を猛スピードで下っていった。

「根津君」

声と共に、雪面を削る音が背後で聞こえた。根津が振り返ると、藤崎絵留が彼を見
下ろしていた。彼女も根津と同様にパトロール員をしている。

「派手に追っかけてたね。かなり目立ってたよ」

「いいんだよ。ルールを破ったらどうなるか、ほかの客にもアピールできただろ」

「それはいいけど、やりすぎるとゲレンデの評判が悪くなるってことで、また営業か
ら文句をいわれるよ」

「構わねえよ。ルールを守れない連中なんか、来てくれなくて結構だ」

「それ聞くと倉田さん、また悲しそうな顔をするだろうなあ」

「なんでだよ。あの人だって、いつもいってるぜ。お客の安全が第一だって」

「そのお客が来なくなったら意味ないでしょうってこと」

「だからルール違反をする奴のことは客とはいわないんだって」

根津が口を尖(とが)らせた時、トランシーバーから男の声が雑音と共に聞こえてきた。

(聞こえますか。こちら本部)

根津はトランシーバーを手にした。

「こちら根津。　聞こえます」

(ダイナミックコースで怪我人(けがにん)発生。女性のスノーボーダーです。桐林(きりばやし)がモービル

で向かいました。そちら、行けますか)

「こちらの現在地、スラロームコースの上です。すぐに向かいます」

(了解。よろしくお願いします)

トランシーバーを戻し、根津は絵留を見て舌打ちをした。

「怪我人だ。どんな無茶をしたんだか」

「ここはね、幼稚園や保育園と同じ」絵留はストックを握り直した。「ふつうに走っ

たり歩いたりするのが精一杯の子供だらけなわけ。そんな相手に怒ってどうすんの」

そういうなり滑り始めた。相変わらず、見事なストックさばきだ。

「幼稚園ね。なるほど」ひとつ頷き、根津もスタートした。

3

　索道事業本部長の部屋は、管理事務所のすぐ隣にある。倉田がノックをすると、

「どうぞ」と低い声が返ってきた。失礼します、といいながらドアを開けた。

　松宮忠明は、机で書類のようなものに目を落としていた。老眼鏡を鼻の上に載せている。頬が垂れているので、老いたブルドッグのように見える。

「リフトの状況はどうだ？　今日から、すべて動かしているはずだが」その頬を揺らせて松宮は尋ねてきた。

「問題ありません。安全に運行しています」

　倉田の返事に、松宮は不満そうに手を振った。

「そうじゃなくて、客の利用状況を訊いてるんだ。特に第2高速クワッドと第1ペアリフトだ。さっき見たら、どっちもがらがらだったぞ。動かす必要はなかったんじゃないのか」

「いえ、そんなことはありません。その二つを動かさないと、センターゲレンデにあ

る二本のリフトが混雑してしまいます」

「混雑といったって、五分やそこら並ぶ程度だろ」

「それはそうですが、常連のお客様から苦情が出ます。どうしてほかのリフトを動か

さないのかと」

松宮は緩んだ口元を歪めた。

「バブルの頃は一時間だって並んでたんだ。五分ぐらい我慢しろといいたいところだ

な」

「いくら何でもそれは……」倉田は、やんわりと反論する。バブルの頃と比べてどう

するんだと思った。

「まあいい。今後の運行については、今日の数字を見てから考えよう。それより、一

つ急用ができた。明日から修学旅行が入ってることは聞いてるな」

「聞いています。たしか、奈良県の高校だとか」

「総勢二八二名、三日間の滞在だ。スキースクールが開かれるのは明後日からの二日

間だが、使用するコースについては決めてあるのか」

「一応考えてあります。初心者の方にはグリーンコースを使っていただいて、初級中

級レベルの方にはアタックコースの一部を──」

松宮は再び顔の前で手を振った。

「ゴールドコースとシルバーコースを使ってもらうことにした」

えっ、と倉田は目を見開いた。

「その二つを全部、ですか」

「そうだ。何か問題があるか」

「問題というか……あのう、安全上、やはり生徒さんたちの滑るエリアは、ほかのお客様とは分けたほうがいいと思うんです。つまり貸切にしていただくのがベストかと」

松宮は不思議そうな顔で倉田を見上げた。老眼鏡を外し、机に置いた。

「もちろん、貸切だ。ゴールドコースとシルバーコースを借り切ってもらうことになった」

倉田は改めて息を呑んだ。

「一般のお客様は、その二つのコースを通れないわけですか」

「当然だ。貸切なんだからな。別に不都合はないだろ。コースはほかにもたくさんある」

「でも、その二つのコースで、センターゲレンデの三分の一を占めます。特に、初心

者にとって、シルバーコースを通れないのは辛いです」

松宮はゆっくりと首を横に振った。

「午前十時から午後二時までだ。その間だけ林道を通ってもらえばいい」

「一般のお客様が狭い林道に集中すれば、かなり混み合います」

「だから事故のないように、よろしく頼む。これは決定事項だ。こういう客を大事にしていかないと、これからはやっていけない」

倉田は口をつぐみ、俯いた。松宮にいわれるまでもなく、修学旅行という大口の収入源を確保したいがための強引な変更だということは察しがつく。

「私からの用はそれだけだ。君からは何かあるか」

「そうですね……じつは今日、北月エリアについてお客様から尋ねられました。どうしてクローズのままなのかと」

途端に松宮は仏頂面になった。

「安全上、問題があるからといったのか」

「そこまではっきりとは……まだ整備不足だと」

「あのエリアについては上と相談中だ。もう少し待ってくれ。何しろあんな事故が起きたんだからな。こちらに落ち度があったわけではないが、慎重になる必要がある」

「それはわかりますが」

「じつは君には話してなかったが、入江さん親子が、近々こちらに来られるそうなんだ」

その名を聞き、倉田はどきりとした。

「入江さんが？　親子ということは、達樹君も？」

松宮は大きく頷いた。

「入江さんから連絡があった。考えるところがあって、達樹君をこのスキー場に連れてくることにした、とのことだ。もちろん、こちらとしては大歓迎だと答えておいたよ。ホテル側にいって、一番いい部屋を用意してもらうことになった」

「考えるところ、というのは一体何でしょう」

「それは話を聞いてみないとわからん。どっちにしても、あの親子が来るって時に、わざわざあそこをオープンさせることなんかは考えなくてもいいだろう。とにかく君は、現状のゲレンデを安全に運営してくれればいい」

「わかりました」

倉田は頭を下げ、部屋を出ていこうとした。すると、あわただしくノックをする音が聞こえた。どうぞ、と松宮がいった。

ドアを開けて入ってきたのは辰巳だった。手に一枚の紙を持っている。

「倉田さんもこちらでしたか。ちょうどよかった」

「どうかしたのか」松宮が立ち上がった。

辰巳は前に歩み出た。

「ホームページを更新していたら、こんなメールが届いたんです」そういって持っていた紙を松宮のほうに差し出した。

松宮は老眼鏡をかけ直してから、それを受け取った。眉間に皺を寄せ、そこに書いてある文字に目を通した。

その顔がみるみるうちに強張っていった。

4

支柱が四本ほど倒れ、そこに張られていたネットは雪に埋もれていた。しかも一部が破れている。どうやらかなり派手に突っ込んだらしい。ネットの向こう側は新雪だった。この中で倒れたのだとしたら、脱出するだけでも一苦労だったはずだ。それを裏づけるように、大きな窪みができていた。もっともその先は林だから、そこで転倒

しなければ木に激突していたかもしれない。

根津は倒れていた支柱を立て、ネットを張り直した。破れているのはみっともないが、張っておかないわけにはいかない。滑走禁止区域を明確にしておくことは、パトロール員の大きな仕事の一つだ。海外のゲレンデでは、すべて自己責任ということで、スキー場側が禁止区域を設けることは殆どないが、日本ではそういう理屈は通らない。何かあれば、必ずスキー場側の責任が問われる。

何しろここは幼稚園だからな、と根津は藤崎絵留の言葉を反芻した。

ダイナミックコースで足を痛めた女性スノーボーダーは、すぐに病院に運ばれていった。先程入った連絡によれば、骨には異状がなかったらしい。無論本人は安心しただろうが、根津たちもほっとしていた。

柵を元通りにすると、ストックを手にしてスキーを装着した。そろそろ日が傾きかけている。すでにゴンドラの営業は終了しており、ナイターゲレンデ以外のリフトも次々と停止していくはずだった。

スタートしようと思った瞬間、目の端で何かが動いた。根津は林の中へ視線を走らせた。木々の間を誰かが滑っている。そのフォームから察するとスノーボードだろう。

「勘弁してくれよ。日没が近いっていうのに」

根津はあわてて滑りだした。

コースを三百メートルほど真っ直ぐに滑った後、柵を越えて滑走禁止区域に入った。

根津のパトロール歴は五年だが、七歳の時からこのゲレンデで滑っている。どこで待ち伏せすればいいのかは熟知している。

木が、ややまばらになっていたところで彼は停止した。必ずここに現れるという確信があった。

案の定、間もなくスノーボーダーの姿が見えた。濃い色のウェアを着ている。根津はホイッスルをくわえた。ひと吹きし、片手を上げた。

ところがスノーボーダーは速度を緩めることなく、根津のほうに向かってきた。根津は身構えた。体当たりされるような危機感を覚えたからだ。

だが今にも当たりそうになった瞬間、スノーボーダーは雪を弾き飛ばしながらターンした。

根津はその雪を頭から浴びた。

「何だよ、この野郎」

雪を払い、追跡を開始した。スノーボーダーは木の間を抜けていく。深い雪だから、スキーでは追いきれないとたかをくくっているのかもしれない。たしかに鋭い滑りはできないが、この山に関しては自分が誰よりも詳しいという自負が根津にはある。ス

ピードで勝てなくても、コース取りで追いつけるはずだった。

それにしても――。

見事な滑りをする奴だ、と後ろから追いかけながら感心した。次々と迫ってくる障害物をよけつつも、身体のバランスは全く乱れない。これだけの腕前なら、パトロールごときは振りきれると思っても無理はない。

根津は重心を沈めた。滑りのギアを上げた。ここで逃げられるわけにはいかなかった。

ところが相手の速度はそれ以上だ。少しずつ後ろ姿が遠のいていく。

やばい、逃げられる――。

根津が唇を嚙んだ時だった。軽快に滑っていたスノーボーダーが、突然バランスを崩した。まるで床運動でもするように縦に回転したかと思うと、そのまま前方に激しく転倒した。雪煙が上がり、一瞬何も見えなくなった。

根津は慎重に近づいた。何か障害物でもあったのかと思ったからだ。だが見たところ、そういうものはなさそうだ。

雪の上にニット帽とゴーグルが落ちていた。それを拾い上げ、根津はさらに進んだ。

十メートル近く先で、スノーボーダーが倒れていた。全く動かない。

「おーい、大丈夫かあ？」根津は声をかけた。怪我でもしているのかと思ったからだ。

やがてスノーボーダーが、もぞもぞと動きだした。顔を上げ、頭についた雪を払っている。根津はぎくりとした。髪が長かったからだ。

「驚いたね。女かよ」近寄りながら根津はいった。「怪我は？」

「タヌキ」

「えっ？」

「タヌキが横切ったんだ。よけようとしたけど失敗した。くそー、タヌキ、出てくんじゃねーよ」女性スノーボーダーは悔しそうに吐き捨てた。吊り上がり気味の目と大きな口は、いかにも勝ち気そうだ。年齢は二十歳前後に見えた。

「その分だと怪我はなさそうだな」根津は帽子とゴーグルを差し出した。「無茶は困りますね、お客さん」

彼女はふてくされた顔で受け取ると、自分の腕からリフト券ホルダーを外した。

「これでいい？」

根津は首を振った。

「ナイター滑走のできないリフト券だろ。そんなものを没収したって仕方がない」

「じゃあ、どうしろっての？」

根津はため息をついて女性スノーボーダーを見下ろした。

「今度見つけたら、住所と名前を教えてもらう。ブラックリスト入りだ」

「それに入ったらどうなるの？　もうこのゲレンデには来るなってこと？」

「来たいなら、ルールを守れ。それだけだ」

彼女は返事をせず、帽子をかぶり、ゴーグルを装着した。立ち上がって、滑りだそ

うとしている。

「待て。勝手に行くな。俺についてくるんだ」

だが彼女は無視し、滑り始めた。正規のゲレンデに出る方向だった。

後ろ姿を見送りながら、根津は小さく頭を振った。

5

倉田は辰巳と共に、ホテルの会議室に移動していた。津野にも声をかけ、同席させ

ることにした。ホテル側からは、ホテル事業本部長兼支配人の中垣、総務部長の宮内、

そして営業部長の佐竹が顔を揃えている。

重苦しい沈黙がしばらく続いた後、中垣が口を開いた。

「悪戯だろう。そうとしか考えられん」

「私も、そう思いますが……」宮内の歯切れは悪い。

「とにかく、社長がどう判断されるかだな」中垣は煙草に手を伸ばした。ホテルの共用スペースは殆ど禁煙だが、この部屋にはまだ灰皿が置かれている。

倉田は机に置かれたA4の紙を手にした。辰巳がプリントアウトしたものだ。彼は当スキー場のホームページ管理人でもある。

そこに並んでいる文字に、倉田は改めて目を走らせた。悪戯だと思いたい中垣たちの気持ちはよくわかる。その内容は、とても正気の沙汰とは思えないものだからだ。

新月高原スキー場の関係者諸君へ、というのが、その文面の出だしだった。さらに次のように続いていた。

『地球温暖化の影響で世界的に雪不足が起きている中、無事に大量の降雪があり、胸を撫で下ろしていることだろうと思う。しかし温暖化は確実に進行しており、諸君たちの悩みが根本的に解消されたわけではない。

忘れてもらいたくないのは、諸君たちは決して温暖化の被害者ではなく、それを引き起こした元凶だということだ。山から大量の木を奪い、土を露出させ、水の流れを変えた。そうした環境破壊の一つ一つが、昨今の異常気象を生み出しているのだ。

したがって毎年のように雪不足に悩まされるのは、諸君たちの自業自得だといえる。しかしそうした大規模な環境破壊に関わらなかった人間も、異常気象という天罰を受けねばならないというのは、じつに不公平なことである。そこでそれを補うべく慰謝料を請求する。

三日以内に三千万円を用意すること。準備ができれば、ゴンドラ山麓駅の屋根に、長さ一メートル以上の黄色い布を結びつけよ。尚、その様子をライブカメラで確認するので、カメラやモニターの故障などには十分に注意すること。

この指示に従わなかった場合のことを記しておく。

諸君たちを有頂天にさせている積雪量たっぷりのゲレンデだが、その下にはタイマー付きの爆発物が仕掛けられている。まだ降雪のなかった時期に、我々が密かにセットしたのだ。我々は遠隔操作によって、いつどこからでもタイマーを作動させることができる。爆発物の規模については想像に任せるが、雪崩対策としてパトロール隊が使用するようなちゃちなものでないことは断言しておく。爆発した際、周囲のスキーヤーやスノーボーダーがどうなるかは、敢えて言及するまでもないだろう。

三日経っても返事がない場合は取引中止と判断し、我々はタイマーを作動させる。止める手段を我々は持っていな断っておくが、一度作動させると後戻りはきかない。

い。

警察に知らせた場合も、取引中止と判断する。また爆発物は圧雪車の作業程度では爆発しないだけの構造になっているが、ブルドーザーなどで無闇に掘り返した場合にどうなるかまでは保証できない。

我々は降雪前から周到に準備を進めてきた。これを単なる脅しだと思うなら、第4ロマンスリフト十二番目の鉄塔から真東に五メートル進んだところを掘ってみるがいい。そこに埋めたメッセージを見れば、我々の実行力を思い知ることになるだろう。

では回答を待っている。尚、このメールに返信してもこちらには届かない。

埋葬者より』

倉田は思わずため息を漏らした。たちの悪い冗談だと思いたいが、文面を読んでいると鳥肌が立ってくる。淡々とした文章だが、それが余計に犯人の自信のように感じられる。

「降雪前から準備を進めてきたって書いてあるけど、実際にはいつ頃のことかな」白髪頭の佐竹が誰にともなく訊いた。

「十二月に入ってすぐの頃じゃないかと思います」倉田が答えた。「もし本当に爆発物が仕掛けられているのなら、という話ですが」

「どうしてそう思う？」

「犯人の気持ちを考えてみたんです。いつ雪が降り始めるかわかりませんから、犯人としては早めに仕掛けておきたいところです。でも仕掛けた後、なかなか雪が降らないと、発見されてしまうおそれがあります。今シーズンは十二月の第二週から降雪があるという予報が出て、実際その通りに降りました。その後、積雪量が減った時期もありましたが、結局そのまま地肌が露出することもなく、順調にオープンにこぎつけました。つまり犯人にとって、最初の降雪の直前が、最も都合のいいタイミングだったはずなんです」

佐竹は渋面のままで頷いた。

「なるほどな。　雪が降ってこっちは喜んでたが、犯人のほうもほくそ笑んでたわけか」

「本当に仕掛けられていると決まったわけじゃないんだ。そういう言い方はやめておこう」中垣が不快そうに窘めた。

「そうでした。すみません」佐竹は白髪混じりの頭を下げる。

「それ、もう一度見せてくれ」中垣が倉田のほうに手を伸ばしてきた。

受け取った脅迫状を読み返し、中垣は舌打ちした。

「どうせ悪戯だと思うが、それにしても勝手な理屈をこじつけたものだ。地球温暖化がスキー場のせいだなんて話、聞いたことがない。それにこいつは、自分は環境破壊に関わってないなどとほざいているが、誰だって大なり小なり原因を作っている。車に乗らん人間はいないし、電気だって元を正せば石油なんだからな」

本部長の言葉に、宮内と佐竹は頷いている。だが倉田は素直には同調できない。スキー場開発が環境破壊だというのは常識だ。だからこそ、廃業する際には元の状態に戻すよう義務づけられている。

「これ、電子メールで送られてきたといったな。どこから送ってきたものなのか、わからないのか」中垣が辰巳に尋ねた。

辰巳は背筋をぴんと伸ばしたままで答えた。

「警察にいえば、調べてもらえると思います」

途端に中垣の顔が曇った。

「警察に？　君のほうじゃ調べられないのか」

辰巳の眉の両端が下がった。説明が面倒だと思ったのだろう。

「ええとですね、電子メールとかの場合、中継役のような会社がありまして、そこに問い合わせればいいんですが、プライバシーの侵害などの問題で、警察の令状がない

と教えてもらえないんです」

「……そういうことか」理解できたのかどうかは不明だが、中垣は納得した様子だ。

「警察には、いつ連絡しますか」倉田は訊いた。「こういうことは、なるべく早いほうがいいと思うんですが」

「まあ待て。社長の判断を仰いでからといってるだろ」

はあ、と倉田は目を伏せる。現在、松宮が電話で社長に報告しているはずだった。

新月高原ホテルアンドリゾート株式会社の事務所は東京にあり、社長の筧 純 一郎は、ふだんそこにいる。彼は広世観光株式会社の取締役でもあるのだ。

倉田は脅迫文を頭の中で再生してみた。犯人は、警察に知らせた場合には取引中止とみなして爆発を起こす、と書いている。通報を躊躇させる一文だ。しかしこういう場合、やはり警察に連絡すべきだと思った。客に事情を話し、安全な場所まで退避させた後、警察に調べてもらうのだ。場合によっては爆発物の専門家を呼んでもらえるかもしれない。そこまでやっておけば、仮に犯人が爆発を起こしたところで死傷者は出ないし、スキー場側の責任が問われることもない。

ただし、イメージダウンは避けられないだろう。ただでさえ減っている客が、さら

に少なくなるのは確実だ。

中垣が警察への通報に消極的らしいのは、そういうことを計算しているからかもしれなかった。

三千万円か――。

大金ではある。だがこうした事件で要求する金額としては決して大きくない。仮にも企業を脅迫するのだから、億単位の金を考えてもおかしくないはずだ。警察に通報した場合のイメージダウンと天秤にかけさせる狙いかな、と倉田は思った。だとしたら、妥当な金額かもしれない。

ぼんやりとそんなことを考えていると、いきなりドアが開いて松宮が入ってきた。額にうっすらと汗をかいている。

「社長に説明したの?」中垣が訊いた。

松宮は頷きながら椅子に腰かけた。

「さすがに驚いてましたよ。あの社長でも、うろたえることがあるんですな」松宮は中垣に対しては敬語を使う。二歳上だからだろう。

「で、社長は何と?」

中垣の問いに、松宮は腕組みをしてから答えた。

「とりあえず、様子を見よう、とのことです」

「様子？　どういうこと？」

「だから」松宮は机の上の紙を指差した。「犯人が書いてるでしょ。脅しだと思うなら、リフトの鉄塔のそばを掘ってみろって。そこを掘って、何が出てくるかを確認してから、もう一度考えようってことです」

中垣は顔を擦り、そのまま頰杖をついた。

「まあ、そうするしかないかな。この状況じゃあ」

「その結果によっては、社長もこっちへ来るそうです」

「本社のほうには知らせるのかな」

中垣がいった「本社」というのは、広世観光のことだろう。

松宮は首を振った。

「現時点では知らせないとのことでした。こっちでも、必要最小限の人間を除いて、箝口令（かんこうれい）を敷くようにといわれました」

「このことを知っている人間が、ほかにいるのかな」中垣が倉田と辰巳を見比べた。

「いないはずです」辰巳が答えた。「メールを受け取った後、すぐに松宮本部長のところへ行きましたから」

「それはよかった。じゃあ、私か松宮さんの許可なく、ほかの人間には話さないこと。それでいいな」

「あのう」倉田は口を挟んだ。「警察への連絡は?」

松宮は仏頂面を向けてきた。

「今いっただろ。まずは犯人がいってる場所を掘ってみて、それから改めて考える」

「まだ通報しないということですか」

「そうだ」

「じゃあ、お客さんのことはどうしますか」

「客? 客がどうかしたのか」

不思議そうに尋ねてくる松宮の顔を見て、その無神経さに倉田は内心愕然（がくぜん）とした。

索道事業本部長は、このスキー場の安全統括管理者でもある。客の安全について、誰よりも考えねばならない立場だ。

「新幹線などで、爆発物を仕掛けたという脅迫電話があった場合、乗客を一旦（いったん）最寄り駅に降ろします。その上で車内を徹底的に調べて、不審なものは何もないと確認されたら、乗客を戻して運転を再開するんです。そうした例に則（のっと）れば、今回の場合も、悪戯だと確認できるまではお客さんをゲレンデには入れないほうがいいと思うのです

が」

　倉田が話している途中から、松宮の顔が歪み始めていた。中垣の口元も曲がっている。

「新幹線とスキー場を一緒にするわけにはいかんだろう」松宮はいった。「あっちは単なる乗り物だ。調べる範囲が、ほんのわずかで済む。ところがこっちはそうはいかない。不審物が埋まってないかどうか、どうやって調べるというんだ」

「調べられないからこそ、何かわかるまではスキー場をクローズにしたほうが——」

「倉田君」中垣が割って入ってきた。「君は、この種の経験がないのだろうが、客商売を長くしていると、こういうわけのわからん脅迫を受けることもあるんだよ。君が例に挙げた新幹線のようにね。しかし大抵の場合、悪質な悪戯だ。　新幹線にしても、実際に爆発物が見つかったという話を聞いたことはないだろう？　この手のいやがらせを受けた時に大切なのは、必要以上に過敏に反応したりせず、毅然とした態度を取るということなんだ。今ここであわててスキー場をクローズにしても、犯人を喜ばせるだけだ。そんなことをしていたら、真似をする連中が増えて、ますます困ることになる」

「それに」松宮が追いかけるようにいった。「もし悪戯でないとしても、今すぐに爆

破されるわけじゃない。三日間の猶予がある。その間に、じっくりと知恵を出せばい

いだけのことだ。違うか？」

倉田は返答せず、机の表面を見つめた。それをどう解釈したか、松宮は妙に明るい

声で続けた。

「まあ君はゲレンデの実質的な責任者だから心配するのはわかるが、本当の責任者は

私や社長なんだ。そんなに神経質にならず、粛々といつも通りの仕事をこなしてく

れればいい」

何も答えないわけにはいかなかったので、倉田は小さく頷いた。爆発物が埋まって

いるかもしれないゲレンデで、どうやっていつも通りの仕事をこなせというのか──

声を荒らげたいところだった。

その思いを嚙み殺し、彼は顔を上げた。

「ほかの人間には一切話さないことといわれましたが、どうしても知らせておかねば

ならない人間がおります。許可をいただけますか」中垣と松宮を交互に見ながら訊い

た。

松宮が眉根を寄せた。「誰だ？」

倉田は真っ直ぐに見返しながら答えた。「パトロール隊です」

松宮は中垣と顔を見合わせている。倉田は続けていった。

「この山を一番よく知っているのは彼等です。今後、何をするにも彼等の力が必要です。

彼等に隠したままで、この問題を解決するのは不可能だと思います」

6

ボーゲンでゆっくりと斜面を下りながら、根津は周囲に視線を走らせた。ナイター営業が終了してから約二十分が経っている。まだしばらく照明は点っているが、転倒して動けなくなっている客がいたりしたら大変だ。

しかし今夜も、そんな心配はなさそうだった。下まで滑り降りると、リフトの後始末をしている係員に声をかけ、パトロール隊の詰め所に向かった。ホテルの横に小さな二階建ての建物があり、その一階が詰め所になっている。二階はスクールの事務所だ。

このスキー場には十二名のパトロール員がいる。根津が詰め所に入っていくと、殆どの者がそれぞれの作業から戻っていた。

「お疲れ様」装備を片づけていた絵留が声をかけてきた。

「お疲れ。全員、戻ってるのかな」

「キリ君がまだ。リフト下にグローブを落としたっていうお客さんがいたから、探し
に行ったみたい」

キリ君というのは桐林祐介といって、今年からパトロール隊に入った新人だ。スキ
ーの腕前は抜群だが、何かというと皆から雑用を押しつけられている。

「それはまた御苦労なことだな」根津は椅子に腰を下ろし、スキーブーツを脱いだ。
締め付けられていた足が解放される時の快感は、いつものことながら格別だ。

机の上の電話が鳴った。内線電話だ。絵留が受話器を取った。

「はい、パトロール隊本部です。……ああ、お疲れ様です。……はい、ちょっと待っ
てください」彼女は根津のほうに受話器を差し出した。「倉田さん」

根津は頷き、受話器を受け取った。

「はい、根津です」

（あ……忙しいところをすまないね）

「大丈夫です。今、最後の見回りを終えてきたところです」

（御苦労様。じつは、君に話しておきたいことがあるんだ。今すぐ、本部長室まで来
てくれないか）

「それは構いませんが」

（疲れているところを申し訳ない。待ってるよ）

そういって倉田は電話を切った。根津は受話器を見ながら首を捻った。

「何かあったの？」絵留が尋ねてきた。

「わからん。本部長室に来てくれってさ」

「本部長室？ 松宮さんが、また何か変なことでもいいだしたのかな」

経費節減で頭がいっぱいの松宮が、時折無理難題を倉田に押しつけることとは、このスキー場で働いたことのある人間なら誰でも知っている。パトロール隊の人数にしても、松宮の提案によってかなり減らされたのだ。

「さあね。とにかく行ってみる」

パトロール隊の装備を所定の位置に戻した後、根津は詰め所を出た。通用口からホテルに入り、索道事業本部長室に向かった。その手前に管理事務所がある。入り口から覗（のぞ）いてみると、索道部主任の津野とゲレンデ整備主任の辰巳（たつみ）が、何やらひそひそと話し合っているところだった。どちらの顔にも笑みがない。一日の業務が無事に終わったのだから、軽口を叩き合っていてもおかしくないところだ。

あの、と声をかけてみた。二人は、ぎくりとしたように根津のほうを見た。

なんだ、と津野が訊いてきた。その表情には余裕がなかった。

「何かあったんですか」根津は訊いた。

津野は辰巳と顔を見合わせた後、視線を根津に戻した。

「どうして？」

「いや、じつは倉田さんから呼ばれたんです。本部長室に来てくれって。それで、お二人が何か御存じかなと思って」

津野と辰巳が再び目を合わせている。その態度は明らかに不自然だった。

「何があったんです？」根津は重ねて尋ねた。

津野は唇を舐めた。

「行けばわかるよ。倉田さんから説明があるだろう。我々も事情を知っているけど、先に話すわけにはいかないんだ」

辰巳は隣で気詰まりそうな顔をしている。根津は自分の体温が上昇するのを感じた。どうやらただ事ではない何かが起きたようだ。

「わかりました。どうも、失礼しました」頭を下げ、事務所を出た。

すぐ隣にある本部長室の前に立ち、根津は様々な想像を働かせた。何か重大な事故が起きたのか。それとも、起きるおそれがあるのか。それがスキー場の過失によるも

のだとしたら、津野や辰巳たちの深刻そうな顔にも納得がいく。

根津は深呼吸をしてからノックをした。どうぞ、と倉田の声が聞こえた。

失礼します、といって根津はドアを開けた。本部長の松宮の姿はなく、倉田が机の

向こう側に座っていた。

「急に悪かったね」

「それはいいんですけど……何でしょうか?」根津は訊いた。

倉田は躊躇うように俯いた。彼の全身には、津野や辰巳たちと共通した、どこか余

裕のない気配が漂っている。

倉田が顔を上げた。その目つきは険しくなっていた。温厚な彼には珍しいことだ。

「これから話すことは、絶対に口外しないでもらいたい。約束してくれるか」目つき

と同様に口調も険しかった。

根津は唾を呑み込んだ。やはり何らかの非常事態が起きたらしい。

「約束します」彼は顎を引いた。

倉田は机の引き出しを開け、中から一枚の紙を出してきた。

「説明するより、これを読んでもらったほうが早いだろう。さすがの君も驚くと思

う」

怪訝な思いで根津は、その紙を受け取った。新月高原スキー場の関係者諸君へ、という書き出しが目に入った。その後に、やけに長い文章が続いている。それを彼は立ったままで読み始めた。

倉田のいう通りだった。そこには、驚かずにはいられないことが記されていた。

「警察に知らせないんですか？　こんな脅迫状が来てるのに？」倉田から会社側の方針を聞かされ、根津は思わず声を荒らげた。

倉田は眉をひそめ、唇に人差し指を当てた。

「大声を出さないでくれ。今もいったように、このことを知っている人間は限られている。外に聞こえたらまずい」

「すみません。でも倉田さん、それはおかしいんじゃないですか。もし悪戯だとしても、こういうのは犯罪です。ネットの掲示板なんかに殺人予告を書き込んだ連中は、たとえ悪戯だとしても逮捕されています。俺は通報すべきだと思います」

「掲示板というのは、不特定多数の人間が目にするだろ？　そんなところに殺人予告なんかを書き込んだら、その時点で世間を騒がせるわけだから、犯罪性は高いといえる。だけど今回の脅迫状は、もし単純な悪戯なら、我々さえ黙っていれば誰も迷惑を

被らない。警察に知らせたりしたら、騒ぎが大きくなって、却って取り返しのつかないことになる」

「そうでしょうか。警察に調べてもらって、悪戯なら悪戯だってことを早く明らかにしたほうがいいんじゃないですか。それに、もし悪戯じゃなかったらどうするんですか。すでにゲレンデの下に爆発物が埋まってるってことでしょ？　それをそのままにして、お客さんにスキーやスノーボーをやらせるわけってことですか。倉田さん、それで平気なんですか。そんなの、倉田さんらしくないですよ」

すると倉田は腕を組み、その両肘を机に載せた。口がへの字になっている。

「君のいいたいことはわかっている。俺だって、それほど馬鹿じゃない。だけど、様々なことを検討した上で、とりあえず警察には通報しないと決まったんだ。君も、その方針に従ってほしい」

目をそらしたままで語る倉田を見下ろし、根津は事情を察した。

倉田も通報しないことには内心反対なのだ。何よりも客の安全を重視する彼が、「とりあえず様子を見る」などという方針を受け入れるには、相当な葛藤があったはずだ。そんな彼を責めるのは酷なことのように思えてきた。

「わかりました。倉田さんがそうおっしゃるなら、俺はもう何もいいません」

すまん、と倉田が呟いた。

「それで、俺は何をすればいいんですか」

倉田が顔を上げた。救われたような表情になっていた。

「まずは明日の朝早くに、犯人がいっている場所を掘ってみようと思う。手伝ってもらえるかな」

根津は脅迫状を読み直した。犯人は、『第4ロマンスリフト十二番目の鉄塔から真東に五メートル進んだところを掘ってみるがいい』と書いている。

「それは構いませんが、ひとつだけお願いしたいことがあります。パトロールの連中には事情を話しておきたいんです。許可してもらえますか」

倉田は厳しい顔で首を振った。

「全員はだめだ。最初は君にさえも話さないことになっていたんだから」

「でも、俺一人じゃ、何をするにも限度があります」

「それはわかっている。君が最も信頼できる者を一人か二人選んでくれ」

「たったの二人ですか。せめて五人というわけにはいきませんか」

「わかってくれ。君の仲間を信用しないわけじゃないが、警察に知らせない以上、このことは絶対に外部に漏らしてはいけないんだ」倉田は頭を下げた。

根津はため息をついた。仕方ないですね。

「わかりました。仕方ないですね」

「すまん。今もいったように、人選は君に任せる」

「そういわれても難しいな。一人は決まってるんですけど」

「誰だ？」

「絵留がいいと思います。女だけど、責任感は人一倍強いし、パトロールの経験は俺と同等です。スキーの腕前に至っては、俺なんか足元にも及びません。まあ、今回の件で、スキーが必要になるかどうかはわかりませんけど」

「わかった。彼女の優秀さは俺もよく知っている。それでいいと思う。あとの一人はどうする？」

「絵留と相談して決めます。それでいいですね」

「結構だ。じゃあ、人選が終わったら連絡してくれ」

「わかりました」

根津はドアに向かって歩いた。だがドアを開ける前に振り返って訊いた。

「倉田さん、もし悪戯じゃないと判明したら、警察に知らせるんですよね」

倉田は即答しなかった。一度目をそらした後、改めて根津を見つめていった。

「当然だ。俺は、そう進言するつもりだ」

「それを聞いて安心しました」根津は口元を緩め、ドアのノブに手をかけた。

パトロール隊の詰め所では、絵留が一人で待っていた。根津が呼ばれた理由が気になっていたらしく、「どうだった?」といきなり尋ねてきた。

「とんでもない話を聞かされた」根津は椅子に腰を下ろした。机の上にウーロン茶のペットボトルが載っている。コップもあるが、彼はボトルを摑んで、そのまま飲んだ。倉田と話しているうちに喉が渇いていたのだ。

「何? 何かトラブル?」

「それ以上だよ。えらいものが送られてきた」

根津は倉田から見せられた脅迫状の内容を、できるかぎり細かく絵留に話した。最初のうち、彼女は椅子にもたれて聞いていたが、そのうちに背筋がぴんと伸びてきた。彼が話し終えるまで、驚きの声を発することもなく、ただ目を見張っていた。

「そういうわけで、今のところは警察を当てにできない。俺たちに何ができるかはわからないけど、とりあえず力を貸してほしい」

締めくくるように根津がいうと、ようやく絵留が唇を動かした。

「今のところはって、それは具体的にいつまでの話?」

「だから、悪戯かそうでないかが判明するまでってことだ」

「でもさ、どうやってそれを判明させるわけ？　爆発物があるかないかってことは、春になって雪が完全に消えるまでは、犯人以外には誰にもわからないんじゃないの？」

「それは何ともいえねえよ。何か方法があるかもしれない」

「そうかな」絵留は浮かない顔で考え込んだ。

「今はそのことを考えても仕方がないだろ。とにかく、明日の朝、犯人がいっている場所を掘ってみる。それで何が出てくるかだ。ただその前に、もう一人の仲間について──」

根津がそこまで話した時だった。ドアの外で何かがぶつかる音がした。

絵留が素早く立ち上がり、入り口に駆け寄ってドアを開けた。

「えっ……何やってたの、こんな時間まで。まさか、グローブを探してたわけ？」驚いたように訊いている。どうやら、外に誰かがいるようだ。

「誰だ？」根津は訊いた。

絵留が答える前に、のっそりと人影が入ってきた。パトロールの制服を着ている。

「すみません」帽子を取り、桐林祐介がぺこりと頭を下げた。「外に立ててあったスキーを倒しちゃったんです」

「そんなことはどうでもいい。——絵留、外にはもう誰もいないか?」

「いないみたい」

「よし、しっかりとドアを閉めてくれ」根津は、直立不動の姿勢でいる新人パトロール隊員に視線を戻した。

桐林は気まずそうな顔で黙ったままだ。茶色に染めた髪の先から滴が垂れている。

「おまえ、俺たちの話を聞いたのか」

客の落としたグローブを探して、雪の中を動き回っていたのだろう。

「どうなんだ。答えろよ」

「聞こえてきたんです。盗み聞きしてたわけじゃないです」絵留がおかしそうにいった。

「根津君の声、大きいからなあ」

根津は鼻の下を擦った。「どこまで聞いた?」

桐林は首を傾げた。「脅迫とか、爆発とか……」

「結構、聞いてるんじゃねえか」

「何も聞かなかったことにします。誰にもいいません。約束します」桐林は固い口調で断言した。

根津は頭を掻きむしった。

「その言葉を信じるしかないかな。絵留、どう思う?」

彼女は腕組みをし、スチール棚にもたれた。桐林を見つめている。

「キリ君なら信用できると思う。でもどうせなら、責任を一緒に背負ってもらったほうが確実かも」

「どういう意味だ」

「もう一人までは仲間を作っていいんでしょ」

彼女の提案を聞き、根津は桐林を見上げた。ひょろりとして見えるが、じつはかなりがっしりした体格をしている。夏はライフセーバーのバイトをしていたという。

「倉田さんに報告するか。もう一人の協力者が決まったってな」根津は立ち上がり、桐林の肩を叩いた。「しっかり頼むぜ」

何のことをいわれているのかわからないらしく、桐林は怪訝そうに首を傾げた。

　　　　7

前日とは違い、アラームの力を借りることなく倉田は目を覚ました。ただし眠ったという実感はなかった。ベッドに入ってからも脅迫状のことが頭から離れず、いつまでも寝返りばかりうっていたのだ。うとうとと微睡むこともあったが、すぐに目が覚

め、そのたびに時計の針を確認するということを繰り返した。

鈍い頭痛を抱えたまま、管理事務所に行ってみた。誰かがストーブの前でしゃがんでいる。辰巳か津野かと思ったが、そうではなかった。その人物はパトロール隊の制服を着ていた。ショートヘアの後ろ姿だけで誰なのかはわかった。

「ずいぶん早いね」倉田は声をかけた。

「あっ、おはようございます」藤崎絵留が立ち上がり、頭を下げてきた。

「事情は根津君から聞いたね」

「聞きました」やや緊張した面持ちで彼女は答えた。「びっくりしました」

「だろうね。世の中には、おかしなことを考える人間がいる」

「せっかく順調にオープンできたと思ったのに、倉田さん、大変ですね。あたしにできることなら何でもしますから、遠慮なくおっしゃってください」

「ありがとう。そういってくれると心強い」倉田は彼女に笑いかけた。

根津が協力者として真っ先に絵留の名前を挙げたことを、倉田は意外には思わなかった。女性だが、冷静な判断力と決断力、さらには大胆な行動力を持っているという点では、パトロール隊の中でも随一だった。大学で法律を学びながら、アルペンスキーでオリンピックを目指したという経歴を持っている。

やがて根津と桐林もやってきた。桐林は今年パトロール隊に入ったばかりというこ
とだが、根津や絵留たちが選んだのだから問題はないはずだった。

「今、ちょうど六時だね。パトロール員が朝の見回りをするのは七時頃だろ？　我々
が例の場所を掘っている間に、ほかのパトロール員が通りかかるってことはないだろ
うか」倉田は気になっていることを根津に訊いた。

「詰め所の黒板に、俺たち三人が倉田さんの手伝いで第４ロマンスリフトの下にいる
ってことは書いておきました。どうして掘ってたのかと訊かれたら、圧雪バーンの厚
みを測る必要があったとか、適当なことをいっておきます。でもみんなで掘ったら、
たぶん一時間はかからないと思います」

どうやら根津は、倉田の懸念を予想していたようだった。

間もなく辰巳と津野も現れた。どちらも緊張した顔つきをしている。

「辰巳君は、いつも通りにゲレンデ整備を始めてください。ただ、第４ロマンスリフ
トの下は、一番最後にしてもらえるかな」

「わかりました」

「じゃあ、行こうか」倉田は辰巳以外の者に声をかけた。

第４ロマンスリフトは、センターゲレンデから少し離れたところに設置されている。

モーグルバーンなどの特殊な斜面に向かうスキーヤーたちがよく利用するリフトだ。

津野がリフトを動かした。パトロール隊の三人が次々に乗っていく。彼等に続いて倉田も乗った。全員がスキーを装着している。

リフトを降りると、十二番目の鉄塔を目指して滑り降りた。夜のうちに少し降ったらしく、雪の感触は柔らかかった。コースは崖と森に挟まれていて、やや狭い。

パトロール隊の三人から少し遅れて、倉田も鉄塔のそばに到着した。スキーヤーやスノーボーダーが衝突した際のことを考えて、鉄塔の根元には黄色いクッションが巻きつけられている。

根津が磁石を取り出し、森のほうを指差した。

「真東っていうと、こっちの方角だな」

絵留がメジャーを使い、鉄塔からの距離を計測した。

「ここがジャスト五メートル」

「よし、とりあえず掘ってみよう」

根津がスコップを雪面に突き刺した。

降り積もったばかりの雪は柔らかそうだが、圧雪された部分に達すると、さすがにスコップの先端が入りにくくなるようだった。それでもパトロール員たちは雪を掘る

ことに慣れている。みるみるうちに直径一メートルほどの穴ができていった。

掘り始めて二十分ほど経った頃、穴はついに地面に到達した。しかもそこにはコンクリート製の溝が設けられていた。排水路だ。

「何かあるかい?」倉田が穴の上から訊いた。

「ちょっと待ってください」根津がしゃがみ込み、排水路から何かを拾い上げた。

「こんなものが置いてありました」

それはビニール袋に入った、直径十センチ、高さ二十センチほどの円筒形の缶だった。倉田はそれを受け取り、ビニール袋から缶を取り出した。蓋はスクリュー式になっている。

蓋を開けようとした時、隣で絵留が息を呑む気配があった。

「これは爆発物じゃないよ」

倉田がいうと、彼女は表情を和ませた。

蓋に手をかけ、捻った。やや固かったが、錆びてはいなかったので、スムーズに開けることができた。倉田は中を覗き込んだ。

その中には電子部品が収められていた。小さな液晶パネルがあり、時刻を表示する数字が不気味に動いていた。

煙草の煙と共に重苦しい空気が会議室内に充満していた。誰も言葉を発しようとしない。口を開いたところで無様な呻きにしかならないことを知っているからかもしれなかった。

だが黙り込んでいては話し合いは進まない。

「どうでしょうか」倉田は二人の事業本部長——松宮と中垣の顔を均等に見ながら尋ねた。

「どうといわれてもなあ」中垣は松宮のほうを見た。「社長は何時頃に着くんだっけ?」

「昼前には着きたいということでしたから、もう間もなくだと……」

「それまでに大体の方針は決めておかないとな。全く厄介なことになった」中垣は忌々しそうな目を机の上に向けた。

そこには倉田たちが雪の中から発見した例の缶と、その中に収められていた手紙と金属部品が置かれている。手紙は無論犯人が書いたもので、その中に収められていた手紙と内容は次のようなものだ

8

った。

『新月高原スキー場の関係者諸君へ

この手紙を無事に君たちが手にしているのなら幸いだ。そのことは、君たちが我々からの最初の通告状を無視しなかったことを意味しているからだ。もし無視していれば、この手紙は壊滅したスキー場の下に埋もれ、永遠に読まれることはなかっただろう。その難を逃れたことを、まずは祝福しよう。

さてすでに気づいていると思うが、手紙と共に小さな装置を同梱した。装置の構成要素は、タイマー、ストロボ、バッテリーとなっている。一見したところ複雑そうに見えるのは、バッテリーの消費を抑える省電力システムを備えているからだ。

本物の爆発物には、これと同等の装置のほか、予備バッテリー、受信機などが付加されている。またストロボの代わりに起爆装置が付いている。いうまでもないことだが、起爆装置は爆薬と繋がっている。

そこで諸君たちにやってもらいたいことがある。タイマーをセットし、装置が正常に動作するかどうかを確認してほしい。もし動作しなければ、我々が埋めた爆発物もまた単なる不燃物に変わり果てているということだ。その場合は、諸君たちは我々の主張など無視し、これまで通りにスキー場経営を続けていけばいい。だがもし動作し

た場合には、君たちのゲレンデの運命は我々が握っているということになる。先日の通告状が単なる悪戯でないことを示すため、このような手順を踏んだ。それでもまだ疑うかどうかは諸君たちの自由である。我々は通告した通りに行動する。

回答を待つ。

　　　　　　　　　　　　　　　　　　　　　　　　　　　　　『埋葬者より』

　文中にある確認テストについてはすでに終わっている。タイマーをセットしたところ、所定の時刻になるとストロボが発光した。根津によれば、それだけの電力がバッテリーに温存されているならば、本物の爆発物に仕掛けられた起爆装置も問題なく動作させられるだろうということだった。彼の実家は建築業を営んでおり、彼自身も冬場以外は建築技師として働いている。発破の知識もあるらしい。

　犯人が、単に悪戯が目的で、これほどの仕掛けを雪が降る前から施していたとは考えにくい。やはり脅迫状の内容は本物で、犯人は本気だと考えてよさそうだった。

　だが倉田からの報告を聞いた二人の事業本部長たちの反応は、予想に反して鈍かった。危機感すら伝わってこない。

　総務部長の宮内や営業部長の佐竹にしても同様だった。ただ苦りきっているだけだ。

「やはり、一刻も早く警察に届けるべきだと思います」煮えきらない態度の上司たち

を見て、倉田は進言した。「犯人は本気です。雪が降る前から準備を進めていたんです。我々は、この缶が埋められていることに今まで気づきませんでした。ということは、爆発物が埋められていてもおかしくないということです」

中垣が顔をしかめ、蠅を払うようなしぐさをした。

「そんなことはわかっている。そう、うるさく騒ぐな」

「でも——」

「倉田君」松宮が、ねっとりと呼びかけてきた。「我々だって、何も考えてないわけではないんだ。そりゃあ君がいうように、何もかも警察に任せてしまえば楽だ。しかしそれが果たして会社のためになるのか、ということも含めて考えなきゃいけないんだ」

「会社のためにはなりませんか。警察に届けるということは」

中垣が、ふんと鼻を鳴らした。

「ほかの者の意見を聞こうか。宮内君、君はどう思う？　倉田君と同様に、警察に届けるのがベストだと思うかね」

指名され、宮内は背筋を伸ばした。

「警察に事情を話せば、間違いなく営業を停止するようにいわれると思います。現在

ホテルに滞在中の宿泊客全員を、ほかの場所に移す必要があります。予約が入っているお客様に対しても、すべて断りの電話を入れることになります。もちろんこっちの都合で断るわけですから、それなりの賠償を求められるでしょう。中には、ほかの宿を手配しろといってくる方もいると思われます。その場合でも、対処するしかありません」

「それは仕方がないんじゃないですか。爆発物が撤去されるまでの辛抱です」

倉田の意見に、宮内は首を振った。

「君は警察というものがわかってない。この広大なゲレンデで、爆発物を探し回ってくれるとでも思ってるのか」

「犯人が逮捕されれば、爆発物を埋めた場所もわかるはずです」

「逮捕されなければどうなる？　犯人が自棄になって爆発を起こすかもしれない。いっておくけど、警察はそれを防いでなんかくれないよ。連中は死傷者さえ出なければいいという考えなんだ。ホテルやスキー場の被害や損失など眼中にない。警察のやることは、皆を避難させて爆発に備えるだけだ。もし犯人が爆破を控えた場合には、警察は、春が来て雪が融けるのを待つだけだろう。もちろん我々に営業許可など出さない。それが自分たちの仕事だと思っている。いずれにせよ、うちは今シーズンを棒に

振るということになる」

「同感だな。で、この事件のことは当然世間に知れ渡る」中垣が後を継いだ。「こういう場合の風評被害は馬鹿にならない。来シーズン以降の経営にも影響してくるだろう。君は、そういうことまで考えた上で、警察警察と喚いてるのか？」

松宮や佐竹も同意見らしく、倉田に威圧的な目を向けてくる。倉田は自分が孤立していることを悟った。

「じゃあ、警察には届けないというんですか」彼は中垣を見返した。

「そうはいってない。警察に届けるというのも一つの選択肢ではある。しかしその選択をした場合にどういうリスクがあるかということも、社長がいらっしゃるまでに検討しておく必要があるということだ」

「ではほかにどういう選択肢がありますか」

「いろいろあるだろう。犯人の指示に従うというのも、その一つだ」

「金を払うということですか」

「場合によってはな。これは一種の誘拐（ゆうかい）事件だ。大勢の人質を取られていると考えれば、金を惜しんでいる場合じゃないだろ」

「その人質というのは、ホテルの宿泊客やスキー場の利用客のことですよね」

「もちろんそうだ」

「では、警察に通報しないとしても、とりあえずはお客さんたちを避難させてはどうでしょうか。その上で犯人と取引するんです。そうすれば、人質の命は守れます」

中垣が、うんざりしたように口元を歪めた。

「何といって避難させる？　地震が来るとでもいうのか」

「それは何か理由を考えなければいけないと思いますが」

「無理だよ。そんなことをしたら大騒ぎになり、警察に気づかれる。それに下手なことをして犯人を刺激したら余計に危険だ。そうは思わないか」

「だからこそ一刻も早く避難を──」

倉田がそこまでしゃべった時、中垣がそれを制するように右手を出した。さらにその手をスーツの内ポケットに突っ込み、携帯電話を取り出した。着信表示を見て、

「小杉君だ」と呟いた後、通話ボタンを押した。小杉というのは社長秘書の名字だ。

「もしもし……ああどうも。……そうかね。……わかった。松宮本部長もそばにいるので、これから一緒に行くよ。では後ほど」電話を切り、中垣は松宮を見た。「社長が到着された。部屋に来てくれということだ」

「わかりました、といって松宮は立ち上がった。

中垣も部下たちを見回しながら腰を上げた。

「私と松宮さんとで説明してくる。君たちはここで待機していてくれ」

よろしくお願いします、と宮内がいった。倉田は無言で頭を下げた。

9

詰め所で根津と絵留が待機していると、上山禄郎が入ってきた。

「どういうことなのかなあ。今日の圧雪、なんかおかしいですよねえ」帽子を脱ぎな

がら首を捻った。

「どうかしたの?」絵留が訊いた。

「ところどころ、圧雪の幅が明らかに狭いんです。いつもなら圧雪するはずのところ

が、全然かかってなかったりする。リフト下とか、特に目立つんですよね。客から文

句をいわれちゃいました。辰巳さんや倉田さんから、何か聞いてますか?」

根津は絵留と目を合わせた。だがすぐに上山のほうを向き、頷きかけた。

「聞いてる。ピステンの調子が悪いとかいってた」

ピステンとはドイツ製の圧雪車のことだ。

「ピステン？　一台ぐらい悪くたって、何とかなるんじゃないのかな」

「俺にいわれても困るよ」

「あっ、そうっすね」上山は肩をすくめた。

「さてと、じゃあ見回りに行ってくるか」根津はトランシーバーを手にし、立ち上がった。

彼が詰め所を出ると絵留も追ってきた。

「仲間に隠し事をしてるのって、やっぱり辛いね」

「仕方ないだろ。倉田さんとの約束だ」

「でも、いつまで隠していられるかな。上山君だって、圧雪のことで怪しんでたし」

「あれは何とかしなきゃな」根津は唇を嚙んだ。

雪の下から犯人の仕掛けた奇妙な装置が見つかったと知り、ゲレンデ整備を担当する辰巳は、たちまち動揺した。爆発物が埋まっているゲレンデ上をピステンで移動することなどできないといいだしたのだ。

彼の言い分はもっともだが、それでは上層部が納得しない。しかも脅迫状には、圧雪程度では爆発しないと書いてある。事実、昨日までは何も知らずに圧雪を続けてきたのだ。

結局、いつも通りに整備は行われることになった。しかし辰巳としては、圧雪をかける範囲をなるべく狭くしたいという思いがあったのだろう。

「ゲレンデを見回ってくる。圧雪をしていないことで危険なようなら、何か考えなきゃいけない」

根津が彼のそばで停止した。

根津がスノーモービルに跨ろうとした時だった。青いウェアを着た一人のスキーヤーが彼のそばで停止した。

「根津さん、藤崎さん、どうも御無沙汰しています」

ゴーグルを外した男性スキーヤーを見て、根津は目を大きく開いた。

「入江さん……いらしてたんですか」

「ついさっき着いたばかりです。まだチェックインもしていません」

「驚いたな。お一人なんですか」根津は相手の背後を見た。

「達樹も一緒です。でもあいつはホテルのラウンジでゲームをしています。ゲレンデには出たくないといいましてね」入江は寂しげな笑みを浮かべた。

「達樹君、ここへ来ることはいやがらなかったんですか」絵留が訊いた。

「じつをいうと、かなり強引に連れてきたんです。親戚にも内緒です。ばれたら、何を考えてるんだと非難されるのは確実ですからね」

根津は俯いた。自分たちが責められているわけではないと思いつつ、後ろめたさは消えない。

「でも、いつまでもそんなことではいけないと思ったんです。今のままでは、あいつはどんなことからも逃げる人間になってしまう。去年、ここで何が起きたのかを、もう一度振り返らせる必要があるんです」

「達樹君に何かあったんですか」根津は訊いてみた。

入江は一瞬ためらいを見せた後、口を開いた。

「この一年、殆ど学校に行ってません。人と接しようとしないんです。精神科の先生に相談したところ、まだ現実を受けとめられないのではないか、ということでした」

「現実、というと？」

「母親が死んだという現実です」入江はいった。「人と接すれば、そのことを思い出さざるをえません。友達の多くは、母親が元気ですからね」

根津は返すべき言葉が思いつかなかった。一年の間、彼等親子は苦しみ続けてきたのだと思い知った。

「入江さん、いつまでこちらにいらっしゃるんですか」絵留が訊いた。

「はっきりとは決めていないんです。ホテル側の厚意で、予定を決めなくてもいいと

いうことになっていますから。といっても、冬中滞在しているわけにはいきません
が」

「どうかゆっくりしていってください。我々にできることがあれば、何でもお手伝い
させていただきます」根津はいった。

「ありがとうございます。今年もあなた方がいると知って、安心しました」そういっ
た後、入江は窺（うかが）うような顔つきをした。「さっき山頂に行ったのですが、北月エリア
へのルートが閉鎖されていますね」

「あ……ええ、現在は閉鎖中です」

「それはもしかすると、例の事故が原因ですか」

根津は絵留のほうをちらりと見た。彼女も気まずそうな顔をしている。

「まあ、そういうことです」根津は答えた。「上の人間も慎重になっているようです」

「そうですか。私の個人的意見としては、そういう問題ではないと思うのですが……。
まあ、スキー場にはスキー場なりの考えがあるのでしょうね。ただ、少し残念だなと
思いましてね。さっきもいいましたように、達樹に現実を受けとめさせるために来た
わけですから」

「入江さんがそうおっしゃっておられたことは、上の者に伝えます」

「いや、それはどちらでも構いません。じゃあ、また後ほど」入江はスキーの方向を変えた。

「お気をつけて」

スケーティングでリフト乗り場に向かう入江の背中を見ながら、根津は昨シーズンの悪夢のような出来事を思い出していた。

その日は朝から雪が激しく降り、視界が悪かった。平日ということでホテルの宿泊客も少なく、ゲレンデはどこもすいていた。

知らせは北月エリアのパトロール員から入った。連絡コースから北月エリアに合流してすぐのところで事故が起きた、というのだった。

その時根津は別の用件で、ゴンドラ山頂駅にいた。本部からの指示を受け、彼はそのまま北月エリアに向かった。

連絡コースは狭い林道で斜度も緩やかだ。雪の量が少ないと、十分な傾斜を作れず、スキーヤーやスノーボーダーたちが途中で止まってしまうこともある。それでもストックを持っているスキーヤーは何とか進めるが、推進力を重力に頼るしかないスノーボーダーたちはどうすることもできない。大抵の場合、片方の足をボードから外し、

その足で雪面を蹴りながら進むことになる。そのせいでこの連絡コースは特にスノーボーダーから評判が悪かった。

だがじつは、その面倒を回避する裏技が存在した。コースが緩やかな上り坂になる手前で、コース外に出てしまうのだ。森の中を少し進めば、新雪に覆われた下り坂が続く。そこを一気に滑り降りれば、北月エリアに到達できるのだ。つまり、ショートカットできるというわけだ。

しかしその方法は単にルール違反というだけでなく、極めて大きな危険を伴うものだった。北月エリアに侵入する際に、斜度の変わり目のせいで、一瞬前方が見えなくなるのだ。そのまま突っ込めば、急斜面を飛び降りるような状態になる。それによって本人が怪我をするのは自業自得だが、問題は、その下に人がいた場合だ。幸いなことに、これまでには一度も事故は起きていないが、一刻も早く何とかしなければならないと根津などは考えていた。

ガスのせいで視界の悪い連絡コースを、根津は慎重にスキーで進んだ。やがて北月エリアに入った。そこから少し下ったところで、前方に人影が見えた。子供がしゃがみ込んでいるようだった。そのそばに誰かが倒れ、スキー板が×印を作るように雪面に立てられている。

根津は、近くまで滑り降りた。子供は十歳ぐらいの男の子だった。　膝を抱えたまま

で、根津のほうを見ようともしない。

「どうしたの？」

　声をかけても少年は反応しなかった。

「パトロールを呼んだのは——」そこまでいったところで根津は声をなくした。　倒れ

ている女性の首から上が、血で真っ赤に染まっていたからだ。　さらに周囲を見渡すと、

数メートル上から、曲がりくねった血のラインが繋がっている。雪が降り続いている

中で、これほどくっきりと残っているということは、出血量は半端ではない。

　根津はあわててスキーを外し、女性の血だらけになった耳に向かって、「聞こえま

すかっ」と呼びかけた。だが女性は、ぴくりとも動かない。　血糊のついていない頰は、

白いというよりも灰色に近かった。

「何があったの？」根津は少年に問いかけた。　しかし少年は俯いたままだ。大きなゴ

ーグルのせいで顔はよくわからなかったが、茫然自失していることは明白だった。

　仲間のパトロール員がスノーモービルで到着したのは、それから間もなくのことだ。

女性はすぐに最寄りの病院に搬送された。だが病院に運び込まれて間もなく死亡が

確認された。頸動脈切断による出血多量が原因だった。

女性の名前は入江香澄（かすみ）といった。夫と息子がおり、前日から三人で新月高原ホテルに泊まっていた。息子の達樹がスキーを始めた二年前から、家族三人でスキー旅行を楽しむようになったという。彼女のスキーの腕前は中級レベルだった。

事故が起きる少し前まで、三人は新月エリアで一緒に滑っていた。北月エリアに行ってみようといいだしたのは夫の義之（よしゆき）で、彼が先導する形で三人は連絡コースを進んだ。

義之はスキー一級の腕前だ。彼が妻や息子よりも少し先を滑り、時折止まって二人を待つ、というのがいつものパターンだった。

異変に気づいたのは、北月エリアに入って、少し滑り降りてからだった。義之は止まって二人を待っていたが、いつまで経っても妻も息子も降りてこない。心配になり、彼はスキー板を外して斜面を登った。

やがて、「おとうさん、おとうさん」と泣き叫ぶ声が聞こえた。達樹の声だった。

義之は雪に足をとられながら、必死で駆け上がった。

達樹の姿が見えた。その傍らで香澄が倒れていた。ようやく二人のそばに辿り着（たど）いた義之は、事態が覚悟していた以上に悪いことを悟った。達樹に事情を訊くと、「急にどこからか人が出てきて、おかあさんにぶつかった」という。それで義之は思い出

した。香澄と達樹を待っていた時、ものすごいスピードで滑り降りていった二人のスノーボーダーがいたのだ。

義之は息子に母親から離れないように告げると、猛然と滑り降りた。約五分後、彼は北月エリアの山麓にあるパトロール隊の分所にコーヒーを飲んでいた。そこでは二人のパトロール員がコーヒーを飲んでいた。彼等は事故のことを全く知らなかった。つまり事故を起こしたスノーボーダーは、そのままどこかへ去ってしまったのだ。

以上の話を聞いた根津は、何が起きたのかを完璧に理解した。連絡コースを使わず、禁断のショートカットを敢行したスノーボーダーが、正規のコースを滑っていた入江香澄に激突したのだ。しかもエッジが頸動脈を切断するという、とてつもない大事故となった。

何ひとつ悪くない被害者が死亡したというのはもちろん悲劇だが、一層根津の心を暗くしたのは、加害者であるスノーボーダーが逃走したという事実だった。たとえ重大な過失を犯したとしても、すぐに救助を求めに行っていれば、まだ救いがある。もしかしたら、入江香澄は助かっていたかもしれないのだ。

スキー場側、すなわち新月高原ホテルアンドリゾート株式会社の対応は早かった。社長の覚純一郎が会見を開き、事故の詳細を説明した上で、当分の間北月エリアの営

業を停止すると発表したのだ。「当分の間とはいつまでか」という質問に対しては、「安全が確認できるまで」と明言した。さらに、被害者から何らかの補償請求があった場合には、誠実に対応していきたいとも述べた。

だが実際には、入江義之がスキー場を訴えることはなかった。事故から二週間後、彼は一人でやってきた。現場に花を供えたい、というのだった。すでにコースを閉鎖してあったので、根津が案内役を務めた。

花を置いた後、スキー場を恨んではいない、と義之はいった。

「コースに問題があったわけじゃないし、事故後の対応が間違っていたとも思いません。あなた方はよくやってくださった。私もそれなりにスキー歴が長いですから、そのぐらいのことはわかります。だからスキー場はもちろんのこと、スキーというスポーツを恨む気にもなれないんです。そもそも妻と出会った場所がスキー場でしたからね」

「そうだったんですか……じゃあ、スノーボードのことも恨んでませんか」

「問題なのは、それをやる人間の心ですからね」そういった後、義之は少し首を傾げてから小声で呟いた。「でも、スノーボードのことは、やっぱり少し恨んでるかな。あんなもの、滑走を許可しなければよかったのにって」

根津は黙ったままで頷いた。義之が恨み言をいいたくなるのも無理はない、と思った。

事故発生後、根津は詰め所に置いてあった自分のスノーボードを片づけた。彼はパトロール員であると同時に、スノーボードクロスの選手でもあったのだ。出場を予定していた大会は、すべてキャンセルした。

この事故は刑事事件となり、警察による捜査が行われた。だが人気の低い北月エリアでの事故だったせいで、目撃者は殆どおらず、手がかりも少なかった。

結局、現在も犯人は見つかっていない。そして今シーズン、根津はまだスノーボードに乗っていない。

10

会議室内の空気は相変わらず重たかった。今は倉田のほかには、総務部長の宮内と営業部長の佐竹がいるだけだが、中垣と松宮が出ていった後は、殆ど会話がない。いやじつは宮内と佐竹は、ひそひそと何やら囁き合ってはいる。だがその会話に倉田を交える気はどちらにもなさそうだった。

この二人に期待しても仕方がない、と倉田は諦めていた。中垣の子飼いで、指示に逆らうことなど最初から念頭にない。

部屋の外で物音がした。間もなくドアが開けられ、中垣と松宮が入ってきた。倉田は宮内や佐竹らと共に背筋を伸ばして座り直した。

「社長と話し合った」そういいながら中垣が席についた。「結論からいうと、犯人の指示に従うことになった。身代金……という言い方が相応しいのかどうかはわからんが、金は明日までに用意する。現金が揃ったところで、脅迫状に書いてあった通りに犯人に回答だ。ええと、どこかに目印を吊すんだったな」倉田に尋ねてきた。

「ゴンドラ山麓駅の屋根に一メートル以上の黄色い布を結びつけよ、ということです」

「そうか。じゃあ、そういう布を用意しておいてくれ」中垣は視線を宮内に移した。

「社長から三協銀行の支店に連絡してもらうことになった。悪いが、準備ができ次第、君が支店まで現金を取りに行ってくれ」

「わかりました。三千万円ですか。少々、緊張しますね」

「ふつうの旅行鞄に入るだろう。──来月には例のクロス大会が控えている。それまでには片を付けようというのが社長のお考えだ」中垣は皆を見回した。

「クロス大会……それがありましたね」佐竹が呟く。

「コースを造るには、雪を掘り返す必要があるだろう。工事に取りかかれない。大会期間中は、すでにホテルも予約がいっぱいになっている。中止なんてことになったら、大損害だからな」

クロス大会というのは、毎年行われているスキークロス及びスノーボードクロス大会のことだ。国内外のトッププレーヤーが勢揃いして技を競い合うだけでなく、一般参加者によるレースも行われる。このスキー場にとって、シーズン最大のイベントだ。

「じゃあ、そういうことでよろしく頼む」中垣は再び立ち上がった。

「あの……」倉田はいった。「社長と話し合われたのは、そのことだけですか。警察に届けるかどうかということについては、何もおっしゃってないんですか」

中垣は露骨に仏頂面を作った。

「もちろん話し合ったよ。その上で、これがベストということになったんだ」

「これ、というのは、警察に届けずに犯人の指示に従うってことですか」

「そういうことだ。今まで何を聞いてたんだ」

「待ってください。金を用意して犯人の指示に従う、ということについては異論はありません。でも、それでもやはり警察には届けるべきです」

中垣は横を向き、蠅を払うように掌をひらひらさせた。

「社長と十分に話し合って決めたことだ。文句をいうな」

「スキー場をクローズにもしないわけですか」

「しつこいぞ」

「しかし……」倉田は松宮のほうを見た。だが松宮も気まずそうに目をそらすだけだ。

中垣は部屋を出ていった。宮内と佐竹もそれに続く。

「爆弾の埋まったゲレンデを、お客さんに滑らせるなんて……」倉田は呻いた。

「本当にあるかどうかはわからんだろう」松宮がいった。「たしかにおかしな装置は埋まっていたが、実際に犯人が爆弾を埋めたとはかぎらない」

「それは本部長、雪崩のおそれはあるけれど、実際に起きるかどうかはわからない、といってるのと同じことです」

返す言葉がなかったのか、松宮の口がへの字に結ばれた。

失礼します、といって倉田は部屋を出た。廊下を足早に進んだ。社長室に乗り込むつもりだった。

だがその必要はなかった。フロント前にあるロビーに、社長の筧純一郎と秘書の小杉友彦の姿があったからだ。筧が何やら話し、小杉がメモを取っている。

「社長」倉田は駆け寄った。「今、いいでしょうか。お話ししたいことがあります」

筧は、狐を連想させる一重瞼の細い目で、じろりと倉田を見た。

「何だ」

「事件のことです」

「倉田さんっ」一九〇センチ近くある小杉が、咎めるように倉田を見下ろしてきた。

「場所を考えてください。周りにはお客様もいらっしゃるんです」

倉田は、はっとして周囲に目をやった。たしかに小杉のいう通りだった。

そこへ、「どうしました?」と松宮がやってきた。

「倉田が、私に何か文句があるそうだ」筧がいった。

「文句だなんて、そんな」

「倉田君は、警察に届けないのなら、せめてゲレンデをクローズにしてはどうか、という意見のようです」松宮が小声で、ぼそぼそと説明した。

筧は、ふんと鼻を鳴らし、尖った顎を倉田のほうに向けた。

「倉田君としては適切な意見だろうね。私が君の立場でも、同じことを主張しただろう。しかし経営者には、もっと多角的視野が要求される。このホテルやスキー場の経営を脅かすかもしれないことを、おいそれと実施するわけにはいかない。

ここで働く従業員たちに対して、社会的責任というものがあるからね。それとも君は、騒ぎが大きくなっても、ホテルやスキー場には影響しないと断言できるのかね。ある

いは、そうなった場合でも問題を速やかに解決できる自信があるのかね」

「いえ、それは……そんなものはありませんが」倉田は俯いていた。

「だったら、最終決断は我々に任せてほしい。経営というのはね、真剣勝負なんだ。無難で安全な手だけを打っていてうまくいくのなら、誰も苦労しない」

倉田は黙り込んだ。納得したわけではなかったが、反論の言葉が思いつかなかった。客の安全が最優先されるべきだといいたかったが、その客が来なくなったらどうするのかといい返されそうな気がした。

「わかってくれたようだね。じゃあ、いろいろとよろしく頼むよ」そういい残し、笠は歩きだした。大柄な小杉が、まるでボディガードのように後に続いた。

松宮が倉田の肩を叩いた。

「君の気持ちはわかるが、正論だけで押し通すってのは、何かと難しいんだ」

倉田は小さく頭を振った。

「それ、どういうことですか。変じゃないですか。あんなものが見つかったのに。悪

戯じゃないとわかったら警察に届ける、そういう話じゃなかったんですか」根津は唇を尖らせて抗議してきた。

「俺も全く同意見だよ。だけど経営者には経営者の考え方があるらしい」

根津は大きく首を横に振り、「納得いかねえなあ」といって雪面を蹴った。

二人はパトロール隊の詰め所の外にいた。中だと、ほかのパトロール員に話を聞かれるからだ。

「黄色い布、ないかな」倉田は訊いた。「一メートル以上ほしいんだ」

「布じゃないとだめですか。黄色いビニールシートならあるんですけど」

「屋根に結びつけられるのならそれでいいと思う。明日までに用意しておいてくれ」

「わかりました」沈んだ顔で答えた根津だったが、ふと何かを思い出したように顔を上げた。「倉田さん、入江さんが来てることを知ってますか。達樹君も」

「入江さんたちが」そういってから倉田は頷いた。「そういえば松宮さんが、そんなことをいってたな」

「今日、来られたそうです。先程、スキーをしておられました」

「スキーを？　親子で？」

「いえ、入江さんだけです。達樹君はさすがに……」後の言葉を根津は濁した。

「まあ、無理ないだろうな」

「一年経った今も、達樹君の心の傷は癒えてないみたいです。それで入江さん、思いきってここに来たんだそうです。息子に現実を受けとめさせる、そんなふうにおっしゃってました」

沈痛な面持ちでいう根津を見て、自分も同程度に暗い顔をしているのだろうと倉田は思った。入江達樹の比ではないだろうが、関係者全員が何らかの形で心に傷を負った出来事だったのだ。

倉田さん、と呼ぶ声が聞こえた。辰巳がホテルの裏口に立っていた。

「ちょっといいですか。お客さんなんですけど」

「すぐに行く」答えてから、倉田は根津のほうを向いた。「じゃあ、藤崎君と桐林君には君から伝えておいてくれるかい?」

根津はため息をついた。

「警察は当てにできない、そういっておきます」

すまない、と顔の前で手刀を切り、倉田はホテルに向かった。

事務所に行くと、丸顔の太った男が待っていた。北月町の観光課長で、岡村（おかむら）といった。倉田を見るなり立ち上がり、毛髪の薄い頭を下げてきた。

「倉田マネージャー、どうも御無沙汰しております。お仕事中、申し訳ありません」

「お世話になっております。ええと、今日はどういった御用件で？」倉田は岡村に問いかけながら横目で辰巳を見る。辰巳がやや困惑しているのがわかる。

「じつは、町長や副町長も一緒なんです。こちらの社長さんが来ておられるという話を伺ったので、是非御挨拶をと思い、やってきた次第です。今二人は、社長室で社長さんや松宮本部長らと会っているはずです。私は、現場の方々にしっかりお願いしておけと命じられまして……」

「ははあ」

もしや事件のことを知って飛んできたのかと思ったが、どうやらそうではなさそうだ。岡村たちの目的を倉田は察した。

「北月エリアのことですか」

はい、と岡村は深刻そうに答えた。

「積雪量は十分ですし、そろそろ考えていただけないか、ということです。このままオープンしていただけないとなると、うちの町は干上がってしまいます。旅館も民宿も、まだ殆ど予約が入ってないんですよ。飲食店だって、どこも開店休業状態でし
て」

倉田は目を伏せ、黙って頷いた。北月エリアを下ったところにある小さな町だ。この北月町は、山の反対側に位置している。北月エリセスが悪く、過疎化も進んでいる。主な産業といえばやはり観光だが、売りは温泉とスキー場ぐらいしかない。ところが北月エリアがクローズのままだと、スキー場利用客が不便な北月町に泊まる理由がなくなってしまうのだ。

「どうか、前向きに検討していただけませんでしょうか」岡村は悲愴な声でいった。

「お気持ちは大変よくわかります。個人的には、早くオープンしたい気持ちはあります。ただ、ああした事故が起きた以上、上の者たちが慎重になってしまうのも当然だと思います。我々はゴーサインが出次第動ける準備はしておきます。ですから、それまでお待ちください、としか申し上げようがありません」倉田は慎重に言葉を選んだ。

岡村は無念そうに口元を曲げた。

「事故といっても、スキー場が悪いわけじゃないのに……」

「それはそうなんですが」

倉田は複雑な気持ちになった。入江親子が来ていると聞いた直後に、こんな陳情を受けている。多くの人間を不幸にした事故、いや事件だった。あの時のスノーボーダ

ーは、今どこで何をしているのか。

不意に岡村が、はっとしたような顔で入り口を見た。それにつられて倉田が振り向くと、町長の増淵が入ってくるところだった。副町長の長井も後からついてくる。倉田はどちらとも面識がある。

「これはどうもお久しぶりです」倉田は頭を下げた。

「お元気そうで何より。ホテルも繁盛しているようでよかったですね」増淵は目尻の下がった顔で笑いかけてきた。

「ありがとうございます」

「おかげさまで、という言葉はさすがに付け足せなかった。

「町長、あちらのほうはいかがでしたか」岡村が訊いた。

うん、と増淵は薄く笑った。

「こちらの実情を話してはおいた。とりあえず考えてくださるようだ。いつから、という回答は貰えなかったがね」

「そうですか」岡村は肩を落とした。

「仕方がない。辛抱強く待つとしましょう。──では倉田さん、いずれまた」

「いつでもどうぞ」

増淵たちが出ていくと、辰巳が近づいてきた。

「社長や松宮本部長にしてみれば、今は北月エリアのオープンどころじゃないでしょうね。元々、お荷物ゲレンデだし」辰巳は倉田の耳元で囁いた。周りには、脅迫状のことを知らない職員が何人もいる。

だろうな、と倉田も小声で答えた。

広世観光が、このスキー場のリニューアルオープンを計画した際、現在の北月エリアにあたる北月町スキー場については買収しない方針だった。利用者が少なく、運営費や維持費とのバランスを考えた場合、メリットがないと判断したからだ。だがそうなれば、北月町スキー場だけが統一リフト券を使えないことになり孤立してしまう。北月町に同情したほかの町村は、一致団結して、すべてのスキー場を買い取らないのならば買収に応じないと主張した。結局、広世観光は北月町スキー場も買い取ることにした。しかし経緯が経緯だけに、北月エリアに対する経営者たちの思い入れは元々薄い。辰巳が「お荷物」といった裏には、こうした事情があった。

「ところで倉田さん、さっき天気予報を確認したら、今夜から朝にかけて、かなりの降雪があるようなんです」辰巳が心配顔でいった。「明日の圧雪、どうしましょう」

倉田は思わず唸った。爆発物が埋まっているかもしれないゲレンデを圧雪すること。当然のことではあるが、圧雪をしないわけにはいかない。辰巳は不安を覚えているのだ。爆発物が埋まっているかもしれないゲレンデを圧雪すること。当然のことではあるが、圧雪をしないわけにはい

かない。ここの利用者には年配のスキー客も多い。彼等は奇麗にグルーミングされたバーンが少ないと不満を漏らす。今日でさえ、いつもに比べて圧雪が手抜きではないか、という苦情がホテルに寄せられている。

「明日の朝、相談しよう。でも、とりあえずは通常通りと思っていてほしい」

「通常通り、ですか」辰巳の表情が不満そうに曇った。

「一応、本部長にはいってみるつもりだ」

はあ、と辰巳は曖昧に頷く。松宮が圧雪をしなくていいなどというわけがない、と諦めた顔だった。

倉田は窓のそばに立ち、空を見上げた。たしかに雪雲の近づく気配がある。皮肉なものだと思った。いつもなら大歓迎の降雪を、今は疎ましく思っている。

11

朝日を浴びて光るゲレンデが見えた途端、ランドクルーザーの中はお祭り騒ぎになった。快人はハンドルを叩いて奇声を発し、後部シートでは幸太が口笛を吹き、足踏みをした。

「すげえじゃん。　思ったより、ずっと広そうだ」快人がはしゃいだ声を出した。

「だからいったでしょ、新月は半端じゃないって。あたし、今シーズンはここを根城にさせてもらうから」そういって瀬利千晶は助手席で足を組み換えた。自分が勧めたゲレンデを褒めてもらうのは、悪い気のすることではない。

「ねえねえ、本当にパウダーを食わしてもらえるわけ?」幸太が後ろから身を乗り出してきた。

千晶は親指を立てた。

「それはばっちり。この前に下見して、最高のパウダーゾーンを見つけといた。ちょっと厄介な場所だけど、あんたらなら楽勝で滑れる。さっきまでずっと降ってみたいだし、この分なら一番乗りは確実だし、期待していいよ」

幸太は、ばんばんとシートの背もたれを叩いた。

「聞いたかよ、兄貴。千晶ねえちゃんがいうなら確かだ。興奮するねえ」

「ああ、一秒でも早く滑りてえよ。だけどさあ千晶、そのパウダーゾーン、どうせコース外だろ。大丈夫なのか」

快人の問いに、千晶はしかめっ面を作った。

「問題はそこなんだよね。パトロールが結構うるさいんだ。この前も見つかっちゃっ

「てさあ、追っかけられた」

ははは、と幸太が笑った。

「そんなの、別にどうってことないじゃん。千晶ねえちゃんのことだから、どうせ振りきって逃げたんだろ」

「それがさあ、そのパトロール、スキーのくせに結構パウダーを攻めてきやがんの。逃げようと焦ってるうちに、目の前にタヌキが出てきて、吹っ飛んじゃったんだ」

「へえー、千晶ねえちゃんが捕まったのか。珍しいじゃん」

「おいおい千晶、本当に大丈夫なんだろうな。一本滑っただけでリフト券没収、なんて御免だぜ」快人が眉をひそめる。

「平気だって。その時は周りをよく見てなかったんだ。滑る前にパトロールが近くにいないかどうかを確認すれば問題ないよ」

「そうだよ、兄貴。びびんなって」

「うるせえな。耳元で怒鳴るんじゃねえよ」

そんなやりとりをしているうちに、新月高原ホテルの駐車場が近づいてきた。千晶は手首のストレッチを始めた。彼女の心も浮き浮きしている。

快人と幸太は千晶の従兄弟（いとこ）だった。歳（とし）が近いせいで、子供の頃から一緒に遊んでい

る。スノーボードを始めたのも同じ時期だ。ただし従兄弟たちが趣味程度に留めているのに対して、千晶だけは四年ほど前から本格的に取り組んでいる。冬の間は、必ずどこかの山に籠もるのだ。そして今年は、先程彼女自身が口にしたように、すでに新月町の居酒屋で、住み込みのアルバイトを始めている。

駐車場は宿泊客専用と外来者用とに分かれていた。当然のことながら、宿泊客用のほうがゲレンデに近い。快人は不平を漏らしながら、外来者用駐車場にランドクルーザーを止めた。まだ朝の七時半だが、駐車場で着替えを始めているスノーボーダーがちらほらいる。

「やべえ、俺たちも急がなきゃ」

幸太が服を脱ぎ始めたので、千晶は車から出た。彼女はすでにスノーボードウェアを着ている。

きらきらと光るゲレンデを見上げた。まだリフトもゴンドラも動いていない。どちらも八時が営業開始時刻だ。

ホテルの横にある小さな建物から、パトロール員らしき人間が数名出てきた。新雪が降り積もったので、雪崩のおそれのある場所がないか確かめに行くのかもしれない。

黒地に赤のラインが入ったワンピースのウェア、帽子は赤いキャップ、それがパトロール員の制服だ。後で快人と幸太にも教えておこうと思った。

千晶は、先日パトロール員から追跡された時のことを思い出した。待ち伏せされていたことにも驚いたが、林立する木々の間をぴったりと追ってくる技術と度胸にも舌を巻いた。幸太がいったように、彼女がパトロールから追われて逃げきれなかったのは初めてだ。タヌキが出てきたというアクシデントはあったが、余裕さえあれば転倒は免れたはずなのだ。

今度またあいつに会ったら――。

絶対に逃げきってやる、と千晶は思った。

12

根津はライトバンの後部ハッチを開け、それを取り出した。四角いケースから一メートルほどの棒が突き出ており、棒の先端には直径約四十センチの円盤がついている。

「どうだい、これ」根津は絵留と桐林の顔を交互に見た。

「意外と小さいのね」絵留がいう。「金属探知機って、もっと大きいのかと思ってた

「大きいのもあるけど、大体これが標準だと思う」

「俺、それよりも小さいやつなら、使ったことがありますよ」桐林がいった。「海水浴場で、金属片が落ちてないかどうかを確かめるために使うんです。瓶の蓋とかヘアピンとか」

「そういえばワイキキで見たことがある。素足だから、踏んだら怪我するもんね」

根津は舌打ちした。

「ワイキキかよ。優雅なことをいってくれるね。うちじゃあこれを、埋まった配管を探すのに使ってるっていうのにさ」

「そうか。根津君の家って、建築屋さんだもんね」

「どうせ冬場は、こいつも出番がない。そこでまあ、こっちのほうに役立てられないかと思ってさ。本当は、これぐらいの規模のスキー場なら、金属探知機の一台ぐらいは常備しておくべきなんだけど、何しろ本部長がケチの松宮さんだからな」

「ちょっと貸して」絵留は機械を受け取り、円盤の部分を上げ下げした。「結構、軽いね」

「重いと作業が長続きしないだろ」

「これ、どのぐらいの深さまで調べられるんですか」

桐林の質問に、根津は首を傾げた。

「仕様書によれば、最大探知深度は百四十センチってことになっている。だけど雪の中だとどうなるかはわからない」

「やってみればいいじゃない」

「そう思って、二人を呼んだんだ。これから実験してみよう。桐林、スコップを取ってきてくれ。ゴンドラ乗り場に集合だ」そういって根津はライトバンのハッチを閉めた。

約三十分後、三人はゲレンデ中腹のコース外にいた。金属探知機の実験をするためには深く穴を掘らねばならない。すでにリフトやゴンドラは動き始めているので、コース内で作業をするわけにはいかないのだ。

昨夜からの降雪で、五十センチ以上は積もったと思われる。昨日と同じように、まずはスコップで穴を掘っていく。掘るのは桐林の仕事だ。しかし何かを掘り出すのが目的ではないから、さほど大きな穴にする必要はない。

「地面が出ました」桐林がいった。

「よし、じゃあやってみよう」

そういって根津が桐林に手渡したのは、壊れたラジオだった。パトロール隊の詰め所に放置してあったものだ。

金属探知機の実験をする際に重要なことは、探すべき対象はどういうものなのか、ということだった。極端な話、金属部品が全く使われていないものを探すのは不可能だ。

しかし犯人はヒントをくれている。昨日掘り出した装置に同封されていた書面には、次のように記されていた。

『本物の爆発物には、これと同等の装置のほか、予備バッテリー、受信機などが付加されている。またストロボの代わりに起爆装置が付いている。いうまでもないことだが、起爆装置は爆薬と繋がっている』

受信機、起爆装置、そしてバッテリー――これらに金属部品が使用されていることは間違いない。ではそれはどのぐらいの大きさのものか。

携帯用のラジオほどではないだろうか、というのは根津がいいだしたことだ。受信機という意味で、同種の部品が使われている可能性が高いからだ。

二人は同意してくれた。どちらも反論の材料がなかったのだろう。

根津にしても自

信があるわけではない。実際にどんなものが埋まっているのかは、犯人しか知らないのだ。

警察に連絡しないということは、絵留と桐林にも話してある。二人は、一層緊張を強めたようだ。無理もない。警察に頼らないということは、自分たちの責任が増すことを意味している。

とはいえ、一体何ができるだろうかと根津は考えた。ただじっと犯人からの指示を待つだけでいいのか。ほかに何か解決策はないのか。そう考えていて、金属探知機を使うことを思いついた。これでもし爆発物が埋まっている可能性があるかどうかだけでも確認できるなら大収穫だ。

ラジオを穴の底に置くと、三人でその穴を埋めた。穴の深さは一メートル以上はある。

「じゃあ、やってみるぜ」根津は傍らに置いてあった金属探知機を持ち上げた。繋いだヘッドホンを耳に付け、スイッチを入れた。メーターを見つめながら、円盤状のアンテナを動かしてみる。

絵留の唇が動いた。どう、と尋ねているようだ。横で桐林も不安そうな顔をしているる。

根津は、雪面を舐めるように何度かアンテナを動かしてみた後、首を振りながらヘッドホンを外した。

「だめだ。全く反応なし。何も聞こえないし、メーターだってぴくりとも動かない」

「この深さじゃだめだってことかな」

「そうかもしれない」

「もう少し、浅いところに埋め直してみますか」

桐林の提案に、根津は顔をしかめながらも頷いた。

「そうだな。やってみるか。スコップを寄越してくれ。今度は俺が掘る」

「いいですよ。体力だけが取り柄ですから」桐林はスコップを手にした。

その時だった。あっ、と絵留が声を上げた。彼女の視線は、そばの林の奥に向けられている。木々の間を、複数の人影が移動していた。

「面倒臭えな。こんな時に違反者かよ」根津は吐き捨てた。

「どうする？　見逃す？」

「いや、ほかの客の目もある。気づいた以上は追っかけよう。このスキー場はほかとは違うんだ。──桐林は、ここにいてくれ」そういうと根津はスキー板を装着し、滑りだした。

すぐに後から絵留も追ってきた。

「あたしは先回りしてる」

「了解」

根津が答えた時には、絵留の姿は数メートル下にあった。まるでスラローム選手のように、木の間を猛スピードですり抜けていく。さすが、元五輪候補だ。

スキー板の先端が新雪に埋まるのを防ぎながら、根津は林の中を進んだ。やがてシュプールが現れた。スノーボードの跡だ。人数は三人か。

それを追っていくと、間もなく前方からはしゃいだ声が聞こえてきた。茶色のウェア、グリーンのウェア、濃紺のウェア、の三人組だ。

その先の林の切れ目で、絵留が待ち伏せしていた。それが見えたらしく、三人のスノーボーダーは一旦速度を緩めた。だが上から根津が来ていることにも気づいたようで、再び雪煙を上げて滑り始めた。二手に分かれて逃げる算段らしい。茶色のウェアだけが、ほかの二人と違うラインを取っている。

絵留が動きだした。どうやら茶色のウェアに照準を合わせているようだ。根津は二人組を追うことにした。

追跡して間もなく、濃紺ウェアの滑りに見覚えがあることに気づいた。一昨日の夕

方、捕まえた女性スノーボーダーに違いない。性懲りもなく、またやってきたらしい。グリーンのウェアは、彼女に比べると滑りが不安定だ。そちらに速度を合わせているせいか、二人の逃げ足はさほど速くない。

不意に濃紺ウェアの彼女が何かを叫びながらブレーキをかけた。グリーンのウェアは、一度振り返った後、やや速度を緩めつつも止まらずに滑り降りていく。

根津が近づいていくのを、濃紺ウェアの彼女は腰に手を当てて待っていた。

「また君か」彼女の前で止まり、根津はいった。「このゲレンデに来る以上はルールを守れ、といったはずだぜ」

「ごめんなさい」彼女は腕からリフト券ホルダーを外した。「名前もいわなきゃいけないんだっけ」

「そんなの、持ってない」

「身分証を持ってるか」

根津はポケットからノートとペンを出した。

「ここに名前と連絡先を書いてくれ」

彼女はグローブを外し、ノートにそれらを書き込んだ。　根津が受け取って確認すると、瀬利千晶と丸い文字で記されていた。　住所は新月町になっている。　しかも根津が

よく知っている居酒屋だ。

「あの店で働いてるのか」

「そう。先週から」

「仲間と一緒に山籠もりか」

瀬利千晶は首を横に振った。

「籠もるのはあたしだけ。彼等は今日東京から来たばかりの、従兄弟なんだ。お願いだから、彼等は見逃してやって。あたしが誘ったの。しびれるパウダーだから、騙されたと思ってついてこいって。せっかく来たんだから、たっぷり滑らせてやりたい」

「そう思うんなら、彼等を危険な場所に誘ったりするなな。ここは雪崩の起きるおそれがある場所だ」

彼女が俯いた時、根津のトランシーバーから声が聞こえた。

(藤崎です。根津君、応答できますか)

根津はトランシーバーを手にし、スイッチを押した。

「こちら根津、違反者一名を捕まえました」

(こちらも確保しています。指示、お願いします)

根津は瀬利千晶を見た。彼女は項垂れたままだ。

トランシーバーに向かっていった。

「よく注意した後、解放してください。リフト券は没収しなくていいです」

（了解）

瀬利千晶が顔を上げた。

「ありがとう」そういって自分のリフト券を差し出してきた。安堵した表情がゴーグル越しに見える。

根津はため息をついた。

「従兄弟たちを案内してやれよ。ただし、大目に見るのはこれが最後だ。わかったと思うけど、うちのゲレンデはよそよりも厳しいんだ。見つけたら、とことん追いかける」

「そうみたいだね。わかった、もうやらない」彼女はリフト券ホルダーを腕に付け、グローブを嵌めた。

「コース外に出なくてもパウダーを食える場所はある。今度、俺が案内してやる」そういって根津が名乗ると、彼女は驚いたように肩をすくめた。

「それってナンパ？　悪いけど、その手には乗らない」そういうとゆっくりと滑りだし、振り返って手を振った。「じゃあ、またね」

根津が思わず頰を緩めた瞬間、トランシーバーから再び声が聞こえてきた。

（こちら本部です。根津さん応答願います）上山禄郎の声だ。

「はい、こちら根津」

（倉田マネージャーが探しておられます。降りてこられますか）

事件に関することだな、と直感した。おそらく、現金の用意ができたので黄色いシートをゴンドラ駅舎の屋根に吊してくれ、ということなのだろう。たった今緩めたばかりの頰が強張った。

「了解、すぐに戻ります」

ストックを持ち直し、ゲレンデへの最短コースを滑走した。

13

ホテルの前まで滑り降りる途中、ウェアの中で携帯電話が鳴りだした。千晶はボードにブレーキをかけ、尻を落として座り込んだ。グローブを外し、ポケットから携帯電話を取り出した。予想した通り、幸太からだった。

「はい、あたし」

「千晶ねえちゃん、どうなった？ リフト券、没収？」心配そうな声で訊いてきた。

「大丈夫。見逃してくれた。次は許さないっていってさ。あんた、どこにいるの？」

「ゴンドラ乗り場の前。兄貴にも連絡した。もうすぐこっちへ来るはずだけど」

「わかった。じゃあ、あたしもそっちへ行くよ」

電話をポケットに戻し、再び滑り始めた。

ゴンドラ乗り場に行くと、茶色のウェアを着た快人とグリーンのウェアを着た幸太が並んで待っていた。遠くからでも、二人は何となくしょげているように見えた。

「お疲れ」幸太が手を上げた。「ごめんな。千晶ねえちゃん、俺を逃がすためにわざと捕まったんだろ」

「気にしなくていいよ。どうせ快人も捕まってたんだし」

「何なんだよ、ここのパトロールは。あんなに必死こいて追っかけてこなくてもいいじゃねえか。だけど兄貴も、あっさりと捕まっちまったもんだな」

すると快人はゴーグルを頭のほうにずらし、首を捻った。

「びっくりした。スピードには結構自信があったんだけど、へこんだ。直滑降でぶっ飛ばしたのに、先回りされてんだぜ。あのパトロールのスキーテクニック、半端じゃねえよ。しかもさあ、女なんだぜ」

「えっ、マジで？」幸太が話に食いついた。

「そうなんだよ。それでまたびっくりだ。おまけにさあ」快人の口元が緩んだ。「結構かわいいっていうか、美人っていうか、はっきりいって俺のタイプなんだよな」

ぎゃはははは、と幸太は笑った。

「パトロールに惚れてどうすんだよ。何考えてんだ。馬鹿じゃねえの」

「いや、本当に美人なんだって。失敗したなあ。名前ぐらい訊いとくんだったよ」

「フジサキさんだよ」千晶はいった。

「えっ、何だって？」

「フジサキさん。トランシーバーで話してるのを聞いたんだ。下の名前は知らないけど」

「ふうん、そうか、フジサキさんか。もう一回、会いたいなあ」

「またコース外を滑ったら、追っかけてきてくれるかもよ」

千晶は冗談でいったつもりだったが、「いやあ、それはまずいよ」と快人は真面目な顔をして答えた。

「ほかのパトロールが来ちゃったら困るし、フジサキさんが来たとしても、違反が二度目となると印象が悪くなる。俺、嫌われたくないもんなあ」

「だったら、怪我をしたとかいって、詰め所に行けば？　手当てしてくれるよ、きっ
と」

「あっ、それいいかも。だけど、どんな怪我がいいかな。本当に血とか出るのは嫌だ
ぜ。捻挫したふりとかか。でもそうすると、明日以降滑れないし、困ったな」

「勝手に悩んでなさい。行こう、幸太。こんな馬鹿兄貴はほっといて」

千晶と幸太がゴンドラ乗り場に向かって歩きだすと、「待ってくれよ。俺も滑る
よ」と快人も追いかけてきた。

パトロール員に見つかって出鼻をくじかれた恰好だが、ゴンドラに乗ると千晶のむ
しゃくしゃした気分も吹っ飛んだ。眼下に広がるゲレンデは起伏に富み、雄大だった。
晴れてきたので、遠方の連峰もくっきりと見える。

すげえなあ、と幸太が呟いた。

「千晶ねえちゃんは、今シーズン、ずっとここで滑れるわけだよな。羨ましいなあ」

「そう思うんなら、あんたも籠もればいいじゃん。大学は休んでさ」

「そんなことできるわけないよ。今度落第したら、俺、親父から首を絞められちゃう
よ」幸太は自分の首を絞めるふりをした。彼は現在大学二年だが、すでに一回落第し
ている。

「千晶さあ、ここで大会があるっていってなかった？ クロスの大会」来春、大学を卒業する予定の快人が訊いた。

「あるはずだよ。来月。それもあって、今年はここに籠もることにしたんだから」

千晶が今最も力を入れて取り組んでいるのはスノーボードクロスだった。ハーフパイプも得意だが、とにかく先にゴールインした者が勝ちというルールのわかりやすさが、彼女の性分に合っていた。

「ふうん。そのコースって、まだ造られてないみたいだな。どこに造るのかな」

「去年までだと、アタックコースっていう中級斜面を使ってたんだよね。今年も同じだと思うんだけどな」

「アタックコースっていうと、あのあたりか。まだ影も形もないな」

「これから造るんじゃない？ たぶん積雪が増えるのを待ってたんだと思うよ」

「そうなのかな。そんなんで間に合うのかな。だって本番までには、選手たちが練習する日もあるわけだろ」

「意地でも間に合わせるんじゃないの。このスキー場としては最大のイベントなんだから」

快人はゲレンデマップを広げ、外のゲレンデと見比べた。

「まあ、そりゃそうだろうな」快人は頷きながらゲレンデマップを畳んだ。

千晶はゲレンデを見下ろした。大会には間に合わせるのだろうが、コース造りが遅れるのは困ると思った。本番までには下見が必要だし、できるかぎりたくさん練習もしておきたい。

その後三人は、最長が四キロ近くになる新月エリアの様々なコースを、それぞれのテクニックを駆使しながら滑りまくった。パークでは幸太がレールテクニックを披露し、千晶はビッグエアでギャラリーたちの度肝を抜いてやった。スピード狂の快人は、コース脇の雪壁を駆け上がり、180、360といった技を決めた。

「ひいい、もう足が動かねえよう」何本か滑ったところで幸太の泣きが入った。「ギブアップ。休憩しようぜ」

「賛成。俺も限界だ」快人もいう。

「何だよ、男のくせに情けないなあ」

「千晶ねえちゃん、さすががアスリート。参った」幸太がボードを抱え、ホテルに向かって歩きだした。

千晶もついていこうとしたが、快人は立ち止まってゴンドラ乗り場のほうを向いている。その視線の先にはパトロール員がいた。例のフジサキという女性らしい。

「何見とれてんの。マジで口説こうとか思ってるわけ?」呆れて千晶は訊いた。

快人はニット帽の上から頭を掻いた。

「いやあ、口説くのは無理でも、何とか俺が東京に帰るまでに話をするチャンスがないかなあと思ってさ。今シーズンは、たぶんもう来れないだろうし」

従兄の言葉に千晶は驚いた。どうやら本気らしい。いわゆる一目惚れというやつだ。

「しょうがないなあ。じゃあ、あたしが何とかチャンスを作ってやるよ」

「本当? 期待していいんだな」

「いっとくけど、話しかけるチャンスを作るだけだからね。その後は自分で何とかしなよ」

「わかってるよ。おお、燃えてきたぞ」快人は改めてゴンドラ乗り場のほうを見た。

「何?」

「あそこだよ。ゴンドラ乗り場の屋根。別のパトロール員がいるだろ」

快人が指差した先に目を向けると、一人のパトロール員が屋根に上っていた。千晶を捕まえた男性パトロール員だ。

やがて屋根から黄色い帯のようなものが吊り下げられた。長さは一メートル以上あ

りそうだ。風を受け、ぱたぱたとはためいた。

「何だ、あれ。何かの目印か」快人が訊く。

さあ、と千晶も首を傾げるしかなかった。

14

ライブカメラの画像に黄色い帯がはっきりと映し出されているのを確認し、倉田は深い息を吐いた。凍った斜面を後ろ向きにゆっくりと滑り落ちていくような不安感が胸に広がった。もう後戻りはきかない。どこへ行くのかもわからない。

通常は管理事務所に置いてあるホームページ管理用のパソコンが、会議室に持ち込まれていた。操作しているのは、ホームページの管理責任者である辰巳だ。

倉田は自分の携帯電話で、ゴンドラ山麓駅の屋根に上っているはずの根津にかけた。

（はい、根津です）

「倉田だ。大丈夫、よく見えるよ。ありがとう。もう下りてくれて結構だ」

（下りた後、そっちへ行ったほうがいいですか）

「いや、詰め所で待機していてくれ」

（わかりました）

電話を切った後、倉田は後ろを振り返った。松宮と中垣が並んで煙草を吸っている。

二人とも、苦い顔をしていた。

「後は犯人からの連絡を待つだけか」中垣が呟きながら煙草の灰を落とした。「どうやって金の受け渡しをする気かな。直接手渡し、なんてことはないと思うが」

「振込じゃないですかね」そういったのは総務部長の宮内だ。「犯人にとっては、それが一番安全です。他人の銀行口座がインターネットで売買されているそうで、振り込め詐欺なんかでも使われています」

「いや、それはないと思います」倉田はいった。

「どうして？」

「犯人としては、一刻も早く金を手に入れたいはずです。でも三千万円を引き出すとなれば、直接銀行に出向く必要があり、しかも本人確認を要求されますから、様々な意味で危険です。キャッシュカードで引き出すにしても、一日に出せる金額に限度があるので、全部おろすまでに一か月以上かかってしまいます」

「振込先が一箇所とはかぎらないだろう。十箇所ぐらいに分けて振り込ませる気かもしれない。犯人が一人じゃなくてグループなら、手分けして引き出すこともできる」

倉田は宮内の顔を見返し、首を捻った。

「そんなことをするでしょうか。誰か一人でもヘマをすれば台無しですよ。リスクが十倍になってしまいます」

「そうかなあ」宮内は釈然としない顔つきだ。

「そもそも犯人は脅迫状に、三日以内に三千万円を用意しろといってきています。銀行振込で事を済ませるつもりなら、そんな表現を使う理由がありません」

「なるほど、たしかにそうだ」中垣が頷いた。「じゃあ、こういうのはどうだ。宅配便で金を送る。あるいは郵便小包で、どこかの私書箱に送る」

ここでも倉田は頷かなかった。

「可能性は低いんじゃないでしょうか。犯人は、こちらが警察に通報していることも考慮しているはずです。荷物の送り先を警察に張り込まれたら、それでアウトです」

「我々が通報していると考えるかな」

「全く考えないとは思えません」

中垣は黙り込んだ。倉田の意見は妥当だと思ったからだろう。

重たい沈黙が続いた。時折、辰巳がキーボードを打つ音だけが響いた。

「ここでじっと待っていても仕方がないな」中垣が立ち上がった。「私は部屋にいる

から、何か動きがあったら知らせてくれ」

わかりました、と宮内が答えた。

「私もそうさせてもらおうかな。やらなきゃいけないこともあるし」松宮も、中垣に

続いて部屋を出ていった。

地位の高い者たちがいなくなったからか、宮内は足を投げ出すように椅子に座った。

「ふっ、やらなきゃいけないことって、一体何なんだろうね」

倉田は吐息をつき、宮内を見下ろした。

「宮内さん、本当にこれでいいと思いますか。警察に知らせる必要はありませんか」

途端に総務部長はしかめっ面になった。

「そのことはもういいじゃないか。君、社長にまで直談判したそうだな。それは越権

行為だぜ」

倉田は唇を噛んだ。宮内は、現金が用意できたことで、もう問題は解決したように

思っているらしい。だが今後犯人がどう動いてくるかは全くわからない。来場者たち

の安全が保証されたわけではないのだ。

根津によれば、今朝早くに金属探知機を試したらしい。だが残念ながら、爆破装置

を発見できる可能性は低いということだった。

倉田は窓からゲレンデを見た。ありがたいことに賑わっている。しかし今の彼は、来場者が多いほど気が気でない。

スキーをつけた一人の男性が、ホテルの前で佇んでいた。その横顔を見て、倉田ははっとした。

「辰巳君、ちょっと席を外してもいいかな。外に挨拶しておきたい人がいるんだ」

「いいですよ。誰ですか」

「入江さんだ。昨日から来ておられるらしい」

ああ、と辰巳は納得したように頷いた。「わかりました」

「最上階のスイートを提供したそうだ」宮内が感情の籠もらない口調でいった。「タイミングが悪いよな。よりによって、こんな時に来なくてもいいのに」

「御本人たちは何も知らないんだから、仕方がないじゃないですか」

倉田がいうと、「まあそうだけど」と宮内は肩をすくめた。

「じゃあ、何かあったら呼んでくれ」辰巳にそういって倉田は会議室を後にした。

防寒コートを羽織って外に出ると、入江義之は先程と同じ姿勢でゲレンデを眺めていた。息子の達樹の姿はない。

入江さん、と声をかけた。

青いスキーウェアを着た入江が振り返り、倉田に気づいて驚きの表情を作った。

「やあ、どうも」

「昨日、来られたそうですね。根津君から聞きました。御挨拶が遅れて申し訳ありません」

「そんなに気遣ってもらわなくて結構です。ホテル代だって、自分で出すつもりだったんです。あんなにいい部屋を用意してもらって、こっちが恐縮します」

「少しでも誠意をお見せしたいということですから、どうか遠慮なさらないでください。それはともかく、息子さんは？」

入江は口元をかすかに緩め、小さくかぶりを振った。

「部屋にいます。雪の上に出るのは嫌だといいましてね」

倉田は足元に視線を落とした。

「そうですか。やっぱり、なかなか心の傷が癒えないのでしょうね」

「でも、必ずあいつを雪の上に立たせます。滑らなくてもいいけど、きちんと現実を直視させないと。それができるまでは帰らないつもりです」入江の言葉には強い決意が込められているようだった。それだけ達樹の精神状態がよくないということなのだろう。

「わかりました。我々に何かお手伝いできることがあればいいのですが」

「ありがとうございます。根津さんにもそういってもらいました。お言葉に甘えるこ
ともあるかもしれません。その時にはよろしくお願いします」

話している間も、入江の目はせわしなくゲレンデに向けられていた。まるで誰かを
探しているようだ。そのことを倉田が尋ねると、彼はばつが悪そうに苦笑した。

「意味のないことをしているんです。単なる気休めです」

「と、いいますと」

「スピードを出しているスノーボーダーがいると、ついそっちに目がいってしまうん
です。あの時の犯人じゃないか――そんなふうに思って。だけど、見つけられるわけ
がないんですよね。私が彼等を見たのはほんの一瞬で、特徴なんて何ひとつ覚えてい
ません。そもそも、彼等が再びこのスキー場に来るとも思えない。だから気休めに過
ぎないんです。そうはわかっていても、探さないではいられない。無意識に目が動く
んです」

ふうーっと白い息を入江は吐いた。

倉田は防寒コートの下で肌が粟立つのを感じた。その父もまた、一年前の悪夢から解放されてはいないのだ。心の病に苦しんでいるのは息子だけではない。

「泣き言をいってしまいました。どうもすみません。身体が冷えてきたので部屋に戻ります。倉田さん、コーヒーでもいかがですか。御存じかもしれませんが、スイートルームにはコーヒーメーカーが用意されているんです」

いや、と断りかけたが、倉田は思い直した。犯人からの回答も気になるが、入江達樹の現在の様子も知っておきたかった。

「じゃあ、少しだけ。でもコーヒーは結構です。達樹君の顔を見たら、戻ります」

「あいつ、倉田さんのことを覚えてるかなあ」

二人はエレベータで最上階の十六階まで上がった。そのフロアにはスイートルームしかない。

入江に続いて倉田も部屋に入った。暖房の効いたリビングルームでは、電子音が鳴り響いていた。テレビの前で、少年がゲームに興じている。

「達樹、ゲームをやめて挨拶しなさい。倉田さんだ。去年、世話になっただろ」

父親にいわれ、達樹は顔を上げた。一年経ち、身体はずいぶん大きくなったようだ。だが顔立ちは幼いままだった。目は倉田に向けられているが、焦点は合っていないように感じられた。

「こんにちは。元気だった?」倉田は笑顔で問いかけた。

　達樹はコントローラを持ったまま、ほんの少しだけ頭を下げた。それが精一杯の挨拶のようだ。

「何とかいったらどうなんだ。もう五年生だろ」

　父親に促されても、達樹は口を開かなかった。それどころかコントローラを床に置くと、立ち上がって奥の寝室に入ってしまった。

　入江は舌打ちした後、すみません、と申し訳なさそうに倉田にいった。

「私のことは気にしないでください。　息子さん自身が一番辛いはずですから。では、何かありましたら遠慮なくおっしゃってください」

「ありがとうございます」

　ではこれで、と会釈して倉田は部屋を出た。エレベータホールで待っていると、扉が開いて老年の男女が降りてきた。二人を見て、倉田は思わず足を止めていた。二日前にゴンドラの中で話しかけてきた夫妻だったからだ。見事なテレマークスキーのテクニックが印象に残っている。

　老人のほうも気づいたらしく、やあ、と声を上げた。

「あなたもこの階にお泊まり……いや、そんなはずはないな。このスキー場の人だものね」老人はおどけていった。

「常連のお客様に、ちょっと御挨拶を。お客様こそ、このフロアでしたか。御利用、どうもありがとうございます」

老人は手を振った。

「そんなことはどうでもいい。それより例の北月エリアですがね、やっぱり当分の間は開けないんですか」

「申し訳ありません。まだ目処が立っていないんです」倉田は謝った。

「そうなんですか。一度見ておきたいんだけどなあ」老人は残念そうに顔をしかめた。

「あなた、無理いっちゃだめよ。それに、こんなところでお引き留めしたら御迷惑でしょ」

夫人に窘められ、老人は、あっと頭に手をやった。

「そりゃそうだ。どうもすみませんでした」

いえ、といって倉田は改めてエレベータのボタンを押した。老夫妻は、入江親子の隣の部屋に入っていく。この不景気な御時世に、スイートに長期滞在とは優雅な話だと思った。リタイヤしているように見えるから、現役時代に相当な成功を収めたのだろう。

エレベータで下に行くと、倉田は会議室に戻った。宮内の姿はなく、辰巳が一人で

パソコンの前にいた。

どうだ、と倉田は訊いた。

辰巳は首を振った。「こっちには何の回答もありません。たしかに前回はメールでしたけど、今回もそうだとはかぎらないんじゃないですか。電話をかけてくる気かも」

「どうかな。犯人としては、どの番号にかけたらいいのかわからないんじゃないか。公開されているのはホテルの番号だ。そんなところにかけて一般の従業員にまで事件のことが知れ渡るのは、犯人としても望まないと思うんだけどな」

「そうか。それもそうですね」

「とにかく待ってみよう」倉田は辰巳の肩を叩いた。

その後、倉田は通常業務をこなすために管理事務所に戻ったが、何をしていても上の空で、仕事はまるではかどらなかった。クロス大会の日程を組むのにカレンダーをまるっきり見間違えていたりして、却って無駄な作業が増えるほどだった。

倉田は頰杖をついた。クロス大会のことを考えると頭が痛かった。国内外の有名選手を招待しているだけに、いい加減なコースは造れない。素晴らしいレースをしてもらうためには、それなりの準備が必要だ。しかし今の状況では、それが十分にできそ

うにない。

遅くとも、二、三日以内には作業を始めないと——倉田の腋(わき)を汗が流れた。いつの間にか外は暗くなり、ナイター営業が始まっていた。倉田は売店で買ってきたパンと缶コーヒーで腹ごしらえをした。食堂でのんびりと食事をする気分ではなかった。

缶コーヒーを飲み干した時だった。倉田の携帯電話が鳴った。辰巳からだった。

「俺だ。どうした」

「来ました」辰巳はいった。「犯人からの回答です。メールで来ました」

胸の内側で心臓が跳ねた。「わかった、すぐに行く」

倉田が会議室に駆け込むと、中垣や松宮たちも来ていて、皆で辰巳の後ろからパソコンを覗き込んでいた。倉田も急いで彼等の傍らに立った。

辰巳がメールの文章を拡大して表示させた。そこには次のようにあった。

『新月高原スキー場の関係者諸君へ

黄色い帯を確認した。こちらの要求が受け入れられたことを喜ばしく思う。お互いにとって最良の選択だということが、いずれ君たちにもわかる日が来るだろう。例によって、こちらから

指示を出させてもらう。

・ゲレンデ内で通話が可能な携帯電話を用意し、その番号を今回こちらが使用したアドレスにメール送信せよ。ただしこのアドレスは、そちらからのメールを受け取った時点で廃棄されるので、携帯電話の変更はないよう注意すること。

・ホテルの一階売店で五百円で売られている、「Happy-Scene Get!」と印刷された防水ケースに三千万円を入れ、運搬係に持たせよ。運搬係はスキーかスノーボードの経験者であること。

・運搬係は腕に黄色いバンダナを巻き、スキーかスノーボードを用意した後、午後八時三十分までにセンターゲレンデ下のリフト券売り場の前に行くこと。また携帯電話の電源を入れておくこと。

今回の受け渡しは信頼関係が成立していなければ実現しない。諸君たちの動きに少しでも不審なものを感じた場合には、即刻取引は中止する。やり直しはない。我々は爆発物のタイマーを作動させ、その後一切連絡しない。そのような事態を招かないためにも、慎重に行動してもらいたい。

　　　　　　　　　埋葬者より』

中垣が唸り声を漏らした。

「犯人は、直接受け渡しをする気らしい」

「だけど、どうするつもりでしょうね。犯人自身が姿を見せるとは思えないのですが」倉田は首を傾げた。「運搬役にスキーかスノーボードの経験者を指定していると

ころを見ると、ゲレンデ内を移動させるつもりかもしれません」

「でも、と辰巳が振り返り、倉田を見上げてきた。

「この時間だと滑れるゲレンデは限られています」

「それもそうだけど……」倉田は沈黙した。

「ああだこうだいってても仕方がない。とにかく、犯人の指示に従おう」中垣がいい放った。「必要なものを揃えるんだ。それから、肝心の運搬役は誰にやらせる？」

「彼等がいいでしょう。彼等に頼むしかない」倉田は答えた。

「俺がやります」倉田が話し終えるなり、根津は即答していた。会議室に来てくれといわれた時から、そういう用件ではないかと薄々予想していたのかもしれない。

倉田は安堵して頷いた。

「ありがとう。そういってくれると思ったよ。犯人の指示に従っていれば、たぶん危険なことはないと思う。連中の狙いは、あくまでも金だからね」

「くれぐれも、勝手なことをするんじゃないぞ。失敗は許されないんだからな」中垣が威圧的にいった。

「わかってますよ、と根津は中垣の顔を見ないで答えた。

ドアが開き、宮内が入ってきた。右手にブルーの防水ケースを提げていた。売店で売られている、このホテルのオリジナルグッズだ。

「犯人の奴、よく調べてますよ。現金を入れてみたところ、この通りぴったりです」

そういって防水ケースを机の上に置いた。

松宮が手に取り、ファスナーを開けて中を確かめた。中垣にも見せ、二人で頷き合った後、根津の前に押し出した。「よろしく頼むよ」

根津は防水ケースの把手を摑んだ。目を見張った後、ファスナーを開けた。一万円札の束が、ぎっしりと詰まっている。彼もまたファスナーを閉じた。

「犯人はスキーかスノーボードの用意をしろといっている。どちらにする?」倉田は尋ねた。

「スキーにします。今シーズン、ボードにはまだ乗ってないので」

「それを持ったままで滑れるかい」

「もちろん滑れますけど、念のためにリュックに入れていきます」

「それがいいだろうな。あと、これを持っていきなさい」倉田が出したのは携帯電話だった。

「誰の電話ですか」根津は訊いた。

「俺のだ。これなら山頂でも繋がることは確認済みだ。まあ、夜だから山頂まで上がることはないだろうけどね」

すでに電話番号は犯人側に伝えてある。

ドアが開き、辰巳が入ってきた。

彼が机に広げたのは、ビニール袋に入ったバンダナだった。その中の一つを根津が選んだ。売店で買ってきたらしい。いずれも黄色を基調にしたものだった。

「黄色一色というのは見つからなかったので、いくつか買ってきました」

「これがいいんじゃないですかね」その中の一つを根津が選んだ。黄色の地に雪の結晶がいくつも描かれたものだった。

「ウェアはどうする?」中垣が訊いてきた。現在、根津はパトロールの制服を着ている。

「詰め所に自分のウェアがありますから、それに着替えます」

「しつこいようだが、余計なことはするなよ」中垣がいう。「君の任務は、犯人の指

示通りに動くことだ。　指示されてないことはするな。　無事に金を渡すことだけ
が——」

本部長、と倉田が声をかけた。

「根津君を信用しましょう。　今回、彼等はよくやってくれています」

その言葉に異存はないらしく、中垣は難しい顔をしつつも、そうだなといって口を
閉じた。

倉田は根津の肩に手を置いた。

「よろしく頼む」

「任せてください」根津は大きく頷き、自分の時計に目を落とした。　つられて倉田も
時計を見た。　午後八時を回ったところだった。

15

ナイター照明の下、ホテル前のセンターゲレンデは適度に賑わっていた。　リフト乗
り場に長い列ができるほどではないが、乗客が途切れることもめったにない。
夜になって冷え込んできたせいで、バーンはしっかりと締まっているようだ。　スキ

　一やスノーボードのエッジが鋭く氷を削っていく音が、そこら中で響き渡っていた。昼間のうちに十分滑っているはずなのに、この時間帯になってもまだ滑りたいということは、余程の中毒者か、少しでも練習して技量を上げたいと願っているのか。いずれにせよ、空気が冷たいのとは逆に、昼間以上にスキーヤーやスノーボーダーたちの熱気が感じられる。

　根津は腕時計を見た。すでに八時三十分は過ぎている。犯人からの連絡はまだない。

　顔を上げ、ホテルのほうを向いた。真正面の二階に大きな窓がある。九時半まで営業しているバーの窓だ。カクテルグラスを傾けながらナイター滑走の様子を眺める、というコンセプトで作られた店だが、繁盛したのはバブル景気の頃だけで、最近ではお世辞にも流行っているとはいえない。こんなところまで来て、洒落た店で安くもないカクテルを飲みたがる者など殆どいないからだ。酒が飲みたければ、ホテル内にある売店で買って、部屋に持ち込めばいいだけのことだ。そのほうが余程寛げる。

　しかしいつもは閑古鳥が鳴くバーも、今は倉田をはじめ何人かのスキー場関係者たちによって席が占められているはずだった。もっとも酒は注文していないだろう。水かソフトドリンクで渇いた喉を潤しながら、根津の様子を見守っているに違いない。

　根津は周囲を見回した。

　犯人もまた、どこかで彼のことを観察しているるに違いないはずだ。ど

のような受け渡し方法を考えているのか、まるで見当がつかないが、何らかのタイミングを計っているものと思われた。

白い息を吐き、もう一度時計を見ようとした時、携帯電話がウェアのポケットの中で鳴った。根津は素早くグローブを外し、電話機を取りだした。着信表示は非通知を告げている。通話ボタンを押して、はい、と返事した。

（第1高速リフトに乗れ。降りたところで待機していろ）

おそらくボイスチェンジャーを使用しているのだろう。その低い声は、明らかに電気的に加工されていた。

「第1高速だな」

根津は復唱したが、その前に電話は切れていた。彼はホテルの二階にちらりと目を向けてから携帯電話を懐にしまった。犯人からの接触があったことは、今の一連の動作で倉田たちにも伝わったはずだ。

傍らに置いてあったスキーを装着し、ストックを手にしてリフト乗り場に向かった。ナイター営業は九時までだ。最後の一滑りを楽しもうと駆け込んできた客たちのせいで、短い列ができていた。

根津の順番が来た。二人の男性スノーボーダーたちと一緒に乗ることになった。彼

等は友人らしく、楽しそうに滑走技術のことなどを話している。もしかするとリフト上で受け渡しをするつもりか、という根津の予想はとりあえず外れた。

リフトの上からゲレンデを見下ろした。犯人は一体何をさせるつもりなのか。こんな時間にリフトに乗ったところで、ほかの場所に移動することなどできない。このリフトより上は、照明がついていないのだ。

リフト降り場に到着した。コースの脇では、数名のスノーボーダーたちがボードの装着のために座り込んでいた。

根津はゲレンデの隅に移動し、犯人からの次なる連絡を待った。直接やってくるつもりかもしれないと思い、用心深く視線を周りに走らせ続けた。

やがて九時を過ぎた。ナイター営業終了のアナウンスが流れている。リフト乗り場の入り口は閉じられたらしく、無人の搬器が連なるようになった。だがその後で、ぽつんと一人でリフトに乗って上がってくる者がいた。パトロールの制服を着ている。

近づくと、桐林だとわかった。ナイター営業を終了した後、パトロール員がゲレンデを見て回るのは通常の手順だ。いつもは根津の仕事だが、今夜は彼に代わってもらったのだ。事情を知らない者だと、根津に気づいて話しかけてくるかもしれないからだ。

携帯電話が着信を告げた。根津は急いで電話に出た。

（防水ケースを第２ロマンスリフトへの案内板の後ろに置け。　置いたら、　速やかにセンターゲレンデを滑り降りろ。リフト券売り場の前に戻り、　次の指示を待て）

またしても一方的にいった後で電話を切った。

根津は後ろを振り返った。ここから百メートルほど斜めに下ると第２ロマンスリフトの乗り場があるのだが、それを示す案内板がたしかに設置されている。彼はリュックサックから防水ケースを取り出すと、指示された通りに案内板の後ろに置いた。人目を気にする必要はなかった。すでにスキーヤーやスノーボーダーの姿はなくなっていた。

やがて桐林がリフト降り場に到着した。　根津のほうを気にしているのがわかる。パトロール員は、客が全員滑り終えた後、見回りを始めることになっている。

根津は彼に向かって頷きかけると、　斜面を滑り始めた。

リフト券売り場の前で停止し、スキー板を外した。携帯電話を取り出し、ホテルの二階に目を向ける。倉田たちが何をしているのかはわからない。向こうは向こうで、根津がリフトに乗って何をしてきたのか、知りたくてうずうずしていることだろう。殆どの客はホテルに引き上げており、根津以外でゲレンデに残っているのはリフトの係員ぐらいだった。

桐林が根津のことを気にする素振りを見せながら詰め所に引き

上げていくのが見えた。

間もなくナイター照明が消された。途端にゲレンデは闇に包まれた。根津のいるあたりはホテルの明かりで辛うじて足元が見えるが、コース上部は完全に真っ暗だ。

犯人はあの防水ケースをどうやって回収するつもりなのか――。

その時、携帯電話が鳴った。

「はい」

（金は確認した。今回の取引はこれで完了とする。今後のことは追って連絡する）

淡々とした口調だった。

「待ってくれ。爆発物の場所だけでも先に――」だが彼の言葉を無視し、電話は切れた。

根津はスキーを装着し、滑り始めた。真っ直ぐに詰め所に向かった。

詰め所に入ると急いでスキー靴を脱ぎ、スノーシューズに履き替えた。絵留や桐林以外のパトロール員もまだ残っている。

「どうしたんですか、根津さん。そんな格好で」早速、上山禄郎が尋ねてきた。根津が自前のスキーウェアを着ているからだろう。

「何でもない。ちょっと遊んできただけだ」そういうと、壁に掛けてあるスノーモービ

ルのキーを手にし、再び外に飛び出した。

スノーモービルに乗り、エンジンをかけていると、絵留がやってきて根津の後ろに跨った。「あたしも行く」

根津は頷き、スノーモービルを発進させた。ヘッドライトで前方を照らし、斜面を駆け上がっていく。ハンドルを操作しながら、犯人からの指示の内容を大声で絵留に説明した。

「あんなところにお金を置いたの？　一体どうするつもりかな」

「わからない」根津は怒鳴って答えた。

第1高速リフトの降り場まで上がったところでスノーモービルを止めた。案内板の後ろを調べたところ、防水ケースはなくなっていた。

「どういうことだ。犯人はどうやって回収したんだろう」根津は呟いた。

「たぶん電話で話している時、犯人はこの近くで隠れてたんだよ。で、誰もいなくなってから回収した。そういうことじゃないかな」

「だけど俺はゲレンデの下にいたんだ。俺と桐林の後に滑り降りてきた人間はいなかった」

「センターゲレンデに関してだけでしょ。犯人は、あっちに行ったんだと思う」絵留

が指したのは、第2ロマンスリフトへの連絡路だ。

「あんなところへ行ったら、真っ暗で何も見えないぜ」

「何か照明器具を持ってたんじゃないの。懐中電灯とか」

「だとしたら、スキーにしろスノボーにしろ、かなりの腕前だ」

根津がそういった時、携帯電話が鳴りだした。しかし倉田から借りたほうではなく、根津自身の電話だった。管理事務所の番号が表示されている。

「はい、根津です」

（倉田だ。一体、どうしたんだ。何かアクシデントでもあったのか）上ずった声には、気持ちの逸りが表されていた。

「アクシデントもトラブルもありません」根津は答えた。「現金の受け渡しは完了しました。物の見事に……」

16

根津の話を聞き終えた後、しばらく誰も言葉を発しなかった。最も正直な感想は、やはり犯人は本気だったのか、というトが思い浮かばなかった。倉田にしてもコメン

間の抜けたものだった。脅迫状を受け取り、現金受け渡しの段取りをしながらも、心のどこかに、これは悪質な悪戯に過ぎないのではないかという気持ちがあったのだ。いや、こうして話を聞いた後も、まだ現実の出来事ではないような気がしていた。

中垣の咳払いが重たい沈黙を破った。

「根津君のいう通りだな。見事にやられたものだ。犯人は、かなり綿密に計画を立てていたということだろう」

「それはそうだと思います。何しろ、雪が降る前から計画していたようですから」そういったのは総務部長の宮内だ。「でもとにかく、無事に金が犯人の手に渡ったようですから、よかったといっていいんじゃないでしょうか」

「そうだな。後は犯人からの連絡を待つしかない」中垣は立ち上がった。「社長に報告してくる。何かあったら知らせてくれ」

私も行きます、といって松宮も腰を上げた。

二人の本部長が出ていくと、ほんの少しだけ会議室内の空気が緩んだように感じられた。宮内がため息をついた。

「三千万か。広世観光からすれば大した金額じゃないが、うちのホテルだけでそれだけの利益を取り戻そうとしたら、かなり大変だ。それでも犯人の奴が本当に連絡して

くればいいが、万一とんずらされたらえらいことになる」

「連絡してこないかもしれない、というんですか」倉田はいった。

「そういうことも考える必要があるってことだ。だって犯人としては、目的は果たしたわけだからな。連絡を取らなくたって、何も問題はない」宮内は会議室の隅に置かれたパソコンのほうを向いた。パソコンの前には辰巳がいて、画面をじっと睨んでいる。

「だけどそれじゃあ、爆発物の場所がわからないままで、掘り出せないじゃないですか」根津が会話に入ってきた。

「そうだけど、そんなことは犯人には関係ないだろ」

「犯人だって、犠牲者を出したくはないはずです」

「起爆スイッチを入れなければいいだけのことだ。春になって雪が融ければ、どうせ爆発物は見つかる」

「スイッチを入れないからといって、爆発しないとはかぎりません」倉田がいった。

「犯人だって、その危険性についてはわかっていると思うんですが」

宮内は肩をすくめた。

「どうかね。そこまで良心的であってくれればいいんだけどな」

「もし犯人からの連絡がない場合は、今度こそ、何がなんでもスキー場はクローズにしないと……」倉田は呟いた。

「きっと君はそういうだろうと思ったよ」宮内が苦笑したが、すぐに真顔に戻った。

「俺も倉田君の考えが正しいと思う。だけど社長はどう判断するかな。今シーズンの営業をすべて中止にすると思うかい？」

倉田は口を真一文字に結んだ。筧が何をいうかは、容易に想像がついた。

「だからいったんだよ。万一犯人にとんずらされたらえらいことになるって。社長のことだ。損失分を何とか取り返そうとするだろう。ゲレンデの下に爆発物が埋まっようが、お構いなしに営業を続けるに違いないからな」

宮内の不吉な予想に、倉田は背筋が寒くなった。そんなことは何としてでも阻止しなければならないと思った。だがあの筧が単なる索道部マネージャーの言葉に耳を貸してくれる可能性は低い。

「もし犯人からの連絡がなければ、警察にも届けないってことですかね」根津がいった。

一瞬意味がわからず、倉田は根津の顔を見返した。だがすぐに意図を理解した。

「そうか。犯人からの連絡がなくて爆発物の場所が不明のままじゃ、警察が営業の続

行を認めるわけがない……」

「参ったな。こうなったら、犯人が連絡してくるのを祈るしかないか。爆発物が埋まってるっていうのは嘘だという内容でも構わないからさ」宮内が苦々しげにいい、改めてパソコンのほうを見た。

午後十時を過ぎたところで、倉田は辰巳に、パソコンの電源を切って引き上げるよう命じた。すでに会議室に残っているのは二人だけだった。犯人からは何の連絡もない。

「困りましたね。明日の整備、どうしますか」パソコンのモニターを消した後、辰巳はゲレンデ整備主任の顔で尋ねてきた。

倉田は両目頭を指先で押さえた後、小さく首を捻った。

「どうなるのかな。松宮本部長と相談して決めることになると思うけど……」

「いつ犯人が連絡してくるかわからないじゃないですか。爆弾の場所がわかったら、すぐに掘り出すわけでしょ。だったら、圧雪をかけるのは、なるべく遅らせたほうがいいと思うんですけど……」辰巳の言葉には切迫感が込められていた。どこに爆発物が埋まっているのかがわからない状態で圧雪車を運転する恐怖は、並大抵のものではない

のだろう。

「わかった。朝になって、もしまだ犯人から何もいってこない場合は、そのように本部長に進言してみよう」

「よろしくお願いします」辰巳は頭を下げた。

会議室の明かりを消し、二人で廊下に出た。管理事務所に寄るという辰巳と別れ、倉田は自分の部屋に向かった。

部屋に戻ると、上着を脱いだだけでベッドに身体を投げ出した。心身共に、ぐったりと疲れていることを自覚した。彼自身は特に何かをしたわけではないのだが、緊張した状況下でただひたすら何かを待ち続ける苦しさは、これまでに経験したことのないものだった。

こんな状態が明日も続くのだろうか――。

今、倉田たちにできるのは、犯人からの連絡を待つことだけだ。連絡がないからといって、次の行動に移るわけにはいかない。いつまで待つか、というリミットもない。連絡がなくても待つことをやめられる日が来るとすれば、それは雪が融けた時だ。しかも、それまでに何かの弾みで爆発が起きないという保証は何もない。

倉田は瞼を閉じた。このまま眠ったら風邪（かぜ）をひくかもしれないと思いながらも、動

く気がしなかった。ぐっすり眠れるならそちらのほうがいいとさえ思った。

しかし彼の淡い期待は裏切られることになった。何度も嫌な夢を見ては目を覚ました。やがて喉の渇きに耐えかねて起き上がり、寝汗で下着が濡れているのを感じながら冷たい水を飲んだ。改めて寝間着代わりのTシャツに着替えてベッドに潜り込んだが、もはや眠れる気配すらない。これではとても身体が保たないと思った。

結局、またしてもアラームが鳴る前にベッドから出ることになってしまった。少しでも頭をすっきりさせようと、シャワーを浴び、冷水で顔を洗った。

テレビをつけ、早朝のニュース番組にチャンネルを合わせた。世間では大きな事件は起きていないようだ。このスキー場で起きていることをマスコミが知ったら、きっと色めき立つだろうなと思った。

だがおそらくそんな日は来ない。事件が無事に解決した後も、筧は警察には届けずに済ませようとするだろう。爆発物がゲレンデに埋まっていることを知りながら営業を続けたことは、絶対に公表できない。

着替えを済ませ、テレビを消した時、机の上に置いた携帯電話が鳴りだした。辰巳からだ。倉田は緊張を覚え、電話に出た。「はい、私だ」

（辰巳です。おはようございます）彼は早口になっていた。

「おはよう。ずいぶん早いね」

（こっちのことが気になったものですから。それで、あの、たった今メールをチェックしたところ……）

倉田は電話機を握る手に力を込めた。「犯人が何かいってきたか」

（はい。メールが届いています。それが、ショックな内容で）

「ショック？　わかった。すぐに行く」

電話を切り、倉田は部屋を飛び出した。ショックな内容とはどういうことなのか。鼓動が速くなっていた。

会議室に行くと、辰巳が一人でパソコンに向かっていた。室内の空気は冷えきっており、彼はスタッフジャンパーの代わりにダウンジャケットを羽織っていた。

「これです」といって彼は画面を指した。

倉田はモニターを覗き込んだ。メールソフトの受信欄に表示された文面は、次のようなものだった。

『新月高原スキー場の関係者諸君へ

三千万円はたしかに受け取った。諸君たちがいたずらに策を弄（ろう）さず、こちらの指示に従ってくれたことを喜ばしく思う。

そこでこちらも誠意を示すことにした。爆発物について情報を提供する。

ファミリーコース、グリーンコース、チビッコゲレンデの下には埋めていない。これら三つのエリアは、存分に使ってもらって結構だ。

これ以上の情報を求める場合は、さらに三千万円を用意し、前回と同様、ゴンドラ山麓駅の屋根に黄色の目印を付けること。三日以内に回答がない場合は、取引不成立と判断する。

　　　　　　　　　　　　　　　　　　埋葬者より』

何だ、これは──倉田は思わず唸っていた。

それから約一時間後、倉田は辰巳や宮内らと共に、中垣と松宮が戻ってくるのを待っていた。犯人からのメールを見た二人は、社長と相談してくるといって出ていったのだ。

「考えてみれば、要求金額自体がおかしかったんだよな。三千万円って、ずいぶんと中途半端な額だ」宮内がプリントアウトされたメール文面を眺めながらいった。

「私もそう思っていました」倉田は同意した。「通報して営業停止になった場合の損失と天秤にかけさせる狙いかなと考えていたんですが」

「最初から分割して要求してくる気だったとはな。三千万を払った直後に、さらにま

た三千万か。さすがに今度は社長も躊躇するかもしれないな」

「警察への通報を決心してもらえるといいんですが」

宮内は腕組みし、苦しげに口元を歪めた。

「もし通報した場合は、今シーズンの営業はパアか。いやそれ以上に、一回目の取引に応じたこととか、今日まで営業を続けてきたことで、確実に世間から叩かれるだろうな。イメージダウンは避けられないぞ。厄介だな」

非難や苦情が殺到した場合、矢面に立たされるのは総務部長の宮内だ。その時のことを想像し、心が暗くなっているようだった。

だからさっさと通報し、スキー場を閉鎖していればよかったのだ、といいたいのを倉田は堪えた。今さら愚痴をこぼしたところで仕方がないし、社長に刃向かえなかったという点では彼自身も同様だった。

「でもどうして犯人はこんなことをするんでしょうね」辰巳がいった。「これなら、最初から六千万円を要求すればよかったじゃないですか。根津君の話を聞いたかぎりでは、金額が倍になっても受け渡しができなかったわけじゃなさそうだし」

「そこだよなあ。たしかにおかしい」宮内も首を捻った。「犯人にとっては、一回目の受け渡しにしても、かなりの大勝負だったはずなんだ。ふつうなら、そんなことは

何度もやりたくない。それとも一回目がうまくいったんで、単に欲をかいただけなのか」

「それはないと思います。この犯人は、それほど単純じゃありませんよ」

倉田と同意見らしく、宮内は黙って頷いた。

その時ドアが開き、中垣と松宮が入ってきた。どちらも硬い表情をしている。

「どうなりました」倉田は両本部長の顔を見比べた。「警察に通報しますか」

中垣は仏頂面のまま、大きな音をたてて椅子に座った後、じろりと倉田を睨め上げた。「それはない」

倉田は目を剝（む）いた。「犯人の要求に従うんですか」

「この規模の脅迫事件なら、元々一億円ぐらいは要求されても当然なんだ。社長も、あっさりとは済まないだろうと予想しておられたらしい」

「犯人の要求が、これで済むとはかぎりませんよ」

「だけど金を払えば、それなりに対応してくることは確認できた。さっさと金を払って、爆発物の埋まっていないコースを聞き出したほうが、結果的には客の安全確保にも繋がるというのが社長の考えだ。私や松宮さんも賛成した」

「しかし──」

「倉田君」横から松宮がいった。「もう決定したことなんだ」

倉田は唇を結び、一度視線を足元に落とした後、再び顔を上げた。

「ではせめて、犯人が安全だと知らせてきたコース以外については、圧雪しないことを認めてください」

「それはだめだ」即座に答えたのは中垣だった。「うちの宿泊客は年配のスキーヤーが多い。彼等は奇麗にグルーミングされたバーンを滑りに来ている。その期待を裏切るわけにはいかない。いつも通りにやってくれ」

倉田は困惑して松宮を見た。ゲレンデの安全統括管理者は彼だからだ。だが彼は、理解してくれ、とでもいうように小さく頷いただけだった。

「昨日と同じ手順でいこう。宮内君、すまないが、また銀行まで現金を取りに行ってくれ」

中垣の指示に、はい、と総務部長も短く答えた。

17

風が少し強くなってきた。ゴンドラ乗り場の屋根から吊した黄色の帯が、裾（すそ）のほう

だけぱたぱたとはためいている。その様子を見上げ、根津はサングラスの位置を直した。

「まさか、またこんなことをしなきゃいけないとはな」隣にいる絵留に話しかけた。

「もう一度、三千万でしょ？　会社としちゃ、大損害よね」

「だけど上の人間は、スキー場をクローズにするぐらいなら払ったほうがいいと判断したんだろうな。シーズンは始まったばかりだ。このまま営業できないとなれば、会社は潰（つぶ）れちまうかもしれないもんなぁ」

「だけど、もしこれで何かあったらどうする気なのかな。犠牲者が出たりしたら大変だよ」

「俺もそれが心配だ。だからこそ、今朝のパトロールだって、いつも以上に念入りにやったよ。爆発物がひょっこり雪から顔を出してないかと思ってさ。残念ながら、空振りに終わったけどさ」

絵留は、足元の雪をつま先でざくざくと掘った。

「積雪は二メートル近くあるもの。春先にならないと出てこないよ」

「だよな。だからまあ、気休めだ」根津はため息をついた。「こんなシーズンになるとはな。今年は雪が多くて喜んでたのに」

「皮肉だよね。雪が少なければ、犯人の思うようにはならなかったかもしれない。

——それより根津君、現金の受け渡しを頼まれたら、またやるの？」

根津は腕組みをし、絵留の顔を見つめた。

「そのことだけどさ、頼みがある。もしまた運び役が必要ってことになったら、今度は絵留がやってほしい」

「あたしが？」

「前回の受け渡しを振り返ってみると、運び役が危険に晒されることはないと思う。

犯人のいう通りにしていれば、たぶん大丈夫だ」

絵留は上目遣いに根津を見上げた。

「根津君、何か企んでるわけね」

「企むってほどじゃないけど、何か俺たちにできることはないかと考えている」

「たとえば？」

「たとえば……どんな些細なことでもいいから、犯人の尻尾を摑めないかと思ってさ。

そのためには、俺が運び役をしてたんじゃまずいと思う。別のところで待機して、い

つでも動けるようにしておいたらどうかな」

途端に絵留は眉をひそめた。

「犯人を捕まえるとでもいうわけ？ それこそ危険だよ」

「そこまでは考えてない。いっただろ、尻尾を摑みたいって。とにかく、犯人にやりたいようにやられてるのが我慢ならないんだ。一泡吹かせてやりたいんだよ」

「そうはいっても——」そこまでしゃべったところで、絵留が言葉を切った。彼女の視線は根津の背後に向けられている。

根津は後ろを振り返った。濃紺ウェアにピンクのニット帽の女性スノーボーダーが、片足だけにスノーボードを装着した状態で、ゆっくりと近づいてくるところだった。

「君はたしか、瀬利……」彼女を指して、記憶を探った。

「千晶。瀬利千晶。へええ、覚えていてくれたんだ」瀬利千晶は、勝ち気そうな顔に屈託のない笑みを浮かべた。「今、ちょっといい？ 教えてほしいことがあるんだけど」

根津は顔の前で小さく手を振った。彼女の用件を察したからだ。

「すまない。パウダーゾーンの穴場なら、今度教えてやるよ。今、俺たちはちょっと忙しいんだ」

瀬利千晶は唇を尖らせ、眉根を寄せた。

「それも教えてほしいけど、今はそんなこといってないよ。クロスのコースについて

「訊きたいんだけど」

「クロス?」

瀬利千晶は頷いた。

「来月、大会があるでしょ。でもクロスのコース、まだ全然造り始めてないよね。いつ頃出来るの?」

根津は絵留と顔を見合わせた後、瀬利千晶に視線を戻した。

「俺たちは担当じゃないからよくわからないけど、たぶんそろそろだと思う」

「ふうん。場所は?」

「えっ?」

「クロスのコースを造る場所だよ。いつもならアタックコースだけど、今年もそうなの?」

「あっ、いやあ、それはどうなのかな。詳しいことは聞いてないんだよな」

「そうなの? ああいうコースを造る時には、パトロールにも相談するっていう話を聞いたことがあるんだけど」

彼女のいう通りだった。大会を行う時に最も気を遣うのは、一般の滑走客といかに切り離すかということだ。どこを立入禁止にし、どのエリアを観戦用に確保するか。

これらを検討する際には、パトロールたちにも意見を求められる。

「今年は少し運営が遅れてるの」口籠もる根津を見かねたらしく、絵留がいった。

「幸い積雪量が豊富で、どこにでもコースを造れそうだから、却って主催者側も迷ってるみたい。なるべくたくさんの人に見てもらいたいもんね」

「そうなんだ。でもこっちとしちゃ、なるべく早く決めてもらいたいんだけどな」

「こっち？ どういう意味だ」根津は訊いた。

だって、と瀬利千晶は顎を少し上げた。「あたし、選手だから」

「選手？ スノーボードクロスの？」

「そう。 一般の部、成年女子Aにエントリーしてる」

どうりで、と根津は合点した。あの滑りのテクニックは、趣味で滑っている程度では手に入らない。

「決まったらすぐに発表されると思うから、それまでもう少し待ってくれ」根津はいった。

「そういうことなら仕方ないかな」そういった後、瀬利千晶は立ち去ろうとはせず、ものいいたげな表情で絵留を見ている。

「何だ。 まだほかに用があるのか」

「うーん、用ってほどじゃないんだけど」彼女は唇を舐め、絵留にいった。「あのー、藤崎さん、ですよね」

「あたし？　そうだけど」

「この間、藤崎さんが捕まえたボーダー、従兄なんです。御迷惑をおかけしてすみませんでした」瀬利千晶は頭を下げた。

「らしいわね。あんまり無茶しちゃだめよ。あなたも根津君から叱られたと思うけど」

「それはわかりました。で、それとは全然関係ない話なんですけど、藤崎さんって独身ですか」

「えっ？　そうだけど」

「彼氏とかは？　いるんですか」

「なんで、そんなことを訊くんだ」根津が横から訊いた。

だが瀬利千晶は彼のほうには見向きもせず、「今度うちの従兄とお茶してやってもらえませんか」と絵留にいった。

「えっ？」絵留は目を丸くした。「彼と？」

「いやー、なんかお恥ずかしい話なんですけど、一目惚れっていうか何というか、ど

うしても一度ゆっくりとお話ししたいとかいってるんですよね。だめですか」

絵留は当惑した顔を根津に向けてきた。彼は肩をすくめた。

「話をするくらいなら構わないけど、彼、たぶんあたしよりもかなり年下でしょ」

「二十三歳です」

「わっ、五つも下」

「二十八ですか。それなら全然大丈夫だと思います。あいつ、年上好きだから。じゃ、後で連絡させます。あのー、ケータイの番号とか教えてもらっちゃっていいですか」

「まあいいけど」

「やった。あいつ、喜ぶぞー」

瀬利千晶と絵留は携帯電話の番号を交換し始めた。その途中、根津の電話が鳴った。

倉田からだった。

「はい、根津です」

〈倉田だ。犯人から連絡があった。会議室に来てほしい〉

「わかりました。すぐに行きます」電話を切り、絵留を見た。「倉田さんからだ。行こう」

絵留は頷き、瀬利千晶に微笑みかけた。「じゃあね」

よろしくお願いします、といって瀬利千晶はぺこりと頭を下げると、片足に装着したままのスノーボードに乗り、ゴンドラ乗り場へと向かった。

「意外なところで見初められたものだな」歩きながら根津はいった。

「びっくりした。でも、あの子もなかなかかわいいじゃない。根津君好みだと思うけど」

「たしかに見た目は悪くない。だけど、あれはかなり気が強いぜ。クロスをやるっていうのを聞いて納得した」

「そのことだけど、彼女もいってたように、そろそろコース造りを始めないとやばいよ。やっぱり、とりあえずは犯人の指示に従って、安全なコースをたくさん聞き出すのが先決だと思う。悔しい気持ちはわかるけど、無茶はよくないよ」

「だから無茶をする気はないって」

通用口からホテルに入り、二人で会議室に向かった。すると途中にある管理事務所の前で、倉田が立ち話をしているのが見えた。相手はスーツ姿の男性だ。倉田が根津たちに気づいて頷きかけてくると、つられたようにスーツの男も振り向いた。まだ二十代前半と思われる若者で、新入社員の雰囲気がある。彼が会釈してきたので、根津も小さく頭を下げた。

「これから会議なんですよ」倉田がスーツの男にいった。「今の話は上の者にもしておきますから、今日のところはお引き取りいただけますか。申し訳ないんですが」

「わかりました。どうか、よろしくお願いいたします」若者は深々と頭を下げた後、もう一度根津たちにも会釈して、廊下を歩いていった。

「誰ですか」根津が訊いた。

倉田は気まずそうな顔で、耳の後ろを掻いた。

「増淵町長の息子さんだよ。大学を卒業して、町役場で働いているらしい。つい先日、町長が来たばかりだっていうのになあ。北月町、相当に焦ってるみたいだな。町長の息子が日参すれば、こっちも無視し続けられないだろうと踏んだんじゃないか」

「早く北月エリアをオープンしてほしいっていう話ですか」

「そういうことだ。北月エリアの人気を高めるアイデアを持ってきたよ」倉田は手にしている書類をひらひらさせた。「モーグル専用バーンを造るとか、巨大キッカーやハーフパイプを造るとか、たしかに客寄せのアイデアとしては悪くないんだが、社長が納得してくれるとは思えない。人件費が増えるのは確実だし、モーグルバーンなんかはすでに新月エリアにあるからなあ」

「でも、北月町の人たちは気の毒ですよね。自分たちが悪いわけじゃないのに」絵留

が眉間に皺を寄せた。

「全くだ。今回の事件が一段落したら、改めて本部長に話してみるつもりだよ」倉田は声をひそめていった。

18

『新月高原スキー場の関係者諸君へ

ゴンドラ屋根のサインを確認した。またしても合理的な結論を下してくれたことに安堵している。お互いにとって、いい結果に結びつくだろう。

今回の指示は以下の通りだ。

・前回使用した携帯電話を用意すること。

・ホテル内にあるスポーツショップで使用している赤いビニール袋に現金三千万円を入れ、口をガムテープでしっかりと閉じること。

・運搬係はスキー場関係者とわかる服装をし、前回と同様に腕に黄色のバンダナを巻き、スキーかスノーボードを用意して、午後三時半までにホテルのゲレンデ出入口の前に行くこと。また携帯電話の電源は必ず入れておくこと。

すでに承知していると思うが、念のために前回と同じ警告を添えておく。諸君たちの動きに少しでも不審なものを感じた場合には、即座に取引は中止する。我々は爆発物のタイマーを作動させる。前回、そちらが三千万円を支払っていることとは関係がない。犠牲者を出したくなければ、そして今後もホテルやスキー場を経営していきたいのならば、こちらの指示に従うことだ。

埋葬者より』

倉田の隣で宮内が細かく貧乏揺すりをしていた。犯人からのメールを読んでいるうちに、苛々してきたのだろう。倉田には同様の癖はなかったが、気分は宮内と同じだった。

この犯人は楽しんでやがる、と感じた。スキー場側が抵抗できないことを確信し、骨の髄までしゃぶり尽くそうとしているのだ。前回の取引に応じたことで、力関係はさらに極端なものになった。もはやスキー場側としては警察に届けるわけにはいかない。そのことを犯人はわかっているのだ。

「三時半ということは、あと三十分もないな」中垣が腕時計を見ながら立った。「とりあえず我々は例のバーに移動するか。あそこからなら、ホテル前のゲレンデは見渡せる。まあ、見渡せたからって、何がどうなるものでもないが」

「社長はどうされますかね」松宮が訊いた。

「同席はされないだろう。逐一報告してくれということだったが」中垣は倉田たちのほうに顔を向けてきた。「受け渡しのことは君たちに任せる。よろしく頼むよ」

わかりました、と倉田は答えた。

中垣と松宮が部屋を出ていった後、宮内が赤いビニール袋を根津に差し出した。

「何度も悪いが、気をつけてな」

「大丈夫です」根津はビニール袋を受け取った。

「じゃあ、俺もバーに行ってるから」宮内はそういって部屋を出た。

倉田は自分の携帯電話を取り出した。「また、この電話の出番だ」

だが根津は電話を受け取ろうとはせず、持っていたビニール袋を隣の藤崎絵留に渡した。

「今回は、絵留に運び役をやってもらいます」

「えっ」倉田は藤崎絵留を見た。「そうなのかい？」

彼女はやや困惑した表情を見せた。

「根津君には、何か考えがあるみたいです」

「考え？　どういうことだ」倉田は根津に尋ねた。

「いや、特に具体的なアイデアはないんですけど、俺が運び役をやったら、何もわからないと思って……」

「わからないって？」

「犯人の手口です。前回、運び役を絵留にやってもらって、俺がどこかで見張っていたら、犯人がどこから現れてどこに消えたのか、確認できたかもしれません。それを後悔しているんです」

倉田は首を振りながら、ため息をついた。

「そんなことはしなくていい。運搬係を藤崎君がすることには文句をつけないが、君は余計なことをするな。下手に犯人を刺激したくない」

「刺激する気はありません。少しでも手がかりを掴んでおきたいだけです。そうしたら、いずれ犯人が逮捕される可能性も出てくるわけだし――」

倉田は根津の顔の前に手を出し、話を制した。

「もし君が何らかの手がかりを得たとしても、犯人逮捕に繋がることはないよ。なぜなら警察は動かないからだ。筧社長は最後の最後まで通報はせず、被害届も出さないだろう。いや、もはや出せない。爆発物がゲレンデに埋まっているかもしれない状態で営業を続けたことなど、口が裂けても公表はできない」

根津は目を険しくした。

「それでいいんですか。こんなふうに好きにやられて、倉田さんは悔しくないんですか」

根津君、と藤崎絵留が窘めるようにいった。

「倉田さんだって、悔しくないわけないでしょ。一番辛いのが倉田さんだってこと、どうしてわからないわけ?」

「それは、わかってるけど……」根津は唇を噛んだ。

倉田は彼の肩を叩いた。

「とにかく、来場者の安全を守ることが第一だ。本当はスキー場を閉鎖したいが、それができないということなら、犯人の指示に従って爆発物の場所を聞き出すしかない。といっても、今回も教えてくれるとはかぎらないがね。前回のように、埋まってない場所をいくつか知らせてくるだけかもしれない。しかしそれでも、何もわからないよりは、はるかにましだ」

根津は納得した表情ではなかったが、小さく頷いた。

「で、どうする? それでもやっぱり藤崎君にやってもらうか」倉田は訊いた。

根津はほんの少し迷いの色を浮かべた後、はい、と答えた。

「営業時間の真っ只中で、万一どこかで事故でもあった場合、俺が動けないのはまずいですから。絵留なら、スキーの腕も確かなので、犯人からどんな指示が出されても対応できると思います」

「それもそうだな。じゃあ、藤崎君に任せよう。よろしく頼むよ」倉田は自分の携帯電話を藤崎絵留に渡した。

彼女は頷いてから口を開いた。

「犯人からの指示に、運搬役はスキー場関係者とわかる服装をしろっていうのがありましたよね。あれはどういう意味だと思いますか」

倉田は首を捻り、根津と顔を見合わせた。

「たしかに奇妙な指示だ。何らかの目的があるのだとは思うが、よくわからないな」

「スキー場関係者ということなら、この恰好のままでもいいということでしょうか」藤崎絵留は自分のウェアを指先で摘んだ。彼女は今、パトロール員の制服を着用している。

「というより、それを着ているしかないだろうね。ほかの係員のウェアを着たら、君のことを知っている人間が変に思う」

そうですね、と彼女は答えた。

根津が彼女の右腕に黄色のバンダナを巻いた。その様子を見ながら、一体犯人はどうやって金を受け取るつもりなのだろうと倉田は考えた。前回と違って、まだ日は高い。ゲレンデにはたくさんの人がいる。仮にうまく奪えたとしても、誰かに目撃されるおそれは十分にある。

今回もスキーかスノーボードを用意しろ、と犯人は要求している。何らかの形で運搬役に滑走させる気なのだろう。人目につかないところまで移動させるということか。

倉田は腕時計に目を落とした。午後三時十五分になっていた。

「そろそろだな」

「はい」藤崎絵留が倉田をじっと見つめてきた。「じゃあ、行きます」

「気をつけて」

三人で会議室を出た。

この時間、店は準備中だが、特別に開けてもらえることになっている。

店内は薄暗かった。窓際に並んだソファに、中垣や松宮の姿があった。テーブルの上には缶コーヒーやペットボトルの茶が置いてある。

倉田は席につきながら、運搬役が藤崎絵留に替わったことを手短に告げた。

「女のパトロール員なんかに任せて大丈夫なのか」中垣が煙草の煙を吐きながらいっ

根津と藤崎絵留を見送った後、倉田は二階のバーに向かった。

た。

「彼女なら信頼できます。それに犯人からの指示に、男性に限るという記述はありません でした」

「まあ、君がそういうのなら信じよう」中垣は窓の外に顔を向けた。

倉田も身を乗り出し、外の様子を見た。ゲレンデは、幾分すいたようだ。三時過ぎ という時間帯は、スキーヤーにしろスノーボーダーにしろ、殆どが四時か四時半には停止する。ナ イターで使用しないリフトやゴンドラは、殆どが四時か四時半には停止する。例の赤いビニール袋は、背中のリュックに入 れてあるのだろう。

すぐ斜め下から、パトロール姿の藤崎絵留が現れた。帽子とゴーグルを装着し、手 にはスキー板とストックを持っている。例の赤いビニール袋は、背中のリュックに入 れてあるのだろう。

「間もなく三時半です」総務部長の宮内が乾いた声でいった。

19

根津は絵留から二十メートルほど離れたところにいた。桐林から借りたスキーウェ アに着替え、スキー板とストックを用意している。自分のウェアは、前回の受け渡し

時に着ているので、万一犯人に気づかれたらまずいと思ったのだ。

絵留はパトロールの制服のままで立っている。ゴーグルのせいで表情はわからない

が、しきりに周囲を見回すのは、不安な心境の表れだろう。

根津は腕時計を見た。三時半になろうとしている。

再び絵留に視線を戻したが、思わず目を見開いていた。スノーボードウェア姿の若

者が彼女に近づいている。さらに彼女の前で立ち止まり、何やら話しかけ始めた。

犯人からの接触か、と思ったが、どうも様子がおかしい。絵留は顔の前で手を振っ

ている。

やがて根津は状況を把握した。若者が着ている茶色のウェアに見覚えがあったのだ。

絵留に一目惚れしたとかいう、瀬利千晶の従兄だ。

よりによってこんな時に──。

根津は付近を見渡した。案の定、少し離れたところに瀬利千晶の姿があった。もう

一人のグリーンのウェアにも見覚えがあった。

根津はあわてて二人に駆け寄った。「おい」

「あっ、こんちは」瀬利千晶が屈託なくいった。「見て見て。今、従兄がアタック中」

「わかってるよ。だから来たんだ。すぐにやめさせろ。呼び戻すんだ」

「えー、どうして？　話をしてもいいって藤崎さんはいったよ」

「今はだめだ。取り込み中なんだよ」

グリーンのウェアの若者が、あっと声を漏らした。根津は絵留たちを見た。絵留は携帯電話を耳に当てたままで歩きだしている。犯人からの連絡があったらしい。茶色のウェアの若者は、とぼとぼと引き上げてくる。

「どうだった？」瀬利千晶が大声で訊いた。

茶色のウェアの若者は、両手で大きく×印を作った。「今は忙しいってさ」

そりゃそうだ、と呟きながら根津は絵留を追った。どうやら彼女はゴンドラ乗り場に向かっているようだ。

絵留は、倉田から預かった携帯電話のほかに、自分の電話も持っている。チャンスがあれば、犯人からの指示がどういうものなのかを知らせてくれといってあった。だが現在の状況では、それは難しいだろう。犯人が、どこかで見ている可能性は十分にある。

絵留はゴンドラ乗り場の階段を上がっていった。ゴンドラの営業は四時までだ。本日最後のロングランを楽しもうとするスキーヤーやスノーボーダーたちが、階段を駆け上がっていく。根津も彼等に続いた。

階段を上がりきった時、すぐ前に絵留がいることに気づいた。だが彼女はゴンドラ

に乗ろうとせず、ほかの乗客たちを先に行かせている。彼女がパトロールの制服を着ているせいか、誰も不審には思っていないようだ。

根津は彼女に近づいた。後ろから誰も来ていないことを確認してから、「何をやってるんだ」と早口で訊いた。

「ゴンドラの営業終了時刻まで、ここで待てって」

「犯人の指示か」

「そう」

根津は唇を嚙み、もう一度後ろを振り返ってから、彼女の前を通りすぎた。こんなところでぐずぐずしていて、犯人に見つかったら面倒だ。

迷いつつ、彼はゴンドラに乗り込んだ。ほかに同乗者はいない。

先に山頂に行っておくのも一つの手だと思った。あんなところで待たせるぐらいだから、犯人は絵留をゴンドラに乗せるつもりなのだろう。ということは、前回と同様、ゴンドラ降り場周辺のどこかに、現金入りのビニール袋を置くよう指示してくる気か。

根津の乗ったゴンドラが山頂駅に到着した。腕時計を見ると、ちょうど四時になるところだった。乗り場では係員が入り口に、『本日の営業は終了しました』と書かれた札を立てていることだろう。

根津が山頂駅を出て、ゲレンデに降り立った時、携帯電話が着信を告げた。絵留からだった。急いで取り出し、通話ボタンを押した。

「俺だ。どうした」

（犯人から連絡があった。ゴンドラの営業終了後、一人で乗り込めって。係の人にお願いして、乗らせてもらった。犯人が、スキー場関係者とわかる恰好をしろっていってたのは、営業終了後に一人で乗せるためだったみたい）

「なるほどな。ゴンドラに乗った後はどうしろと？」

（指示を待ってって。また電話がかかってくるんだと思う）

「オーケー。じゃあ、絵留がゴンドラに乗っている間は、この電話は切らないでおこう。もし犯人からの連絡があったら、倉田さんの電話に絵留の電話をくっつけて話してくれ。たぶんこっちにも聞こえるはずだ」

（わかったけど、根津君、どうするつもり？　まさか、変なことは考えてないよね。無茶しちゃだめだよ）

「安心しろ。受け渡しの邪魔をする気はない。ただ、何か摑めればいいなと思ってるだけだ」

（摑んだとしても無駄だよ。だって、社長は最後まで警察には知らせない気だもの。

「そんなこと、やってみないとわからないだろ」

（だけどさ──）絵留がそういった時、着信音が根津の耳に飛び込んできた。犯人から電話がかかってきたのだ。

絵留が息を呑み、通話ボタンを押す気配があった。はい、と答える。根津は唾を呑み込み、反対側の耳を手で塞いだ。

（現金入りのビニール袋を取り出せ）くぐもった声が聞こえた。前回と同じく、ボイスチェンジャーで加工された声だった。

（出しました）絵留がいった。

すると間髪を容れずに犯人はいった。（ゴンドラの窓を開けろ）

根津は目を剝き、携帯電話を耳に押し当てたままでスキー板を装着した。空いたほうの手で二本のストックをまとめて摑み、スケーティングを始めた。

開けました、と絵留が答えた。

（間もなく十三番目の鉄塔に近づくはずだ）犯人はいった。（その鉄塔にさしかかった時、窓からビニール袋を落とせ）

根津は奥歯を嚙みしめた。思った通りだ。犯人はゴンドラの索道下に潜んでいるの

だ。そこは滑走禁止区域で、一般の人間は近づかない。

十三番か——。

　根津はゴンドラの索道下を目指して滑った。当然、その手前にはロープが張られている。自分たちが張ったものだ。それをくぐり抜け、林に侵入した。木々の間を縫うように滑り、索道下に出た。綿のように柔らかい雪にスキー板が沈んだ。

　滑走禁止区域だが、何人かが滑った跡はある。地形をよく知っている地元のスキーヤーやスノーボーダーたちの仕業だろう。地形を知らずにこんなところに入ったら、ゲレンデに戻れないどころか、下手をしたら沢に落ちるおそれさえある。

　根津はすぐそばの鉄塔を見上げた。『17』という表示が見える。十三番の鉄塔は、もっと下だ。

　スキーの先端を少し浮かせ気味にし、根津は再び滑り始めた。新雪滑走特有の浮遊感があるが、今はそれを楽しんでいる場合ではない。

　『14』の鉄塔を過ぎたところで根津は止まった。これより先に行けば、ここから先にはなかった。理由は明確だ。違反者たちの滑走跡が、もう戻ってこられないからだ。沢に落ちるか、その手前で止まり、延々と雪の中を歩くしかない。

　根津はゆっくりと滑りだした。十三番の鉄塔下にビニール袋を投下させたのだから、

犯人は何としてでもそこに近づかねばならない。その後、どうやって逃走する気なの
か、それを確認したいと思った。

十四番と十三番の鉄塔の間は、急勾配になっていた。殆ど飛び降りるような感覚
で根津は滑走した。間もなく、十三番の鉄塔の下に辿り着いた。

目を凝らし、雪面を見回した。鉄塔のすぐそばに、雪を掘り返した跡がある。さら
にそこから一本のシュプールが、林に向かって走っていた。スノーボードの跡だ。

その跡を辿るように根津はスキーを走らせた。もしも犯人に追いついたらどうする
か。その答えは出せないまま、彼は滑走を続けた。

いや、このままなら本当に追いつく――そう思った。彼はこのスキー場の地形を熟
知している。今進んでいる先には逃走ルートなど存在しないはずだった。斜面は途切

れ、崖になっている。崖の下は沢だ。

林を抜けた。白い斜面に一本の筋が走っている。その先には誰もいない。

まさか、と思った。根津はブレーキをかけた。崖の縁に立ち、見下ろした。

沢を挟んだ向こう側に、木の生えていない小高い丘がある。もちろんゲレンデの一
部ではなく、圧雪も成されていない。そもそも、そこへ行くルートが存在しない。だ
がふっくらと積もった新雪の上に、明らかにたった今誰かが滑ったと思われるシュプ

ールが一本、下に向かって走っていた。

ここから跳んだのか――。

それしか考えられなかった。だが根津の立っている地点からそこまでは、幅も高低

差も三十メートル以上はあるだろう。

俺のスキーの腕前では到底だめだ、と根津は思った。

20

犯人からの連絡があったのは、ナイター営業が終了した直後だった。例によって各

部門の責任者たちは会議室に集まり、辰巳がプリンタで打ち出した犯人からのメール

文を読んだ。その内容は以下のようなものだった。

『新月高原スキー場の関係者諸君へ

追加情報料の三千万円はたしかに受け取った。今回、こちら側の運搬者を追跡する

ような動きが見られたが、警察ではないようだから目をつぶってやろう。本来ならば

取引不成立とするところだ。以後、気をつけるように。

さて、追加情報だ。次のコース及びエリアには爆発物はない。

・シルバーコース
・ウッディコース
・スラロームコース
・ダイナミックコース
・すべての林道
・北月エリア

いずれも初心者から上級者まで楽しめるコースだ。これで諸君たちも、かなり安心できたのではないだろうか。

今後のことについては、また連絡する。

『埋葬者より』

どん、と大きな音がしたので、倉田は顔を上げた。向かい側に座っている中垣の拳が、机の上にあった。どうやら思いきり叩いたようだ。

「ふざけてやがる。どういうことだ」中垣は舌打ち交じりにいった。

「やはり、肝心なことは教えられないってことでしょうね」松宮が首を振りながらいう。

「いや、しかし」倉田は二人の本部長を交互に見た。「これでかなり危険区域を絞れ

ました。犯人が本当のことを知らせてきているとすれば、爆発物の埋まっているおそれのあるコースは、それほど多くはありません」

さらに彼はポケットに入れていたゲレンデマップを机の上で広げた。

「前回知らせてきたファミリーコース、グリーンコース、チビッコゲレンデと今回知らせてきたコースを足しますと、ゲレンデ全体の半分ほどにはなります。どうでしょうか。ほかのコースは、滑走禁止ということにしませんか」

「そんなこと、出来るわけがないだろう」中垣が吐き捨てた。「客に何といって説明するんだ。雪はたっぷりあるし、雪崩が起きているわけでもない。なぜ滑らせないんだと苦情をいわれるのはこっちなんだ」

倉田は松宮のほうを向き、「だめですか」と訊いた。中垣はホテル事業本部長に過ぎず、スキー場の安全統括管理者は松宮なのだ。

だが松宮は倉田が期待した反応は見せなかった。論外だとばかりに顔の前で手を振った。

「中垣さんのいう通りだ。客が納得するわけがない。君はゲレンデ全体の半分だというが、センターゲレンデで安全なのはシルバーコースだけだ。ホテルの真ん前にある広大なゲレンデの殆どを滑走禁止にしろというのか。それは無茶だろう」

　倉田は黙り込み、唇を噛んだ。客の安全を考えれば、多少の無茶は仕方がないではないかと思った。だがどうやら松宮たちは商売のことしか考えていないようだ。

「追跡、と書いてあるな」中垣がメール文を見て、ぽつりといった。「運搬者を追跡するような動き、とはどういうことだ。そんなこと、誰がやったんだ」

「根津君、かもしれませんね」倉田はいった。「藤崎君はゴンドラの中にいたわけですから、彼しか考えられないと思います。ほかにこの件を知っているのは、桐林君というパトロールだけですが、彼は本来の仕事をしていたはずです」

「根津か。どうしてそんな余計なことをしたんだ」

　さあ、と倉田は首を捻った。

「詳しい事情はわかりません。後で聞いておきます」

「ちゃんと注意しておくんだぞ。あいつがそんなことをしなければ、犯人はもう少し情報をくれたかもしれないんだ」

　まさかそんなことはないだろうと思ったが、倉田は黙っていた。それに根津に釘を刺しておかねばならないのは確かだ。余計なことをするなではなく、危険なことをするな、と。

「あのう、ちょっといいですか」辰巳がおずおずと切りだした。全員の視線が彼に集

まった。それを瞬きして受けとめた後、彼はいった。「クロスのコース、どうしましょうか」

はっとして倉田は二人の本部長を見た。

松宮が顔をしかめた。「それがあったか」

「何か問題があるのか」中垣が訊いた。「安全なコースがいくつか判明したんだ。どこかに造れるだろ」

「いえそれが、といって辰巳は倉田を見た。それで中垣も彼のほうに顔を向けた。

「どういうことだ？」

倉田は唇を舐めた。

「クロスのコースを造るには、幅、長さ、斜度といった条件が揃っている必要があります。うちのゲレンデで国際大会レベルのコースを造るとなれば、アタックコースかゴールドコースしかありません。ところがその二つは、犯人が安全だと挙げたコースには入っていません」

中垣の渋面が、さらにひどいものになった。

「そういうことか。何とかならないのか」

「シルバーコースとかグリーンコースはどうだろう」そう訊いてきたのは松宮だ。索

道事業本部長だけに、中垣よりはコースレイアウトが頭に入っているらしい。

「残念ながら、どちらも斜度が不足しています。長さも足りません」

「そうか……」松宮は腕組みをし、唸った。

「何とかならないのか」中垣が、先程と同じ台詞を繰り返した。「雪不足の時、君たちは別の場所から運んできた雪を盛ったりして、いつもうまくゲレンデを仕上げるじゃないか。ああいうふうにはいかないのか」

「お言葉ですが、斜度不足を補うほどに雪を盛ることは不可能です」馬鹿馬鹿しい質問だと思いつつ、倉田は真面目に答えた。

「じゃあ、どうすればいいんだ」

仏頂面で訊く中垣に答える者はいない。それがわからないから、辰巳が質問したのだ。

「犯人からの連絡を待つしかないってことかな」松宮が皆を見回した。「安全なコースを小出しにしてくるのは、こちらを何度も脅迫するつもりだからだろう。ということは、また金を要求してくるはずだ。それでまたこっちが要求通りに金を出せば、いくつかの情報を寄越してくる。その中にアタックコースかゴールドコースが入っていれば、そこにクロスのコースを造ればいい」

「入ってなかったらどうするんですか。もし入ってなかったら、アタックコースとゴールドコースは本当に危ないってことになります」

倉田の問いに、松宮は答えない。ただ不愉快そうに口元を歪めただけだ。

「ちょっといいですか」今まで発言していなかった総務部長の宮内が、小さく手を挙げながらいった。「今回、どうして犯人は勿体をつけてるんですかね」

「勿体？　どういう意味だ」中垣が訊いた。

宮内はメール文が印刷された紙を指した。

「今後のことについては、また連絡するって書いてありますよね。もしまだ金を要求してくる気なら、前回と同様、さらに情報が欲しいなら三千万円を用意しろとか書いてくるはずじゃないでしょうか。どうして今回は、そうじゃないのかなと思って」

もっともな疑問であり、倉田も気になっていたことだった。犯人は何を考えているのか。

「犯人が一人じゃないからだろう」中垣があっさりといった。「仲間うちで、いろいろと相談してるんじゃないか。要求する金額とか」

誰も反論しなかったが、同意もしなかった。倉田は的外れだと感じた。この犯人は周到に計画を練っている。仮に複数犯だとしても、この段階で揉めるとは思えなかっ

た。

「まあ、いずれにせよ、犯人からの連絡を待つしかないんじゃないかな」とりまとめるように松宮がいった。

「すみません。それで、クロスのコースはどうしたらいいですか。じつのところ、もう作業に入らないと間に合わないんですけど」辰巳がいった。その声からは切羽詰まった思いが滲み出ていた。

中垣も松宮も黙り込んでいる。この二人に結論を求めるのは無理だった。どのみち、社長の筧に相談せねばならない問題だ。だが相談するにしても、何らかの案が必要だ。一番妥当な案はクロスの大会を中止にすることだが、この二人がそのように進言するとは思えなかった。もししたとしても筧に却下されるだろう。

筧はどんな結論を出すか。何としてでも大会を開けるようにしろというだろうが、コースを造れないのでは話にならない。

倉田は犯人からのメールに目を向けた。安全が保証されたコースを眺めているうちに、ある考えが閃いた。

「北月エリアはどうでしょうか」彼はいった。「あそこの斜面なら、長さも幅も十分です。斜度もあり、いいコースを造れると思います」

「あっ、それはいいかもしれません」辰巳の表情が途端に明るくなった。

「いや、それはだめだ。それはまずいだろう」松宮が目を見開き、唇を尖らせた。

「あそこは閉鎖中じゃないか。オープンさせることにはいろいろと問題がある。それは君たちが一番よくわかっているはずだ」

「わかっています。でも、背に腹は代えられないんじゃないでしょうか。今、入江さん親子が来られていることは御存じですよね。少し話をしたのですが、息子さんに現実を受けとめさせるために来たから、北月エリアがクローズなのは残念だとおっしゃってました。どうか、考えていただけませんか」

松宮は困惑した様子で、隣の中垣と顔を見合わせた。

「昼間、増淵さんが来られました。息子さんのほうです。北月エリアを充実させるためのアイデアをいくつか持ってこられました。あちらの役場と協力すれば、大会を盛り上げられると思うのですが」倉田は懸命に語った。

松宮と中垣は何やら囁き合った。やがて中垣が、倉田の予想通りの台詞をいった。

「わかった。その件も含めて、社長に相談してみよう」

21

キッカーから跳び出した瞬間、ちょっとまずい、と思った。角度が上に向き過ぎている。これでは滞空時間が延びてしまう。足を引きつけ、着地に備えた。グラブを入れる程度の余裕はあるが、今日は遊びで跳びに来たわけではない。空中姿勢をチェックしながら、近づいてくるランディングバーンを睨んだ。

両足に少し衝撃を感じた。重心がボードの真ん中にあることを確認した後、やや後方に体重をかける。着地後、どれだけロスなく板を走らせるか——それがクロス競技でジャンプした時の勝負の分かれ目だと千晶は考えている。

少し滑ったところでエッジを切り、鋭くターンしてから停止した。

幸太が上から滑り降りてきた。

「すっげえスピードで入ったから、どんだけ跳ぶんだと思ったけど、千晶ねえちゃんにしてはおとなしかったじゃん。どうしたんだよ」

千晶は腰に手を当てた。

「いわなかった？　もうしばらく、ビッグエアはおしまい。今は、いかにして跳ばな

いかっていう練習をしてんの」

「キッカーで跳ばないのかよ」ゴーグルの下の口が尖る。「テンション上がんねえな」

「しょうがないでしょ。クロスの練習をしようにも、まだコースができてないんだから」千晶は幸太の後ろに目を向けた。「ところで快人は?」

「一人で滑りに行った。たぶん、あの美人パトロールを探しに行ったんだと思うよ」

「へええ。あいつ、かなり本気だね」

「本気なんてもんじゃないよ。延泊しようっていわれた。俺は予定があるっていったら、じゃあ一人で帰れってさ。参っちまうよ」

横内兄弟は新月駅のそばにあるリゾートマンションに泊まっている。彼等の父親の友人が、バブル期に購入した1LDKの部屋だ。誰も使わないと傷む一方だからということで、殆どただ同然で泊まらせてもらっているらしい。建物は古いが、温泉やジムがついた、なかなかの高級マンションだ。

「延泊してまで口説こうっていうガッツには感心するけど、あのおねえさんはどうかね。脈はなさそうだよ。昨日だって、軽くあしらわれてたし——」

そこまでしゃべったところで千晶は言葉を切った。キッカーに向かって滑り始めた一人のスノーボーダーに注目したからだ。ほかの者とは明らかにフォームが違う。バ

ランスは完璧で、柔軟性を感じさせる。

そのスノーボーダーが跳んだ。高い。飛距離も出ている。それ以上跳んだら斜度がなくて危険、というぎりぎりのところで着地した。体勢は全く崩れない。空中で派手な技を決めたわけではないが、周りからはどよめきの声が上がった。シンプルでも迫力のあるエアは、時に最高のパフォーマンスとなる。

ひゅうっと幸太が声を裏返した。

「やるねえ、あいつ。ローカルかな」

「地元の人間か、という意味だ。

「どうかな。昨日まではいなかったと思うんだけど」

そのスノーボーダーはボードを外し、ゆっくりとキッカーの上部を目指して登り始めた。その様子を千晶たちが目で追っていると、視線に気づいたように顔を向けてきた。さらに、彼女たちのほうに近寄ってくる。

「あれ。なんか、こっちに来る感じだぜ。喧嘩でも売る気かな」

「えっ、なんでこんなところで喧嘩を売られなきゃいけないわけ」

「知らねえよ。俺たちがじろじろ見てたからじゃないか」

「感心して見てただけなのに、文句をいわれる筋合いないよ。大体こんなところで跳

んでる奴なんて、人に見られてなんぼのはずじゃん」

「わかんねえよ。あいつにいえよ」

やがて大柄のスノーボーダーは千晶たちの前まで来て足を止めた。

よう、と声をかけてきた。「何やってるんだ」

「別に。おたく、誰?」ぶっきらぼうに訊いてみた。

「俺だよ」

「そうか、わかんねえか」男はゴーグルを外した。相手はパトロールの根津だった。

あっ、と千晶は声を漏らした。

「根津さん、ボードもやるんだ」

「こういっては何だけど、こっちのほうが本職でね。パトロールだから、いつもは仕方なくスキーを履いてるけどさ」

「そうなんだ。で、今日はパトロールの仕事は休みなわけ?」

「いや、そういうわけじゃないんだけど、ちょっと足馴らしをしておこうと思ってさ。今シーズン初だ」

じつをいうと、ボードに乗るのは久しぶりなんだ。今シーズン初だ」

マジで、と驚きの声を上げたのは幸太だ。しかし千晶も同感だった。

「それにしては、すっごいのを見せつけてくれたよね。根津さんだとわかって悔しいけど、思わず見とれちゃったよ」

だが根津は顔をしかめ、首を振った。

「全然だめだ。着地点が奇麗に固められているからごまかせたけど、下が不整地とか新雪だったら、たぶん足をとられてただろう。感覚が戻るには、もう少し時間がかかりそうだ」

その口調を聞いたかぎりでは、謙遜しているわけでも、恰好をつけているのでもなさそうだった。あの滑りとエアで本調子でないというなら、相当な腕前だ。

「ずいぶんと気合いが入ってるね。まさか、今度の大会に出るんじゃないだろうね」

半ば本気で訊いてみたところ、根津は蠅を払うように手を振った。

「そんなことは考えてない。仕事で必要になるかもしれないから練習を始めただけだ」

「仕事？　パトロールの仕事でボードが必要になる時って、どういう時？」

千晶の問いに、根津は気まずそうな顔をした。その表情を隠すようにゴーグルを付けた。

「俺たちの仕事にも、いろいろとあるんだよ。まあ、大したことじゃない。忘れてくれ」

彼はボードを抱え、登り始めた。その背中に、「ちょっと待って」と声をかけた。

「クロスのコース、まだ何も決まらないの？」

根津が立ち止まり、振り返った。

「今日か明日には決まると思う」

「本当？　どこになりそう？」

「決まったら、教えてやるよ」そういうと根津はくるりと前を向き、再び歩き始めた。

22

瀬利千晶たちに背を向け、雪の上をざくざくと歩きながら、本当にやばい、と根津は思った。今日か明日には決まるといったが、口からでまかせだった。実際には、そんな情報は入っていない。

今朝、倉田から聞いた話によれば、金の受け渡しがうまくいったので、犯人はまた新たに安全なコースをいくつか知らせてきたらしい。だがその中に、クロスのコースを造れるようなところは含まれていないということだった。アタックコースかゴールドコース――新月エリアでレースを実施するとなれば、この二つしか考えられない。北月エリアを考えている、と倉田はいった。それを聞き、根津は所謂「目から鱗が

落ちる」ような思いがした。その手があったか、と指を鳴らした。ホテルからのアクセスは悪く、ところどころ観戦しにくい場所がありそうだが、レースを中止にできないということなら、今や最善の策だと思われた。

しかし上の人間には、あれこれと思惑があるようだ。どう考えてもグッドアイデアだと根津などは思うのだが、二人の本部長はあまり乗り気ではなさそうだという。一応社長と相談してみるといっていたらしいが、望みは薄いだろうと倉田はいった。

たしかに会社としては、採算の合わないゲレンデを今さら開けたくない、というのが本音に違いない。昨年の死亡事故のせいでイメージもよくない。今でもホテルには時折事故に関する問い合わせがあり、安全対策はどうなっているのかと訊かれることが多いという。そんな時には、「あのエリアは現在使用しておりません」と答えるのが、一番手っ取り早く相手を納得させられるのだ。

ようやく根津はキッカーのスタート地点に辿り着いた。全身が汗ばんでいる。意外に重労働だった。一回跳ぶたびに、いちいちリフトに乗るために下まで滑り降りていたら面倒だと思ったのだが、次からはそうしたほうがいいかもしれない。

キッカーの順番待ちをしているスノーボーダーたちが七人ほどいた。根津は彼等の後ろに並んだ。

こんなところを倉田や絵留に見られたら何をいわれるかわからないな、と思った。

まさか、次に犯人を追いかけた時には逃げられないよう練習しているのだ、とはいえない。

実際、自分でも何をしているんだろうと思う。こんなことをする意味があるのかどうか、全くわからないままに始めてしまっている。強いていえば、あのシュプールに刺激を受けたということになるだろうか。

犯人は三十メートル以上のギャップを飛び越え、はるか先の雪面に着地した。無論、転倒した気配はない。ものすごいテクニック、驚くべき身体能力、そして類い稀な精神力を持っている人間というほかない。

あんなことが俺にできるだろうか——そう考えた途端、根津の中にあるスイッチが、かちりと音をたてて入った。忘れかけていた何かが蘇り、心の隅ですっかり冷えていたはずのものが、少しずつ熱を帯び始めた。その温度は瞬く間に高くなり、やがては彼自身にはどうすることもできないほど、全身の血をたぎらせるようになった。

もはやじっとはしていられなかった。昨夜、寝床に入った後もまるで寝付けず、夜中にごそごそと起き出した。封印していたはずのスノーボードを引っ張りだし、ホットワックスをかけ始めた。そんなことをしていると、一層頭が冴えてきた。

俺は一体何がしたいんだろうな、と根津は思った。この局面でスノーボードの技術を磨いたところで、何の解決にもならない。犯人を捕まえられるわけでもない。いやそれどころか、昨夜倉田からは、もう決して危険なことはしないでくれと釘を刺された。

「犯人からのメールによると、彼等は君の追跡に気づいてたんだ。今回は特別に見逃すと書いてあったけど、今後は絶対にそういうことはしないでくれ。犯人を刺激したくないということはもちろんあるけど、君のことも心配だ。仮に君の追跡がうまくいって、犯人に迫っていたら、あわてた犯人が君に何をするかわからないからね」

倉田のいうことはもっともだった。根津は頭を下げ、もう二度としません、と答えるしかなかった。

あんなふうに約束したにもかかわらず、俺はここで何をしているんだ——改めて自問した。

もしかしたら言い訳を探していたのかもしれない、と思った。北月エリアでの事故をきっかけに、スノーボードには乗らないようになった。遺族である入江親子の気持ちを考えると、このスキー場でパトロール員として勤務する以上、それは最低限の礼儀だと思ったのだ。次に乗ることがあるとすれば、それは犯人が逮捕された時、と決

めていたはずだった。

ところが昨日、脅迫犯のシュプールを見た瞬間から、その決意がどこかへ吹き飛んでしまった。

この事件を解決するには俺もスノーボードに乗るしかない、緊急事態だ——そんなふうに都合よく考えて、昔のボードを引っ張り出してきた。だが結局のところ、俺は滑りたかっただけではないのか。自分を納得させられる理由を探していただけではないのか。

しかしスノーボードに乗ること自体が悪いわけではない、という誰にでも思いつく正論が根津の中に常にあったのは事実だ。悪いのは人間であって、スノーボードというスポーツに非はない。ルール違反、マナー違反を犯す人間はスキーヤーにだってたくさんいる。滑走禁止区域に入るのはスノーボーダーだけではないし、偽造リフト券を使おうとしていたスキーヤーを警察に突き出したこともある。

いつの間にか根津の順番がきていた。早くスタートしなよ、とでもいうように、後ろの若者たちが見ている。

根津は低い姿勢を取り、キッカーに向かった。ぐんぐんと加速していくのがわかる。ワックスの効きは悪くないようだ。

高速でキッカーを一気に滑り上がる。タイミングを合わせ、空中に跳び出した。

だめだ、タイミングがずれた――。

これではあいつに敵（かな）わない、と思いながら着地の姿勢を作った。

23

松宮は眉間に皺を寄せていた。倉田の反論を封じるように、全身から拒絶の気配を漂わせている。彼のほうを見ようともしない。

倉田は索道事業本部長室にいた。社長からの指示を受けるためだった。松宮は中垣と共に、昨日に引き続き、今朝も社長の篤と協議を行っていたはずなのだ。

「なぜだめなんですか。ほかに、もう手はないんですよ」倉田は机に両手をつき、渋面を作って座っている松宮を見下ろした。

「だから、だめだとはいってない。慎重になるべきだといってるんだ」松宮はいった。

「同じことじゃないですか。北月エリアは使えないというんでしょ。クロスのコースを造るわけにはいかないと」

「現段階では、時期尚早だ」

倉田は首を振り、頭を掻きむしった。

「考えられない。本部長、クロスの日程は御存じですよね。世界中から有力選手がやってきて、コースがまだ造られてないとなったら、来年からはどんなに招待しても来てくれませんよ。いやそれどころか、開催できるかどうかも怪しい。もちろん、今年の話です」

松宮が目だけでじろりと見上げてきた。

「北月エリアを稼働させたら、一日にどれだけの経費が必要になるか、君だって知らないわけじゃないだろう。整備は必要だし、連絡の悪いロマンスリフトを二基動かさなきゃいけない。一旦あっちに滑り降りたら、新月エリアには戻れないから、そういう客のためにシャトルバスを用意する必要がある」

やはりそういうことか、と倉田は合点した。これまでは昨年の死亡事故を理由に挙げていたが、結局のところ竟としては、北月エリアを切ってしまいたいのだ。

「大会を中止にするよりはいいんじゃないですか」彼はいった。「経費が問題だということなら、大会の間だけ開けるというのはどうでしょう。終わったら、再びクローズにするということで」

松宮は首を振った。

「いやあ、一度開けてしまったら、途中でまた閉めるというわけにはいかんだろう。客への説明が難しくなる」

「そうでしょうか」

ホテル側から北月エリアは全く見えない。整備上の問題だとでもいえば、客たちは納得するしかないはずだった。

とにかく、と松宮は声のトーンを上げた。

「もうしばらく犯人の出方を待つ。一両日中には、必ず何かいってくるはずだ。社長は、あと三千万なら払ってもいいとおっしゃっている。金を出せば、犯人から新たな情報が提供されるだろう。それを見てから、クロスコースをどうするか判断しよう」

「本部長、それでは整備がとても間に合いません」

「間に合わせるんだ。それがプロというものだろ」

プロという言葉を聞き、倉田は力が抜けそうになった。プロだというのなら、本気で来場者の安全を最優先にしたらどうなのか。

「では、準備だけはさせてください。北月エリアの圧雪と、リフトの点検整備を始めていいですね」

「それはだめだ。そんなことをしたら、北月町の連中から、オープンするんだろうと

「期待されてしまう」

「別にそれでもいいじゃないですか」

「しかし、結局オープンしないということになったら、またいろいろとうるさいぞ」

「本部長、大会に間に合わなかったらどうするんですか」

お願いします、と頭を下げた。

松宮は仏頂面で深くため息をつき、口元を歪めた。

「圧雪ぐらいはまあいいだろう。ただし、誰かに何か訊かれたら、雪崩対策だと答えるんだ。リフトについては点検に留めてくれ。整備は、まだ始めるな」

「我々は索道事業主ですよ。リフトの運転が本来の業務です」

「だからこそだ」松宮はじろりと睨め上げてきた。「鉄道会社が電車を走らせる予定もないのに線路の整備をすることはないだろう？　金が余ってるわけじゃないんだ」

今度は倉田がため息をつく番だった。わかりました、と力なく答えた。

本部長室を出て、管理事務所に戻った。ゲレンデ整備主任の辰巳と索道部主任の津野に声をかけ、松宮とのやりとりを話した。

「ピステンを何台か回さないといけませんね」辰巳がいった。「今、北月エリアには小さいピステンが一台あるだけです」

「それは動かせるのかな」

倉田が訊くと、辰巳は白い歯を見せて笑った。

「もちろん、燃料を入れれば動きます。周辺の除雪には時々使っていますから」

北月エリアがクローズ中とはいえ、定期的に建物などを見回る必要がある。ゲレンデ周辺の除雪を怠るわけにはいかないのだ。

「じゃあそれを使って、一度エリア全体を見て回ったほうがいいな。何しろ、一度も整備をしてないからなあ」倉田はいった。

「誰かパトロールの人間を連れていきたいですね。雪崩の起きそうな地点とかは、彼等が一番よく知っているし」

辰巳の進言に倉田は頷いた。

「根津君か藤崎君に声をかけてみよう。あとはリフトの点検だな。人数は確保できるかな」

「最低でも四、五人はほしいですね」津野が腕組みをした。「でも、結構こっちも手一杯なんですよね。今は殆どのリフト整備係を動かしてるから」

本来は仕事が別のはずのリフト整備係が、運転係や監視係も兼ねているから、手が離せないということだ。人員削減の皺寄せといえた。

「何とかならないかな」

「ならないことはないです」津野がきっぱりといった後、窺うような目をした。「勝手にバイトを雇うことになりますけど、構いませんか」

気心の知れた経験者に声をかけるということなのだろう。

「構わない。俺が責任を取る」倉田はいいきった。

細かい打ち合わせを終えた後、倉田はパトロールの詰め所に行った。藤崎絵留が外にいて、ロープを片づけているところだった。

声をかけ、「根津君は？」と訊いた。

「二時間だけ遊んでくるということでした。呼びましょうか」

「いや、君でもいいんだ。ちょっと頼まれてくれないか」

事情を話した。藤崎絵留の顔が明るく輝いた。

「それってラッキーですね。誰も滑ってない新雪のバーンを、一人で滑っていいということでしょう？」

倉田は苦笑した。

「まあそうだけど、あくまでも点検が目的だ。あまり楽しんでもらっちゃ困る」

「わかっています。今すぐに出発されますか」

「うん、できるだけ早く出たい。辰巳君はすでに向かっている」

「わかりました。五分で準備します」

「駐車場にいるよ」

ホテルの従業員用駐車場に止めてあるハイエースに乗りこみ、エンジンを暖めていたら、すぐに藤崎絵留がやってきた。片手にスキーブーツを、もう片手にスキー板とストックを持っている。

荷物を後部シートに置いた後、彼女は助手席に乗り込んできた。

「すみません。ワイドの板を探してたら遅くなっちゃって」

新雪を滑るから、なるべく幅の広いスキーのほうがいいと思ったのだろう。

「大丈夫。日暮れまでには何時間もある」倉田はエンジンをかけた。

降り積もった雪のせいで、ただでさえ細い道が一層狭められていた。対向車とすれ違うのが困難な場所がいくつもある。この道がスキーヤーたちにとって北月町を縁遠いものにしているのは明白だった。運転に自信がない人は避けたほうがいいでしょう──インターネットの掲示板には、こう書かれている。

倉田はハイエースのハンドルを慎重に操作しながら、ふと疑問に思ったことを口にした。

「遊んでくるって、どういうことなのかな」

だが何のことをいわれているのかわからないらしく、助手席の藤崎絵留は戸惑ったように黙っている。

「根津君のことだよ。二時間だけ遊んでくるといってたそうだけど」

ああ、と絵留は漏らした。

「スノーボードを抱えてましたから、久しぶりに滑ってるんだと思います」

「スノーボード？　本当かい」

「ブーツも履き替えていました」

「ふうん、どういうことかな」

倉田はエンジンブレーキを効かせて速度を落とした。小さな橋にさしかかったからだ。見た目は何でもなくても、こういう場所では凍結していることがよくある。

「彼、ボードはしばらくやらないといってたよね」

昨シーズン、北月エリアで死亡事故が起きた直後、根津がそう宣言したことを倉田は覚えている。同じスノーボーダーとして、逃げた犯人のことが許せなかったのだろう。

「たぶん、刺激を受けたんだと思いますけど」藤崎絵留はいった。遠慮がちではある

が、確信の籠もった口調だった。

「刺激？」

「犯人に、です。追跡した時のこと、お聞きになりませんでしたか」

「聞いたよ。そういえば、犯人はスノーボードで逃げたとかいってたな」

「かなりの腕前だそうです。自分のスキー技術では対抗できないいって、根津君はいってました」

「おいおい、まさかスキーじゃ対抗できないからって――」

「大丈夫です。彼が何かやろうとしたら、あたしが絶対に止めます。危ないことはやらせません」

「そうはいっても、今回みたいに彼が勝手に暴走したらどうしようもない」

「今回は、あたしがいけなかったんです。根津君のいうことを聞いて、ケータイで状況を報告したりしたから。でも次は、そんなことはしないつもりです。あたしを信用してください」藤崎絵留は語気を強めた。女性ではあるが、パトロール員としての責任感の強さは根津に負けていないことを倉田は知っている。

「もちろん君のことは頼りにしている。しかし責任を君一人に押しつけるわけにはいかない。根津君には、俺からも改めて釘を刺しておこう」

「あたしからも注意しておきます」

「彼は負けん気が強いからな。金が奪われるのを黙って見ているのが、悔しくて仕方がないんだろう」

「悔しいのは、あたしも同じです。こんなことが起きるなんて、少し前までは考えもしませんでした。雪がたくさん降って、順調にオープンできてよかったと喜んでたんですけど」

「同感だよ。ところが犯人も、雪が降り積もるのを待ちこがれていたわけだ。世の中にはとんでもないことを考えつく奴がいる」

「あの脅迫状に書いてあったことは本心なんでしょうか。地球温暖化を招いたことに対する慰謝料を要求するってありましたけど、本当にそれが動機だと思いますか」

倉田はハンドルを握ったままで肩をすくめた。

「違うだろうね。スキー場開発が環境破壊を伴うのは確かだけど、慰謝料云々は後付けだろう。うまい脅迫方法を思いついたから実行することにした——単にそれだけのことじゃないかな」

「やっぱりそう思いますか」

「本気で環境破壊のことで腹を立てているのなら、慰謝料なんか要求しないで、爆発

物の存在を公表すればいいんだ。そうすればスキー場を営業するわけにはいかなくなる。仮に営業したところで、世間から非難されるだけで客は来ない。スキー場の経営者にとっては、そっちのほうが余程打撃だ」

「たしかにそうですよね。犯人はきっと、スキー場側が警察に届けないことも見越してたんでしょうね」

藤崎絵留の呟きを聞き、倉田はため息をついた。

「情けない、と思ってるんじゃないのか」

「何がですか」

「俺が上司のいいなりになっていることさ。本来なら、首をかけてでも来場者の安全を守らなきゃいけないところだ」

「倉田さんのお立場はよくわかっています」

「いや、本来なら、何とかして社長たちを説得すべきなんだ。辞表を叩きつけて、脅迫状のことを公表しないのなら自分が勝手にやる、ぐらいのことをいえばよかった。だけど最初にそうしなかったばかりに、何もかもが後手に回った。根津君が悔しがるのも無理はない。今や、上司のいいなりになっているだけでなく、犯人のいいなりだ」

「倉田さんのせいじゃありません。あたしはわかっています」藤崎絵留の言葉からは真摯な思いが伝わってきた。

倉田は、ちらりと彼女のほうに視線を走らせた後、ありがとう、と小声でいった。

細い道がようやく広くなり、右斜め前方にゲレンデが見えてきた。道路に近い部分は除雪されている。倉田は空いたスペースにハイエースを止めた。車を降り、まずは周囲を見回した。

更衣室や休憩所のある建物は、雪に覆われてひっそりと建っていた。リフト券売り場の小さな小屋は、窓のあたりまで埋まっている。搬送機のかかっていないリフトの鉄塔も、存在感が薄かった。

完全に遊休施設だな、と倉田は思った。このまま放置しておけば、廃れる一方だろう。

しかし新月高原ホテルアンドリゾート株式会社としても、ここを完全に閉鎖するわけにはいかなかった。スキー場の閉鎖の際には、リフトを撤去して植林などで元の状態に復帰させなければならない、と林野庁によって規制されているからだ。いうまでもなく、それを実行するには何億もの金がかかる。

つまり現在のように閉鎖はせずに遊休状態にしておくのが、会社にとっては一番都

合がいいわけなのだ。そして昨年に起きた死亡事故は、それを実践する恰好の言い訳となっている。

それだけに、一時的にせよ北月エリアをオープンさせたくないという彼たちの考えは、倉田にも十分に理解できた。一度開けてしまうと、再び閉鎖するには別の理由が必要になるからだ。もちろん、無駄な経費を使いたくないという経営者としての本音もあるだろう。

だがもう待ってはいられなかった。大会を行う以上、完璧に近いコースを造らねばならない。試合を素晴らしいものにするためというのもあるが、それ以前に選手たちの安全を確保する必要があった。安全が保証されてこそ、選手たちも最高のパフォーマンスを発揮できる。

遠くからエンジン音が近づいてきた。音のするほうを見ると、一台のピステンが斜面を降りてくるところだった。どうやら辰巳が、早くも上の様子を見てきたらしい。

ピステンは倉田たちから十メートルほど離れたところで止まった。運転席から辰巳が降りてきた。

「どうしますか」辰巳が訊いてきた。吐く息が白い。

「上はどんな具合かな」

「ざっと回ったかぎりでは、雪崩の心配がありそうなところは見当たりません」

「よし。じゃあとりあえず、上がってみるか」そういって倉田は、すでに車から降りている藤崎絵留を見た。「出番だ。スキーを持って、一緒に行ってくれ」

はい、と彼女は元気よく答えた。気分が悪いはずがなかった。今シーズン、まだ誰も滑っていないゲレンデに自分のシュプールを刻むのだ。

辰巳に続いて、倉田はピステンの助手席に乗り込んだ。キャビンは二人乗りだ。そこで藤崎絵留は後部の荷台に乗ることになった。

「犯人からの連絡、ありませんね」走りだして間もなく、辰巳がいった。

「そのようだね」

「一体、犯人はどうするつもりなんでしょうか。これまでは次々と要求を出してきたのに、急に何もいってこなくなったというのは変だと思いませんか」

「たしかに気にはなる」

「もし、このまま何もいってこなかったら、社長や本部長たちはどうしますかね。今のままで営業を続けろってことになるんでしょうか」

「ふつうに考えればそうだろうな。だけど、犯人がこのまま何もいってこないという ことはないと思う。こっちが警察に届ける気がないっていうことは犯人だってわかってい

る。いうなれば、いくらでも金を要求できる状態だ。それをほうっておく手はないだろ」

「そうですよね。すると、どこかでまた三千万円か。次のボーナスは期待できそうにないな」辰巳が嘆息を漏らした。

エンジン音を響かせながら、ピステンは降り積もった雪の上を進んだ。雪は柔らかく、まるで波をかき分けて進むクルーザーに乗っているような感覚を倉田は覚えた。実際には時速にして二十キロも出ていないのだが、すぐ目の前を細かい雪が流れていくので、スピードが出ているように錯覚するのだ。

「やっぱり、こっちのゲレンデはちょっと単調ですね」辰巳がいった。「斜度変化が少ないし、幅も広くない。何本か滑ったら、飽きてしまうかもしれない」

うん、と倉田は答えた。その意見には反論できなかった。

おまけに一旦下まで滑ってしまったら、二本のリフトを乗り継いでも、新月エリアへの連絡路に行くには、さらに二十メートル以上を歩いて登る必要があった。これではスキーヤーやスノーボーダーたちに毛嫌いされても仕方がない。

新月高原ホテルアンドリゾート株式会社が買収した時点では、新たに長いリフトに付け替えるという計画があった。だが結局、投資に見合うだけの効果は期待できない

ということで見送りになったのだ。

平均斜度が二十度ちょっとの斜面を、ピステンは力強くぐいぐいと登っていった。上部リフトの降り場付近まで到達したところで、辰巳はキャタピラを止めた。ドアを開け、倉田は雪の上に降り立った。空は曇っているが、雪の白さは目が痛くなるほどだった。ポケットに入れてあったサングラスをかけ、改めて周囲を見た。

「このあたりは問題なさそうだな」

辰巳も降りてきて、横に並んだ。

「危ないとしたら、リフトのすぐ上にある壁でしょうね。毎年春になると、真っ先に亀裂(きれつ)が入りますから」

倉田はその壁に目を向けた。斜度は四十度ほどある。パウダーマニアなら涎(よだれ)を垂らしそうだが、そこは滑走禁止区域だ。そもそも、その上まで登る手だてがない。そうしたところも、このゲレンデはちぐはぐなのだ。

藤崎絵留もスキーを担いで下りてきた。

「どのあたりを見て回ったらいいでしょうか」

「まずはメインコースを見回ってもらおう。ただし、段差のある場所には近づかないようにな」倉田はいった。

「わかりました」

藤崎絵留はスキーを装着すると、柔らかい雪の中を滑り始めた。圧雪されていないので、腰のあたりまで沈んで見える。それでも彼女はスキーの先端が沈まぬように巧みに操作し、雪煙を上げながら遠ざかっていった。

「じゃあ、我々も一回りしてみよう」倉田は辰巳にいった。

ピステンに乗り込み、少しコースを変えて斜面を下っていった。よく見ると、スキーやスノーボードで滑った跡がところどころにある。新月エリアからの連絡路は閉鎖されているが、新雪を滑りたい連中が、どうにかして侵入してきたのだろう。ただし一旦ここを滑り降りたら、車を使わないかぎりは新月エリアに戻れない。

一番下のリフト乗り場付近まで戻ると、すでに藤崎絵留の姿があった。満足そうな笑みを浮かべている。

「気持ちよく滑れたみたいだね」ピステンから降り、倉田はいった。

「最高でした」

「それはよかった。特に変わったことはなかったかい」

「大きな問題はないと思います。ただ、いくつか雪庇のせり出しているところがあります。あれは先に崩してやったほうがいいんじゃないでしょうか」

「なるほど。クロスのコースを造るとしたらどうかな。物足りなくないだろうか」

藤崎絵留は頷いた。

「大丈夫だと思います。斜度も長さも手頃だし、観戦スペースも確保できそうです」

「それならよかった」

クロスの大会については、これで解決できそうだ――倉田は安堵した。

その時だった。辰巳が、「倉田さん」といって彼の背後に目を向けた。倉田は振り返った。防寒具に身を包んだ二人の男が近づいてくるところだった。どちらも知っている顔だ。北月町観光課の岡村と増淵町長の息子英也だ。

二人は倉田たちの前まで来ると、深々と頭を下げた。

「ピステンを動かしておられると聞いたものですから、見に来たんです」岡村が媚びるような笑みを浮かべていった。「こちらをオープンしていただける目処が立ったということなんでしょうか」

松宮が心配していた通りの展開だ。ここで迂闊に首肯したら後が面倒だ、ということは倉田にもわかっている。

「いや、残念ながら、そういうことではないんです。パトロール員の報告で、新月エリアから滑走禁止区域を抜けて、こっちの斜面を降りる者がいるとわかったものです

から、状況を確認しに来ただけです。そういう人たちが雪崩に巻き込まれたりしたら大変ですから」

倉田の説明に、二人は失望感を露わにした。

「そうなんですか。私はてっきり、オープンしていただけるものと。——なあ」岡村は隣の増淵英也のほうを向いた。

増淵も頷いた。

「昨日、北月エリアの利用方法について、いくつかアイデアをお持ちしましたけど、その後検討していただけたのでしょうか」

「いやあそれが」倉田は辰巳たちのほうをちらりと見た。「こちらもいろいろとありまして、すぐに検討するというわけにもいかないんです。もちろん、全く考えてないということではなくて、上の者たちの判断次第では、近々オープンすることもありえます」彼はしゃべりながら気恥ずかしくなった。役所の人間に対して、それこそ役人のような答弁をしてしまったからだ。

「倉田さん、どうでしょうか」岡村が一歩前に出た。「せっかくここでお会いできたわけですし、少しだけ我々の話を聞いていただけませんか」

「うーん、今はちょっと……」

倉田は困惑した。こんなところで陳情されてもどうしようもない。

すると岡村がさらにいった。

「じつは、お尋ねしたいことがあるんです」

倉田は相手の丸い顔を見返した。

「どういったことですか」

「それが、立ち話で済ませられるような内容ではないんです。三十分で結構ですから」

岡村は食い下がってくる。

倉田は黙考した後、小さく頷いた。北月エリアで大会を開くことになれば、町役場にも協力してもらわねばならないのだ。

「わかりました。じゃあ、三十分だけ」

「ありがとうございます」岡村は相好を崩した。

倉田は辰巳と藤崎絵留のほうを向いた。

「そういうことだから、俺はちょっと行ってくる。悪いけど、君たちだけで見回ってもらえるかな」

「わかりました。大丈夫です」辰巳が答え、横で藤崎絵留も頷いた。

岡村たちは町役場の車で来ていた。倉田は自分のハイエースを運転し、彼等の後に

ついていくことになった。もっとも、北月エリアのゲレンデから北月町までは一本道だ。

二、三分走ると、前方に町並みが見えてきた。だが真っ先に目に飛び込んできたのは、入り口が封鎖された建物だった。看板は外され、地面に放置されている。かつてそこが旅館だったことを倉田は思い出した。半年ほど前に、廃業が決定したという話を聞いていた。

その後も宿や商店がちらほらと見られたが、どこも開店休業というほかない状態だった。スキーやスノーボードのレンタルを扱っているはずなのに、店内が廃材置き場のようになっている店もある。

岡村たちの車が止まった。小さな食堂の前だ。その店は営業しているようだ。倉田も彼等の車の隣にハイエースを止め、エンジンを切って外に出た。岡村が食堂の引き戸を開けて中に入っていく。増淵英也は倉田に向かって、どうぞ、と促すしぐさを見せた。

店内には四人掛けのテーブルが六つほど並んでいて、客はいなかった。マンガや雑誌の入った棚があり、その上には十四インチのテレビが載っている。岡村を見て、かすかに笑った。奥から六十歳前後と思われる小柄な女性が出てきた。

顔見知りらしい。

「ええと、コーヒーでいいですか」岡村が倉田に尋ねてきた。

「私は何でも」

「じゃあ、コーヒーを三つ」岡村は女性に注文してから、「どうぞ、おかけになってください」と倉田に椅子を勧めてきた。

倉田は彼等と向き合って座り、店内を見回した。メニューには麺類や丼物、定食などがある。観光客相手の店ではなく、地元の人間たちが重宝しているのだろう。だからこそ、辛うじて営業を続けていられるというわけだ。

「倉田さんは、めったにこっちのほうには来られないのではないですか」岡村が訊いてきた。

「そうですね。春以来……かな」

「驚かれたでしょう。すっかり寂れちゃってますから」

「そんなことはない、と否定したところで空々しいだけだ。

「たしかに、閉まってる店が多いですね」

「開けたって、経費がかさむだけなんですよ。何しろ、お客さんがいませんから」

倉田は黙って頷いた。返す言葉が思いつかない。北月エリアが閉鎖されている以上、

スキー客たちがこの町に泊まろうとしないのは当然のことだ。

先程の女性がコーヒーをトレイに載せて運んできた。各自の前にカップを並べると、頭を一つ下げて奥に消えた。

倉田はブラックのままでコーヒーを啜った。深い香りが鼻腔を刺激して、思った以上にコクがあった。

「それで、尋ねたいことというのは?」カップを置いてから彼は訊いた。

岡村が身を乗り出してきた。

「じつは妙な噂が流れているそうなんです」

「どういう噂ですか」

岡村は店の奥を気にする素振りを見せた後、一層声を落としていった。

「新月高原スキー場が売りに出されている、という噂です」

「えっ」倉田は目を剝いた。「まさか。どこでそんな噂が?」

「ネット上です」そう答えたのは増淵英也だ。「見つけた知り合いが教えてくれたんです。ただ、ソースはよくわかりません。いくつかの掲示板に書き込みがされて、それが広まったということなんですけど、今では元の書き込みも削除されているらしいんです」

「具体的にはどういう内容なんですか」

「だから、今申し上げたようなことです」岡村が続けた。「新月高原ホテルが経営難

からスキー場の売却先を探している、早ければ今シーズン終了時には決定するかもし

れない——そういう内容です」

24

駐車場でスノーボードとブーツを車に積み込んだ後、根津は詰め所に戻った。詰め

所では数人のパトロール員が休憩をしていた。その中には桐林もいる。彼は根津を見

上げて目を丸くした。

「どうしたんですか、その恰好」

根津の着ているウェアがスノーボード用のものだったからだろう。最近ではスキー

ウェアとスノーボードウェアの違いは少なくなってきているが、やはり見慣れた人間

にはすぐにわかる。

「ちょっと遊んでたんだ」根津はゴーグルとグローブを外し、ウェアを脱ぎ始めた。

「そういえば根津さんは、元々ボーダーだったんですよね。今まで滑ってるのを見た

ことがなかったけど」

「今日が今シーズン初滑りだ」根津はパトロールの制服を引き寄せた。「そういえば、キリはあまりボードの話をしないな。夏はサーフィンをするんだろ。だったら、スキーよりもボードじゃないのか」

「それが不思議なもので、雪の上だと横乗りはだめなんです。なぜなんでしょうね」

「ふうん、そういうものなのかな。俺はサーフィンのことは全然わかんないけど」根津は制服を着て、椅子に腰を下ろした。「北月です」

桐林は指で遠くを示すしぐさをした。「北月です」

「北月？　どうして？」

「倉田さんたちが点検するので、その手伝いだそうです。未圧雪用の板を持って、嬉しそうに出かけていきましたよ」

根津は頷いた。

「なるほどな。じゃあ、本格的に準備を始めるのかもしれない」

「北月エリアをオープンさせるってことですか」

「クロスの大会があるからな。倉田さんは、あっちにコースを造ることを考えている

みたいだ」

根津の声が聞こえたらしく、上山禄郎が近づいてきた。

「それ、本当ですか」

彼等に聞かれることは承知の上だったので、根津はあわてなかった。事件のことは話せないが、クロスのコース造りが遅れていることについては、いずれ何らかの説明をしなければならないと思っていたのだ。

「詳しいことはわからないんだけど、会社側は例年とは違うところにコースを造ることを考えているそうだ」根津は曖昧な言葉でごまかした。

「例年とは違うって……アタックコースやゴールドコースには造らないってことですか」

「そうらしい」

上山は腕組みをして、首を縦に振った。

「それでか。いつもに比べて工事の始まるのが遅いと思ってたんですよね。でもどうしてそんなことをするのかな」

「理由は俺も知らない。とにかくそれで北月エリアを検討することになったようだ」

「へえ。でも、あっちのエリアがオープンされたら、それはそれで面倒ですよね。

またきっと、客からいろいろといわれますよ」上山は唇を尖らせた。

昨シーズンの事故のことをいっているのだ。スキー場の責任ではないとはいえ、事

故のあったコースをオープンさせるとなれば、あれこれ質問してくる客もいるだろう。

クローズのままのほうが面倒がなくていいというのは、パトロール員たちの本音でも

ある。

「仕方がないだろ。そういう客に説明するのも俺たちの仕事なんだからさ」

「それはわかってますけどね」上山はため息をついた。

「キリ、ちょっといいか」根津は桐林に声をかけ、親指をドアに向けながら立ち上が

った。ついてこいという意味だ。

いいですよ、と桐林も腰を上げた。

詰め所を出て、ゲレンデに面したベンチに二人で並んで腰掛けた。近くに誰もいな

いことを確かめてから、根津は口を開いた。

「じつはちょっと相談があるんだ。もちろん、例の事件のことでな」

桐林の顔が引き締まった。「何ですか」

「その前に約束してくれ。今からいうことは絵留や倉田さんたちには内緒だ。俺とお

まえだけの秘密ってことにしたい」

桐林はサングラスをかけた後、改めて顔を上げた。目に緊張の色が浮かんでいる。

「なんだか、やばそうな話ですね」

「悪いことを企んでいるわけじゃない。どうなんだ。約束できるか」

桐林は少し黙った後、小さく頷いた。

「わかりました。約束します。これで話の続きを聞かなかったら、余計に気になるし」

「オーケー。じつはおまえのいう通りなんだ。少々やばいことを考えている」

桐林は身構えるように顎を引いた。

「何ですか、一体」

ここで根津はもう一度周囲に目をやった。さらに声を落としていった。「犯人の尻尾を摑んでやろうと思っている」

「えっ、と桐林は一瞬背筋を伸ばした。「摑むって、どうやって？」

「これまで犯人は、現金を手にした後、閉鎖後のコースやコース外を滑って逃げているだろ。警察の監視がないと見越しているからだと思うけど、たぶんこれからも似たような手で来るだろうと思う。奴は滑りの技術に自信を持っていて、誰にも追跡できないと踏んでるんだ。そこで、その自信を逆手に取る」

「まさか、二人で捕まえようっていうんじゃないでしょうね。根津さん、それはまずいですよ。犯人が一人ならいいけど、もしほかに仲間がいたら、ゲレンデを爆破されちゃうかもしれない」

今にも目を血走らせそうな桐林の顔の前で、根津は手を振った。

「そうじゃない。話を最後まで聞けよ。誰が捕まえるなんていった。犯人の尻尾を摑むといっただけだ」

「じゃあ、何をする気ですか」

「これだよ」根津はカメラのシャッターを押すふりをした。「写真を撮る」

桐林の口が半開きになった。意図が理解できないからだろう。

「もっと厳密にいえば、写真を撮るふりだけでもいいんだ。肝心なことは、犯人側に撮られたと思わせることだ」

「何のためにですか」

「それはもちろん、犯人の動きを封じるためだ。写真を撮られたと思ったら、犯人としては、もう下手に動かないほうがいいと考えるんじゃないか。スキー場側が、絶対に警察には届けないなんていう保証はないんだからさ。写真には、犯人を特定できる何かが写っているかもしれないわけだろ」

「それはわかりますけど、そんなことをしても大丈夫ですかね。犯人が、怒って爆破を実行するなんてことはありませんか」

根津は肩をすくめた。

「そんなことをして、犯人側にどんなメリットがある？　罪が重くなるだけだ。万一人が死んだら殺人罪だぜ。当然、被害者からの届けがあろうがなかろうが警察は動きだす。そうなったら、会社としてもすべてを白状するしかない。写真があるんだから、犯人が割りだされる可能性も高い。どうだ？　どう考えたって、犯人側にはデメリットしかないだろ。俺が犯人なら、そんな馬鹿なことはしない。これからもスキー場側が警察に届けないことを期待して、さっさと退散する」

桐林は腕を組み、唸った。

「なるほど。いわれてみれば、たしかにそうかもしれません。だけど、もし犯人がそこまで考えない奴だったらまずいですよ」

根津は苦笑し、ふんと鼻を鳴らした。

「そんな単細胞なら、今度みたいな事件は起こさない。この犯人は、かなり周到に考えて行動している。大丈夫だよ」

桐林は眉間に皺を寄せてしばらく黙った後、わかりました、と頷いた。

「そういわれてみれば、そうかもしれませんね。で、具体的にどんなことをすればいいんですか」

「その通りだ。ふつうに追っかけるのでさえ大変なんだからな。だけどそれは俺一人だったからだ。こっちが二人なら、何とかなるんじゃないか。コース外を滑る連中を追っかける時だってそうだろ」

「何か作戦があるんですか」

「作戦ってほどのものじゃない。俺の考えでは、次もたぶん絵留が現金を運ぶことになるだろう。これまでと同様、犯人はケータイを使って、彼女をあちこちに移動させるはずだ。そこで、まず俺たちのうちのどちらか一方は、彼女の行き先を察知した時点で先回りをしておく。もう一人は、彼女の後からついていく。たとえば犯人からの指示で絵留がリフトやゴンドラに乗ったら、一人が彼女よりも先に乗り、もう一人が後に乗るって具合にさ。前回、もしそうしていれば、彼女よりも後に乗ったほうが、犯人が現金を回収するところを目撃できたかもしれないんだ。その間、ケータイは繋ぎっぱなしにして、常に連絡を取り合うことにする。どうだ。これならどんな手を打たれても、

にはいかないと思いますけど」

にはいかないと思いますけど」

だったからだ。こっちが二人なら、何とかなるんじゃないか。コース外を滑る連中を

どちらかが犯人を追跡できる可能性が高いんじゃないか」

頭の中で状況を思い浮かべているのか、桐林は少し考え込むように黙った後、「ど

うですかねえ」と呟いた。「その時になってみないとわからないな……」

「もちろん俺だってそうだ。相手がどう出るか、予測できないんだからな」

「だめで元々ってことですね」

「何もやらないよりはましだろ。でもうまくすれば、一方が犯人を追いかけて、もう

一方が待ち伏せるっていう形になれるかもしれない。その時が来たらチャンスだ。カ

メラを構えて、撮影してるってことをアピールする。さっきもいったけど、実際には

撮れてなくてもいいんだ。犯人側に撮られたと思わせることが大事なんだからな」

桐林は身体を細かく揺すった。

「大体わかりました。でも、そんなふうに追跡して、後で倉田さんたちに叱られませ

んか。余計なことはするなって釘を刺されたんでしょ」

「注意はされるだろうな。でも結果的に犯人の動きを封じられたなら、俺たちの意図

も理解してもらえるはずだ。それに、仮にうまくいかなくても、おまえが心配するこ

とはないよ」根津は桐林の肩を叩いた。「責任は全部俺がとるから」

すると桐林は瞬きし、根津さん、と真剣な眼差<ruby>眼差<rt>まなざ</rt></ruby>しを向けてきた。

「何だよ、俺、何か変なことをいったか」

「いや、そうじゃなくて」桐林は頭を掻いた。「根津さんは、真剣にこのスキー場のことを考えてるんだなあと思って。だって、こんなとんでもない事件に巻き込まれて、ふつうなら責任逃れをしたいところなのに……」

根津は苦笑して片手を振った。

「そんな恰好のいいもんじゃねえよ。俺はただ、これ以上犯人のいいなりになるのが我慢ならないだけだ。遠いところからスキーやスノーボードを楽しみに来てる人たちを、いわば人質にとってるわけだろ？　あの人たちには何の罪もないのに、危険に晒している。そんな汚いやり方、許せねえよ。そうは思わないか」

彼の語気に圧されたように少し身を引きつつ、思います、と桐林は答えた。

「わかりました。じゃあ、今度何かあったらすぐに教えてください。俺、いつでも出動できるように準備しておきます」

「うん、頼むよ」

「でも、犯人はまた何かいってきますかね。もう六千万円も手に入れてるわけだし、そろそろ引き際じゃないですか」

「それは……」根津は両手を広げた。「俺にもわからない」

「もう何もいってこなきゃ、一番いいわけですよね」

「そんなことはないぞ。爆発物がどこに埋まっているのか、それをはっきりさせないと事件解決とはとてもいえないだろ」

「あ……そうですよね」

根津はゲレンデに目を向けた。今日もなかなかの賑わいを見せている。楽しそうに滑っている人々は、自分たちの足元に何が潜んでいるのか、全く知らない。

このまま犯人からの連絡が途絶えてしまったら困る理由が、じつはほかにもあった。

だがそちらは根津の個人的理由だ。

あいつともう一度勝負したい——。

三十メートルの飛躍を成し遂げて逃げた犯人とは、一体何者なのか。是非とも自分の目で見てみたいと思っていた。もちろんそんな本音を桐林に語るわけにはいかなかったが。

25

倉田が藤崎絵留と共に新月エリアに戻った時には、すでにナイター営業が始まって

いた。パトロールの詰め所に戻るという彼女とは駐車場で別れ、倉田はホテルの通用口から中に入った。だが管理事務所は素通りし、本部長室をノックした。どうぞ、と松宮の声が聞こえたので、ドアを開けた。松宮は席で煙草を吸っていた。机の上に広げられているのは、宣伝用のポスターだった。『ダイナ・クロス！』の文字が躍っている。今度行われる大会の愛称だった。

「北月エリアに行ってきたのか」

「はい。辰巳君たちと見回りましたが、特に問題はありません。クロスのコースを造ることは可能です。ただし、リフトの準備はそろそろ始める必要があります。人員を確保するよう津野君に指示しましたけど、構いませんよね」

松宮は灰皿の中で煙草の火を消した。

「人員確保は認める。ただし今朝もいったが、まだ作業には入るな。あと、二日待て」

「二日？　本部長それはちょっと──」

倉田が意見を述べようとするのを、松宮は手を出して制した。

「いいたいことはわかっている。もうぎりぎりなんだろ。そこを何とか堪えてほしい。君たちの力なら、二日間の遅れなど挽回できるはずだ。そのかわり、工事開始となれ

ば、最大限のバックアップをする。それは社長も約束してくれた」

倉田は深く俯き、ため息をついた。それから顔を上げ、改めて松宮を見た。

「北月町で、岡村さんに会いました。観光課長の岡村さんです」

松宮は片方の眉を上げた。「彼が何か？」

「妙なことを訊かれました。広世観光がスキー場の売却を検討しているというのは本当か、と」

松宮が大きく息を吸い込む気配があった。背中を反らせるようにして倉田を見上げてくる。その目は少し充血していた。

「何だ、それは」

「インターネット上で、そういう噂が流れたんだそうです。増淵町長の息子さんが、知り合いに教えられて見つけたとか」

松宮は、頰を揺らして首を振った。

「そんな話、聞いたことないぞ。俺は知らん」

「私も岡村さんにはそのように答えました。でも火のないところに煙は立たないという諺もあります。本部長には、何か心当たりはありませんか」

「ない。全くない」松宮は煙草の箱を引き寄せ、中から一本を抜き取った。火をつけ

るのに何度か手こずった後、白い煙を吐いた。「スキー場といえば、今や斜陽産業の

代表格だ。それでどこかの誰かが、単なる憶測を書き込んだだけだぞ。ネッ

ト上には、その手のデマ情報のほうがたくさん流れているという話だぞ」

「たしかにそうですが、今回の噂の場合、売却先として複数の社名が挙がっていたり

して、かなり具体的な内容が含まれているらしく、気になります」

松宮は煙草を指に挟んだままで手を横に振った。

「気にするな。俺が知らないんだから、そんな話が進んでいるわけがない。余計なこ

とは考えず、君は現時点での問題に取り組んでくれ。今我々が考えなきゃいけないの

は、次に犯人は何をいってくるか、それに対してどうすべきかってことだ。違うか?」

「それは……そうだと思います」

「わかったなら持ち場に戻ってくれ。噂については、何かの機会に社長の耳に入れて

おこう。一笑に付されると思うがね」

「わかりました。どうも失礼しました」頭を下げ、倉田は出口に向かった。だがドア

を開ける前に振り返った。

「最近、北月町には行かれましたか」

「北月町? いや、行ってないな。どうかしたか」全く興味がない、という口ぶりだ。

「かなりの寂いようです。あれでは、やっていけないでしょう。何とかしてやりたい、と思ってしまいました」

松宮は苦いものを呑み込んだような顔をした。

「この御時世だ。苦境に立たされている地域は、日本中どこにでもある。残念ながら我々には、ボランティアをやっている余裕はない。明日は我が身なんだからな」

予想された答えだった。倉田は反論せず、失礼します、といって部屋を出た。

管理事務所に戻り、今日のこれまでの業務内容などの見直しを始めたが、なかなか仕事に集中できなかった。無論、岡村から聞かされた話が気になっているからだ。親会社である広世観光は、ここ数年でいくつかのスキー場を売却あるいは閉鎖している。新月高原スキー場は経営が安定しているといわれているが、だからこそ今が売り時と首脳が考えたとしても不思議ではない。

椅子にもたれ、ぼんやりと窓からゲレンデを眺めた。この時期は、あっという間に日が落ちる。ナイター照明の下、スキーヤーやスノーボーダーたちが楽しそうに滑っている。

知っている人物の姿を発見し、倉田は身体を起こした。青いスキーウェア姿でゲレンデの下部に立っているのは、たしかに入江義之だった。さらにその傍らには、子供

の姿もある。入江達樹だろう。

倉田は防寒コートを手にして立ち上がった。　懸念すべきことは山ほどあるが、入江親子のこともほうってはおけなかった。

ゲレンデに出て、彼等に駆け寄った。入江親子は、どちらもスキーを装着していた。

入江さん、と倉田は声をかけた。入江義之は顔を上げ、小さく会釈してきた。

「息子さん、ようやく滑る気になったんですか」親子を見比べながら倉田は訊いた。

だが入江は首を振った。

「無理矢理、ここまで連れてきただけです。　昼間は人が多いから嫌だというので、ナイターならすいていると思いましてね。でも、これでもやっぱり怖いらしい」

「怖い……というと？」

入江はゲレンデを見渡した。

「次から次へとスキーヤーやスノーボーダーが滑り降りてくるでしょ？　特に夜は、エッジの音がよく響きますよね。あれが後ろから近づいてくると、怖くて仕方がないみたいなんです。たぶん、母親が事故に遭った時のことを思い出すんでしょうね」

この話に、倉田はぎくりとして入江達樹を見下ろした。彼はじっと下を向いている。

母親が後方から激突され、血を流す場面を目撃しているの

無理もない、と思った。

だ。

「どこか、自分たちだけで滑れる場所があればいいんですけどね。まあしかし、雪の上に立てるようになっただけでも前進です。ぽちぽちやります」そういうと入江は、

「じゃあ、もう帰ろうか」と息子に声をかけた。

入江達樹は頷き、スキーを外し始めた。その手つきは慣れたものだ。事故に遭うまでは、スキーに親しんでいたということがわかる。

入江親子は、と入江義之がいった。お疲れ様でした、と倉田は返した。

ではまた、と入江義之がいった。お疲れ様でした、と倉田は返した。

入江親子は、スキー板とストックを持って、ホテルに向かい始めた。その後ろ姿を眺めているうちに、一つのアイデアが浮かんだ。ほんの思いつきだったが、悪くないアイデアだと思った。

倉田は二人を追った。背中に声をかけようとした。

だがその時、防寒コートの下で携帯電話が着信を告げた。彼は足を止め、電話を取り出した。かけてきているのは辰巳だった。彼もすでに北月エリアから戻ってきている。

「はい、倉田です」

（辰巳です。倉田さん、すぐに戻ってきてください）彼の声には余裕がなかった。

26

ある予感を抱いた。倉田は電話を握る手に力を込めた。

「どうかしたのか」声が上ずりそうになるのを堪えて訊いた。

一拍置いてから、辰巳は倉田が予想した通りのことをいった。

「連絡が来ました。犯人からです。新たな要求をしてきました」

『新月高原スキー場の関係者諸君へ

次なる取引を提案させてもらう。要求金額は五千万円だ。

今回無事に支払いが行われた場合は、爆発物の場所を具体的に明かす。そして当然のことながら、我々と諸君との取引は、これを最後とする。

条件を受け入れるのなら、次の指示に従うこと。

・二十四時間以内に現金五千万円を用意せよ。用意ができたら、いつものようにゴンドラ屋根に黄色の目印を付けること。二十四時間が経過しても合図がない場合は、取引に応じる意思がないと見なす。

・五千万円を持ち運べる防水バッグ、前回使用した携帯電話を用意し、いつでも現金

を運べるようにしておくこと。運搬係は、スキーかスノーボードの経験者であること。

毎回警告していることだが、この取引は信頼関係がなければ成立しない。諸君たちの動きに少しでも不審な点がある場合、即刻取引は中止する。場合によっては爆発物のタイマーを作動させることもありうる。そのことを決して忘れないように。

では回答を待つ。

　　　　　　　　　　　　　　　　　　　　　　　　埋葬者より』

プリントアウトされた脅迫状を会議机の中央に置き、いつもの顔ぶれが並んでいた。もはや見慣れた光景といえる。しかしこれまでは誰よりも苦々しさを発散していた中垣でさえ、その顔には無力感が漂っていた。もはやここで怒ろうが喚こうがどうにもならない、と諦めてしまっているように倉田には見えた。

「──というわけで」その中垣が重々しく口を開いた。「社長は金を払おうとおっしゃっている。今夜中に、本社の許可も得られるだろうということだった」

倉田は小さく頭を振った。

「三千万、三千万で、次は五千万ですか。それだけの金があったなら、もっといろいろとスキー場のサービスを充実させられるのに」

「仕方がないだろ。サービスよりも、まずは安全確保だ」

もっともらしい顔でそんなことをいう松宮を、倉田は思わず眉をひそめて見返して
いた。安全を口にするのなら警察に届けるべき、という台詞を呑み込んだ。今さらそ
んなことをいっても遅い。

「それにしても、どうして分割なんですかねえ」総務部長の宮内が首を捻る。「一億
一千万という額が中途半端なのはまあいいとして、なぜ一回の取引で奪おうとしなか
ったんでしょう。取引の回数を増やせば、それだけ危険が増すとは思わないのかな」

「最初は三千万だけでやめておくつもりだったんじゃないか」中垣がいった。「とこ
ろが思った以上にあっさりと金を奪えたものだから、さらに要求することを思いつい
た。で、二度目もまたうまくいったので、ますます欲が出てきた。そんなところじゃ
ないか。たしか前回のメールでは、今後のことについてはまた連絡すると書いてあっ
ただろう。きっとあの時点では、どうするべきか犯人自身も迷ってたんだ」

「なるほど。今回少し間が空いたのも、そう考えれば筋が通りますね」宮内が納得顔
で頷く。

「だろ？　警察に通報されるおそれがないと見越して、図に乗ってきてるんだよ」

「そう考えると癪ですねえ」

「癪だが仕方がない。ほかに選択肢はないんだからな」

中垣と宮内のやりとりを横で聞きながら、倉田は釈然としないものを感じていた。警察に通報されていないことは、一回目の現金授受の際に犯人は確信したはずだ。当初の予定を変更してさらに一攫千金（いっかくせんきん）を狙う気になったのだとしたら、その次で勝負をかけてきたのではないか。

犯人が取引の回数を増やすのは、何か全く別の理由があるからではないかと倉田は思った。しかしそれは何かと問われると、彼にも答えられなかった。

「これまでと同様、明日は宮内君に銀行まで現金を取りに行ってもらう。倉田君たちは、犯人の指示通りに準備を進めておいてくれ」中垣がとりまとめるようにいった。

「何か質問は？」

「ひとついいですか」倉田は手を上げた。

「しつこいようですが、クロスのコースはどうしますか。今日、辰巳君たちと北月エリアの下見をしてきました。あちらにコースを造ることには何の問題もないと私は判断したのですが」

「そのことなら、夕方にも話をしただろう」松宮が横からいった。「二日待てといったはずだ。こうして犯人が連絡をしてきたんだから、あわてて作業に入らなくて正解だったじゃないか」

「しかしこの取引の結果がどうなるかはわかりません。犯人が爆発物の位置を知らせてこなかったらどうするんですか。私としては、北月エリアも使えるようにしておくのがベストだと思います」

松宮は苦いものを口に入れたような顔で中垣のほうをちらりと見た後、倉田に視線を戻した。

「君の言い分はわかった。とにかく二日待とう。明後日の午後までだ。その時点で犯人からの連絡がなければ、北月エリアでのコース造りに取りかかってくれていい」

「その指示に変更はありませんね」

「ああ、約束しよう。ただし、犯人からの連絡があった場合は、話は別だぞ」

「わかっています。私も、できれば爆発物を除去してからコース造りを始めたいですから」

「どうやら話はついたようだな」中垣が立ち上がった。「金を払えば爆発物の場所はわかる。それがわかれば、除去もできる。あと少しの辛抱だ。がんばろう」

鼓舞するような台詞に倉田は虚しさを覚えた。何をどうがんばればいいのかと思ったが、黙って頷いておいた。

会議室を出た後、倉田は根津に電話をかけた。まだ帰らずに残ってくれるよう頼ん

であったのだ。彼はパトロールの詰め所にいた。藤崎絵留も一緒らしい。新たな脅迫
状が来たということで、とても帰る気にはなれなかったのだろう。管理事務所に来て
くれといって倉田は電話を切った。

管理事務所には誰もいなかった。倉田がインスタントコーヒーを淹れる準備をして
いると、程なく二人が現れた。すでに私服に着替えている。倉田は彼等にもコーヒー
を淹れてやりながら、新たに送られてきた脅迫状のことを話した。彼等を最も驚かせ
たのは、五千万円という金額だった。

「完全に舐められてる。どんなにふっかけても、こっちはいいなりになるしかないと
思ってやがるんだ」コーヒーカップを手にして、根津は吐き捨てるようにいった。

「その脅迫状って、見せてもらえますか」

藤崎絵留にいわれ、倉田は上着のポケットに折り畳んで入れてあった脅迫状を取り
出した。辰巳がプリントアウトしたものをコピーしたのだ。

彼女は真剣な眼差しで脅迫文を読み始めた。根津も横から覗き込んでいる。

「今度も、スキーかスノーボードのできる人間を運搬役にしろといってきてますね」
また、ゲレンデ内を移動させる気ですよ、きっと」根津が悔しそうにいう。「次はど
ういう手を使うつもりだろう」

「それはわからんが、またしても君たちに運搬役を頼むしかない。やってもらえるね」

根津は、すぐに藤崎絵留を見た。

「絵留、いいよな?」

彼女はじろりと根津を見返した。

「あたしはいいんだけど、根津君はどうする気?」

「どうって?」

「何度もいうようだけど、変なことは考えないでね」

根津はげんなりした顔を作った。

「俺はスキー場のためを思ってるんだけどな。それを、変なことといわれるとはね」

「わかってくれ。無事に取引を終えることが、現時点では最もスキー場のためになるんだよ」倉田はいった。「犯人のいいなりになるのは悔しいが、仕方がない」

根津は無念そうに眉根を寄せた。

「わかりました。でも離れたところから様子を窺うことは許可してください。決して犯人を刺激しないよう気をつけますから」

「君のことだ。犯人の姿を見たら、追跡したくなるんじゃないのか」

「そんなことはしません。約束します。犯人の手口を見届けたいだけなんです」

「そうすることに何か意味があるのか。前にもいったけど、社長は今度の事件について警察に届ける気は全くない。君が何か手がかりを摑んだところで、何の役にも立たないんだ」

「そうかもしれませんが、自分の気が済まないんです。お願いします」根津は頭を下げた。

倉田は吐息をついた。根津の気持ちは彼にもよくわかった。

「本当に見守っているだけなんだな。手は出さないな」

「出しません」

「わかった。それなら認めよう。ただし、約束は守ってくれよ」

はい、と根津は頷いて答えた。嘘をついているようには見えなかった。

「それと、もう一つ頼みがある。事件とは関係のない話だ」倉田は二人を交互に見ながらいった。「入江さんたちのことだ」

倉田は、ナイターゲレンデで入江親子と会った時のことを話した。「達樹君がゲレンデに出られるようになったのはよかったと思いますけど、その分だと、スキーをできるようになる

「そうですか」根津が難しい顔つきで腕組みをした。

までには、まだかなり時間がかかりそうですね」

「ナイターは雪面が硬いから、エッジの音が特に大きく聞こえますものね。慣れてな
いと怖いかも」藤崎絵留がいう。「でも人が多くて嫌だということなら、昼間のほう
が断然いいんですけどね。ナイターはゲレンデが狭くなる分、人口密度が高くなるか
ら」

「理屈はそうなんだけど、達樹君にしてみれば、広大なゲレンデのあちらこちらで人
が滑っているという状況が怖いのかもしれない。どこから人が飛び出してくるかわか
らない、という恐怖があるんだと思う。何しろほら、事故が起きたのは昼間だった
し」

「あれは特殊な状況だったんだけどなあ」根津が悔しそうにいった。「くそっ。今さ
らながら、腹が立って仕方がない。滑走禁止区域を滑ったこともそうだし、先を見な
いで飛び降りたこともそうだけど、何より、逃げたというのが、どうにも許せねえよ。
あの事故のせいで一人の男の子が未だに苦しんでるってことを、どうにかしてわから
せてやりたいよ」

「同感だな。しかも苦しんでるのは達樹君だけじゃない」

倉田の言葉に、根津は瞬きした。

「もちろん入江さんも……お父さんのほうも苦しんでおられるでしょうね。急に奥さんを失ったわけだし」

倉田は首を振った。

「そういう意味じゃない。入江さん親子だけが被害者じゃないといいたかったんだ。あの事故のせいで、いろいろな人たちが苦境に立たされている」

倉田は昼間に見てきた北月町の様子を話した。根津たちの表情が一層暗くなった。

「あの町のことなら、俺も結構聞いています。かなり厳しいって……」

あたしも、と藤崎絵留もいった。

「筧社長が北月エリアの営業に消極的なのは、今に始まったことじゃない。はっきりいって、うちの会社が買い取った時から、切り捨てたかったはずなんだ。だけどその口実がなかった。ところがあの事故が起きたものだから、堂々と閉鎖にしておける。それがスキー場側の安全意識だと評価してもらえる。今のままじゃ、北月エリアはいずれ廃止になるだろうな。そうなったら、北月町の人々は一体どうなるのか……。考えるだけで憂鬱(ゆううつ)になってしまうよ」

倉田の話を聞き、若い二人は黙り込んだ。自分たちにはどうすることもできないだけに、歯痒(はがゆ)い思いを噛みしめているのだろう。

「あ、いや、そういう話をしたいわけではないんだ」倉田は手を振った。「話を戻そう。入江さんたちのことだ。そんなわけで、ほかの人たちが滑っていると、達樹君は怖くて動けないらしい。そこで、彼等のために貸切ゲレンデを用意しようと思う」

「貸切？」根津が目を丸くした。「そんなこと、勝手にやってもいいんですか。しかも二人だけのために」

「こっちのゲレンデでは無理だろうね」

「こっちって……」

「ああ、そうかっ」藤崎絵留が手を叩いた。「わかりました。そういうことですね。それ、すごくいいと思います。グッドアイデアです」

「えっ、何、どういうこと？」根津がきょろきょろした。

「さっき話したでしょ。今日、倉田さんたちと一緒に北月エリアに行ってきたって。見回りってことで、ピステンで上まで乗っけてもらって滑ってきたって」

「あっ、なるほど……」根津が倉田に顔を戻した。「入江さんたちを北月エリアに連れていこうってことですね」

「そういうわけだ。あそこならほかに人がいないから、達樹君でも思いきって滑れるんじゃないかな。残念ながら、まだリフトは動かせないが、スノーモービルで二、三

回ぐらいは運べると思うし。入江さんは君たちにおっしゃってたんだろう？　もう一度達樹君をあの場所に連れていって、何が起きたのかを正面から受けとめさせたいって。そういう意味でも、ちょうどいいんじゃないだろうか」

「たしかにグッドアイデアですね。安全確保には万全を期す必要がありますけど」

「その通りだ。そこで君たちの出番だよ。入江さんたちを連れていく時、君たちのどちらかが同行してほしい。パトロール員も一緒となれば、本部長の許可も取りやすいだろうからね」

「わかりました。お安い御用です」根津は藤崎絵留と共に頷いた。

うな顔を作った。「ところで、クロスのほうはどうするんですか。　北月エリアにコースを造るかもしれないということでしたけど」

そのことを考えると倉田も頭が痛い。　冴えない表情になるのが自分でもわかった。

「あと二日待てといわれたよ。それまでに爆発物の場所が特定できなければ、工事を始めていいということだった」

「結構、きついスケジュールになりそうですね」

「スタッフたちには徹夜覚悟でがんばってもらうことになるかもしれないが、仕方がない。　君たちにも無理をお願いすることになると思う」

「俺たちは大丈夫です。——なあ」

根津に同意を求められ、藤崎絵留も深く顎を引いた。

「倉田さんこそ無理をしないでくださいね。何もかも一人で責任を負おうとされてるみたいで心配です」

「ありがとう。自分一人で背負い込める問題でないことはわかっているよ」そういって倉田は窓の外に目をやった。細かい雪が降っている。この分だと明日もゲレンデコンディションはよさそうだ。

「本当に犯人は教えてくれるでしょうか。爆発物の場所を」根津が、ぽつりといった。

何とも答えようがなく、倉田は黙って首を傾げた。

27

ホテルから出てきた入江達樹は、明らかに乗り気ではなさそうだった。眉間に皺を寄せているのは、雪の反射が眩しいからだけではないだろう。それでもスキー靴を履き、スキー板とストックを手にしているのは、父親から強く命令されたせいに違いない。

北月エリアの一部を入江親子のために開放することについては、今朝早く、倉田が松宮の許可を取ったらしい。あくまでも特例であり、入江親子以外の人間は絶対に滑らせないこと、というのが条件だった。

「何だか、申し訳ないですね。私たちだけのために」入江義之は気まずそうな表情で根津にいった。

「気にしないでください。みんな、何とかして入江さんたちの力になりたいんです。達樹君に、早くスキーの楽しさを思い出してほしいし」親子の顔を交互に見て、根津はいった。

ありがとうございます、と入江は頭を下げた。だが息子のほうは目を合わせてくれない。

「ほら、おまえも礼をいわないか」

「いや、いいんですよ、そんなのは」

「いえ、そういうわけにはいきません。達樹、お礼をいうんだ」

父親に命じられ、ようやく達樹はこくりと頭を下げた。ありがとうございます、と弱々しい声が漏れた。

「なんだ、その声は」

「もういいじゃないですか。さあ、行きましょう」

根津は二人を、駐車場に止めてある自分のライトバンまで案内した。車の屋根には、スキー板を積めるキャリアを装着してある。そこにスキー板とストックを取り付け、二人を後部座席に座らせた後、根津は運転席に乗り込んだ。エンジンをかけ、ゆっくりと車をスタートさせる。タイヤが、昨夜降り積もった雪を踏んでいった。

「十分ほどで着きますから」根津は後ろの二人にいった。

雪はやんでいるので視界は良好だった。幅の狭い道を、慎重に進んでいく。前後に車はいない。反対側から来ることもない。

「この道は、あまり使われてないんですか」入江が訊いてきた。

「いえ、北月町に行くには、この道しかありません」

「そのわりに車がいませんね」

「そうですね。向こうのゲレンデがオープンしたら、状況は変わると思うんですけど」

「やっぱり、当分の間は今のままなんでしょうか」

「さあそれは、自分には何とも……」根津は言葉を濁した。

「何だか複雑なんですよね。あの事故のせいで、いろんな人が困ってると思うと」

「お気持ちはわかります。でも一番の被害者は入江さんたちですから、そんなふうに思う必要はないですよ」

そうかもしれませんけど、といって入江は口を閉ざした。

細かった道が突然広くなり、右手前方にゲレンデが見えてきた。ピステンが止まっていて、その横に辰巳たちの姿がある。

根津は車を止め、スキー板を下ろした。　辰巳が近づいてきたので、入江親子を紹介した。

「昨日、絵留ちゃんが見回ってくれたから、危険なポイントはわかってるよ。中腹の緩斜面なら大丈夫だ」辰巳はいった。

「達樹君、見てごらん」根津は腰を落として少年と目線を合わせ、ゲレンデのほうを指差した。「誰もいないだろ。今日は貸切だ。達樹君とお父さんだけのゲレンデだから、何も怖がらなくていい。思いきり滑っていいよ」

達樹は相変わらず不機嫌そうな顔つきだったが、その目は雪面を見ることを拒絶してはいなかった。ほんの少しではあったが、彼自身が何かを期待している気配を根津は感じた。この試みはうまくいくのではないか、と思った。

辰巳が二人乗りのスノーモービルを用意してくれていた。根津が運転し、まずは入

江を後ろに乗せて出発した。雪を散らし、斜面を駆け上がっていく。

「根津さん、大変ですね。二人いるから、何度も往復しなきゃいけない」後ろで入江がいった。

「大丈夫です。パトロール中は、何度も行ったり来たりするんですから」

斜面がやや急になる手前で止まった。達樹にとっては久しぶりのスキーだ。まずは緩やかなところで練習したほうが無難だろう。

入江を降ろすと元の場所に戻り、今度は達樹を後ろに乗せた。スノーモービルが動きだすと、後ろで達樹が身体を硬くしたのがわかった。雪の上を移動するというだけで怖いのかもしれない。だがしばらくすると、彼の上げる声が根津の耳に入ってきた。それは悲鳴ではなく、明らかに驚きと興奮によるものだった。

28

ココアの入ったカップを前にして、快人は腕組みを始めた。カップの横には空になった皿がある。つい数分前まで、その皿にはショートケーキが載っていた。男のくせにどれだけ甘党なんだ、とわけもなく苛々した。千晶はコーヒーをブラックで啜った。

「いろいろ考えたんだけどさあ、いきなりケータイにかけるのはまずいと思うんだよなあ」快人が難しい顔つきでいう。

やっぱりそのことか、と千晶は脱力する。このところこの従兄は、口を開けば同じ話題ばかりだ。

「まだそんなこといってんの？　かなり焦れったいんだけど」

「だって、千晶だってそう思うだろ。知らない男から電話がかかってきたら、気味悪いだろ」

「まあ、あたしなら出ないね」

「ほらみろ」

「だから、あたしのケータイを使えっていってるじゃん。番号を交換したから、藤崎さんのケータイにはあたしの番号が入ってる。それなら気味悪がられないよ」

「いやあ、そのやり方はどうかなあ」快人は大きく首を捻る。

「何だよ、何が気に入らないわけ？　せっかく番号をゲットしてやったのにさあ」

隣で幸太が、けけけと笑った。

「兄貴はさあ、昔から電話が苦手なんだよな。緊張すると、何しゃべってるのか自分でもわからなくなっちゃうんだ」

「馬鹿いうな。それほどじゃねえよ」

「だけど元カノと仲直りしようとした時もそうだったじゃないか。謝るつもりだったのに、結局は余計に喧嘩がひどくなって、別れるしかなくなったわけだろ」

「あれはまあ、そうだったな」快人はしかめっ面で頭を掻く。「とにかくさあ、電話だと俺の良さをアピールしにくいんだ」

ふんと鼻を鳴らし、千晶は椅子の背もたれに掛けてあったウェアを取った。快人のいいたいことはわかっている。彼の自慢は容姿なのだ。たしかに従妹の目から見ても、なかなかかっこいいほうだとは思う。表参道の交差点でスカウトされたという話も、まるっきりの嘘ではないだろう。これまでに付き合った相手は、殆どの場合、向こうから言い寄ってきたらしい。それだけに、いざ自分からアタックしようと思っても、やり方がわからないのだ。

こんな情けないナルシストに付き合っている暇はない。千晶はウェアを着込み始めた。

「何だよ、もう行くのかよ」快人が口を尖らせる。「協力してくれねえのか」

「十分協力してるでしょ。これ以上、何をしてほしいわけ?」

「それがよくわからないから困ってるんだろ。二人きりじゃなくてもいいから、一緒

に飲みに行くチャンスがあればいいんだけどな」

「あたしが合コンでもセッティングすればいいわけ?」

冗談でいってみただけだが、快人は目の色を変えた。

「あっ、それ、理想」

「ばーか」ニット帽をかぶり、ゴーグルとグローブを手にした。「幸太、食器の片づ

けをお願いね」彼にはコーヒーを奢ってやった。そのお返しだ。

「千晶ねえちゃん、またキッカー?」

「うん、少しフリーランやる。こんところ、滑り込んでないから」

従兄弟をレストランに残し、千晶はゲレンデに出た。空は青いのに、どこからか粉

雪がちらちら落ちてくるという絶好のコンディションだ。これでクロスのコースが完

成していたなら理想的だが、そこまで贅沢はいえない。

レストランの前に立てかけてあったボードを抱え、一人でゴンドラ乗り場に向かっ

た。屋根に一人のパトロール員が上がっている。片方の手に黄色い帯のようなものを

持っていた。そういえば何日か前にも同じような光景を目にした。あの時、屋根に上

がっていたのは根津だったが、今は違う人物のようだ。

何をやってるんだろうと思いつつ、千晶は乗り場の階段を上がっていった。

ゴンドラはすいていた。彼女の前には年配のカップルがいるだけだった。彼等をやりすごせば、一台のゴンドラを独占できる。だがすぐ後ろから何人かやってきたので、結局年配カップルに続いて乗り込んだ。珍しいが、最近ゲレンデでよく見かけるようになった。手にしているのはテレマークスキーだ。

ングスキーにテレマークスキー、スノーボードにスノースクート、最近のスキー場は様々な乗り物が行き来きしている。

「お一人ですか」男性のほうが話しかけてきた。日本人男性は口べただといわれるが、こんなふうに高齢のカップルと乗り合わせた際、声をかけてくるのは大抵男性のほうだ。妻と一緒にいるので心強いのかな、と思ってしまう。

「連れは、まだ休んでるんです」千晶は答えた。

「そうですか。スノーボードは疲れそうだからなあ。この山には、よく来られるんですか」

「今シーズンから籠もってます」

「籠もる？　それはすごい」ゴーグルのレンズの向こうで、男性の目が笑った。「じゃあ、北月のほうにも行くことがあるんですか」

「北月って、裏山ですか。いえ、行ってません。あっちは閉鎖されてますよね」

「うん、それはそうなんだけど、この前どこかのボーダーの人たちが、あっちの話をしているのを聞いたものだから」

「北月を滑ったといってたんですか」

「そんなようなことをいってたな。結構、大変らしいけど、向こうは圧雪がされてないから、新雪の上を思う存分に滑れるそうだよ。スノーボードというのは、新雪を滑るのが一番気持ちいいんでしょ」

「最高です。へえ、そんな裏技があるんだ。ちょっと行ってみようかな」パトロール員たちの目も、そこまでは届かないのかもしれない。

「でも、戻ってこれないんでしょ」ここで初めて隣の女性が発言した。「そのことも教えてあげないと」

「ああ、そうだな。じつは、そういうことなんだよ。どうにかして北月エリアに行くことはできるらしいんだけどね、下まで滑って降りたら、反対側の町に出てしまって、こちら側には戻ってこれんそうなんだ」

「あ、そうなんですか」楽しそうな話なので食いつきかけたのに、いきなり落胆した。

いくら新雪を滑れても、戻ってこれないのでは意味がない。

「だからね、そういう人たちは、あらかじめ向こうに車を置いておくんだそうだ。そうすれば、帰ってこれるからね。だけど、一日に何度もやれる方法ではないね」

「へえ」

なるほどそうか、と千晶は納得した。それならばやれない話ではない。快人と幸太を誘って、と考えたところで問題に気づいた。車は一台しかない。つまり誰か一人が運転して、裏山の麓で、あとの二人が滑り降りてくるのを待つわけだ。そんな提案を、あの二人のどちらかが承諾してくれるとは思えない。

「北月エリアからこっちに運んでくれるバスか何かはないんですか」千晶は訊いてみた。

「本来はあるんだそうだよ。でも今はあっちのゲレンデがクローズになってるから、ホテルとしてもバスを出す必要はないってことらしいねえ」

「そうなんですか。それは残念」

「私らも、残念だなあといってるんですよ。滑ってきた人たちの話を聞いたかぎりでは、結構いいゲレンデらしいから」

その噂は、千晶も時折耳にしていた。一般受けはしないが、マニアたちには人気があったらしい。それでもオープンしないのは、採算が合わないというスキー場側の都

合があるからだろう。近頃はどこのスキー場でもある話だ。

ゴンドラが山頂駅に着いた。千晶はボードを装着して滑り始めた。奇麗に圧雪されたバーンで高速ターンをいくつか決めた後、不整地斜面に入っていった。スキーヤーたちによって、大小様々な形のコブが形成されている。モーグルコースほどにはコブのピッチが細かくはないが、並び方が不規則なところが、臨機応変に滑るためのトレーニングになる。両脚を素早く曲げ伸ばしし、車のサスペンションのように雪面変化を吸収しながら滑った。時には跳ぶことも必要だ。殆ど速度を落とすことなく凸凹の斜面を滑走していると、周りの視線を感じる。不整地斜面を好んで滑るスノーボーダーは稀だ。スキーヤーでも、かなりの技術を要する者でないと近づかない。体力を要するトレーニングではあるが、千晶は快感を覚えていた。

途中、気紛れを起こし、これまでに滑ったことのない斜面を降りた。何か新しい発見があるかもしれない、と期待したからだ。だがこうした期待は、往々にして失望に変わる。シュプールが全くない斜面を見つけて一瞬喜んだが、その先に待ち受けていたのは細い林道だった。しかも傾斜が全くない。みるみるうちに速度が低下し、ついには停止してしまった。千晶は諦めてボードを外し、抱えて歩きだした。ここは一体どこだろう、とあたりを見回した。

間もなく、前方に見覚えのある光景が広がり始めた。すぐ手前にある小屋は、パトロール員たちの詰め所だ。ずいぶんと端まで来てしまったらしい。

詰め所のそばに、一人のパトロール員がいた。帽子をかぶらず、サングラスもかけていない。だからすぐに、それが藤崎絵留だと気づいた。

快人とのやりとりを思い出した。合コンをセッティングしてやる気はさらさらないが、みんなで飲みに行くという話なら悪くない。従兄のためだ。ひとつ骨を折ってやるかと思い、千晶は近づいていった。

藤崎絵留のほうは千晶に気づいていない様子で、建物の向こうに消えた。詰め所に入られたらまずいな、と千晶は思った。わざわざ途中で訪ねていくのは気が重い。

急いで建物に近づいた。すると女性の声が聞こえてきた。藤崎絵留の声に違いなかった。

「それで根津君は、いつ頃こっちに戻ってくるの？　そう。……うん、黄色の帯でしょ。あれはキリ君に取り付けてもらった。……うん、まだ犯人からの連絡はないみたい」

千晶は足だけでなく、全身の動きを止めた。犯人？　何のことだ。それより根津君、

「……うん、防水バッグはクラタさんたちが用意してくれるって。それより根津君、

やっぱりあたしが身代金の運搬係をするの？　……嫌なわけじゃないけど、根津君のことが気になるわけ。キリ君から聞いたけど、犯人のことを追っかけるつもりだったでしょ。……キリ君のことを怒らないでよ。彼だって一生懸命なんだから。……本当ね？　無茶なことはしないよね。とにかくお客さんたちの安全確保が第一なんだから。

……わかった。じゃあ、そっちのほうよろしくね」

藤崎絵留は、どうやら根津と電話で話していたようだ。一体何のことなのか。単なる保安に関する打ち合わせか。

いや、そんな感じではなかった。身代金。そう、身代金といった。やっぱりあたしが身代金の運搬係をするの――断じて聞き間違いなどではない。

千晶はおそるおそる建物の陰から顔を出した。反対側に歩いていく藤崎絵留の背中が見えた。おそらく彼女は、誰にも聞かれたくないから、こんなところで電話をかけたのだ。

千晶はボードを抱え、その場にしゃがみ込んだ。胸の鼓動が速くなっている。こめかみのあたりに血の流れる感覚があった。妙に身体が熱い。

思考が混乱していた。何とかして、たった今聞いた内容を楽観的なものにすり替えようとした。犯人？　身代金？　まるでドラマかゲームだ。そうだ、ゲームの話に違

いない。彼等はその種のゲームに凝っていて、その話をしていたのだ。

だがそう考える一方で、そんなわけないじゃないか、と否定してもいた。藤崎絵留は黄色の帯のことを話していた。あれが何か関係しているのだ。現実について、彼等は話し合っていたのだ。ゲームの話なんかじゃない。現実について、彼等は話し合っていたのだ。ゲームの話なんかじゃない。お客さんたちの安全確保が第一なんだ、と。

ぶるぶると身体が震えた。寒い中でじっとしていたからだろうが、わけのわからない不安感が芽生えているのも事実だった。快人や幸太に話すべきかどうか迷いつつ、千晶はのろのろと動きだした。

29

カービングスキーは奇麗な弧を描き出していた。まさにカービング──刻む、だ。真っ白な雪面に、二本のシュプールが残った。ひらがなの『し』を書き終えたところで入江達樹の履いたスキーは停止した。まだ少し腰が引けているが、これだけ滑れば立派なものだ。自然な笑みが、達樹の顔からこぼれた。

「いいじゃないか。何も問題ないよ」スノーモービルに跨ったままで根津はいった。

達樹は少し照れ臭そうにしている。

北月エリアに連れてきたのは正解だった。最初は戸惑っていた達樹だったが、周囲に誰一人いないとわかると、怖がりつつもスキーを滑らせ始めたのだ。それでも途中、何度も後ろを振り返った。突然誰かが滑り降りてこないかと怯えているからだ。母親が激突されたことが、今も忘れられないのだろう。

そういうことを何度か繰り返すうちに、少しずつではあるが達樹は大胆さを取り戻していった。入江義之によれば、事故以前の達樹は、どんな斜面でもターンできる程度の腕前を持っていたらしい。スキー技術は自転車と同じで、一度身につけてしまえば忘れない。要は気持ちの問題なのだ。

入江も滑り降りてきた。こちらは見事なテクニックを披露した後、達樹のすぐそばで止まった。「だいぶ思い出したみたいだな。気持ちいいだろ」

父親にいわれ、達樹も頷いた。しっかりとした意思表示だったので、根津はほっとした。

「もう一本行きましょうか」根津は親子に声をかけた。

「まだ大丈夫ですか」入江が訊く。「そろそろ戻ったほうがいいんじゃないですか」

「いえ、あと一本ぐらいなら平気です」

ついさっき、絵留と電話で話した。現金の用意ができて、例の黄色い目印は桐林が
ゴンドラ乗り場の屋根に取り付けたらしい。いつ犯人からの連絡があるかはわからな
いが、少なくとも午前中は動きはないだろう。

入江は息子を見下ろし、しばらく何事か考えていた。やがて顔を上げた。

「だったら、あそこに連れていってもらえませんか」

根津は思わず背筋を伸ばした。「あそこ……というと」見当はついていたが、念の
ために確認した。

「新月エリアから合流してくるところです。要するに……あの場所です」入江も言葉
を濁しているが、どこのことをいっているのかはもはや明らかだった。事故のあった
場所だ。

「お連れするのは構わないんですけど、大丈夫ですか」根津は親子を交互に見た。
「あそこに行くことが今回の目的でしたから」ゴーグルのせいで表情はわからないが、
入江の口調は真剣そのものだった。「お願いできますか」

それなりの覚悟を決めて、入江はここへ息子を連れてきたのだ。ならば根津として
も、協力してやりたい。わかりました、と答えた。

例によって入江を後部席に乗せ、根津は斜面を上がっていった。中腹を過ぎ、さら

に進む。斜面の角度が少しきつくなった。

「ああ、そうだ。こういう感じだった」後ろで入江が呟いた。「この少し上に、合流地点があるんですよね。こういう感じだった」

懐かしい、という言葉に根津は意表をつかれた。入江にとってこの場所は、ただ辛い思い出があるだけだろうと決めつけていた。だが事故が起きるまでは、家族と楽しく過ごした場所だったのだ。そちらの思い出が胸をよぎったとしても不思議ではない。

スノーモービルは問題の地点に到着した。事故を検証するために何度も訪れたところだ。

「そうだ、ここだった」スノーモービルから降り立ち、入江は周囲を見回した。その顔には、もはや過去を懐かしんでいる気配はない。血まみれの妻を発見した時のことを思い出しているに違いなかった。

入江を残し、根津は元の場所に引き返した。達樹はゲレンデの真ん中で、ぽつんと待っていた。その顔に怯えの色はない。これなら大丈夫かな、と根津は思った。すでに何往復かしているので、少年も慣れたものだ。

達樹を乗せ、スノーモービルを発進させた。

入江はまだスキーを装着せず、寒そうに身体を動かしながら待っていた。そのすぐ

横でスノーモービルを止めた。

根津は達樹が降りるのを手伝った。寒さのせいで彼の頬は少し赤くなっていた。そ
れ以外、顔つきに変化は見られない。

「達樹、この場所を覚えてるか」入江がいった。「周りをよく見てみろ。ここに来た
ことがあるだろ」

だが達樹は視線を大きく回すことなく、すぐに一点を凝視し始めていた。彼が見つ
める先にあるのは、雪に覆われた林だった。この斜面より、一段高くなっている。

根津は察した。達樹の母親に激突したスノーボーダーは、そこから飛び出してきた
のだ。恐怖で頭が混乱しながらも、そのことだけは覚えているらしい。

「そうだよ、達樹。おかあさん、おかあさんは、ここで死んだんだ」入江は息子の前で跪いた。
「覚えてるだろ？ おかあさん、ここで倒れてただろ」

達樹は弱々しく首を横に振った。その口から、知らない、という言葉が漏れた。

「そんなわけないだろ。一緒にいたじゃないか。思い出せ。目をそらすんじゃない」

入江は息子の両腕を摑み、前後に揺すった。

だが達樹は無言だった。その顔に表情はなかった。視点は定まらず、黒目は揺れて
いた。

入江がグローブを外し、スキーウェアのポケットのファスナーを開けた。取り出してきたのは、ビニール袋だった。中に押し花のようなものが入っている。

「ほらこれ、庭でおかあさんが育てたパンジーを押し花にしてもらったんだ。これを、この場所に埋めてやろう」入江は押し花を差し出した。

宙をさまよっていた達樹の大きな目が、ようやく押し花を捉えた。じっと見つめるが、手を出そうとはしない。

「どうしたんだ？ さあ、早く埋めてやろう。おかあさん、きっと喜ぶぞ」

しかし達樹は凍りついたように動かない。押し花と父親の顔を見比べている。

「さあ」入江は息子の右手を取り、押し花を持たせようとした。

だが次の瞬間、達樹は父の手を振り払った。押し花が、ひらひらと雪の上に落ちた。

「達樹……」

「知らないもんっ」達樹は顔を歪めて怒鳴った。「そんなこと、知らないもん」

「何をいってるんだ。おかあさん、ここで死んだじゃないか」

「知らない、知らない」達樹は両手を激しく振り回したかと思うと、あーあーあーと奇声を発し、駆けだした。しかし雪の斜面で、おまけにスキーブーツを履いているので、うまくは走れない。やがて転倒し、雪に埋もれた。

スノーモービルを使うほどの距離ではなかった。根津は駆け寄った。達樹は小動物のように背中を丸くしてうずくまっていた。ひいひいと泣く声が聞こえた。

入江がやってきた。「弱ったな……」

「とりあえず、戻りませんか」根津は提案してみた。

「そうするしかなさそうですね」入江は力なく頷いた。

根津は達樹を抱きかかえ、スノーモービルに乗せた。彼は抵抗することも、喚くこともなかった。一刻も早く、この場から立ち去りたがっているように感じられた。

駐車場に戻り、来た時と同様、ライトバンの後部座席に入江親子を座らせて出発した。太陽が眩しく、根津は運転席のサンバイザーを下ろした。

車内の空気は重たかった。入江親子は無言だ。

「達樹君、久しぶりにスキーをやってみてどうだった？　気持ちよかったんじゃない？」根津は努めて明るい声を出した。

「どうだったんだ？　わざわざ連れてきてもらったんだから、何とかいいなさい」入江が責めるようにいう。それではますます萎縮してしまう、と根津ははらはらした。

「ありがとうございました」単調なトーンで達樹は答えた。魂が抜けてしまっているように聞こえた。

「お礼はいいんだ。達樹君が楽しめたんならよかったんだけど」

「楽しめたよな」入江が促す。「なあ」

うん、と低い声が聞こえてきた。

「それを聞いて安心したよ。——また近いうちに行きましょう。上の者と相談しておきます」ルームミラーに映った入江に向かっていった。

入江は沈んだ顔つきのままで無理に笑みを作り、頭を下げた。先程の息子の反応に、うちひしがれているようだった。

30

ホテルの駐車場に戻ると、根津は入江親子が車から降りるのを手伝った。達樹は無言だ。スキーをしていた時の明るい表情が、すっかり消えてしまった。

「この後、どうされますか」根津は親子を交互に見て訊いた。「こっちのゲレンデで滑ってみるということでしたら、リフト券を御用意させていただきますけど」

達樹は不機嫌そうな顔で俯いている。そんな息子を見下ろした後、入江義之は首を小さく振った。

「いや、今日はここまでにしておきます。いつも疲れたと思いますから。それに、まだこっちは無理じゃないかな」ゲレンデのほうを向き、眩しそうに目を細めた。

「そうですね。焦る必要はないですね。さっき車の中でもいいましたけど、また北月エリアにお連れすることも可能だと思います。詳しいことがわかり次第、お知らせいたします」

「ありがとうございます。よろしくお願いします」入江が礼をいいながら、達樹の頭を手で押さえた。達樹は無表情のまま、ぺこりと頭を下げた。

親子がホテルに向かって歩きだすのを見届け、根津はパトロール隊の詰め所に戻った。中には三人のパトロール員がいた。そのうちの一人が桐林だ。絵留の姿はない。

「キリ、ちょっと来てくれ」そう声をかけてから外に出た。

すぐに桐林も出てきた。

「絵留は？」

「見回り中です。もうすぐ戻ってくると思います」

「あれ、キリがやってくれたそうだな。お疲れ」根津はゴンドラ乗り場のほうを顎でしゃくった。屋根の上からは黄色い帯が下がっている。

だが桐林は頭に手をやり、申し訳なさそうな顔をした。

「すみません。例の作戦のこと、絵留さんにしゃべっちまいました。ほら、二人で犯人を追いかけて、何とかして写真を撮ろうっていう作戦のことです」

根津は、ふんと鼻を鳴らした。

「さっき電話で絵留から聞いたよ。誘導尋問でもされたのか」

「いや、俺がしくじったんです。現金の運び役は絵留さんですよねって、つい先に訊いちゃって、それで怪しまれたみたいです。どうしてそんなことを確認するのかと問い詰められて、しどろもどろになっちまったんです。すみません」

根津は顔をしかめた。状況が目に浮かぶ。桐林のことを迂闊だなと思うと同時に、絵留の勘の良さが憎らしくもあった。

「まあ、仕方ねえよ。でもさ、絵留のことを遠くから見守る分については構わないって、倉田さんから許可を貰っている」

「本当ですか」桐林の顔が明るくなった。

「ああ。だから、全くノーチャンスってことはない。一応、カメラは用意しておこうぜ」

「わかりました」桐林は大きく頷いた後、「根津さん、今回の取引について、どう思いますか。俺、おかしいと思うんですけど」声をひそめていった。

「おかしいって？」

「今回の犯人からの指示ですよ。一体、何を企んでるんだと思います？」

根津はゲレンデを眺めながら肩をすくめた。

「企むって、どういうことだ。これまでの取引がうまくいったから、味をしめて、最後にもう一回大金をせしめようってことだろう」

桐林は隣で、うーん、と唸っている。根津の意見に納得できないらしい。

「何だ？　いいたいことがあるなら、はっきりいえよ」

「いやあ、それほどはっきりとした意見があるわけじゃないんですけど、もしスキー場側が取引に乗らなかったら、犯人はどうする気だったのかなあと思って」

「乗らなかったら……」

「もし、あのゴンドラ乗り場の屋根に黄色の目印を付けなかったらって話です。今回犯人は、爆発物が埋まっている正確な場所を知りたければ金を払えって要求しているだけですよね。一回目と違って、取引に応じなければ爆発させるといってるわけじゃない。クロスのコースは北月エリアに造るっていうアイデアも出てきたことだし、スキー場側としては犯人の要求を無視するという選択肢もあったわけです。もしそうしていたら、犯人はどうしたと思います？」

根津は眉間に皺を寄せ、腕組みをした。たしかにその選択肢はあった。その場合、犯人はどうしていたのか。それとも、スキー場側は必ず要求を呑むとたかをくくっていたのか。

「そんな要求、突っぱねればよかったのに」桐林はいった。「犯人だって、だめもとだったんじゃないかなあ。だからこれまでよりも要求額を増やして、五千万にしたと思うんです。断られることを予想していたんですよ」

「そうはいっても、やっぱり爆発物の在処を突き止めて、きちんと処理したいっていうのが、会社側の本音だろう。そうしないと安心して営業できねえもんな」

「それはわかるんですけど……」桐林は不服そうに首を捻っている。

納得できないのも無理はない、と根津は思った。彼自身が理不尽に感じているのだ。スキー場にとって五千万円は大金だ。それだけの儲けを出すには、どれだけの入場者数が必要なのかと考えると気が遠くなる。

そんなことを考えながらも、根津はゲレンデに目を走らせた。危険な行為をしている者がいないか無意識に監視している。長年パトロール員をしてきたことによる習性だろう。

ゲレンデに、見覚えのある二人組がいた。瀬利千晶の従兄弟だという若者たちだ。

緩斜面でグランドトリックの練習をしている。目で千晶の姿を探したが、周囲には見当たらなかった。

その時、ウェアの下で携帯電話が震えた。ポケットのジッパーを開け、取り出す。

倉田からだった。

「はい、根津です」

（倉田だよ。君は今、どこにいる？　まだ北月か）

「いえ、こっちに戻ってきています。入江さんたちはホテルに戻られました。何かありましたか」

（犯人からの連絡があった。すぐに会議室に来てくれないか）

「わかりました。絵留も連れていったほうがいいですよね」

（そうしてくれ。なるべく目立たないようにな）

「了解です」

電話を切り、桐林に事情を説明していると、スノーモービルに乗った絵留が戻ってきた。グッドタイミングだ。彼女にも事情を伝えた。

「いよいよね。これが最後だといいんだけど」絵留は切れ長の目を一層吊り上がらせた。

「最後に決まってるだろ。そうでなきゃ困る」

「いや、わかんないですよ。金を受け取った後、やっぱりもう少し払えって要求して
くることだって考えられます」桐林がいった。「何しろ、あっちはいいたい放題なん
だから」

根津は口元を歪めた。

「もしそうなったら、そうなった時のことだ。判断するのは俺たちじゃない。──行
こう、絵留。──キリ、ほかの者に俺たちのことを訊かれたら、うまくごまかしとい
てくれ」桐林の胸を手の甲で叩き、ホテルに向かって歩きだした。絵留も後からつい
てきた。

「今までキリ君と何を話してたの？」

「大した話はしてない。五千万は大金だってことを話してた。だから悔しいってな」

「犯人を追っかけることなんか計画してないよね」

「してねえよ。しつこいぜ」絵留の顔を見ないでいった。

会議室のドアをノックすると、どうぞ、と倉田の声が聞こえた。ドアを開け、中の
様子を窺う。倉田のほかには、総務部長の宮内、ゲレンデ整備主任の辰巳がいるだけ
だ。全員、机を囲むようにして立っている。中垣と松宮の本部長コンビがいないので、

根津はほっとした。

「犯人からの連絡があったそうですけど……」

宮内が無言で机の上にあった書類を摑み、差し出してきた。根津は受け取り、そこに印刷された文面に目を落とした。横から絵留が覗き込んでくる。

『新月高原スキー場の関係者諸君へ

そちらからの回答を確認した。迅速かつ冷静、そして妥当な判断に高い評価を与えたい。お互いにとって、いい取引になることだろう。

では早速指示する。

・五千万円入りの防水バッグと前回使用した携帯電話を運搬役に持たせろ。尚、運搬役には、その状態でスキーあるいはスノーボードによる斜度四十度バーンの滑走が可能な者を選ぶこと。

・運搬役は、右腕に黄色のバンダナを巻くこと。

・運搬役は、本日午後四時ちょうどに第4ロマンスリフトに乗れ。リフトを降りたら、ダウンヒルコース入り口付近で待機すること。

毎回警告していることだが、改めて繰り返す。そちら側に不審な動きがあった場合には、即刻取引は中止する。場合によっては最悪の結果を招くかもしれないが、そち

らの責任だ。そのことを決して忘れるな。では午後四時に。

　根津は書類から顔を上げ、絵留のほうを見た。彼女と目が合った。双方が瞬きした。

「まあ、そういうことだ」宮内がいった。「で、どっちがやってくれる？」根津と絵留とを見比べた。運搬役のことをいっているのだろう。

　根津は机の上を見た。リュックサックが載っている。膨らんでいるから、すでに現金が入っているのだろう。

「近づき、持ち上げた。意外に重かった。

「五キロほどある」根津の考えを察したらしく、倉田がいった。「三千万円の時と、ずいぶん違う。三千万なら、約三キロだ」

「そうか。それで犯人は、身代金を分割して要求してきたのかな」

「そうじゃないかって、今も話していたところだ。一億円だと十キロ。嵩張る上に、かなりの重さだ。ただ、そうすると今回五千万に値上げしてきた理由がわからない。五キロでも運べると踏んだのなら、最初から五千万を要求していたはずだ」

「そうか」

「ちょっといい？」絵留が近づいてきたので、リュックを渡した。彼女は両手で上げ

下げし、頷いた。「そうね。結構、ずっしりしてるね」さらに彼女はそれを背負い、その場で軽く膝を屈伸させた。

「どうだ？」根津が訊いた。

「うん、これなら大丈夫。何の問題もないと思う」

「本当か。ここはやっぱり、男のほうがいいんじゃないか」

「いや、絵留に任せて大丈夫でしょう」根津は否定した。「こいつを背負った状態で、斜度四十度の斜面を滑れること、と指定しています。俺も滑ることぐらいはできるけど、そこから何をやらされるかわからないとなると、やっぱり絵留のほうがいいです。スノーボードよりスキーのほうが安定していると思うし。――絵留、いいよな」

彼女は一旦リュックを下ろし、頷いた。「うん、大丈夫」

「たしかに、この点は引っかかるよな」犯人からの指示書を手に取り、宮内は難しい顔をした。「斜度四十度といったら、かなりの斜面だ。一体何をやらせるつもりなんだ」

辰巳が、机の上に広げてあるゲレンデマップを指差した。

「目的はわかりませんが、スーパースラロームコースを滑り降りろってことだと思います。ダウンヒルコースの途中に一箇所、枝分かれしているところがあって、ふつう

の人は広い中級者斜面を滑りますが、腕に自信のある人は狭い上級者斜面を行きます。

ここは最大斜度が四十度を超えます。積雪量が十分ない場合はクローズしますが、今日は開いています。それがスーパースラロームコースです」

辰巳の話が根津には手に取るようによくわかる。なぜなら彼等パトロール員が、毎朝特に重点的に見回るコースだからだ。斜度が大きい分、雪崩も起きやすいのだ。

「そいつを降りたら、どこに出る?」

宮内の質問に、辰巳は無表情のままマップ上で指先を動かす。

「ふつうに降りた場合、ゴールドコースと合流して、最後にはファミリーコースに出ます。そこをさらに滑り降りたら、ホテルのすぐ西側です」

「その途中で、現金の受け渡しをするということか」

「いや、今回の犯人が、単純な受け渡しをさせるわけないですよ」根津はいった。

宮内がぎょろ目を剝いた。「じゃあ、どうすると思う?」

「俺は、ここがポイントだと思います」根津はゲレンデマップ上の一点を指した。

「スーパースラロームコースの西側に林があります。もちろんコース外です。でもここを横切れば、下山ルートは無数にある。これを使うんじゃないかと思います」

「その先は?」

「わかりません」根津は肩をすくめた。

倉田が腰に手を当て、頷いた。

「大いに考えられることではあるな。現金受け渡しの一回目はナイター照明のないゲレンデ、二回目はゴンドラ下の滑走禁止エリアと、犯人は一般客が絶対に来ない場所を逃走経路に使っている。急斜面のコース外というのは、いかにも目をつけそうだ」

「するとそこで待ち伏せしておけば……」宮内が企みのある目つきになった。

「宮内さん、それはちょっと」倉田が困惑したように顔をしかめた。

「ああ、わかっている。いってみただけだ」宮内は大きく手を振った。

二人のやりとりを見て、根津は意外な感じがした。全員が倉田と同様、身代金を無事に犯人に渡すことだけを願っていると思っていたからだ。だがよく考えてみれば、そんなはずはないのだ。会社の金を無関係の人間に獲られて平気な人間など、どこにもいないだろう。その損失は、いずれ自分たちに跳ね返ってくる。

「君たちにも改めていっておくけど」倉田が根津と絵留を交互に見ながらいった。「大事なのは、取引を成立させておくことだ。一刻も早く爆発物の在処を犯人から聞き出し、ゲレンデの安全を確保することだ。そのことを忘れないでくれよ」

二人にいっているが、根津に対して発せられた言葉であることは明白だった。

「わかっています。手は出しません」根津は約束した。

四時までは、まだ時間がある。それまで待機しているという絵留を残し、根津は会議室を出た。詰め所に戻ろうと廊下を歩いていたら、後ろから足音が追ってきた。

「根津君」声がした。

振り返ると、宮内が近づいてくるところだった。胸に何かを含んだような顔をしている。

「ちょっといいかな」

「いいですけど、何ですか」

宮内は周囲をさっと見回した後、「喫煙所に行こう」と顎をしゃくった。

ゲレンデに出る通用口の手前に、空気清浄機を備えた喫煙所がある。飲み物の自動販売機も並んでいる。今は誰もいなかった。宮内は煙草に火をつけた。

「今回のことでは、いろいろとすまないね。社長からも、よく労（ねぎら）うようにいわれているよ」

「いや、そんな……特に大したことはしてませんし」根津は戸惑いながら答えた。こんなふうにいわれるとは予想していなかった。

「全く悔しい話だよなあ。五千万だぜ、五千万。それがメール一本で手に入るなんて、

こんなふざけた話があるかよ。何とか、犯人に一泡吹かせてやりたいとは思わないか」

勢いよく煙を吐き出す宮内を、一層意外な思いで根津は見返した。

「何だ？　俺の顔に何か付いてるか」

「いえ、宮内さんがそんなことをおっしゃるとは思わなかったので……」

ふふっと宮内は唇の端を曲げた。

「俺はさ、今回のことで、三回も銀行に行ってる。現金を受け取るためだ。三千万、三千万で、今度が五千万。正直、馬鹿馬鹿しくなったよ。金なんて、あるところにはあるもんだよなあ。会社は不景気だ不景気だと繰り返すばっかりで、もう何年も給料は据え置きなのにさ。十分の一、いや百分の一でもいいから、こっちに回してほしいと思ったよ。で、犯人に猛烈に腹が立ってきた。あっさり渡すのが悔しくてしょうがないんだ。もちろん客の安全が第一っていうことはわかってる。だけどさあ、犯人の立場になって考えてみたら、そう簡単には爆発させないと思う。死人でも出てみろ、とんでもない重罪だぜ。しかも、そうなったら必ず警察が乗り出してくるしな」

まさに根津も同意見だった。大きく頷いた。「俺もそう思う」

「だろ？　そこでだ」宮内はもう一度周囲を見回し、顔を近づけてきた。「犯人が現

れたら、もう一度追ってみてくれないか。捕まえなくてもいい。正体を突き止める手がかりがほしいんだ」

根津は瞬きした。「いいんですか」

「ただし、犯人には気づかれないようにな。金を奪い返すのが目的じゃない」

「倉田さんが何といいますかね」

宮内は苦笑を浮かべ、煙草を指に挟んだままで手を振った。

「彼にはいわないほうがいい。本部長たちにもな。受け渡しの場所は、下からは見えない。君が何をしたって、わからないさ」

さすがに様々なトラブルに対応してきただけあって、総務部長の考えることとは大胆だ。だが根津としても、元々桐林と二人で手がかりを摑もうと思っていたのだ。こんなふうにいってもらえると心強い。

「わかりました。やってみます」

「頼むよ。ただし、深追いは禁物だからな」宮内は根津の肩に手を載せてきた。

詰め所に戻り、雑用をいくつかこなしながら約束の時刻が来るのを待った。桐林も時折姿を見せるが、やはり落ち着かなそうだ。二人きりになった時、宮内からの指示を話すと目を丸くした。

「会社にも、そんなことを考える人がいるんですね」

「気持ちはわかるよ。総務部長とはいえ、たぶん給料は大したことないと思うしさ」

大企業の部長クラスとは雲泥の差があるだろう。

「じゃあ、予定通りにやりますか」桐林が訊いてきた。

「もちろんだ。犯人の逃走ルートは大体予想がついている。どこかで待ち伏せして、写真を撮ろう。その後は追跡だ」

「わかりました。面白くなりそうですね」桐林は笑みを浮かべたが、やはり緊張の色が滲んでいた。

午後三時半を過ぎると、根津は桐林と共に詰め所を出た。どちらも私用のウェアに着替えている。桐林はスキーを手にしたが、根津は少し考えてからボードを持っていくことにした。宮内は犯人を追ってもいいといった。犯人がボードで逃走した場合、自分のスキー技術では追えないと思ったからだ。

ホテルから絵留が出てくるのが見えた。リュックサックを背負い、黄色いバンダナを右腕に巻いていた。彼女は根津たちのほうを見たが、何もいわずに詰め所に入ると、スキーブーツに履き替えて出てきた。

「しっかりな」根津は声をかけた。

絵留は黙ったままで頷くと、自分のスキー板を取り付け、見事なスケーティングで滑り始めた。

31

誘拐事件じゃないか、と快人はいった。

「だって、身代金っていったんだろ？　藤崎さんが身代金の運搬係をやるって。だったら、誘拐事件だよ」いかにも自信ありげな口ぶりだ。藤崎さんが身代金の運搬係をやるって。だっ

「誰が誘拐されたわけ？」千晶は訊いた。

「そんなのわからないけど、たぶん客の誰かだよ。お客さんの安全が第一って藤崎さんはいったんだろ？」

「お客さんじゃなくて、お客さんたちっていってた」

「じゃあ、複数だ。何人かが誘拐されたんだ」

「えー、そんなことあるかな。誘拐するなら、一人で十分じゃん」

「成り行きってやつだよ。よくあるんだ。一人だけ誘拐するつもりだったけど、犯人の予想外のことが起きて、ほかの人間も連れていかなきゃいけなくなるってパターン

「が」

「それって、小説とかドラマの話でしょ。あたしは現実の話をしてるんだけど」

「現実でもあるんだって。ほら、外国の戦地でさ、避難勧告を無視して残ってた日本のボランティアが、揃って攫われたことがあったじゃないかっ。単なる脅しじゃないっていっところを見せるには、一人ぐらいは本当に殺したほうがいいから、わざと複数の人間を攫うことだってあるんだ」

千晶は眉根を寄せた。

「そんなすごいことが起きてるわけ？　このスキー場で」

「だって、大変なことになってるっていいだしたのは千晶だぜ」

「そうだけど……」

二人はレストランで話し合っていた。藤崎絵留が電話で話していたことについて、千晶は従兄弟たちに相談してみたのだった。幸太には、パトロールの詰め所を見張らせている。

その幸太がゴーグルも外さず、レストランに駆け込んできた。

「藤崎さんがパトロール小屋から出てきたぜ。背中にリュックを背負ってる。あれ、たぶん身代金じゃあ──」

千晶は拳で従弟（いとこ）の脇腹を突いた。

「馬鹿、声がでかいよ」

「あっ、いや、だって……」

「藤崎さんはどこへ向かった？　ゴンドラ？」幸太はグローブを嵌めたままの手で口を押さえた。

「いや、ゴンドラに乗る感じじゃなかった。ファミリーコースのほうに向かってるみたいだったけど」

千晶はニット帽をかぶり、立ち上がった。向かいに座っている快人の隣の椅子から、茶色のウェアを引き寄せる。

「快人、ウェアを借りるよ」

「えっ、なんでだよ」

「あたしのウェア、覚えられてるもん。上だけでも変えたら、印象が違うでしょ」

「一体、何する気だ」

「そんなの決まってるじゃない。藤崎さんの後を追ってみる。どういうことなのか、突き止めないと」

「俺も行くよ」幸太がいった。

「だめ。足手まとい」ウェアを羽織ると、ゴーグルとグローブを手にし、レストラン

の出口に向かった。急がないと見失ってしまう。

外に出ると、片方の足にだけボードを装着し、スケーティングでファミリーコースに向かった。軽い上り坂なのが忌々しいが、進み辛いのはスキーも同様のはずで、藤崎絵留もそれほど先には行っていないと思われた。

「千晶」後ろから声が聞こえた。

グリーンのウェアを着た青年が追いかけてくる。一瞬幸太かと思ったが、パンツの色が違っていた。快人だ。

「足手まといだっていったのに」

「そういうなよ。藤崎さんは俺の憧れの的なんだぜ。その人が危険なことをしてるっていうのに、レストランでのんびりしてられっかよ」息をきらしながら生意気なことをいう。

「しょうがないな。だけど、もたもたしてたら置いてくからね」

やがてファミリーコースに到着した。急いで周りを見回したが、藤崎絵留の姿はない。すでに、いくつかあるリフトの一つに乗ったということか。

「ちくしょう、遅かったか」快人が悔しそうにいった。

その時だった。千晶は前方に見覚えのあるスノーボーダーがいることに気づいた。

「あっ、あの人」そういって後ろ姿を指差した。「あれ、根津さんだ」

「えっ、マジで？」

「たぶん間違いない。キッカーで跳んでるのを見たんだ。それに、一緒にいるスキーヤーも見たことがある。今日の午前中、ゴンドラ乗り場の屋根に上ってた人だ。だから、根津さんたちと同じくパトロール員だよ」

「パトロールの二人が、なんでこんなところにいるんだ。しかも私服で」

「わかった。あの人たちも藤崎さんの後を追ってるんだよ。だって、身代金を運んでるんだよ。誰も見張ってないなんてこと、あるわけない」

「てことは、あの人たちについていけば……」

「藤崎さんにも追いつけるってことだ。急ごう」千晶は雪を蹴る足に力を込めた。

根津たちは、ファミリーコースの端にあるリフトに乗った。二人乗りのリフトだが、分かれて一人ずつ乗っている。時間差をつけることで、様々な局面に対応しようとしているのかもしれない。

「あたしたちも分かれて乗ろう」そういって千晶は乗り場に向かった。

時間が遅いので、ゲレンデはすいてきている。根津の乗った搬器は千晶よりもずいぶん先だが、彼女が降りる時に彼等がまだ近くにいたら見つかるかもしれない。その

時はその時だ、と思った。別に悪いことをしているわけではない。

それにしても一体何が起きているのだろう、と千晶は考えた。　快人の説は一理ある

が、何か少しずれているような気がする。

ふと思いついたことがあり、彼女は後ろを振り返った。何を思ったか、快人が手を

振ってきた。それを無視し、さらに後方に目をやる。　空の搬器が並んでいた。

やっぱりおかしい——。

警察が見張っている気配がまるでないのだ。もちろん制服を着用するわけがなく、

一般客に化けるケースだろうが、それにしても千晶たち以外に追っている人間が見当

たらないのは、どう考えてもおかしい。そもそも身代金の運搬について、藤崎絵留が

根津と電話で相談していたこと自体が不自然だ。そんなことは警察が決めることでは

ないか。

つまり何らかの事件が起きているにせよ、スキー場は警察に届けていないというこ

とになる。もし客が誘拐されたとして、そんなことがありうるだろうか。それとも、

「警察に知らせたら人質の命はない」とでも脅されているのか。

自分たちは今、とんでもない状況に立ち会っているのかもしれない。そう考えると、

体温が少し上昇するようだった。そのくせウェアの下では鳥肌が立っている。

リフト降り場が近づいてきた。先に降りた根津たちは、すでに滑りだしている。ど

うやら、さらに上へ行く第4ロマンスリフトに乗るようだ。

千晶もリフトから降りた。すぐに後から快人も追ってきた。

「千晶、第4ロマンスだ」

「わかってる。急ごう」

手早くボードを装着し、二人は滑りだした。

根津が第4ロマンスリフトに乗った時、時計の針は午後四時を二分ほど過ぎていた。

このリフトの本来の営業時間は四時までだが、乗ろうとしている客を制止してまで係

員が入り口を閉めることはない。通常、十分程度は遅れる。犯人の指示に従って四時ちょうどに

前方に並ぶ搬器に、絵留の後ろ姿はなかった。

乗ったはずだから、かなり先にいるのだろう。

リフトの右側に幅のあるコースが広がっている。かつて国際大会で使われたことも

あるダウンヒルコースだ。人気のあるコースで、今もひっきりなしにスキーヤーやス

ノーボーダーたちが滑り降りてくる。

やがてリフト降り場が迫ってきた。ダウンヒルコースの入り口に絵留が立っている

のが見えた。彼女も根津のほうを見ている。どうか余計なことはしないでくれと願っているに違いない。

リフトを降りると、根津はベンチに腰掛け、ボードを装着した。桐林もやってきた。

「どうしますか」絵留のほうを見ながら尋ねた。

「あまりあっちを見るな。どこで犯人が見張ってるかわからない。俺たちが彼女の仲間だとばれたら厄介だ」

「あっ、そうか」桐林はあわてて視線をずらした。

「辰巳さんの読みでは、犯人は絵留にスーパースラロームコースを滑らせるつもりじゃないかってことだった。俺も同感だ。とりあえず、先に行ってみよう」

「スーパースラロームですね。わかりました」

桐林が先に滑り始めた。根津も立ち上がり、スタートする。ダウンヒルコースに突入すると、ボードの先端を真下に向けた。エッジを立て、身体を沈める。速度が急激にアップする感覚があった。

途中、コースは枝分かれしている。右側には上級者用という表示が出ていた。迷わず、そちらにターンした。

前方で桐林が停止した。

その先の斜面は根津の位置からだと見えない。斜度が大き

く変化しているからだ。

根津も桐林の横で一旦止まった。スーパースラロームコースの最大斜度は四十度だが、上から見下ろすと垂直に感じる。時間が遅いこともあり、滑っている者はいなかった。

「ここをただふつうに滑らせるとは思えない。この斜面の途中で、身代金の受け渡しをやろうってことじゃないかな」

「それは……大胆不敵ですね」

「問題はその後だ。犯人は、あの森を突っ切るつもりじゃないかと思う」そういって根津は右側の森を指差した。

「あれを横切れば、ゲレンデに戻らずに下山できるからな」

「なるほど。じゃあ、どうしますか。ここで待ち伏せしますか」

「いや、こんなところにいたら目立ってしようがない。犯人に怪しまれるだろう。一か八かだ。先に入っていよう」

「入るって?」

「森の中だ。キリは真ん中あたりで隠れててくれ。俺は、もう少し先にいる。カメラは持ってきたよな。犯人の姿を撮れそうだったら撮ってくれ」

了解、という言葉を残し、桐林が滑り始めた。斜滑降で森に向かうが、エッジのずれる音が響いた。日が暮れてきて、バーンがかなり硬くなっているようだ。

根津も滑りだした。スピードをコントロールし、ミドルターンを繰り返しながら下っていく。途中で斜面を横切るように森に向かった。森の手前にはロープが張ってある。

ほかでもない、根津たち自身が張ったものだ。それをくぐり抜け、森に入った。

木の間の雪は柔らかい。

数メートル進んだところで止まった。コースのほうを向き、身体を屈めた。

誰かが滑り降りてくる音が聞こえた。絵留かと思い、根津は緊張した。だが間もなく姿を見せたのはスノーボーダーだった。茶色のウェアを着ている。

見つからないようにやりすごそうと、根津はさらに頭を低くした。ところがそのスノーボーダーは、真っ直ぐに根津のほうに向かってきた。それだけではない。さっき彼がやったようにロープをくぐり抜け、森に入ってきたのだ。

馬鹿野郎、どうしてよりによってこんな時に――。

だが相手は単に新雪を楽しみたくてコース外に出たのではなかった。女の声だった。しかも聞き覚えがある。根津のそばまで来ると、「どういうこと?」と訊いてきた。

「君は……」

「あたしだよ」瀬利千晶だった。「それよりさ、ねえ、どういうこと？　教えてよ」

「コース外に出ていることなら、これにはわけがある。説明している暇はないが——」

「——」

「それはわかってる。藤崎さんのことを見張ってるんでしょ。身代金を持ってるから」

さらりといわれ、ぎょっとした。

「どうして知ってる？」

「そんなことはどうだっていい。訊いてるのはこっち。一体何なの？　誰かが誘拐されたわけ？」

「誘拐？　誰がそんなこといった」

「だって、身代金を運ぶってことは、誰かが誘拐されたってことでしょ」

「いや、そうじゃなくて——」

その時、上のほうから滑走する音が聞こえてきた。根津は見上げた。今度は間違いなかった。絵留が滑り降りてくる。しかもかなりの速度だ。ほかには誰もいない。

殆ど減速することなく、絵留は根津たちの前を通り過ぎていった。背負ったリュックサックは膨らんだままだ。つまり、受け渡しはまだ行われていない。

「しまった。森を横切るんじゃなかったのか」

根津は小さくジャンプしてボードの向きを変えた。木の間を抜けるように滑りだす。

「ちょっと待ってよ」後ろから千晶の声が追ってくる。

「後で説明する。このことは絶対誰にもいうなっ」滑りながら叫んだ。説明は？

絵留の姿は、はるか彼方にあった。すでにスーパースラロームコースを抜け、ゴールドコースに入っている。彼女が止まらないかぎり、追いつけそうにない。だがどうやらコース外に出る気はなさそうだ。

やがて、そのままファミリーコースに出た。ここまで来ると、まだ人気が多い。安全のことを考えてか、絵留が速度を緩めた。根津もブレーキをかけ、一定の距離を保ちつつ後を追った。

「根津さん」後ろから桐林が追いついてきた。「どうなってるんでしょうね。絵留さん、まだお金を背負ったままですよ」

「俺にも、わけがわかんねえ。とにかくついていくしかない」

気がつくと、すぐそばを千晶が滑っていた。一緒についてくるつもりらしい。根津が手で追い払うしぐさをすると、唇を尖らせ、スピードを落とした。

「なんですか」桐林が訊いてくる。

「関係ない。ただの野次馬だ」

結局、絵留はホテルの前まで行って止まった。スキーを外し、リュックサックを下ろしている。根津は彼女に近づいていった。

「おい、どういうことだ」

絵留は首を横に振った。「中止」

「何だって？」

「電話がかかってきて、今日の取引は中止にするっていわれたの」

「どうして？」

すると絵留は根津のほうを向き、ため息をついた。「ギャラリーが多すぎる、だって」

「えっ？」

「周りに変な見張り役をつけるな。今度やったら承知しない──そういわれた」

「俺たちのことか」

「ほかに誰がいるわけ？」そういうと絵留はホテルの入り口に向かった。

32

倉田が会議室を出て管理事務所に戻ると、根津と藤崎絵留の姿があった。二人とも悄然(しょうぜん)としている。倉田を見て、根津が椅子から立ち上がった。

「いや、座っててていい」倉田は頷きながら手を小さく上下させた。

それでも根津は立ったままで、頭を下げた。「どうもすみませんでした」

倉田は頭を掻いた。

「まあ、仕方がない。藤崎君から聞いたかぎりでは、君たちがそれほど無茶なことをしたわけではなさそうだし」

「そうなんです。本当に俺たち、遠くから見ていただけなんです。スーパースラロームコースでは、ずっと森の中にいたし……」

「だから、それが気に食わなかったんじゃないの? 犯人としては」藤崎絵留がいう。

「まあそうなんだろうけど、納得いかないんだよな」根津は倉田を見て続けた。「俺たち、絵留には近づいてないし、ダウンヒルコースからスーパースラロームコースまで、周りには誰もいなかったんです。一体犯人は、どこから見ていたのか……」

「単に根津君たちが気づかなかっただけでしょ。どこかに隠れて、遠くから見ていた
のよ」

「そうかな。隠れるところなんてないぜ。だから俺たちもスーパースラロームコース
まで行くしかなかったんだ」

「そんなことないよ。小さな繁みぐらいなら、あちらこちらにあるじゃない」

「それなら気づくって。ぼんやり滑ってたわけじゃないんだ」

「だけど、実際犯人に見られてるわけじゃないんだ――」

まあまあ、と倉田は二人を宥めた。

「君たちがいい争ってどうするんだ。何の意味もない」

すみません、と根津は再び小声で謝った。「あのう、本部長たちは何と……」

倉田は口元を緩め、ふっと息を吐いた。

「機嫌がいい、とはいえないね。取引がうまくいかなかったわけだから。だけど事情
を説明したら、多少はわかってもらえた。ただし、次は絶対におかしなことをさせる
なといわれたよ」

「次……次のチャンスって、ありますかね」根津が呟く。

倉田は藤崎絵留のほうを向いた。

「犯人は、今度やったら承知しない、そういったんだろ?」

はい、と彼女は頷いた。

「だったら、次のチャンスがあるということだ。ただし、そう何度もない。次がラストチャンスだと考えるべきだろうね。だから、絶対に失敗はできない」

「そうですね」根津は唇を結んで俯いた後、再び顔を上げた。「次は俺が身代金を運びます。それなら本部長たちも納得してくれるんじゃないでしょうか」

「そうだな。それがいいかもしれない。じゃあ、その時にはよろしく頼む」

「わかりました」と気合いのこもった声で答えると、根津はもう一度頭を下げてから、部屋を出ていった。藤崎絵留も彼に続きかけたが、途中で思い直したように引き返してきた。

「どうかしたかい?」倉田は訊いた。

「少し気になることがあるんです」

「何だ?」

「根津君には、ああいいましたけど、もしかしたら彼のいっていることは正しいのかもしれません。犯人は、あの場にはいなかったのかも」

「どうしてそう思う?」

「電話です。かすかにですけど、ホテルの館内放送が聞こえてきました」

倉田は藤崎絵留の顔を見つめ、瞬きした。「本当に？」

「間違いないと思います。あの時、犯人はホテルの中にいたということになりますよね」

「犯人は一人とはかぎらない。現場で受け渡しをする係と君に連絡をする係が別だったということも考えられる」

「そんな面倒なことをするでしょうか」

「ありえないことじゃない。それに君のいう通りだとすると、犯人は最初から取引する気がなかったことになる。なぜそんな意味のないことをする？」

「それはわかりませんけど……もう一つ、気になることがあるんです」

「何？」

「犯人の声です。前回はボイスチェンジャーを使ってましたけど、今回は口にハンカチか何かを当てて声をくぐもらせている感じでした。口調も違っていたように思います」

「連絡係が代わった、それだけのことじゃないか」

「なぜ代わったんでしょう。それになぜボイスチェンジャーを使わなかったんでしょ

うか」

　倉田は息を吸った。何か妥当性のある推理を述べようとしたが、思いつかなかった。

　そんな彼に手助けするように藤崎絵留はいった。「特に気にすることではないのかもしれませんけど」

　倉田は腕組みし、何気なく窓の外に目をやった。小雪が舞い落ちてきている。今シーズンは雪不足に悩まされることはなさそうだ、とぼんやり思った。

33

　ホテルを出て、パトロールの詰め所に戻る途中で根津は足を止めた。茶色のウェアを着た瀬利千晶が雪の上に立っていたからだ。ゴーグルを頭にずらし、腕組みをしている。

　根津はため息を一つついてから近づいていった。「何か用か」

　「はあ？」信じられない、というように瀬利千晶は目を剝いた。「このまま何の説明もしないで済むと思ってんの？　あたしを舐めてるわけ？　何も教えてくれないんなら、自分の知ってることをネットに書き込んじゃうよ。それでもいいの？」

根津は顔をしかめた。

「わかったよ。教えてやるから、ぎゃあぎゃあ騒ぐな」

「誰のせいで騒いでるんだと思ってんのさ」唇を尖らせた。

「とにかく場所を変えよう。ここじゃ、まずい」根津はナイター営業が始まっている

ゲレンデに向かって歩きだした。

「外で立ち話？　パトロール小屋でもいいよ、あたしは」

根津は足を止め、振り返った。

「ほかのパトロールには内緒の話なんだ。パトロールで知っているのは、俺を入れて

三人だけだ」

「どうしてそんなことに……」

「だからそれを説明するっていってるんだ。　黙ってついてこい」

根津が再び歩き始めると、瀬利千晶はおとなしくついてきた。

ゴンドラの営業はすでに終わっているので、乗り場周辺に人影はなかった。階段の

下に灰皿が置いてあるが、わざわざこんなところまで煙草を吸いに来る者はいない。

「まず、こちらから訊きたいことがある。君はなぜ、絵留が身代金を運ぶってことを

知ってたんだ」ホテルに背を向けた状態で根津はいった。傍からは、暗がりの中で喫

煙をしているように見えるだろう。

「藤崎さんが電話で話しているのを聞いたの。でも、盗み聞きじゃないよ。パトロール小屋のそばにいたら、たまたま聞こえてきたんだ。話してた相手は、たぶん根津さんだと思う。今日の午前中のことだけど」

「あの時か」根津は鼻の上に皺を寄せた。覚えがあった。入江親子を連れて北月エリアに行った時だ。たしかに絵留と電話で話した。会話の中で彼女が身代金という言葉を使ったことも記憶にある。

「ねえ、やっぱり誘拐なの？」瀬利千晶が真剣な表情で尋ねてきた。「そうなんでしょ。でなきゃ、身代金を運んだりしないもんね」

どうやら彼女は詳しいことは何ひとつ知らないようだ。いっそのこと、誘拐事件だと答えようかと根津は考えた。ホテル関係者の子供が誘拐され、犯人から身代金を要求されている。人質の安全を優先した結果、警察には通報せずに身代金を支払うことになった。そう説明したほうが相手が納得するように思ったのだ。

だがすぐにその考えを打ち消した。この瀬利千晶という娘は馬鹿ではない。誘拐されたのはどこの誰なのか、身代金はどこから出ているのか、といったことも質問してくるに違いない。この場だけで取り繕ったところで、いずればれてしまうだろう。そ

してこの期に及んで根津が嘘をついたと知れば、それこそ激怒してネット上に何かを書き込んでしまうおそれもあった。この娘は馬鹿ではない上に、やたらと気が強いのだ。

「何を考えてるわけ？　まさか、あたしをうまく騙そうとか企んでないよね。そんなことしても無駄だよ。本当の話かどうか、徹底的に確かめちゃうから」瀬利千晶は目を一層吊り上げていった。まるで根津の心を読んだかのようだ。

「そういうことも一瞬考えた」

彼女は舌打ちをした。「やっぱり」

「一瞬だけだ。すぐに君には嘘をつかないほうがいいと思い直した」

「その通りだよ」

「ただし約束してくれ。これから話すことは絶対に秘密だ。ほかには漏らさないでほしい」

瀬利千晶は白い息を大きく吐いた。

「従兄弟たちにはいいよね。だって、身代金のことは話しちゃったから」

根津は天を仰いで頭を振った後、改めて彼女を見つめた。

「彼等は信用できるのか。君にそそのかされて滑走禁止区域を滑ったり、自分たちを

取り締まったパトロールに一目惚れしたり、どうにも軽そうに感じるんだけどな」

「軽いのは事実。否定しない。でも、あいつらのことなら大丈夫。あたしが秘密だといえば、絶対に約束を守ってくれる。もし守らなかったら、あたしが責任を取る」瀬利千晶は真剣な眼差しを向けてきた。　滑走禁止の林の中で従兄弟たちは見逃してやってくれといった時と同じ目だった。

わかった、と根津は答えた。

「君の言葉を信用しよう。このスキー場で何が起きているのか、彼等にも話してやるといい。おそらく腰を抜かして、もうここへは来たくないというだろうけどね」

「どういうこと？」　一体、どこの誰が誘拐されたの？」

「誰も誘拐なんかはされてない。ただし、人質はいる」

瀬利千晶は眉間に皺を寄せた。「意味わかんないんだけど。誰が人質なの？」

それは、といって根津は彼女を指差した。「君たちだ」

えっ、と彼女は目を見張った。

「同時に、俺たちでもある」根津は親指を自分の胸に押しつけた。「このスキー場にいるすべての人々が人質なんだ。ゲレンデ全体が乗っ取られたんだよ」

まだ話の行方が摑めない様子の瀬利千晶に、根津は事件の概要を最初から話し始め

た。犯人から送られてきた脅迫状の内容あたりから、彼女は声を発しなくなった。小

さく頷くのが、唯一の相槌だ。

これまでに二度の身代金受け渡しが行われたこと、それによって爆発物の埋まって

いないエリアがいくつか判明したが、まだ正確なことはわかっておらず、そのせいで

クロスのコースも造れないでいることも話した。この時には、「そういうことだった

んだ」と彼女は小声で呟いた。

犯人から三回目の要求があり、それによる受け渡しが、先程未遂に終わった一件だ

ったということまで根津は話した。「これが事件のすべてだ」そういって締めくくっ

た。

話を聞き終えた後も、瀬利千晶はしばらくの間動かなかった。夜の冷気で凍りつい

たのかと思うほどだった。彼女の帽子に薄く雪が積もっている。いつの間にか、また

細かい雪が降り始めていたのだ。

やがて瀬利千晶は、ふーっと白い息を吐いた。そして、「びっくり」と続けた。

「そりゃ、驚くだろうな」

「映画のストーリーを聞いてるみたい。全然現実感がない。いきなり聞かされてたら、

たぶん信用してなかったな」

「だろうな。話してる俺自身が、これは本当に現実なのかって疑いながらしゃべってる。でも現実なんだよ、紛れもなく」

瀬利千晶はナイターのライトによって明るく照らされたゲレンデに目を向け、一歩二歩と近づいた。そこでは昼間の滑走だけでは満足しきれなかった大勢のスキーヤーやスノーボーダーたちが、楽しそうに腕を競っている。

「あの人たちの下に爆弾が埋まってるかもしれないんだね」

「そういうことだ。それがわかってて、どうしてクローズにして警察に通報しないのかという話だけど、俺たち雇われ側にはどうしようもない」

「スキー場としては、事件がおおっぴらになれば、確実に今シーズンは営業できなくなるもんね。隠すのも無理ないかも」

「今シーズンだけじゃない。事件が明るみに出れば、確実にスキー場のイメージは地に落ちる。もし犯人が捕まらなければ、尚のことだ。来シーズン以降も、また狙われるんじゃないかと思って、客からは敬遠されるだろう」

「それはいえるね。だけど、一体どこの誰がそんなことをしたんだろう。どうしてこのスキー場が狙われたんだろう」

根津は首を振った。

「それが全くわからない。最初の脅迫状には、地球温暖化については環境を破壊したスキー場にも責任があるから、その慰謝料を要求するなんていう理由が書いてあったけど」

瀬利千晶は驚いた顔で振り向いた。「マジで？」

「本当だ。でも、そんなのはたぶんこじつけだ。犯人には、何かほかの理由があって、このスキー場を狙ったんだと思う」

「ここがほかよりも儲かってるから、とか？」

「まさか」根津は肩を揺すり、笑い顔を作った。「経営難で何年間もずっと右肩下がりなのは、ほかのスキー場と変わらない。親会社のおかげで、辛うじてやっていけるという状況だ」

「でも結局、一億円以上もの身代金を払うわけでしょ。このスキー場なら払えると思ったから、犯人は狙ったんじゃないの？」

「どうかな」根津は首を傾げる。「そもそもこんなに手間をかけてスキー場を狙うという発想が理解できない。金目当てで企業を脅すなら、ほかの業界を狙ったほうがいい。この御時世でも、一億円程度の金を出せる会社はいくらでもある」

「犯人の目的はお金じゃないっていうの？」

「俺は、そう思う」

「じゃあ、何が目的？　単に嫌がらせがしたいだけってこと？」

「それがわからないから困ってるんじゃないか。目的がわかれば、おそらく犯人の正体も摑めるんだと思う」

瀬利千晶は再びゲレンデのほうを向いた。「恨みがあるとか」

「何だって？」

「恨み。このスキー場に何か恨みがあって、それを晴らすためにやってるわけ。お金なんかはどうでもいい。とにかくスキー場を苦しめたいの。最終的には営業ができなくなるくらいに」そういってから彼女は振り返り、ぺろりと舌を出した。「そんなこと、あるわけないか」

そうだよあるわけない、という台詞を根津は発せられなかった。来場者たちが心から楽しめるよう、自分たちは最大限の努力をしているという自負はある。だがそれでもすべての人には満足してもらえないというのが現実だ。スキー場では毎日のようにアクシデントやトラブルが発生する。そのことでスキー場自体に反感を持つ者も中にはいるだろう。

たとえば――。

根津は一人の男性の顔を、いや、一組の親子を思い浮かべていた。

34

「それはありえないよ。考えすぎだ」携帯電話を耳に当て、窓からゲレンデを眺めながら倉田はいった。時刻は午後八時五十分。ナイター営業は、そろそろ終わりに近づいてきている。

（俺も、そうは思うんですけど、ふと気になったものですから。タイミングもいいし）電話をかけてきているのは根津だった。パトロール員は交代制で、この時間帯は遅番の担当だから、彼は自宅に帰っているらしい。

「タイミングというと？」

（事件が起きたのと、入江さん親子がホテルに来た日です）

「馬鹿な。偶然だろ」

（だといいんですが）

根津は、今回の事件の首謀者は入江義之ではないか、というのだった。動機は無論、亡き妻のことだ。事故の原因がスキー場の不完全な安全対策にあったと思い込んだと

すれば、復讐（ふくしゅう）を果たそうとする理由にはなる。

「忘れたのか。事故から二週間後ぐらいに、入江さんが現場に花を供えるためにいらっしゃったことがあったじゃないか。あの時案内したのは君だったね。入江さんは、スキー場のことは恨んでいないときっぱりとおっしゃったんだろ。君がそういってたよ」

（もちろん覚えています。だけど、あの時点ですでに今回のことを計画していたということも考えられます。事件が起きた時、自分に疑いがかからないように伏線を張っておいた──深読みしすぎでしょうか）

「しすぎだね。そんなふうに疑いだしたらきりがない。スキー場の責任を問うつもりなら、事故の直後に訴えていたはずだ。脅迫なんかじゃなく、裁判で堂々と賠償金を手に入れればいいじゃないか」

（目的は金じゃなく、スキー場を追い詰め、最終的に閉鎖に追い込むことだとしたら……）

「ありえない、と改めていうよ。いいか、根津君。入江さんは事故が起きた直後でさえ、スキー場を責めるようなことは一言もおっしゃってない。ふつうなら取り乱して、心ないことまで口にしてしまうものだ。それとも事故が起きた瞬間から、入江さんが

今回のことを計画していたとでもいうのかい」

(それは……そこまではいいませんが)

「なあ根津君、君はこのスキー場では誰よりも入江さんたちと親しいはずだろ。彼等だって、君のことを一番信用しているし、信頼している。君がそんなふうに考えていると知ったら、彼等はどれだけ悲しむと思う?」

(そりゃあ、俺だって疑いたくないです。でも可能性がないわけでもないと思って、こうして電話したんです。正直いって、いい気持ちはしません)

「わかっている。君の気持ちはわかるよ。今もいったけど、君は誰よりもあの親子と親しく、二人のことを理解している。彼等の無念な思いがわかるからこそ、犯人である可能性にも思い至ったんだろう。君の説はたしかに聞いた。しかしこれから先、入江親子に関して、君は余計なことは考えなくていい。この件については私に任せてほしい」

根津は数秒の沈黙の後、わかりました、と答えた。

(これからもあの親子とは顔を合わせるわけだし、俺が腹の中でおかしなことを考えてたら、きっと向こうにも伝わるでしょうからね。責任を押しつけるようで申し訳ないのですが、それでは倉田さんにお任せします)何かが吹っ切れたような声と口調だ

った。

「そうしてくれ。　明日は、犯人から次の指示が来る可能性が高い。今度こそ取引を成立させなければ、クロスの大会に間に合わない。余計なことは考えず、今夜はゆっくり休んでくれ」

（そうします。お疲れ様でした）

「ああ、お疲れ」

電話を切り、倉田は椅子に座った。管理事務所に残っているのは彼だけだった。根津の意見を馬鹿げたことだとは思えなかった。じつは同じようなことを倉田自身も考えていたのだ。

単独犯か複数犯かは不明だが、犯人はこれまでに二度、このゲレンデに現れている。今日にしても、藤崎絵留に「ギャラリーが多すぎる」と電話をしてきたわけだから、すぐ近くにはいたはずだ。なぜ常にゲレンデを取引場所にするのか。受け渡しにトリッキーな方法を使えるという利点があるからかもしれないが、スキー場側が警察に通報していないことが明らかな今、もはやそんな凝ったやり方は必要ない。どこか人気のないところまで現金を運ばせ、運搬係が立ち去ったのを確認してから回収すればいいのだ。そもそもこれまでに犯人が行った受け取り方法は、いずれも警察が見張って

いれば成功しなかったと思われる。

取引場所をゲレンデ内にするのは、犯人側に何らかの事情があるからではないか、と倉田は考えた。ではどんな事情か。そこで思いついたのが、犯人はこのホテルに宿泊しているのかもしれない、ということだった。

これまでは、犯人は外部からやってきて、現金を回収した後はスキー場から立ち去っているものと思い込んでいた。しかし考えてみれば、内部に潜入していたほうが、スキー場側が警察に通報したかどうかなどを確認しやすい。

犯人は宿泊客か——そう考えた時、真っ先に思い浮かんだのが入江義之のことだった。

根津にはああいったが、入江がこのスキー場を恨んでいないとは断言できない。事故直後にはそういう気持ちはなくても、時間が経つにつれ、徐々に憎しみが増していった可能性はある。

しかし倉田はこの推理を誰かに話す気はなかった。現時点では何ひとつ証拠がない。単なる想像だ。それでも聞いた者は、入江たちに疑念の目を向けるようになるだろう。

そんなことは何としてでも避けねばならない。

ナイター営業終了を告げるアナウンスが聞こえてきた。今日も無事に一日の営業を

終えられそうだ。あくまでも表面上のことではあったが。

倉田は管理事務所を出ると、二階のバーに向かった。飲酒ではなく、店の窓からゲレンデを眺めるのが目的だった。リフトが止まり、ゲレンデに残っている最後のスキーヤーあるいはスノーボーダーが滑走を終えてから約十分後、雪面を照らすライトが消されることになっている。それを見届けようと思った。

倉田が入っていくと、顔見知りのウェイターが笑顔で会釈してきた。彼が酒を注文しないことは、この店では知られている。

店内には一組の客がいるだけだった。窓際のテーブルを挟み、三人で座っている。彼等を見て、倉田は足を止めた。一人が入江義之だったからだ。さらに彼と向き合っているのは、いつかゴンドラの中で会った老夫婦だった。

入江が倉田に気づいたようで、小さく手を上げてきた。老夫婦たちの視線も彼に向けられた。

倉田は近づいていき、こんばんは、と挨拶した。「達樹君は?」

「部屋で寝ています。今日は久しぶりに滑りましたから、疲れたんでしょう。それで一人でここへ飲みに来たら、お二人がいらっしゃって」入江は老夫婦を見た。

「誰か話し相手が来ないかと思って、待ち構えておったところだったんですよ」老人

が笑った。顔の皺が深くなった。

「たしか、お二人ともロイヤルスイートの御利用でしたね。入江さんとは同じ階の」

そうそう、と老人は頷いた。「いい部屋で、のんびりさせてもらってますよ」

老人は名刺を出してきた。倉田の知らない会社名と共に、『相談役　日吉浩三』と印刷されていた。日吉は隣にいる妻のことも紹介した。友恵というらしい。

「日吉さんはスキー歴五十年だそうです」入江がいった。

「それは素晴らしい」倉田は演技でなく、目を見張った。

いやいや、と日吉は顔の前で手を振った。

「長くやってるというだけです。腕前のほうは二十年前からちっとも進歩しておりません。むしろ、年々だめになっていくようで」

「そんな御謙遜を。一度、滑っておられるところを拝見しましたが、お二人とも見事なものです。あれほど奇麗にテレマークスキーを扱える人は、そうそういません」

「そうですか。スキー場の人にそういってもらえると自信がつきますなあ」

「馬鹿ね、お世辞に決まってるでしょ」友恵が顔をしかめる。

「いえ、本心です」倉田はいった。「しかもあのテレマークは、少し幅広でしたね。深雪なんかもよく滑られるんですか」

「ええ、深雪は大好きです。ちょうどよかった。今、その話を入江さんとしていたところでしてね」日吉が意味ありげな笑みを浮かべた。「北月エリアを滑れるそうですね」

倉田は、えっと驚いて入江を見た。彼は、ばつの悪そうな顔をした。

「日吉さんが北月エリアのことを気にしておられるので、つい話してしまったんです。今朝、息子と二人で滑ってきましたって」

「そういうことでしたか」倉田は呟いた。入江を責めるわけにはいかない。

「羨ましいですなあ。誰もいない広大なゲレンデ、しかも未圧雪のところを滑るなんて、まるで天国でしょうなあ」そういって日吉は身を乗り出した。「どうでしょう。その特別ツアーに、どうか私らも参加させていただけませんか」

「いやあ、それは……」

迂闊には承諾できなかった。入江親子以外には誰も滑らせるな、と松宮からはきつくいわれている。

「もちろん、ただでとはいいません。それなりの代金は支払います」

「いやそんな代金だなんて。元々、そういうツアーは存在しないわけで」

「倉田さん、私からもお願いします。私たちだけがあの素晴らしいゲレンデを独占す

るのは、やっぱり気が引けます。どうか日吉さんたちも連れていってもらえませんか」

こんなふうに入江にまでいわれ、倉田は困惑した。ただでさえ事件のことで頭がいっぱいなのだから、余計な雑務を増やしたくないというのが本音だった。松宮を説得するのも難しそうだ。

だが入江義之の顔を見返した時、ふと一つのアイデアが閃いた。

35

千晶の話に、従兄弟たちは絶句した。缶ビールを持ったまま、マネキン人形のように動かない。やがて幸太の持った缶から噴き出した泡がこぼれ、胡座をかいている彼の膝を濡らした。

「わわわ、冷てっ」あわてて缶に口をつけた。

「何やってんの。ドジ」千晶はそばにあったタオルを投げた。

時計の針は零時を過ぎている。彼女は居酒屋でのバイトを終えた後、従兄弟たちが借りているリゾートマンションに来ていた。ガラスのテーブルを囲み、スナック菓子

などを肴に酒盛りを始めることになったが、先に根津から聞いたことを二人に話して

おこうと思った。案の定、ゲレンデの下に爆弾が埋まってるんだって、の台詞だけで

彼等は固まったのだった。

「それ、本当かよ」快人が訊く。「本当だったら、やばいじゃん。それ、めっちゃ

ばいじゃん」

「そんなに何度もいってくれなくてもわかってるよ。だから、絶対にほかの人にいっ

ちゃだめだからね。大騒ぎになって、スキー場が閉鎖なんてことになったら、あんた

らだってもうあそこを滑れなくなるんだから」

「いやあ、悪いけど、俺はもう新月高原で滑る気なくなった。スキー場なんて、ほか

にいくらでもあるし」

さらりという快人の顔を千晶は睨みつけた。

「あのスキー場がどうなってもいいってわけ？」

「そうじゃないよ。俺は滑りたくないといってるだけだろ。わかってるよ。ほかの人

間にはしゃべらないって」

「本当だろうね。　裏切ったら承知しないよ」

「信用しろよ。だけどさ、マジでそれ大丈夫なのか。今までは何もなかったけど、何

かの拍子に爆発するっていう可能性もあるんじゃないの？」

「それはあるかも」

ひゃあ、と幸太がのけぞった。「やばいよ、それ。千晶ねえちゃんも、もうあそこで滑るのはやめたほうがいいよ」

だが千晶は答えず、缶ビールを傾けた。いつもよりも味が苦く感じられた。

「えっ、何だよ。千晶ねえちゃん、まだあそこへ行く気かよ」

「悪い？」

「悪くはないけど、危ないよ。やめたほうがいいって」

千晶は、がんと音をたてて缶ビールをテーブルに置いた。

「そういう卑怯なことはしたくないんだよね」

「えっ、卑怯かな」幸太が意見を求めるように兄のほうを向いた。

快人は首を振った。

「そんなことねえよ。命に関わる問題だぜ。危ないところに立ち寄らないことの、どこが卑怯なんだ」

千晶は深呼吸を一つしてから従兄弟たちを見た。

「あたしは根津さんと、あんたたち以外の人間には話さないって約束した。あんたた

ちにも、誰にもいうなって誓わせた。でもあのゲレンデには、明日も大勢のスキーヤーやボーダーたちがやってくる。その人たちには何も知らせず、自分だけが安全なところにいるなんて、卑怯だと思わない？」

二人は顔を見合わせた。

「そういう言い方をしたら、そうかもしれないけど……」幸太がぼそぼそいった。

「どういう言い方をしたって同じこと。危険なことを知ってて黙ってるんだから、それなりの責任を負わなきゃいけないと思う」

「じゃあ、俺や兄貴も行かなきゃ卑怯ってこと？」

千晶はふっと息を吐き、口元を緩めた。

「あんたらはいいよ。あたしに口止めされただけだから」

「だけどそれをいったら、千晶だってそうだろ」快人がいった。「誰にもいうなって根津さんに無理矢理約束させられたわけじゃないか」

「無理矢理じゃないよ。約束してなくても、あたしはあんたたち以外の人間にはいわなかったと思う」

怪訝そうに眉を寄せた二人に、「苦しいんだよ」と彼女は続けた。「あたしはいろいろなスキー場を渡り歩いてるから、よくわかってる。今、スキー場

はどこも経営が苦しいの。新月みたいに儲かってるように見えてるところでも、一つ間違えたら危機に陥っちゃう。雪が少ないと人が来ないし、多すぎると今度はアクセスが大変になって、また客足が減る。ただでさえウインタースポーツの人口が減ってるって時に、今度の事件。あたし、スキー場側が警察に通報しないのは無理ないと思う。あたしが社長でも、やっぱり同じように考えたかも」

彼女の話を聞き、二人は黙り込んだ。幸太はポテトチップスの袋に手を伸ばし、ビールを飲んだ。

「でもさ、その取引はもう終わるんだろ?」快人が訊いた。

「うん、根津さんによれば、明日こそ終わるだろうし、終わらせなきゃいけないってことだった」

「だったらさ、千晶も明日ぐらいは行くのをやめればいいじゃん。一日ぐらいなら、卑怯ってことにはならないよ」

千晶は苦笑して首を振った。

「一日だろうが十日だろうが、危険を知ってて自分だけ逃げるのは卑怯だよ」

「そうかなあ」

「それに、見届けたいっていう気持ちもあるんだ。無事に取引が成立するのかどうか

をこの目でね。根津さんや藤崎さんたちが命がけでゲレンデを守ろうとしてくれてい
るのに、部屋でぼんやりしてるなんてこと、あたしにはできないよ」

快人は顔をしかめ、「藤崎さんか……」と呟いた。「その名前を出されると弱いな」

「あんたは気を遣う必要ないよ。これはあたしの問題なんだから」そういうと千晶は
自分を納得させるように、うんと大きく頷き、缶ビールの残りを飲み干した。

幸太が立ち上がり、窓に近づいた。ガラスの結露を指で擦り、外を見ている。

「また結構降ってきた。今シーズンはどうなってんのかな。雪不足の長期予報、大は
ずれだよ」

千晶は二本目の缶ビールを開けた。幸太の後ろから窓を見上げ、明日の受け渡しが
うまくいくことを祈った。

36

根津が自分の車を駐車場に止めた時、時計のデジタル表示が六時三十分になった。
そのまま詰め所に行くと、すでに藤崎絵留と桐林の姿があった。ほかのパトロール員
は、まだ来ていない。

「何か変わったことは……」根津は二人の顔を交互に見てから続けた。「ないようだな」

「さすがに、犯人が夜中に連絡してくることはないと思うよ」絵留がいった。「でも、今日は必ず何かいってくるはず。あたしたちは、いつどんな要求が出された場合でも対応できるようにしておかないと」

根津は頷いた。

「現金の受け渡し時に、三人とも出払ってたら話にならないからな。絵留は、なるべく管理事務所にいてくれ。ほかの者に何か訊かれたら、倉田さんから手伝いを頼まれたとか何とか適当にいっておけばいい。キリは、ここで待機だ。通常のパトロール業務をしてくれ」

「了解です」と桐林は敬礼のポーズを取った。

それから間もなく、ほかのパトロール員たちがやってきた。いつものように手分けして、始業前のゲレンデ点検に出かけていく。根津も桐林が運転するスノーモービルの後部席に跨った。

主にゴンドラに沿ったコースを二人で点検して回った。昨夜もかなりの降雪があったので、見た目の地形がずいぶんと変わっている。雪崩の起きるおそれがないかなど

を慎重に調べた。現金の受け渡しを控えているとはいえ、本来の業務をおろそかにするわけにはいかない。

新雪が降り積もった斜面を眺めながら、根津は今日行われるに違いない身代金受け渡しのことを考えた。今回は自分が運搬役をやろうと決めている。犯人はこれまでと同様、ゲレンデ内のどこかを受け渡し場所に指定してくるのだろうか。もしそうだとして、今度はどんな手を使うつもりなのか。

点検を終え、詰め所に戻った。すると入り口の前で倉田が待っていた。

「御苦労さん。今、ちょっといいかな」

根津は、ぴんと背筋を伸ばした。「犯人から連絡が?」

「いや、それはまだだ。だけど先に相談しておきたいことがある。ホテルのロビーにいるから、来てくれないか」

「わかりました」

点検用の荷物を詰め所に置いた後、根津はロビーに行った。倉田が隅の席に座っていた。根津も向かい側に腰を下ろす。

「相談というのはほかでもない。昨夜、君が電話をかけてきた件だ」近くに人はいなかったが、倉田は声を落とした。「入江さんが今回の事件と関係があるんじゃないか

って君は疑っていただろ?」

根津は苦笑いを浮かべて手を横に振った。ばつが悪かった。

「あのことならもういいです。倉田さんがおっしゃった通り、俺だけはあの人たちを疑っちゃいけないと思います。すべて倉田さんにお任せします」

「それはわかっている。だけどあれから少し考えて、はっきりさせられるものなら、はっきりさせておいたほうがいいんじゃないかと思ってね」

倉田のいわんとしていることがよくわからず、根津は小首を傾げた。

「ロイヤルスイートに、ヒヨシさんという老夫婦が泊まっている。長期滞在している人たちで、俺も何度か言葉を交わした。ところが厄介なことに、その人たちが入江さんの話を聞いて、自分たちも北月エリアを滑りたいといいだしたんだ」

「はあ……」根津は曖昧な相槌を打つ。たしかに厄介な話だと思ったが、事件と何の関係があるのかが見えない。

「最初はほかの人間を滑らせるのはまずいと思ったんだけど、少し考えた後、了承することにした。ただし、条件を二つ付けた。まず、入江さん親子が一緒であること。さらに、彼等を連れていかないのであれば上役たちの許可を取れないからといってね。

実施時間はこちらに調整させてほしいといった。つまり、いつ連れていって、いつ連れ戻すかは、こっちが決めるというわけだ」

根津にはまだ倉田の狙いが理解できなかった。入江たちを北月エリアに連れていくことに、どんな意味があるのか。

すると倉田は企み顔で身を乗り出した。

「わからないか？　この約束によって、我々はいつでも入江さんたちを北月エリアに隔離できるようになったわけだ。老夫婦という証人も確保できた」

あっ、と根津は声を漏らした。

「そういうことか。犯人が指定してくる取引の時刻前に入江さんたちを北月エリアに連れていき、現金の受け渡しが終わった後で連れ戻すことにすれば、入江さんにはアリバイがあるってことになるわけだ」

「もちろん、共犯者がいる可能性は残るけれど、それは限りなくゼロに等しいと思う。もし入江さんが犯人なら、受け渡し時に北月エリアに行くこと自体に同意しないだろう。何か理由をつけて中止にしようとするはずだ」

根津は何度も首を縦に振った。

「いいじゃないですか。特別ツアーのサービスができて、さらに入江さんへの疑いを

払拭できるなら一石二鳥だ」

「松宮本部長のことは何とかして説得するよ。君のほうでは、入江さんたちを北月エリアまで案内して、さらにスノーモービルで引っ張り上げる係を用意してほしい」

「わかりました」

よし、と気合いを入れるようにいって倉田は立ち上がった。

「今日が勝負だ。失敗は許されない。何とか乗り切ろう」

はい、と根津も気持ちを込めて返事をした。

37

表情を強張らせた辰巳が管理事務所に入ってきたのは、間もなく正午になろうという頃だった。通常業務をこなしていた倉田だったが、すぐに手を止めて彼を見上げた。犯人からの連絡があったのか、と目で尋ねてみる。だが辰巳は渋い顔でかぶりを振った。

「だめです。まだ連絡が来ません」倉田のそばに来て、小声でいった。

倉田は思わず舌打ちをした。

「この時間になっても音沙汰なしか。いつまで勿体をつける気かな」

「まさか犯人のやつ、計画を中止にしたんじゃないでしょうね」

その可能性は皆無ではない。倉田は唇を噛んだ。

時計を見つめた後、すぐ横で待機している藤崎絵留のほうを向いた。

「根津君にいって、入江さんたちを北月エリアに案内するよう手配してもらってくれ。あまり時間が遅くなると不自然だ」

すでに詳しい事情は彼女にも話してある。わかりました、といって事務所を出ていった。

「辰巳君は会議室に戻って、引き続きメールを待ってくれ。犯人はぎりぎりの時間を指定してくる気かもしれない。少しでもタイムをロスしたくない」

「はい」辰巳も急ぎ足でドアに向かった。

倉田は再び時計を見つめ、机を指先で叩いた。万一犯人が連絡してこなかった場合のことを考えた。クロス大会のコース造りには、明日の早朝からとりかからなければ間に合わない。いやそれ以前に、爆発物がどこに埋まっているのかがわからないままで、一体いつまで営業を続ければいいのか。

しばらくすると入り口から誰かが駆け込んできた。藤崎絵留だった。顔つきが厳し

い。

どうした、と倉田は訊いた。

「根津君によると、入江さんたちが捕まらないらしいんです」

ぎくりとした。「何だって?」

倉田は自分の携帯電話を出し、入江義之にかけてみた。番号はずいぶん前に教えてもらっている。

「部屋にはいないみたいで、ケータイにかけても繋がらないそうです」

だが藤崎絵留のいう通り、電話は繋がらなかった。

「根津君は、今どこに?」

「駐車場にいます。日吉さんという御夫妻と一緒です」

そちらのほうとは連絡がついたらしい。倉田は防寒着を手にし、席を立った。

藤崎絵留と共に駐車場に行ってみると、一台のワンボックスワゴンの前に根津の姿があった。運転席にいるのはパトロール員の上山禄郎だ。彼が北月エリアの案内役に選ばれたらしい。ワゴン車の後部座席には日吉夫妻が乗っているようだ。

「一応、入江さんのケータイの留守電に、ここで待っているってことは入れておきました」根津はいった。「部屋にいないということは、ホテル内のどこかにいるか、あ

るいはゲレンデで滑ってるってことだと思うんですが」

「昨夜入江さんには、いつでも連絡を取れるようにしておいてくれといったんだけどな」倉田はそばのゲレンデに目を走らせる。だが入江親子の姿は見当たらない。

「あたし、場内アナウンスをお願いしてきます」

藤崎絵留の提案に、よろしく、と倉田は答えた。

ワゴン車の運転席の窓ガラスが下がり、上山が顔を出した。

「どうしましょうか。日吉さんたちだけでも、先に御案内しておきましょうか。入江さんたちが見つかったら、俺がまた迎えにきますよ。その間、日吉さんたちには休憩してもらってるってことでいいんじゃないですか」

「いや、それはまずい」倉田はいった。「向こうで日吉さんたちだけにしておくのはよくない。悪いけど、もう少し待ってくれ」

「はあい。俺はどっちでも構わないっすよ」そういって上山は窓ガラスを閉めた。事件のことを知らない人間の台詞は、どうしても能天気に聞こえてしまう。

「一体どういうことだと思いますか」根津が声をひそめていった。「このタイミングで行方がわからないなんて、ちょっと変だと思いませんか」

倉田は小さく首を振った。「結論を急ぎすぎるな」

でも、と根津が口を開きかけた時、倉田の服の下で携帯電話が震えた。取り出して着信表示を見る。辰巳からだった。

「はい」

（倉田さん、来ました。犯人からのメールです）辰巳の声は上ずっていた。

「受け渡しに関する指示か？」

（そうです。すぐに来てください）

「わかった。宮内さんたちにも知らせてください」電話を切り、根津を見つめた。

「犯人から連絡があった。俺は会議室に行く。君は、もうしばらくここにいて、入江さんたちを待ってくれ」

だが根津は返事をせず、一歩近寄ってきた。ワゴン車のほうをちらりと見た後、何かいたそうにした。

倉田は手を出し、それを制した。

「君のいいたいことはわかっている。もし入江さんが現れなければ、その時また考えればいい。今、最優先すべきことは、金の受け渡しを成功させることだ。そうだろ？」

根津はごくりと唾を呑み込むように喉を動かし、深く頷いた。「そうですね」

「じゃあ、よろしく頼む」倉田は足早にその場を離れた。

　会議室に向かって廊下を歩いていると、中垣に続いて宮内が部屋に入っていくのが見えた。ただならぬ雰囲気がある。

　会議室では辰巳がプリンタから何枚かの用紙を取り出しているところだった。さらにそれを集まってきた者たちに配っている。倉田も受け取るなり、文面に目を走らせた。

　『新月高原スキー場の関係者諸君へ

　昨日の諸君らの行動には失望した。なぜこの期に及んであのような不誠実な行動をとったのか、理解に苦しむ。

　こちらとしては、取引不成立とみなし、このまま袂を分かつ選択肢もある。それをしたところでこちらは何も困らないし、損もしない。そちらが、六千万円もの大金を投じたにもかかわらずゲレンデ内の爆発物を処理できない、という事態に陥るだけである。

　だが熟慮の末、もう一度だけチャンスを与えることにした。ただし、これで不成立に終わった場合には、もう次はない。また不成立の原因がそちらにあった場合には、それなりの報復をさせていただくつもりなので覚悟しておくように。

　では指示を出す。

・すでに用意したはずの五千万円は前回と同様に防水バッグに入れろ。
・これまでと同じ携帯電話を用意しろ。
・運搬係も前回と同じ人物が務めること。
・以上の準備を整え、午後三時にセンターゲレンデにて待機すること。
次こそ、お互いにとって理想的な結末が訪れることを祈る。

『埋葬者より』

38

雪上に落ちた自分の影が濃くなっていることに根津は気づいた。見上げると、分厚い雲が割れ、その隙間から青い空が出現しつつあった。

「おっ、晴れてきましたね」ワンボックスワゴンの運転席から、上山がにこやかに声をかけてきた。

そうだな、と気のない返事をした時、根津の携帯電話が着信を告げた。表示を見ると、かけてきているのは倉田だった。

「はい、根津です」

（倉田だ。入江さんたちは現れたか？）

「いいえ、まだです」

（……そうか）

「倉田さん、これはやっぱりおかしいですよ」

（結論を急ぐなといっただろ。現時点では、犯人がどこの誰であろうと、我々のすることは一つだ。犯人の指示に従って現金の受け渡しを成し遂げる——そうだろ？）

「おっしゃってることはわかりますが……」

（それ以外のことは考えないでくれ。頼む）

根津はため息をついた。その息は彼の顔の前で白く広がった。

「では、北月行きについてはどうしますか。中止にしますか」

（そうしてくれ。入江さんたちを連れていけないのでは意味がない。それに、今日の北月行きについては、まだ松宮本部長の許可を取っていない。何かあったら、後が面倒だ）

「わかりました。じゃあ、日吉御夫妻には俺からそのように説明します」

（すまない。よろしく頼む）

「それで、犯人からの指示はどうでしたか？」ワゴン車から離れながら根津は小声で

訊いた。上山たちに聞かせるわけにはいかない内容だ。

倉田が息を整える気配があった。

（午後三時にセンターゲレンデで待機するように、といってきている。金額や準備内容は、前回とほぼ同じだ）

「了解です。じゃあ俺は、すぐに詰め所に戻って支度を始めます」

（いや、申し訳ないが君ではだめだ。犯人は、運搬係は前回と同じ人間にさせろと指示してきている）

根津は息を呑んだ。

「どういうことですか。何のために、その必要があるんです？」

（わからんよ、俺には。とにかく犯人が、そのように指示してきているんだ。藤崎君には、俺のほうから連絡しておく）

根津は携帯電話を握り直した。たった今まで、自分が現金の受け渡し役をやろうと決めていた。今回にかぎって、なぜ犯人はそんな指示を出してきたのか。

「俺はどうすればいいでしょうか」

（何もしなくていい。昨日のことを覚えてるだろ？　犯人たちはこちらの動きを見張っている。おかしなことをすれば報復するとも書いている）

「倉田さん、昨日もいいましたけど、俺たちの姿が犯人から見えたはずがないんです。信用してください」

（もちろん、君のことは信用している。だけど、今一番大切なことは、目の前の危険を取り除くことだ。そのためには無事に金を犯人に渡すしかない。指示に従うしかないんだ）

釈然とせず、根津は黙っていた。すると倉田は、わかったか、と念押しをしてきた。

（悔しい気持ちはわかるが、我慢してくれ）

倉田の立場はよくわかった。最初の脅迫状が届いた時、彼は即刻スキー場を閉鎖し、警察に通報すべきだと主張したのだ。上役たちの賛同を得られず、犯人の要求に応えるしかない今となっては、一刻も早くそれを成し遂げることが自分の使命だと考えているのだろう。悔しいのは彼だって同じのはずだ。

わかりましたと根津は答えた。声に力が入らなかった。

（うん、ではまた連絡する）そういって倉田は電話を切った。

根津は再びため息をつき、電話を見つめた。自分の無力さを痛感する思いだった。

「倉田さんからですか」車の中から上山が訊いてきた。不安そうな顔をしている。

根津はワゴン車に近づき、上山と日吉夫妻に、入江親子が見つからないので、北月

行きは中止する旨を告げた。

「そうですか。それは仕方がないですねえ」日吉浩三は残念そうな表情を作ったが、その口調は穏やかだった。入江親子がいなければ実施するわけにはいかない、ということは理解していたからだろう。

「でも、心配ね。どうして連絡が取れないのかしら」日吉友恵が車から降りながらいった。

「わかりません。どこか電波の届かないところに行ってらっしゃるのかもしれません」

「居場所が判明したら、私たちにも知らせてもらえませんか。このままじゃ、気になる」そういって日吉浩三は、スキーウェアのポケットから携帯電話を出してきた。自分の番号を表示させると、根津のほうに画面を向けた。

了解です、といって根津は番号を登録した。

日吉夫妻と別れると、ワゴン車の片づけを上山に任せ、詰め所に戻ることにした。

頭の中では二つの考えが交錯していた。一つは入江義之のことだ。彼と達樹はどこへ行ってしまったのか。そしてもう一つは取引のことだ。

やはり彼が犯人だったのか。やはり倉田の指示に従って、犯人に金を奪われるのを黙って見過ごすしかないのか。

ホテルの脇を通った時、根津君、と呼ぶ声が聞こえた。　総務部長の宮内が、通用口のそばに立っていた。

根津は小走りに駆け寄った。「何でしょう」

宮内は髭の感触を確かめるように顎を撫でた後、意味ありげな視線を向けてきた。

「例の件だ。今回も、やってくれるんだろう？」

「やるって、何をですか」

宮内は、腰砕けするしぐさをした。

「もう忘れたのか。昨日、話したじゃないか。犯人の正体を突き止めたいから、受け渡し場所を見張って、何かヒントを摑んでほしいって」

根津は総務部長の強面を見返した。

「宮内さんこそ、昨日のことを忘れたわけじゃないでしょう？　俺たちが見張っているからといって、犯人は取引を中止にしたんですよ」

「しかし君は納得していないわけだろ？　倉田君から話を聞いたよ。絶対に犯人には見つかっていないという自信があるそうだね」

「絶対に、とはいいませんけど……」

「私はね、君のその直感を信じていいと思っている。再挑戦する価値はある」

「でもたった今、倉田さんからは、何もしないでくれといわれました」

宮内は肩を揺らすって苦笑した。

「倉田君はそういうだろうさ。物事には本音と建前がある。彼としては建前を重視するしかない。ゲレンデの責任者だからな。客の安全確保が最優先だ。そこで本音の部分は俺が引き受ける。貴重な会社の金を、どこの馬の骨ともわからぬ輩には渡したくない。できれば正体を突き止めて、すべて回収したい。わかるか?」

「わかりますけど」根津は首を捻った。「もしまた犯人が難癖をつけてきたらどうしますか。今度は承知しないっていってるんでしょ」

宮内は顔をしかめ、苛立ったように首を横に振った。

「いってるだけだよ。昨日もいったが、本気で爆破させる気なんかはない。そんなことをしたって、犯人側には何のメリットもないじゃないか。奴らはすでに六千万円を奪っている。こちらの出方に文句があるなら、取引を中止にして、さっさと手を引けばいいだけのことだ。どうしても、もっと金が必要だということなら、改めて要求してくるだけのことだ。実際に爆破させてしまえば警察沙汰になるだけでなく、脅迫のネタがなくなる。そんな馬鹿なことはしないと俺は思う。そもそも、本当に爆発物が埋まってるのかどうかも怪しいもんだ」

「その考えには俺も同感ですが……」

「だろ？　だったら、何も躊躇うことはない。犯人の正体を暴く手がかりが得られるのは、金の受け渡しの時だけだ。つまりこれが最後のチャンスかもしれない。指をくわえて見ている手はない」

「だけど、もし取引がうまくいかなかったらまずいでしょう？　爆破はされないかもしれないけど、そのまま犯人が何もいってこなければ、爆発物の場所はわからないままです」

宮内は仏頂面をし、懐から煙草を取り出した。一本をくわえ、ライターで火をつける。近くに灰皿はない。どうする気かと思って根津が見ていたら、反対側の内ポケットから携帯灰皿を出してきた。

「その時はその時、じゃないかな。むしろそれでも構わない、と俺は考えてるけどね」

煙と共に吐き出された台詞に、根津は目を剥いた。

「それ、マジでおっしゃってるんですか」

「マジだよ、もちろん」宮内はさらりという。「無論、大きな声ではいえないがね。五千万円の純利益を上げるためには、どれだけの来場者数が必要考えてみるといい。五千万円の純利益を上げるためには、どれだけの来場者数が必要

だと思う？　どうしても安全を確保したいというのなら、営業エリアは犯人が安全宣言をしているコースに限定し、そうでないコースについてはクローズにすればいい。うちのスキー場は広い。いくつかのコースが滑れないからといって怒りだす客はいない」

どうやら宮内は、易々と大金を奪われることが我慢ならないようだ。昨日も自分の給料について愚痴をこぼしていたのを根津は思い出した。

「でもそれは宮内さんの意見ですよね。社長や本部長たちがどう考えておられるかはわかりません」

宮内は煙草を吸い、煙を吐きながら口元を曲げた。

「さっきもいっただろ。本音と建前があるって。あの人たちの立場じゃ、無茶なことはいえない。犯人から金を要求された以上、支払うという姿勢を見せるしかない。だけど内心では、支払いたくないと思っている。だから俺みたいな人間が必要なんだよ」

「じゃあ、本音では宮内さんと同意見だと？」

「そうでなきゃ、昨日の件で、君たちはもっと責められていただろうな」宮内は、にやりと笑った。

そういえば、と根津は現金の受け渡しが失敗に終わった直後の倉田の話を振り返った。取引が成立しなかったことで本部長たちの機嫌はよくなかったが、根津たちの行動については理解してもらえたということだった。

「どうだ、やる気になってくれたか」

「そういうことなら。でも倉田さんには──」

「わかっている。彼にはいわないでおく。じゃあ、任せていいな」

「どこまでうまくできるか、わかりませんけど」

「何もできなくて元々だ」宮内は煙草の火を消し、吸い殻を携帯灰皿に入れた。「聞いたと思うが、三時にセンターゲレンデだ。ウェアは着替えたほうがいいだろうな」

そういうとホテルの中へ入っていった。

総務部長の、やや猫背の後ろ姿を見送りながら、根津は不思議な思いを抱いていた。

倉田のような慎重派もいれば、一方には大胆なことを考える人間がいる。いずれにせよ、宮内が後押ししてくれたとなれば心強い。根津は急いで詰め所に戻った。桐林がいたので、手招きして外へ連れ出すと、たった今いわれたことを話した。

「宮内さんが、またそんなことを？　昨日、あんなことになっちゃったのに」意外そうな顔で桐林は首を捻った。

「犯人に爆発させる気はないと踏んでるみたいだ。俺もそう思う。倉田さんから絶対に余計なことをするなと釘を刺されたんだけど、宮内さんからお墨付きをもらえたから勇気百倍だ。今度こそ、うまくやってやろうぜ」

だが桐林は返事をせず、なぜか浮かない顔つきだ。どうした、と根津は訊いた。

「根津さん、俺はやめておきます」

桐林の言葉に、根津は耳を疑った。聞き違えたのかと思った。

「何だって？」

桐林は真っ直ぐに根津の顔を見つめてきた。

「やめるといったんです。根津さんもやめたほうがいいです。倉田さんがいうように、手を出すべきじゃないと思います」

「ちょっと待てよ。どうしてそうなるんだ。昨日は俺に賛成してくれたじゃないか」

「でもそのせいで取引が中止になりました。今日こそは無事に終えなきゃいけないと思います」

「終えられるさ。取引を邪魔しようっていうんじゃない。犯人の尻尾を掴みたいだけだ」

「昨日だって、そのつもりだったじゃないですか。でも、結果的にあんなふうになっ

た」

「昨日の一件は、おまえだっておかしいと思うだろ？　俺は、昨日に関していえば、犯人は自分の都合で取引を中止したんだと思う。俺たちが隠れてたことは関係ない」

「だけど、そうだとは断言できないでしょ？　やめましょう、根津さん。今回は、黙って下で見守りましょうよ」

根津は首を振った。

「断る。このまま犯人を逃がすわけにはいかない」

「でも俺たちは警察じゃないんです。何か手がかりを摑んだところで、捕まえることなんて不可能です」

「いや、そうでもない。じつは、犯人に心当たりがある。後は確認するだけだ」

桐林は目を大きく見開いた。「……誰だというんですか」

根津は周囲を見回し、声を落としていった。「入江さんだ」

「まさか……どうしてですか」

「入江さんの奥さんの話は聞いてるだろ？　あの人にはこのスキー場を狙う動機がある。しかも、北月エリアへ連れていく約束をしてたのに、時間になっても現れなかった。犯人から新たなメールが届いたのは、そのすぐ後だ。そして今も連絡が取れない。

取引のためにどこかで準備をしてるんじゃないかと俺は思う」

「でもそれなら、最初から北月に行く約束なんかしないんじゃないですか」

「その時点では何とかなると思っていたんだ。ところが、行き帰りの時刻はこちらで決めることになったものだから、やむなく約束をすっぽかすことにした——そんなところじゃないかな」

桐林は険しい顔で首を振った。「俺は違うと思います」

「どうしてだ？　あの人以外、このスキー場を狙う人間なんかいない」

「それは……わからないと思うんですけど」桐林は頭を掻きむしった。「とにかく、犯人を刺激することはやめましょう。今回だけはおとなしくしていましょうよ」

「そういうわけにはいかない。おまえがやらないのはわかった。だけど、俺は一人でもやる」根津は踵を返し、歩きだした。

「どこへ行くんですか」桐林が訊いてきた。

「駐車場だ。一旦、家に帰る。別のウェアに着替えなきゃいけないからな」

「待ってくださいっ。根津さん、先輩っ」

桐林の声が後ろから飛んできたが、根津は足を止めなかった。

駐車場に行くと、一直線に自分の車に向かった。ライトバンの運転席側に回り、ド

アを開けた時、根津さんと遠くから呼ぶ声が聞こえた。女の声だ。きょろきょろと見回していると、茶色のウェアを着た瀬利千晶が駆け寄ってくるところだった。もうちょっとですれ違いになるところだった」

「よかった。パトロール小屋に行こうと思ってたところだったの。もうちょっとですれ違いになるところだった」

「驚いたな。まさか、来るとは思わなかった」

「どうして？　爆弾が怖くて、もうこのスキー場には近寄らないと思ってた？」瀬利千晶は目に勝ち気そうな光を宿らせた。「馬鹿にしないでよね」

「そういうわけじゃないが、俺に何の用だ」

彼女は少しすましたように鼻先を上げた。「連れてって」

「何だって？」

「どうせ、昨日みたいに身代金の受け渡しをどこかで見張るんでしょ？　だったら、あたしも付き合う。一緒に連れてって」

根津は虚を衝かれた思いで彼女の顔を見返した。つい笑みを漏らしていた。

「何？　あたし、何かおかしいこといった？」

「いや」根津は笑いながらかぶりを振った。面白いことになってきた、と思った。

腕時計の針は午後二時四十三分を示していた。藤崎絵留は五千万円の入ったリュックを背負い、倉田の携帯電話をウェアのポケットに入れた。さらには帽子をかぶってゴーグルを付け、グローブを両手に嵌めた。

「根津君はどこにいる？」倉田は訊いた。

「わかりません」彼女は首を振った。「ずっと姿が見当たらないんです。パトロールの仲間には、行方のわからなくなったお客さんを捜すといってたらしいんですけど……」

入江親子のことだな、と倉田は察した。やはり根津は入江義之のことを疑っているのか。たしかに、彼等がこのタイミングで突然姿を消したのはおかしい。

39

だが、と倉田は思った。この期に及んで、あれこれ考えている余裕はない。今回は、何があっても取引を成立させねばならないのだ。

「では、行ってきます」そういって藤崎絵留は居合わせた者たちを見回した。会議室には倉田のほか、中垣、松宮、宮内がいる。

「頼んだぞ。スキー場の安全は君にかかっている。

「あたしは犯人のいう通りにするだけです。特別なことは何もできません」

「それでいいんだ」倉田はいった。「余計なことはしなくていい。いわれたところへ行って、いわれた場所に金を置いてくれればいい」

「そうします」藤崎絵留は腕時計で時刻を確認すると、もう一度全員を見渡し、最後に倉田に一礼してから部屋を出ていった。

「さて、どうなるかな」

中垣が椅子に腰かけ、煙草に火をつけた。

「あと何分だ」中垣が煙草をくわえたままで宮内に訊いた。

「約十分です」

「うまくいくといいですがね」松宮も腰を下ろす。

「そうか。それですべて片付くな」

あのう、と倉田は上役たちを見下ろした。「二階へは行かなくていいんですか」

「二階？　なぜだ？」中垣が怪訝そうに眉根を寄せた。

「もちろん、藤崎君のことを見守るためです。バーの窓から見えますから」

「ああ……そうだったな」中垣は火をつけたばかりの煙草を灰皿の中で揉み消した。

落ち着いているように見えても、やはり全員が緊張のあまりかなり浮き足立っているようだ、と倉田は感じた。

全員で二階のバーへ行き、窓際に並んで座った。センターゲレンデに目をやると、ちょうど藤崎絵留が歩いているところだった。スキー板を担ぎ、もう一方の手にはストックを持っている。

彼女を眺めながら倉田は、なぜ犯人は運搬係を昨日と同じ人物にしろと指示してきたのだろう、と考えた。昨日は、斜度四十度の斜面を滑走できること、という条件があったから彼女が選ばれた。その条件が依然として必要だということか。

後方でドアの開く音がしたので、倉田は振り返った。入ってきた人物を見て、思わず腰を上げた。

社長の筧純一郎が、悠然と近づいてきた。

「社長……」中垣が立ち上がった。

松宮や宮内も続いたが、筧は彼等を宥めるように手を上下させた。

「座ったままでいい。で、どういう状況だ?」

倉田は座らずに一歩前に出た。

「パトロールの藤崎君が、指示された場所で待機中です。間もなく犯人指定の三時に

なります」

　筧は頷きながら窓に近づいた。中垣が自分の隣のソファを勧める素振りを見せたが、筧はそれを無視して手近な席に腰を下ろした。

「今日こそ、終わりにしてくれるんだろうな」

　誰に向かっての質問かはわからなかったが、「そのはずです」と倉田が答えた。「犯人側も、これが最後の取引だと明言していますし、爆発物の場所も具体的に教えると書いています。これまでのことを考えると、信用していいと思います」

　筧は窓越しにゲレンデを見つめたまま、身体を揺すった。

「爆弾を使って脅迫してくるような奴を信用するしかないわけか。全く情けない話だな。まあしかし、これで終われるんなら一安心だ。一億一千万か。それだけの収益を上げるのは簡単じゃないが、怪我人や死人が出ることを考えたら安いものだ」

　それを心配するなら、事件が起きた時点で閉鎖にし、警察に通報するべきではなかったか、といいたいのを倉田は堪えた。もはや、ここでいい争っても遅い。

　するとその心の声が届いたかのように、倉田君、と筧がいった。

「今回のことでは、君にはいろいろと苦労をかけたな。君は私のやり方には賛成できなかったはずだ。しかし結果的には従ってくれた。そのことを評価したいと思う」

「私は何もしていません。ただ犯人のいいなりになっただけです」

「私がそう命じたからだろう？　それでいいんだよ。ここ新月高原スキー場では、爆弾による脅迫事件なんぞは起きなかった。期待通り、オープン前に降雪に恵まれ、予定通りに営業を始められた。本格営業に入ってからも、何も問題はなし。大雪の影響などで多少スケジュールが狂うことはあっても、クロスのコースは計画通りに造られ、大会も順調に開催される。そして四月半ばまで、いつも通りに営業を続ける。そういうことでいいな」

筧の小柄な体格に似合わない低い声が店内に響いた。淡々とした口調ではあったが、倉田は威圧感を覚えた。今後もこの件については沈黙を続けろ、と改めて釘を刺してきているのだ。

「聞こえたのか、倉田君」筧が顔を巡らせてきた。狐を連想させる細い目で見つめてくる。

「社長、事件はまだ終わっておりません」倉田はいった。「まずは取引が無事に終わることを祈りたいと思います」

ふんと鼻を鳴らし、筧は前を向いて座り直した。その直後だった。「あれを見てください。犯人が連絡してきたんじゃないですか」あっ、と宮内が声を上げた。

倉田は藤崎絵留を見た。たしかに彼女は携帯電話を手にしていた。耳に当て、何か話しているようだ。

通話していたのは数十秒間だった。携帯電話をポケットにしまうと、藤崎絵留はスキーを担いで移動を始めた。

「どこへ行くんだ?」中垣が呟いた。

「ゴンドラだと思います」倉田はいった。「リフトに乗るのなら、スキーを装着するはずですから」

「やれやれ、取引場所はまたしても山の上か。ということは、報告を待つしかないってことだな」筧は片手を上げた。「ウェイターはいるか? せっかくバーにいるんだ。ブランデーでも持ってきてもらおう」

40

絵留が動きだしたのを見て、根津はそばに立ててあったボードを手にした。行くぞ、と声をかけた相手は瀬利千晶だ。二人はホテルのゲレンデ用出入口のそばにいて、絵留の様子を窺っていたのだった。

「滑らないのかな」千晶もボードを抱え、根津と並んで歩きだした。

「それならスキーは置いていくだろう」

二度目の受け渡しのことを思い出した。たぶんゴンドラだと思う」

棄させた。だがそのやり方が可能だったのは、あの時犯人は、ゴンドラの窓から現金を投

して、営業終了直後のゴンドラに乗り込めたからだ。絵留がパトロール員であることを利用

で、犯人は現金を回収するところを誰にも見られないで済んだ。だが今はまだ、ほか

の客が乗っている。

それに、と根津は思った。この犯人は用心深い。同じ手を使ったりはしないだろう。

「どうする、根津さん」千晶が訊いてきた。

彼は少し考えてから、「君は絵留より少し遅れて乗ってくれ」といった。「できれば

すぐ後ろのゴンドラに乗ってほしいけど、それが無理なようなら二、三台後でもい

い」

「わかった。根津さんはどうする?」

「俺は逆に、絵留より前のゴンドラに乗る。先に山頂に行って、様子を窺う。もし何

かあったら、いつでもいいからケータイにかけてくれ」

「了解」

千晶の返事を聞き、根津は足早に進んだ。前方を行く絵留の姿がどんどん近づいてくる。やがて彼女を追い抜き、ゴンドラ乗り場を目指した。彼女が根津に気づいた様子はない。彼が着ているウェアは彼女の知らないものだし、顔はゴーグルとフェイスマスクで完全に隠している。まず、ばれる心配はなかった。

ゴンドラ乗り場で待っていると、予想通りに絵留もやってきた。建物に入るとすぐにポケットから携帯電話を取り出している。いつ犯人から連絡があってもいいように、ということだろう。

ゴンドラは係員によって、数名による相乗りになっていた。根津は三人組のスキーヤーと一緒だった。後ろを振り返ると、絵留もほかの客と相乗りさせられそうな気配だ。この状況を犯人が知らないはずはないから、彼女がゴンドラに乗っている間は連絡してこないのではないかと思われた。やりとりを同乗者に聞かれるおそれがあるからだ。

窓ガラスに顔を寄せ、ゲレンデを見回した。まだ多くのスキーヤーやスノーボーダーたちが気持ちよさそうに滑っている。犯人は、どんな気持ちでこの光景を眺めているのだろうか、と思った。万一爆発が起きたら、というふうには考えないのか。

根津のウェアの下で携帯電話が震えた。ただし、電話ではない。メールを受信した

のだ。ほうっておこうかと思ったが、パトロール仲間からだとまずいと思い、チェッ
クすることにした。

メールを送ってきたのは千晶だった。彼女もまた相乗りしているので、電話をかけ
にくかったのだろう。中身を見ると、『エルさんの2台後ろに乗りました。今のとこ
ろ異状なし』とあった。Vサインをした女の子のイラストが動いている。大した余
裕だな、と心の底から感心した。

やがて根津の乗ったゴンドラが山頂駅に到着した。建物を出ると、なるべく斜面を
下らないよう注意しながら、二十メートルほど離れた位置まで移動し、絵留が出てく
るのを待った。

間もなく絵留が建物から出てきた。彼女はスキー板を雪上に置いたが、装着するこ
とはなく、周囲を見回している。ここから先の行動はまだ指示されていないようだ。

やがて千晶も出てきた。根津のほうに顔を向けてきたが、近づいてはこなかった。
ボードを置き、そばに座り込んだ。傍目には、仲間を待っているように見えるだろう。

根津の携帯電話が着信を告げた。千晶がかけてきているのだった。はい、と応じる。

（ねえ、もしこのまま絵留さんが動かなかったらどうする？　あたしたちだけがいつ
までもここにいたら、そのうち絶対に怪しまれるよ。　絵留さんからも、犯人からも）

彼女のいう通りだった。ゴンドラ小屋からは次々にスキーヤーやスノーボーダーたちが出てくるが、彼等は板を装着すると、さっさと滑り去っていく。つまり人の流れができているのだ。それだけに、あまりに長い時間留まっていると目立ってしまうのだ。

「あと五分だけ待とう。それぐらいなら不自然じゃない」

（その後は？）

「……それまでに考えておく」

（わかった）

電話を切り、バインディングの具合を確かめる素振りなどをしながら絵留の様子を窺った。彼女はまだ、根津や千晶の存在には気づいていないはずだ。だがいつまでもこうしてはいられない。五分経っても動きがなければどうするか。根津は懸命に頭を働かせるが名案は出ない。

五分が経過した。千晶が座ったままでこちらを見ている。根津はボードの装着を始めた。これ以上、ここに留まっているのはまずいと判断した。せめて絵留の視界からは消える必要がある。それを見たからだろう、千晶も同じようにボードを付け始めた。

だがいよいよ滑り始めようとする時になって絵留に動きがあった。携帯電話に連絡

があったらしく、何か話している。やがて彼女は電話をポケットにしまい、スキー板をブーツに装着した。ストックを持ち直し、ダイナミックな動きでスケーティングを始めたかと思うと、スムーズに滑走姿勢に入った。

根津は千晶に目配せし、スタートした。すでに絵留の後ろ姿は、かなり前方にある。彼女を追いかけるとなれば、全速力で滑らねばならない。殆ど直滑降で飛ばした。

最初の分かれ道で絵留は左側のコースを選んだ。それを見て、まずいな、と根津は思った。難易度の高い上級者コースで、そちらに行くスキーヤーやスノーボーダーは非常に少ないのだ。

分かれ道に入ったところで減速した。千晶がやってきたので、そのまま停止した。

「まずいね。この先は不整地斜面だよ。しかも、結構斜度がある。大雪が降った直後ならともかく、この時間だと余程の物好きでなきゃ滑らない。あたしたちが行ったら、確実に目立っちゃうよ」

彼女も同じことを懸念しているらしい。

「様子を見ながらゆっくり進もう。絵留の姿が見えたら、一旦ストップだ」

「わかった」

緩やかで細い連絡路を二人は進んだ。やがて幅の広い斜面の上部に出た。絵留の姿

ない。すでにここを滑り降りたということか。

　根津は周囲を見回しながら進んだ。絵留だけでなく、ほかの人影もなかった。斜面の縁に近づき、見下ろした。大小様々な自然のコブが斜面いっぱいに広がっている。凹凸の差は、大きいところでは一メートル近くありそうだ。

　見渡したところ、絵留はいなかった。もっと下へ行ったのかもしれない。

「どうする？　少し下りてみる？」

　そうだな、と根津が答えた時、携帯電話に着信があった。ポケットから取り出し、着信表示を見て驚いた。入江義之からだった。あわてて電話に出た。

「はい、もしもし」そういいながら周りに視線を走らせた。やはり入江が犯人で、どこかで自分たちを見ているのではないかと思ったからだ。

「あっ、根津さんですか。私です。入江です。すみません、連絡が遅れてしまって」

　だが携帯電話から聞こえてきた声は、拍子抜けするほどに緊張感のないものだった。

「入江さん……今、どちらに？」

「ええと、たぶんここは北月エリアだと思います」

「北月エリア？　どうしてそんなところに」

（いや、それが、今朝になって達樹が急に北月エリアに行くといいだしたんです。そ

れも、妻が命を落としたあの場所に。あの時のスノーボーダーたちのように、コース外を滑ってです。それで二人でゴンドラに乗って山頂へ行き、北月エリアを目指すことにしたんです。お知らせしなかったのは、コース外滑走を許可してもらえないだろうと思ったからです。約束の時間までには戻ってこられるだろうと思いましたし。本当に申し訳ありませんでした）

「それで、今まで北月エリアを滑っておられたんですか」

（いえ、じつは今まで山の中にいました）

「山の中？」

（はい。息子と二人でコース外に出たまではよかったのですが、道に迷ってしまいまして、ずっとさまよっていたんです。疲れて息子は動けなくなってしまうし。連絡しようと思ったのですが、携帯電話が繋がらず、参りました。たった今、北月エリアのゲレンデらしきところに出てきたところです）

「そうだったんですか……」

入江の言葉は嘘には聞こえなかった。こんな嘘をつく理由もないはずだった。

「わかりました。では、十分気をつけて滑り降りてください。雪崩のおそれもありますから。下まで行けば、タクシーを呼べばいいと思います」

（ええ、少し休んでから二人で下ります。どうも御心配をおかけしました）

電話を切った後、千晶に事情を手短に話した。

「容疑者が一人いなくなったってことだね」彼女はいった。

「よかったよ。本音をいえば、あの人を疑いたくはなかった。それより──」根津は携帯電話をしまいながら斜面の下を見つめた。「絵留を探そう。もうかなり先に行かれてしまったかもしれないけど」

「この斜面、かなり手強そうだけどね」そういうなり、千晶はスタートした。不規則に繋がっているコブの間を縫うように滑っていく。上半身は全く動かず、下半身だけがバネのように伸び縮みしている。スノーボードクロス選手の面目躍如といったところか。

根津も滑りだした。こちらは起伏など無視し、ひたすら直線的に攻めていく。大きな段差があったりすれば、ジャンプして越えてしまう。

斜面を半分ほど滑り降りた時だった。根津の視界の端で何かが動いた。咄嗟（とっさ）に減速し、そちらを見た。

絵留が立ち上がるところだった。今まで座っていたらしい。それで上からは見えなかったのだ。彼女は根津のほうを向いた後、スキー板を装着し、滑り始めた。

根津も再び速度を上げた。下では千晶が待っている。絵留が一直線にそちらに近づいていくのが見えた。まずいな、と彼は思った。

その予感は当たった。絵留は千晶の前で止まり、スキー板を外した。さらには根津を待ち受けるように、腰に手を当てて彼を見た。ゴーグルのせいで目元は見えないが、表情が険しくなっているのはわかる。

根津は近づいていき、二人の前で止まった。

「やっぱり根津君ね。そうじゃないかなと思った」

根津はフェイスマスクを外した。「いつわかったんだ」

「ゴンドラを降りて、しばらくしてから。体格と身のこなしから、何となく似てるなあと目をつけてたの。連れがいる様子はないのに、なかなか滑りだたさないのも怪しかった」絵留は千晶のほうを向いた。「瀬利千晶さんでしょ。あなたのことも気づいてた。自慢じゃないけど、ウェアを覚えるのは得意なの。従兄弟たちのウェアを上下組み合わせても、あたしの目はごまかせないわよ」根津に目を戻した。「で、だめ押しがさっきの滑り。上からすごい勢いで滑ってくるのを見て、間違いないと思った。根津君のフォーム、特徴があるからね」

参ったな、と根津は顔をしかめた。「あんなところにいるとは思わなかった。一体、

「何をしてたんだ」

「そんなの決まってるでしょ。犯人の指示に従って、お金を入れ替えてたの」

「入れ替える？」そういわれて根津は初めて、絵留の背負っているリュックサックが平たくなっていることに気づいた。

「ゴンドラを降りたところで待っていたら、犯人から電話があったの。スーパーテクニカルコースを滑れ、途中に旗を立ててあるから、その下を掘って、指示に従ってね」

スーパーテクニカルコースというのは、今まさに滑り降りてきた斜面のことだ。

「それで旗はあったのか」

「さっきあたしが座っていたところに立ってた。下を掘ってみたらリュックとビニール袋に入れたメモが出てきたってわけ」絵留はポケットから白い紙を出してきた。そこには、『金をそこのリュックに詰め替えたら、そこに置いて、おまえはすぐに立ち去れ』と印刷されていた。

「そういうことか……」根津は凹凸だらけのコースを見上げた。すでに五千万円は絵留の手を離れていたというわけだ。

あっ、と千晶が声を上げた。「根津さん、あそこっ」

彼女が指した方向に視線を移すと、灰色のウェアを着たスノーボーダーが滑り降りてくるところだった。しかも、ついさっきまで絵留がいた地点に向かっているように見える。

予感は当たった。そのスノーボーダーは、まさにあの場所で停止したのだ。

絵留が双眼鏡を取り出し、ゴーグルを外して覗いた。

「どうやら、犯人みたい。例のリュックを背負ってる」

「こっちを見てるか」

「ゴーグルを付けてるし、よくわからない」絵留は双眼鏡から目を離した。「滑りだした」

スノーボーダーが滑り始めたことは肉眼でもわかった。だが当然のことながら根津たちのところへ降りてくる気配はなく、ほぼ真横に移動している。その先には滑走禁止区域がある。そこへ侵入し、下山する気だろう。

「やられたな」根津は呟いた。脱力感が襲ってくる。「これじゃあ、手の出しようがない。絵留に気づかず、滑り降りた時点で俺たちの負けだ」

「これでよかったの。とにかく取引を無事に成立させることが先決なんだから」絵留がそういった直後だった。

彼女のウェアの下で携帯電話が鳴りだした。

「犯人からの電話らしいぜ」根津はいった。「金はたしかにいただいた、とでもいう気かな」

「違う。……鳴ってるのは、あたしの電話」絵留は急いで電話を取り出し、繋いだ。「藤崎です。……ああ、倉田さん……えっ、そんなはずないです。だって、たった今犯人がお金を……えっ、でも確かに……」彼女の表情はみるみるうちに強張っていった。

珍しく、目が泳いでいる。

「どうしたんだ」根津は絵留の肩を揺すった。

彼女は電話を耳に当てたままで彼を見上げた。

「犯人からメールが来たんだって。またしても邪魔者が入ったので取引は中止。こちらは報復行動に出るって」

「何だって？　だけど、犯人は金を奪っていったじゃないか」

「でもそういうメールが――あ、はい。今、根津君がそばにいます」絵留は電話で話し始めた。倉田が何か問いかけているのだろう。

「ちょっと、根津君っ、どこ行くの？」絵留が大声で訊いてきた。

ぐずぐずしている暇はなかった。根津は滑り始めた。

「さっきのボーダーを追いかける。捕まえて、どういうことか問い詰めてやる」

「だめだよ、それ。ちょっと待って」

しかし根津は絵留の言葉を無視し、加速していった。金を奪ったスノーボーダーが、どういうルートを選びそうかは大体察しがついている。近道をすれば、この位置からでも十分に追いつけると判断した。

「根津さんっ」後ろから千晶が追いかけてきた。「そっちじゃなくて、こっち」

その声に根津は減速した。彼女が、まるで違う方向に滑っていくのが見えた。

「そっちは斜面が切れてるぞっ」根津は叫んだ。

「いいからついてきてっ」叫び返してきた。

いわれた通りについていったが、やはり斜面は切れている。どうする気なのかと思って千晶を見ていると、彼女は何かを探すように崖下を覗き込んでいる。

根津も彼女の隣に行って下を見た。すると十メートルほど下に、古いリフト小屋があった。今は使われていない設備だ。三角屋根の上には、雪がたっぷりと積もっている。

根津は千晶を見つめた。「まさか、あれを?」

彼女は口元を緩めたかと思うと、そのまま滑降し、再び跳んだ。最後は見事に着地を決め、屋根に着地したかと思うと、次の瞬間には空中に跳び出していた。屋根に着地し、ガッツポ

「しょうがねえな」根津はため息をつき、跳び降りた。

ーズをしている。根津を見上げ、早く来いとばかりに手招きしてきた。

41

（だめだよ、それ。ちょっと待って）

藤崎絵留が悲鳴混じりに叫んでいるのが聞こえてきた。無論、電話の相手である倉田に対して発せられた言葉ではない。

「どうした？　何があった？」倉田は訊いた。

（根津君たちが犯人を……お金を奪ったスノーボーダーを追いかけていったんです）

「金を奪った？」

（あたしは犯人の指示に従って、スーパーテクニカルコースの途中に現金を置きました。そこに埋めてあったリュックに入れたんです。で、たった今、どこからか現れたボーダーがそれを持っていきました。たぶん滑走禁止区域を通って下山する気です）

「それは確かなのか。本当にそいつが犯人なのか」

（だと思います。だって、犯人じゃなければ、そんなことしないと思いますから）

状況がよくわからない。倉田は苛立ちを覚えた。

「とにかく、急いでこっちに戻ってきてくれ」

（わかりました）

倉田が電話を切ると同時に、がたんと音がした。筧が椅子から立ち上がったのだ。持っていた紙を放り出す。それはひらひらと倉田の足元に落ちた。

「こんな馬鹿な話があるか。一体どういうことだ。どうなっているんだっ」

倉田は紙を拾い上げた。そこには犯人からのメールが印刷されている。次のようなものだった。

『新月高原スキー場の関係者諸君へ

前回注意したにもかかわらず、またしても邪魔者がいるようだ。

取引を中止する。以後、こちらからは連絡しない。

この不誠実な行為に対しては報復措置をとる。

埋葬者より』

このメールが届いたのは、ほんの数分前だった。辰巳が持ってきてくれたのだ。そこで藤崎絵留に電話をかけたわけだが――。

「また、あのパトロールだろう?」中垣が倉田に訊いてきた。「根津とかいう奴だ。

あいつがまた何か余計なことをしたんじゃないのか」

「近くにいたのは確かなようです」

倉田の答えを聞き、中垣はテーブルの脚を蹴った。「馬鹿たれがっ」

「何をやってるんだ、君たちはっ」筧が怒鳴った。「あれほど慎重にやれといったのに、どうしてこんなことになるんだ」

すると今まで黙っていた宮内が筧のほうに歩み出た。

「申し訳ありません。もしかすると、私のミスかもしれません」

「君が？　何をやったんだ」

「根津君に、できれば犯人の正体を知る手がかりを摑みたい、というようなことをいいました。いやもちろん、取引の邪魔をしていいとはいっておりません。現金の受け渡しを成立させることは最優先で、その上で何とかしたいという意味のことを述べました。それほど強く要望したわけではなかったのですが、彼が拡大解釈した可能性はあります」

筧は大きな音をたてて舌打ちした。

「なぜそんな余計なことをしたんだ。パトロールといったって、所詮は素人なんだぞ。警察官じゃない。そんな奴に手がかりを摑めといったら、無茶なことをするに決まっ

てるだろう」

「申し訳ありません。スキー場の損失を少しでも減らしたいと思ったものですから

……」

「一億や二億、どうってことないだろ。取引に応じると回答した以上、金が犯人の手

に渡らなきゃ意味ないだろうが」

「おっしゃる通りです。軽率でした」

「ちょっとすみません」倉田は二人のやりとりに割って入った。「藤崎君の話では、

金は犯人が持っていったらしいのですが」

筧と宮内の視線が同時に倉田のほうを向いた。二人とも、虚を衝かれたような顔を

している。

「何? どういう意味だ」筧が訊く。

「彼女が犯人からの指示通り、コースの途中に金を置いたら、どこからか現れた犯人

がそれを持ち去ったそうなんです。金は間違いなく犯人の手に渡っています。それな

のに、なぜこんなメールを送ってきたのか……」倉田は改めてメールを見て首を捻っ

た。「犯人の意図がわかりません」

「犯人が現れた? 倉田君、それ、本当かい」宮内が疑念の籠もった目を向けてき

た。

「藤崎君はそういっています。彼女が嘘をいう理由はありません」

「いや、しかし……」宮内の視点が揺れている。

「違う。そいつは犯人じゃないんだ」そういったのは中垣だった。「たまたま通りかかった、関係のない人間に違いない。あの藤崎とかいう女子パトロールが雪の上に何か置いたものだから、興味本位に持っていったんだよ」

「ありえませんよ。だって、藤崎君たちは、まだその場にいたんですよ。盗む気なら、彼女らが去った後にするでしょう。そもそも、そんな偶然が起こるとは思えません」

「だがそいつが犯人だという確証もないわけだろ」中垣は早口になっていた。こめかみから汗が流れている。

「単なる手下かもしれませんが、金を持ち去ったのだから、犯人の仲間であることは確かでしょう？　わからないな。どうしてそう考えないんですか。なぜ犯人じゃないと思うんですか」

倉田の問いに答える者はいない。筧が険しい顔つきで中垣を睨んでいた。中垣はわけがわからない、といったように首を小さく振った。その隣では松宮が途方に暮れたような顔で黙り込んでいる。

とにかく、と宮内がいった。

「こういうメールが届いたということは、取引が不成立に終わったってことだ。金を持ち去ったのが何者かはわからないが、犯人が報復を考えているのは確かだ。——社長、大至急何らかの対策を講じたほうがいいのではないでしょうか」

「うん、そうだな」筧は頷き、細い目を倉田に向けてきた。「本日の営業は、すべて終了してくれ。ナイターも中止だ。理由は適当につけられるだろ」

「しかし、社長——」

「時間がないんだ。犯人が次にどう出るかわからんのだぞ。さっさと動いてくれっ」筧は怒鳴り、出口を指差した。

倉田は一礼し、踵を返した。営業を即刻終了したほうがいいのは事実だ。だが管理事務所に向かって駆けながら、黒い疑念が膨らんでくるのを感じた。何かがおかしい。この事件の裏には、自分の知らない何かがある——。

42

林立する木々の間を、根津は殆どスピードを緩めずに滑走していた。広がる枝が、眼前をかすめて後方に飛んでいく。一つ間違えれば木に激突しそうだ。だがここで速

度を落とすわけにはいかなかった。現金を奪った犯人が、どこかで停滞しているとは思えない。それに根津たちが滑っているのは厚みが二メートル以上ある深雪の上だ。こんなところで下手に止まったりしたら、たちまち足元が埋まってしまい、今度は滑りだすことさえできなくなるだろう。

すぐ後ろから滑走音が追ってくる。瀬利千晶だ。振り返らなくても、彼女が一定の距離を保って後をついてきていることはわかった。いつだったか、彼女を森の中で追跡した時のことを思い出した。あのテクニックがあれば、この程度のスピードで根津を追尾することも難しくはないだろう。

ついに森を抜けた。シュプールが殆ど走っていない真っ白な斜面が現れた。だが中央に、巨大な鉄塔が立っている。ここはゴンドラ下の滑走禁止区域内だ。二度目の取引の時、絵留がゴンドラから現金を落とした場所に近い。

「根津さん、あそこっ」

後ろから千晶の声が聞こえたが、根津も気づいていた。鉄塔の脇に人影がある。しかも二人いる。一方は、灰色のウェアを着ていた。リュックを持ち去ったスノーボーダーだ。そしてもう一人は黒いウェア姿だった。体格から察するに男だろう。灰色ウェアが持ち去ったリュックを、今は黒色ウェアが背負っている。

根津たちに気づいたらしく、二人はあわてた様子で滑走を始めた。黒色ウェアもスノーボードに乗っている。やがて二人は左右に分かれた。灰色は左へ、黒色は右の森の中へ。

根津は、ぴんときた。右側の森を抜けた先は崖だ。

また、あそこから跳ぶ気だな──。

「俺は黒を追うっ」大声で叫び、根津はボードの向きを変えた。黒色ウェアを追い、森へと突っ込んでいった。今日は逃がさない。

黒色ウェアのテクニックには瞠目すべきものがあった。低い姿勢を維持し、下半身だけで斜度変化に対応しながら、瞬時にして方向を切り替えていく。しかも減速要素は殆どない。追跡しつつ、根津は全身から冷や汗が出るのを感じていた。恐怖心に負けて少しでもスピードを緩めれば、忽ち引き離されてしまう。だからといってボードをコントロールできなくなるほど暴走するわけにはいかない。集中力が途切れたら、途端に破綻してしまうだろう。

そして再び森を抜けた。白い斜面が広がっているが、その向こうには空しか見えない。だが黒色ウェアが速度を緩める気配はなかった。むしろ、姿勢を一層低くし、空気抵抗を減らそうとしているように見える。

迷いや躊躇いを全く感じさせないまま、黒色ウェアは空中へ跳び出していった。自信に満ちた飛躍だった。

根津もまた、その軌道上を滑走していた。みるみる崖が近づいてくる。その真下には沢がある。そこへ落ちたら単なる怪我では済まないだろう。ここで跳ばないなら、追いかけてきた意味がない。

やめるか、どうする？――千分の何秒か迷い、決断した。

全身の神経を研ぎ澄ました。テイクオフのタイミングを計る。これはパフォーマンスのエアじゃない。サバイバルのジャンプだ。

身体が空中に放たれた。空気の層をくぐり抜けていく感覚がある。聴覚は麻痺していた。根津は着地点を凝視した。白い斜面がある。柔らかい綿のような雪が積もっている。そこへ到達してみせると念じた。

次の瞬間、彼の身体は念じた場所より数メートル手前に着地していた。ずしん、という衝撃はあったが、覚悟したものよりはずっと軽かった。そのまま板は深雪を滑走した。雪煙が両側で舞う。

視線を前方に向けた。黒色ウェアの姿が、すぐ前にあった。彼もまた白い煙を上げていた。だがスピードは根津のほうが少し勝っている。気配を察したらしく、黒色ウ

エアが振り返った。焦りの気配が表れたように感じられた。

追いつける——そう確信した。

その時だった。突然根津はボードの裏に衝撃を感じた。まずいと思った時には遅かった。彼の身体は宙に飛ばされていた。空と雪面が逆になった。

背中から雪面に落ちる。少し転がった後、止まった。雪に埋まり、身動きがとれなかった。しかもゴーグルが雪だらけで何も見えない。

ゴーグルを帽子ごとむしり取り、両足からボードを外した。懸命に這い出し、周囲を見回した。

十メートルほど離れたところで黒色ウェアも雪に埋まっていた。根津は自分たちの滑ってきた跡を見た。太い木の幹が横たわっていて、その上に雪がかぶさっている。

どうやらこいつに乗り上げてしまったようだ。

黒色ウェアは今も雪の中でもがいていた。ボードが雪に埋まり、動けないらしい。

根津は近づいていった。足が埋まるので、ひどく歩きにくい。それでもどうにか辿り着けた。

おい、と声をかけた。

観念したのか、黒色ウェアはじっとしていた。黙って俯いている。フェイスマスク

とゴーグルのせいで、顔は全く見えない。

「覆面、外せよ」根津はいった。「それとも、腕ずくで剝がさなきゃいけないのか」

黒色ウェアはため息をついた。諦めたようにフェイスマスクを外し、次にゴーグルを取った。

その顔を見て、根津は思わず目を剝いた。「おまえ、どうして……」

「どうも」

根津を見上げて力なく苦笑を浮かべているのは、桐林祐介だった。

43

灰色ウェアのスノーボーダーは、千晶より約二十メートル先を疾走していた。追跡されていることには、当然気づいているはずだった。だからこそ黒色ウェアと分かれた後、反対側の森の中へ入っていったのだろう。樹木が立ち並ぶ中なら、追跡者を振りきれると踏んだに違いない。

しかしいくら木々の間隔が狭かろうと、四人の選手が曲がりくねったコース上で鍔(つば)迫り合いを繰り返すスノーボードクロスに比べれば、ツリーランなど千晶にとっては

何でもない。瞬く間に灰色ウェアの背後に近づいた。

すると何を思ったか、灰色ウェアは森を出てロープをくぐり、正規のコースを滑り始めたのだ。しかも真っ直ぐに滑り降りようとはせず、ゆったりとエッジで弧を描きだした。ロングターンからミドルターン、ショートターンをしてからまたロングターンに戻る。まるで滑りを楽しんでいるかのようだ。

気味が悪くなり、千晶は速度を緩めた。今も、つかず離れずといった状態で滑り続けているのだった。

灰色ウェアがちらりと振り返った。追跡者の存在を確認したらしい。距離がある上にフェイスマスクをしているので、表情はよくわからない。だが不意をついたというふうではなかった。むしろ千晶には、ついてこいよ、というメッセージが発せられたように感じられた。

どこへ行くってんだよ——呟きながら追いかける。

灰色ウェアは時折振り返りながらコース上を移動していく。やがて千晶にも行き先の見当がついてきた。マジかよ、と再び呟く。

予想通りだった。灰色ウェアはパークを目指しているのだった。二連キッカーがあり、ボックスがあり、最後にはレールが待っている。

時間が遅いせいか、スタート地点には人がいなかった。これ幸いとばかりに、灰色ウェアはスピードを緩めることなく一つめのキッカーに突っ込んでいく。飛び出した瞬間は、ストレートエアかなと思わせた。だがすぐにゆったりと横に回転し始めた。長い滞空時間を使ったバックサイドの一八〇だ。

灰色ウェアは危なげなく着地した。そのまま次のキッカーに向かっていく。この局面で何を考えてこんなことをしているのかは不明だったが、千晶は併走しながら技を見守ることにした。

二つめのエアはスイッチスタンスからのバックサイド５４０だった。リップの抜けからグラブ、着地まで、すべて一連の流れの中で行っている。

次に灰色ウェアはボックスに挑んだ。腰をしっかりと落とし、ノーズプレスする。さらに浮いたボードを右手で摑む。バックサイドノーズスライドで決めてきた。

千晶はゴール地点で待ち受けた。灰色ウェアに逃げる気がないことを確信したからだ。

最後のレールを灰色ウェアは、ノーズプレス・トゥ・バックサイド一八〇で締めくくった。レールから着地した後は、グラトリの技をいくつか披露し、雪上に座り込んだ。相当疲れたらしく、肩が上下している。

千晶は右足だけをボードから外し、灰色ウェアに近づいていった。

「拍手でもすればいい？」

灰色ウェアは首を振った。

「着地はごまかしたし、ボックスはスピードが死んでた。はっきりいって、最低の出来」若い男の声だった。

「ふうん、意外と謙虚なんだ。それとも理想が高いのかな。まあ、どっちでもいいや。あなた、犯人だよね」

「犯人？　何のことだ」

「とぼけたってだめ。あたし、見てたんだから。あなたがリュックを持っていくところを」

灰色ウェアは首を傾げた。

「覚えがねえなあ。だってほら、リュックなんて持ってないし。誰かと見間違えたんじゃないのか。このウェア、地味だしさ」

顔の表情が見えない分、余計にむかついた。

「そんなことをいっても無駄だよ。あなたの仲間は、たぶん今頃捕まっている」千晶はウェアのポケットから携帯電話を取り出し、根津にかけた。

（俺だ。どうなった？）

「捕まえた。でもこいつ、とぼけてるんだけど。人違いだとかいって」

（じゃあ、そいつにいってやれ、キリバヤシも捕まったって）

「キリバヤシ？　うん、わかった」

千晶は電話を繋いだままで、根津からいわれた通りのことを灰色ウェアにいってみた。灰色ウェアの表情は相変わらずわからない。だが黙り込んだ様子は、悄然としているように見えた。

「ねえ、あんた。　諦めなよ」千晶はいった。

やがて灰色ウェアはゴーグルを外し、フェイスマスクも取った、現れたのは、まだ少年っぽさの残る痩せた顔だった。

「名前は？」

「マスブチ」

「マスブチ？」千晶は首を捻った。「どっかで聞いたことがある」

男はかすかに口元を緩め、続けた。

「親父のことだろ。マスブチヤスヒデ。北月町の町長だよ」

44

瀬利千晶から話を聞き、根津はますます混乱した。灰色ウェアの男は町長の息子、増淵英也だというのか。

（どうしたらいい？　警察に知らせる？）瀬利千晶がせっついてきた。興奮しているのが口調でわかる。

「待て。とりあえず、そのまま待機していてくれ。あっ、でも、逃げられるなよ」

（大丈夫。こいつ、もう逃げる気はないみたいだから。方針が決まったら連絡して）

「わかった」電話を切り、根津は前を見た。桐林はボードを外し、ようやく身体を起こすことに成功していた。

根津はため息をついた。

「共犯者は増淵町長の息子か。おい、キリ、これはどういうことだ。どうしてこんなことをした」

桐林はニット帽の上から頭を掻いた。

「説明するのは、すごく難しいんですけど……」

「そうだろうけど、説明してもらわなきゃ困る。なぜ爆弾なんかを埋めた？　金のためか。金が欲しかったのか」

「そうじゃありません」桐林は首を振った。「違うんです、根津さん。俺たちじゃないんです」

「何が違うんだ」

「爆弾を埋めたのは俺たちじゃありません。別の人間です」

「何？　おまえ、いい加減なことをいうなよ。じゃあ、脅迫状を書いたのも自分たちじゃないとでもいうのか」

桐林は苦しげに顔を歪めた。「脅迫状は……俺が書きました」

「何だ、それ。舐めてんのか」根津は桐林のウェアを摑んだ。「脅迫状を書いて、金を奪って、それで自分たちは犯人じゃないといい張ろうってのか。そんな話が通用するとでも思ってんのか」

桐林は、また首を激しく振った。

「俺たちは犯人です。それは認めます。だけど俺たちだけじゃないんです。最後の取引に関しては、俺たちがやったことではないんです」

「嘘をつけ。現にこうやって、金を奪ってるじゃねえか」

「これは取引を成立させるためです。でないと、爆弾が爆発させられるから……」

「何をいってるんだ。さっき犯人からメールが届いたって聞いたぞ。取引は不成立、報復行動に出るって。おい、あれは一体どういうことだ」

すると桐林は大きく目を見張った。「それ、本当ですか」

「本当も何も、おまえたちの仲間が書いたメールだろ」

「大変だ。根津さん、大変だ」桐林は血相を変え、逆に根津のほうに迫ってきた。

「北月エリアが危険だ。北月エリアが爆破される」

45

増淵英也が立ち上がるのを見て、千晶は身構えた。

「どこへ行く気?」

「北月エリアだ。ぐずぐずしてるとゴンドラが止まってしまう」

「北月? 何のためにあんなところへ行くわけ? あたしは根津さんと約束したんだからね。あんたのことを逃がさないって」

千晶は英也の腕を摑もうとした。だが彼は素早くよけた。

「確かめたいんだ。北月エリアが無事かどうかを。信用してくれ。俺は逃げない。正体まで明かしたんだ。逃げたって無駄だろ」

「……北月エリアが無事かどうかって、それどういうこと？　あそこには爆弾はないんでしょ」

「君は事情を知っているようだから教えてやる。爆弾が埋まっているのは北月エリアだ。そしてたぶん奴らは、今日、爆破する気だったはずだ。だけど現金は犯人が奪っていった。これで爆破の口実がなくなったはずなんだけど」

「ちょっと待って。何のことをいってるの？　奴らって誰よ」

「ごめん。説明している暇はない。話を聞きたかったら一緒に来てくれ。君の腕前ならついてこれるだろ。ただし、安全は保証できない」そういうと英也は滑りだした。ゴンドラ乗り場を目指しているようだ。たしかに、そろそろゴンドラが止まる時間だ。

ここまで来て、引き下がれるかよ——口の中で呟きながら千晶はボードを装着した。

46

「北月エリアが？　一体どういうことだ」根津は怒鳴った。

「爆弾が仕掛けてあるのは北月エリアなんです。最初から、あそこを壊す気だったんです」

「何をいってるんだ。犯人からの回答じゃ、北月エリアは安全ってことになってたぞ」

「そうじゃないんですっ」桐林は苛立ったように足踏みした。「北月エリアは安全だと書けば、連中は爆破させられなくなる——そう考えたんです」

根津はお手上げのポーズをした。

「おまえのいってること、全然意味がわかんねえぞ」

桐林は何かを迷っているらしく、俯いて苦しげに唇を嚙んだ。だがすぐに意を決したように顔を上げた。

「根津さん、大至急倉田さんに電話をしてください。そうして社長たちに、俺たちが捕まったことを知らせるよういってください。そうすれば爆破を中止してくれるかもしれない」

「社長に？ おまえ、何をいってるんだ」

「社長なんです。いや、社長だけじゃない。二人の本部長も、増淵町長も、みんな仲間なんだ。みんなで北月エリアを壊そうとしているんだ」

桐林が喚く内容を聞き、根津は混乱した。依然として意味がよくわからない。

「落ち着いて話せ。おまえの言い方だと、社長たちが犯人のように聞こえるぞ」

「そうなんです。犯人なんです。実際に爆弾を仕掛けたのが誰なのかは知らないけど、指示したのは社長です。そうして、みんなぐるなんだ」

「馬鹿いうな。なんで社長が自分のところのスキー場を爆破させなきゃいけないんだ」

「邪魔だからです。北月エリアがあるかぎり、新月高原スキー場には買い手がつかない。筧社長は、スキー場を丸ごと売りに出そうとしているんです」

「まさか……そんな話、信用できるか」

「本当なんです。英也から……増淵英也から聞いたんです。あいつは町長たちが話しているのを盗み聞きしたそうです」

「どうして北月町の町長が、北月エリアの爆破に加担するんだ。あのスキー場が閉鎖されて、一番困ってるのは北月町のはずだぞ」

「増淵町長は、元々北月町の人間じゃありません。今住んでる家だって、仮住まいみたいなものなんです。任期が満了したら、さっさと出ていく気です。その前に、今回の話に乗って、金を手にしようっていう魂胆なんだ」

「ふざけるな。仮に北月エリアが爆破されたら、警察だって消防だって黙ってない。誰の仕業だってことになるんぞ」

「ところがそうはならないんです。誰もいない雪山が崩れたって、爆破によるものだとはふつう思わない。自然に雪崩が起きたと考えます。もしそうは思わない人間がいたとしても問題ないんです。だって、北月町の警察や消防の署長たちも、今回の計画のことは知っているんですから。新月高原スキー場側から、使用していないエリアで雪崩が起きた、死傷者はゼロ——そういう報告を受けた後は、ろくな調査をしないまで幕を引くという手筈なんです。全員ぐるなんです」

「何だって……」

「お願いです、根津さん。今すぐに倉田さんに電話をかけてください。爆破を中止させるよう、頼んでもらうんです」

根津は懸命に頭の中を整理しようとした。今の話を聞いただけでは、まだまだ腑に落ちないことがたくさんある。ではあの脅迫状は何だったのか。現金受渡にはどんな意味があったのか。しかし桐林が嘘をいっているのでなければ、それらの疑問点に拘っている余裕はなかった。

「おい、キリ。脅迫状を書いたのがおまえなら、当然倉田さんの電話番号は知ってる

よな」

「知ってますけど……」

「じゃあ、おまえが電話しろ。俺はそんなことをしている暇がない。これから北月エ
リアへ行く」

「そんな……危険です。何のために?」

「入江さんたちが、あっちにいるんだよ。雪崩に巻き込まれたら大変だ」

桐林は目を剝いた。言葉を発しないまま自分の携帯電話を取り出した。

根津はスノーボードを装着した。

「俺は後でゆっくりと聞かせてもらうけど、倉田さんには何もかも包み隠さず話すん
だぞ」

「わかっています。根津さん、これを」桐林はウェアのポケットから何かを取り出し、
根津のほうに投げてきた。

根津がキャッチしたものは、スノーモービルのキーだった。

「この下の林道に止めてあります。北側の斜面を登っていくのが、北月エリアまでの
最短コースです」

「わかった」キーを握りしめ、根津は滑りだした。

47

倉田は索道部主任の津野に、今すぐにすべてのリフトを停止させ、ナイター営業も中止するように命じた。津野は詳しい事情を知らなかったが、急を要する事態が起きていることはわかったようだ。やや顔をひきつらせ、近くの電話を手にした。

藤崎絵留が駆け込んできたのは、その直後だった。「倉田さんっ」

「ああ、御苦労だ。根津君たちがどこへ行ったかは、やはりわからないか」

すると藤崎絵留はじれったそうにかぶりを振り、携帯電話を差し出してきた。犯人との連絡用に使っていた倉田の電話だ。

「繋がっています。話してください」

倉田は電話と彼女の顔を交互に見た。「誰と?」

彼女は真剣な目をしていった。「犯人と、です」

「犯人?」ぎくりとした。「犯人が電話をかけてきたのか」

「単なる犯人というわけではなさそうです。ずいぶんと複雑な事情があるみたいで……。あたしも詳しいことは聞いていません。とにかく話してください。誰なのかは、

声を聞けばわかると思います。倉田さんの知っている人間です」

わけがわからないまま、倉田は電話を受け取った。もしもし、と呼びかけてみた。

躊躇うような沈黙の後、倉田さん、と相手がいった。男の声だ。しかもどこかで聞いたことがある。すると相手は続けた。（俺です。桐林です）

倉田は息を呑み、藤崎絵留を見た。彼女は、こっくりと頷いた。

「桐林君……どうして君が」

（すみません。いろいろと事情があるんです。なるべく手短に話しますから、聞いてもらえますか）

「そりゃあ、聞くよ。一体どういうことなんだ」

（……シーズンが始まる一か月ぐらい前のことです。友達の英也からとんでもない話を聞かされました。英也というのは増淵英也、北月町の町長の息子です）

「彼なら知っているが……。どんな話だったんだ」

それが、といって桐林が話し始めた内容は、たしかにとんでもないものだった。

数分後、倉田は二階のバーに駆け込んでいた。そこにはまだ筧たちの姿があった。

社長、と倉田は詰め寄った。

筧は眉をひそめた。

「何だ、一体。スキー場の営業はすべて停止したのか」

「あなたがそれを指示するのはおかしいでしょう。その前に計画を中止してください」

「計画？　何のことだ」

「とぼけないでください。北月エリアを爆破する計画です。すべて聞きました」

笈の顔つきが変わった。頬が強張っているのがわかった。

「誰から何を聞いたというんだ」声が尖っている。

「根津君が捕まえた犯人からです。彼等は自分たちの罪を認めています。でも同時に、爆弾を埋めたのが誰なのかも教えてくれました。あなたたちの計画のすべてを聞きました。社長、どうか思い留まってください」

「何をいってるんだ。そんな奴のいうことを信用するというのか。君はそれでもうちの社員か」

「あなたこそ、それでも社長ですかっ」

「何だとっ。貴様、自分の立場がわかってるのか」

「立場がわかってないのは、あなたでしょうが」

笈は目を吊り上がらせると、大きな音をたてて立ち上がった。そのまま出ていこう

とする。倉田は追いかけた。だが、「やめろっ」と右腕を摑まれた。中垣だった。

「離してください」

「だめだっ。おまえはじっとしてろ」

「あなたたち、こんなことをして恥ずかしくないんですか」

「うるさい。おまえなんかに会社経営のことがわかるものか」

「これのどこが会社経営だ。犯罪じゃないか。離してください。離せっ」倉田は中垣の手を振り払い、その勢いで相手の顔面に右の拳を叩き込んだ。中垣は後ろに吹っ飛んだ。

松宮が怯えの色を見せて後ずさりした。

筧は憎悪の目を向けてきた。

「そんなことをして、ただで済むと思ってるのか」

「クビで結構です。ここを出た後、警察に向かいます。もちろん県警本部です。小さな町の警察署長は買収できても、県警本部長はそういうわけにはいきませんよ」

筧は言葉に詰まったように黙り込んだ。倉田は大股で近づいていき、筧の上着のポケットから携帯電話を取り出した。

「爆破を中止してください。どうせ、秘書の小杉あたりに命じたんでしょ」

筧は顔を歪め、自分の携帯電話を手にした。不承不承といった感じでボタンを操作し、電話を耳に当てた。だがすぐに首を振った。「だめだ。繋がらない」

「小杉はどこに？」

「爆弾のあるところ……北月エリアの上部だ。リフト降り場より、さらに上だ」

「爆破させるために、わざわざそんなに近くで？」

「爆弾は遠隔操作でタイマーのスイッチを入れるようになっている。ただし、雪の中だから通常の電波は届かない。マイクロ波による送受信を行う仕組みだが、それでも数十メートル以内にまで近づかないと起動させられない」

倉田は舌打ちした。

「繋がるまで、電話をかけ続けてください。何としてでも爆破を中止させるんです。そうしないと、あなた方全員が刑務所に行くことになります。下手をすれば殺人罪だ。

現在、北月エリアには人がいるんです」

筧が驚いたように口を半開きにするのを見届け、倉田は出口に向かった。バーを出ると藤崎絵留が廊下で待っていた。

「根津君から連絡はあったか」

ありません、と彼女は首を振った。

「そうか」

倉田は足を止めず、階段を下りた。管理事務所で防寒着を手にし、再び廊下に出た。藤崎絵留が後からついてくる。「倉田さん、どちらへ?」

「北月エリアへ行く。俺が行ってもどうしようもないかもしれないがね」

「あたしも行きます」

「いや、君は——」危険だから来ないほうがいい、という言葉を倉田は呑み込んだ。彼女の真剣な眼差しを見るかぎり、あっさり引き下がるとは思えなかったからだ。

よし行こう、といって倉田は小走りになった。

48

ゴンドラを降りると、増淵英也はゲレンデとは反対の方向に進んだ。その足取りに迷いの色はなかった。

「連絡路は閉鎖してあるんじゃないの?」後を追いながら千晶は訊いた。

「正式なルートはね。森を抜ける近道があるんだ。大丈夫、ここは地元だ。俺はガキの頃から遊んでる。木の一本一本の位置だって覚えてる」

自信たっぷりにいって前へ進む英也の背中を見ながら、それだけ思い入れのあるゲレンデを切り捨てられるのは苦痛だろうな、と千晶は想像した。そして先程ゴンドラの中で聞いた、驚くべき話を思い返した。

十一月の某日、増淵康英の家に筧純一郎が訪ねてきた。その日、たまたま康英の家にいた英也は、二人の会話を盗み聞きした。スキーシーズンを一か月後に控え、北月エリアがどうなるのか、個人的に気になっていたからだ。

だが二人の間で交わされた会話は、英也が想像もしていないものだった。新月高原ホテルアンドリゾートの親会社である広世観光は、スキー場を手放そうとしていた。すでに売却先も決まりつつあるという。順調に進めば、この冬を最後に新月高原ホテルアンドリゾートという名称は消えるわけだ。

だがこの交渉を難航させる要因があった。それが北月エリアだ。採算が合わないお荷物ゲレンデを抱えたままでは、有利に交渉を進められないだけでなく、売却話自体が御破算になってしまうおそれがあった。とはいえ、北月エリアだけを切り離しての売却ができないことは、広世観光がスキー場を買収した時の契約書に明記されている。一番まともなやり方は、北月エリアを完全に閉鎖した上で売却することだが、その場合には林野庁の規制があるため、リフトの撤去や植林等を行い、山を完全に元通りに

しなければならない。当然のことながら、それらには莫大な費用がかかる。

そこで筧たちが目をつけたのが、広世観光がスキー場を買収した時に交わした契約書の例外事項だ。それによれば、雪崩や地震等の自然災害によって甚大な被害が出た区域に限っては、転売時に切り離すことも可能となっていた。つまり北月エリアで大規模な雪崩を起こせばいいわけだ。

筧たちは爆薬を使い、雪崩を起こすことを考えた。無論、専門家が調査すれば、すぐにばれてしまうだろう。だがすでに手は打たれていた。警察や消防の責任者たちも、この計画に引き込んであるのだ。広世観光にしてみれば、一つのゲレンデを完全に元通りにする費用を考えれば、町長や役人たちに渡す金など微々たるものなのだろう。

スキー場をオープンさせた後も北月エリアだけは閉鎖にしておき、誰にも近よらせない。昨シーズン起きた死亡事故が、恰好の口実になる。そして積雪量がピークに達した頃を見計らって爆発、すなわち雪崩を起こす――それが筧たちの計画だった。

英也は友人の桐林に相談した。何としてでも阻止しなければならない、というのが二人の出した結論だった。だがどうすればいいのか。真っ先に思いついたのはネット上に書き込むことだったが、単なる悪戯だと思われるおそれがあった。ではマスコミに情報を流すか。しかし自分たちの身元を隠したままでは信用してもらえないだろう。

それに英也としては、なるべく警察沙汰になる前に計画を断念させたかった。父親を犯罪者にはしたくなかったのだ。

仕掛けられた爆弾を自分たちの手で回収してしまうことも考えたが、場所が不明ではどうすることもできない。だからといって、四六時中見張っていることなど不可能だ。

知恵を絞った末に思いついたのが、爆弾を逆手にとってスキー場を脅迫するというアイデアだった。筧たちとしては警察に通報するわけにはいかない。そんなことをすれば、スキー場を閉鎖しなければならない上、警察による本格的な爆弾捜索を受け入れることになってしまうからだ。それほどの大事件となれば、北月町の警察署レベルで処理できるわけがなく、県警本部が乗り出してくるだろう。それでは裏から手を回して揉み消すこともできない。

自分たちの計画と関連があるのかどうかを決めかねたまま、筧たちは脅迫状の指示に従うだろうと予想された。そうなってしまえばこちらのものだ。

英也たちは脅迫状によって現金を要求したが、じつは狙いは別にあった。真の目的は、北月エリアをオープンさせることだった。クロス大会の会場に使えるのはアタッククコースかゴールドコースだ。だがこの二つのコースについて、犯人側から安全宣言

が出なければ、スキー場としては北月エリアにコースを造るしかない。そしてコースを造る以上、大会後もゲレンデを閉鎖する理由がなくなる。営業しているゲレンデで雪崩が起きたとなれば、たとえそれが夜中や明け方で被災者が出なかったとしても、警察や消防による大々的な調査が必要となる。下手をすれば国土交通省も乗り出してくるだろう。つまり筧たちは爆破計画の実行を断念せざるをえないというわけだ。

以上のような作戦を立て、英也と桐林は周到に準備を始めた。桐林がパトロール員としてもぐり込むことも、その一つだった。また、雪が本格的に降りだす前に、起爆装置を模した仕掛けをゲレンデ内に潜ませておく必要もあった。

増淵英也の話を聞き、千晶は目眩がしそうになった。会社というものを彼女はよく知らない。だが各地のスキー場が経営に苦しんでいることはわかっていた。新月高原にしても同様だろうと思った。しかしまさか裏でそんなことが行われていようとは夢にも思わなかった。スキー場の経営者がスポーツを冒瀆していたと知り、ショックだった。

一方で、腑に落ちたこともあった。国際的なクロス大会が迫っているにもかかわらず、一向にコースが造られないこともその一つだ。責任者は、何としてでも北月エリアだけはオープンするなと社長から厳しくいわれていたのだろう。

もちろん納得できないこともある。たとえば、現金を三回も要求したことだ。二回目の時、北月エリアは安全だというメールを英也たちは送ってきた。北月エリアをオープンさせることが目的なら、あれでやめておけばよかったのではないか。

すると英也は答えた。三回目は自分たちがやったことではないのだ、と。「あれは社長たちの仕事なんだ。たぶん連中は、途中で俺たちの狙いに気づいたんだと思う。

そこで、さらに俺たちの作戦を逆手に取って、自分たちが犯人になりすますことにしたんだ」

千晶は首を傾げた。そんなことをして、何になるのか。

「社長たちの計画は、たぶんこうだ。三度目の現金要求を行う。だけど今回は受け渡しを成立させない。邪魔者がいるとか何とか難癖をつけて中止にするんだ。それを二回ほど繰り返した後、取引は不成立だといって、報復措置として爆弾を爆発させる。

だけどスキー場側としては、脅迫のことを警察に届けていない以上、爆破されたことを公表するわけにはいかない。結局、原因不明の雪崩が起きたことにしようということになる。倉田さんや根津さんたちも後ろめたさがあるから、社長の命令に従うしかない。当初の計画通りに事が運ぶわけだ」

千晶は唸った。信じがたい話ではあるが、見事に筋が通っている。これまで変だと

思っていたことにも説明がつく。たとえば根津によれば、宮内とかいう人物から、犯人の尻尾を摑まえろという意味のことをいわれたらしい。社長たちにしてみれば、根津におとなしくしていられたら困るので、そんなふうにけしかけたのだろう。また、前回の受け渡しでは、やけにあっさりと取引中止の連絡をしてきた。何のことはない。最初から中止にするつもりだったのだ。

英也によれば、運搬役に「荷物を背負った状態で斜度四十度の斜面を滑走できること」という条件をつけてきたのも、そうすれば必ず藤崎絵留が選ばれると見越したからだろうとのことだった。運搬役が根津になれば、受け渡し時にちょっかいを出す人間がいなくなってしまうからだ。今日の受け渡しに関して、「運搬役は前回と同じ人物であること」などと指示してきたのも同じ理由からだ。

すべてが計算ずくなんだ、と英也はいった。

では筧たちのそんな策謀に対し、英也と桐林はどう対抗しようとしたのか。

「それは決まってるよ。またしても、こっちが犯人になりすますんだ」

筧たちが爆破を実行するためには、犯人との取引が不成立に終わった、という事実が必要だ。そこで英也たちは、取引が成立したように見せかけることを考えた。どうせ筧たちは、藤崎絵留に大した指示も出さないまま、唐突に中止を宣言する気だ。そ

れならば先に指示を出し、藤崎絵留や根津たちの見ている前で現金を奪取しようというわけだ。その報告を受けた筧は、北月エリアを爆破できなくなる。

うまく考えたものだ。しかし千晶は、彼等のプランが爆破しなかったことを告げざるをえなかった。スキー場には、「もう一方の犯人」からのメールがすでに届いている。「取引は中止、報復行動に出る」という内容だ。

彼女の話を聞き、英也はゴンドラの中で頭を抱えた。

「どうする？ それでも北月エリアを見に行く？」

「当たり前だ」英也は即座に答えた。「奴らのすることを見届けてやる」

49

爆音が轟いた。白い海の上をジェットスキーで疾走しているようだった。速度を維持しなければ、スノーモービルの車体は深雪に埋まりそうだ。根津はアクセルをふかし続けた。バックミラーが付いているので時折目を向けるが、後方に舞い上がる雪煙のせいで殆ど何も見えない。

スタートしてから何分経っただろうか。ようやく北月エリアの中腹に到着した。そ

こから根津は、周囲を見ながら下っていった。やがて複数の滑走跡を発見した。見た

ところ、付けられたばかりという感じだ。

入江義之が、北月エリアにいると連絡してきたのは、今から三十分近く前だ。少し

休んでから下りるといっていた。このシュプールが彼等親子のものだとしたら、二人

はすでに下山したことになる。

幾分安堵しながら根津は斜面を下っていった。前方にリフト乗り場や、現在は使用

されていないスキーハウスなどが見えてくる。そのそばに一台のスノーモービルが止

まっていた。しかも、すぐ横に人影がある。

根津は訝りながら近づいていった。相手も気づいたらしく、彼のほうを見た。その

顔は、根津のよく知っている人物――上山禄郎だった。

「あれっ、どうしたんですか、根津さん」上山はいった。

「それはこっちの台詞だ。こんなところで何してるんだ」

「いや、大した理由はないんです。今日はほら、入江さんたちをこっちに連れてくる

っていう話になってたでしょ。中止になっちゃいましたけど。でも、北月のほうはど

うなってんのかなあと個人的に気になって、様子を見に来たんです。そうしたら、入

江さんたちがいるんで、びっくりしましたよ」

「入江さんたち？　会ったのか」

「ええ。入江さんの話じゃ、山頂から回ろうとして道に迷ったそうですね。相当長い時間、山の中を歩き回ってたみたいですよ」

「それで二人はどうした？　帰ったのか」

「いえ、上にいますよ」

「上に？」心臓が跳ねた。「どうして？　どうして上にいるんだ。滑り降りたいんじゃないのか」

「降りてきましたよ。ここで会ったんですから。だけど達樹君が楽しそうでね、もっと滑りたいといいだしたんです。それで、じゃあ俺が上まで連れていってあげますよといったんです」

「連れていったのか」

「ええ。まず入江さんを乗せて上まで行って、次に達樹君を乗せて……」上山は戸惑った顔で答えた。何がいけないのか、という表情だ。

馬鹿野郎、といいたいのを堪えて根津はスノーモービルを発進させた。何も知らない上山を責めるわけにはいかない。

Uターンすると、斜面を猛スピードで駆け上がった。爆破まで、一体どれだけの時

間が残されているのかはわからない。しかしこのまま後戻りはできなかった。

前方には無人の白い斜面が広がっていた。だが不意に雪煙が現れた。それはものす

ごいスピードで下ってくる。根津は目を凝らした。入江義之かもしれないと思った。

しかし違っていた。入江よりもはるかに大柄だ。

根津はあることを直感した。同時にスノーモービルの向きを変えた。スキーヤーが

下りてくるコースを塞ぐ位置に移動した。

スキーヤーは数メートル手前で停止した。様子を窺うように黙っている。

「スイッチを入れたのか」根津は訊いた。

「何のことだ」スキーヤーが答えた。その声で、根津は気づいた。何度か見かけたこ

とがある。筧の秘書の小杉という男だ。

「とぼけるな。全部わかってるんだ」

ごまかしても無駄だと悟ったらしく、小杉は肩をすくめた。

「答えてくれ。あと何分で爆発する?」

「そんなに時間はない。おたくも早く逃げたほうが——」

「だからあと何分だと訊いてるんだよっ」根津は怒鳴った。「さっさと答えろ」

小杉は腕時計を見た。「十分ぐらいかな」

根津はスノーモービルをスタートさせた。ここで小杉なんかに構っている余裕はない。

不整地の急斜面を駆け上がった。車体が大きくバウンドし、そのたびに根津の身体も跳ねた。思わず呻き声が漏れる。それでもアクセルを緩めなかった。

視界の隅で何かが動いた。明らかに人だ。しかも一人ではない。斜面の途中に黒い塊がある。咄嗟に速度を落とし、素早く視線を走らせる。

近づいていった。二人いる。一人は雪上で座り込んでおり、もう一人はそのそばに立っていた。残念ながら入江親子ではなかった。立っているほうは白のウェアで、座っているほうは茶色のウェアを着ている。どちらのウェアにも見覚えがあった。

「日吉さん……」根津は声をかけた。座り込んでいるのは日吉浩三だった。

「ああ、根津さん。こいつは助かった」日吉はいった。

「どうしたんですか」

「いやあ、あの後、どうしてもこっちのコースを滑りたくなってね。どうにかこうにかして辿り着いたわけですが、滑りだした途端に膝をやっちゃったんです。それで、休み休みここまで下りてきたというわけなんですが」

「準備運動をしっかりしないからよ」日吉友恵がげんなりしたようにいう。だが根津

としては、それどころではなかった。

「後ろに乗ってください。早くっ。奥さんは滑り降りてください。絶対に途中で止まらないように。間もなく雪崩がきます」

二人は、ぎょっとしたように目を見開いた。

「雪崩？　どうしてこんなところで……」日吉が呟く。

「説明は後でしますっ」根津は叫んだ。「はやくっ。早くしてください」

ようやくただ事でないと悟ったか、日吉が動きだした。膝が痛いのか、顔をしかめている。根津はスノーモービルから降り、彼が乗り込むのを手伝った。ところが友恵は心配そうな顔で、横に突っ立ったままだ。

「何やってるんだっ。さっさと滑って」声を荒らげた。言葉遣いを気にしている余裕などなかった。

友恵があわてた様子で滑り始めた。テレマークスキーの技術は安定している。問題なく下まで行けるだろう。

根津はスノーモービルに跨った。「しっかり摑まっててくださいよ」そういうなり、発進した。すぐさまトップスピードまで上げる。日吉が後ろで何かを叫んでいるようだが聞きとれない。

少し走ったところで、前方に人影が現れた。青いウェアの男性スキーヤー——入江
義之に違いない。そばには達樹らしき姿もあった。

入江さん、と叫びながら近づいた。入江は停止し、ゴーグルを上げた。その顔は笑
っている。

「ああ、どうも。御心配をおかけしました」

のんびりとした口調が根津を苛立たせた。

「急いで下りてください。雪崩が発生します」

えっ、と入江は背後の山を振り返った。

「爆発が起きるんです。時間がない。急いでっ」

わけがわからないといった様子だったが、入江は頷いた。後ろにいる達樹を見た。

「達樹、滑れるな。しっかりついてくるんだぞ」

達樹は、こっくりと首を縦に動かした。それを見て、義之が滑りだす。達樹もすぐ
に父親に続いた。

根津も再びスノーモービルで走りだした。これなら大丈夫だ、と安心した時だった。

ずんっ、と、まさに山を揺るがすような音が響いた。さらに、ずんっ、ずんっ、と
二回続いた。その震動は大きくて低く、耳だけでなく内臓にまで響きが達した。

根津はバックミラーに視線を走らせた。だが彼の目が捉えたのは雪崩ではなく、転倒している達樹の姿だった。あわてて急停止し、振り返った。

達樹は尻餅をついていた。今の衝撃音で狼狽したのかもしれない。怪我はないようだったが、スキー板が外れ、下に流されていた。

根津は戻ろうとした。だが次の瞬間、轟音と共に遠方から雪の壁が押し寄せてくるのが見えた。

雪崩の速度は時速百キロにまで達することがある——パトロールの教育を受けた時に聞いた話が根津の脳裏を横切った。

50

倉田たちがその音を耳にしたのは、北月エリアの駐車場に車を止めた時だった。腹に響くような重低音が続けざまに三回聞こえた。

倉田は藤崎絵留と顔を見合わせた。爆破が実行されたに違いなかった。

「行ってみよう」

二人でゲレンデに向かった。リフト乗り場の近くに上山禄郎の姿があった。そして

少し離れたところに、なぜか日吉友恵が佇んでいる。

こんなところで何を、と二人に尋ねようとした時だった。斜面の上部から、地響き

が伝わってきた。倉田は声も出せず、ただ見上げていた。

それは十数秒間続いた。大きな雪崩が生じたことは確実だった。問題は、彼等が無

事かどうかだった。

倉田は上山のそばに止まっているスノーモービルに近づいた。「これ、借りるよ」

返事を待たずに乗り込んだ。

「あたしも行きます」藤崎絵留が後部席に跨った。

倉田はエンジンをかけ、発進した。斜面を上がり始めた。

だがそれから間もなくのことだった。前方からスノーモービルが近づいてきた。さ

らにその後ろから何人かが滑り降りてくる。スキーヤーもいれば、スノーボーダーも

いる。

倉田はスノーモービルを止めた。

根津の運転するスノーモービルが最初に近寄ってきて、停止した。後ろのシートに

日吉浩三が座っている。

スキーヤーは入江義之だった。スノーボーダーは二人いる。小柄なほうは女性だ。

そして灰色ウェアのスノーボーダーは増淵英也だった。彼は入江達樹を背負っていた。

雪上に下ろされた達樹は、「ああ、怖かった」と子供らしい声を出した。

倉田は根津を見た。「全員、無事だったんだな」

「危ないところでしたけど」根津は頷いて笑った。「雪崩が間もなくやってくるって

時に、達樹君が転んじゃったものですから」

「よく助かったね」

「ええ、彼が」根津は増淵英也を指した。「彼がどこからか現れて、達樹君を抱きか

かえたんです。そのまま見事な滑りで逃げきってくれました。雪崩は中腹の斜面あた

りで止まりました」

「そうだったのか。まさに間一髪だな」

入江義之が達樹の背中を押しながら増淵英也に近づいた。

「ありがとうございました。本当に命の恩人です」

義之の隣で達樹も、ありがとうございました、と頭を下げた。

すると増淵英也は、なぜか激しく頭を振り始めた。顔を歪め、雪に膝をついた。そ

して二人に向かって土下座をした。

「違います。恩人なんかじゃない。俺は人殺しです。達樹君のお母さんを殺したのは

「俺なんです」

51

会議室のドアを開けると、全員の視線が倉田に集中した。ここにいるのは、根津、藤崎絵留、瀬利千晶、桐林、増淵英也、日吉夫妻、そして入江義之の八人だ。達樹は部屋で休んでいる。

「説明は終わったのかな」倉田は根津に訊いた。

「大方聞きました」根津は桐林と増淵英也に目を向ける。「こいつらの気持ちもわかりますよ。社長たちも、ひどいことを思いついたものだ」

今回の事件に関わった者たちに、桐林たちから事の真相を話してもらうことにしたのだった。日吉夫妻や入江にも同席してもらったのは、あの不自然な雪崩について説明しておく必要があったからだ。

「それにしても、おまえにはまんまと一杯食わされたよ」根津は桐林にいった。「何がスノーボードは苦手だ。あんなところから跳びやがって」

すみません、と桐林は身体を縮めている。

「俺と絵留が事件のことで詰め所で話してた時、おまえ立ち聞きしてたよな。それでおまえを仲間にせざるをえなかったわけだけど、あれも計算だったのか」

「いえ、あれはどっちかというと誤算だったんです。本当は、何も知らないふりをして、根津さんたちとは別行動を取っていたかったんです。ただ、一回目の受け渡しでは、パトロール員として一番最後にリフトに乗れたので、英也が現金を回収するのを、ほかの人間に見られずに済んだんですけど」

「そうか。そういえばあの時、おまえが最後にリフトに乗ってきたんだよなあ」根津は顔をしかめた。「犯人から三回目の取引が持ちかけられた時、おまえは応じるべきじゃないといったよな。社長たちの企みだとわかったからだったのか」

「そうです。ただ、あの時点では狙いはよくわからなかった。だけどあっさりと取引を中止にしてきた時、もしやと思ったんです。さらに、根津さんが宮内さんから犯人の尻尾を摑まえろというようなことをいわれたと聞いて、確信しました。取引不成立の形を作りだして、北月エリアを爆破させる気なんだって」

「もっと早く俺にいってくれりゃあ……いや、それは無理か」根津は頭を搔きむしっ た。

「それで、社長たちは何と?」藤崎絵留が倉田に訊いてきた。

倉田は吐息をつき、椅子に腰を下ろした。たった今まで、例のバーで筧たちと話し合ってきたのだ。

「取引を持ちかけられたよ」

「取引?」根津が意表を衝かれた顔でいった。「どういう取引ですか」

「早い話、内密に願えないか、ということだ。黙っておいてくれれば、スキー場の売却後も各自の立場は保証する。桐林君たちの脅迫状の件も不問に付すとのことだ」

「何いってるんだ。脅迫状のことを警察に届けたら、向こうだって困るくせに」根津が吐き捨てた。

「でも、警察沙汰にしたら、このスキー場はもうおしまいね」藤崎絵留がいった。

「爆破事件のあったスキー場……誰も寄りつかない」

それはそうだけどさ、と呟いた根津の声が、やけに大きく響いた。

その時、ノックの音がした。はい、と倉田が答えると、ドアが開いて辰巳が顔を覗かせた。これを、といって一枚の書類を差し出してきた。倉田はそれを一瞥した。や驚きの事実が、そこには記されていた。

「北月エリアの被害を辰巳君に調べてもらったんだ」倉田は皆にいった。「彼が見たかぎりでは、リフト小屋の一部が破損しただけで、大きな被害は殆どなかったようだ。

リフトも、ほぼ無事だということだ」

おう、という声が誰からともなく上がった。

「ということは、北月エリアを切り離して売却することはできなくなったってわけだ」根津が手を叩いた。「ざまあみろだ。くそ社長め」

「でもそうなると、これからもあの面々と付き合っていかなきゃいけないわけね」

藤崎絵留の言葉に、根津は顔をしかめて唸った。ほかの者たちも黙り込んだ。

「ちょっといいですか」そういって手を挙げたのは日吉浩三だ。「要するに、北月エリアを切り離さずに売却できれば、誰も文句ないってことですね」

「そうですが。それは難しいと社長らは——」

倉田の言葉の途中で日吉は手を振った。

「スキー場売却を持ちかけている相手は星雲興産です。あの会社を説得すればいい」

「説得って、一体どうやって……。そもそも、どうしてあなたが売却先のことを知っているんですか」

「それはまあ年の功というやつで」

そんなふうにいう日吉の袖を、隣の友恵が引っ張った。

「勿体をつけてないで、さっさといいなさい。どうせいうんだから」

「ははは、まあそうだな」日吉は咳払いをしてからいった。「星雲興産は、私が会長をやっている会社です」

一瞬奇妙な沈黙があり、その後全員が老人のほうを向いた。誰もが声を出せないでいた。

「しかし名刺にはそんなふうには……」

「そりゃあ倉田さん、スパイが名刺に本当の身分を書くわけないでしょう」

「スパイ?」

「ええ、スパイなんですよ」日吉は全員を見回して続けた。「星雲興産内でも、このスキー場の買い取りに関しては議論が起きています。やはり北月エリアがネックになっているんです。あれを何とかできないか、という具合にね。そこで私が自分の目で見ることにしたんです。妻と二人でね。ところが実際に来てみると、北月エリアはクローズのままだ。これでは、どんなコースなのか確かめることもできない。やきもきしていたところ、今回の騒動に出くわしたというわけです」

「そうだったんですか」

この夫婦に初めて会った時のことを倉田は思い出した。そういえば最初から北月エリアのことを気にしていた。

「今日、ようやく北月エリアに行けました。なるほど、たしかに問題はある。採算を考えたら、切り離したいところだ。しかしスキー場を経営するとは、そういうことだけではないと私は思う。北月エリアは素晴らしかった。切り捨てるのは惜しい。それに」日吉は根津に目を向けた。「私は今日、命を助けられた。無断で滑走禁止区域に入っていたにもかかわらずね。その恩返しはしなければなりません」

「じゃあ、本当に……」

ええ、と日吉は倉田に頷きかけてきた。表情は穏やかだが、目には決意の光が宿っている。

「会社に戻ったら、早速指示するつもりです。北月エリアも一緒に買い取れとね。どうです。これで何も問題はなくなったでしょう？　ただ、一つだけ皆さんにお願いがある。どうか今回のことは、皆さんの胸の内にしまっておいていただきたい。さっきどなたかがおっしゃったように、爆破事件があったスキー場となれば、星雲興産としても買い取るわけにはいかなくなる」

雲間から陽光が差すように全員の表情が明るくなった。だが言葉を発する者はいない。この歓びをどう表現していいかわからないからだろうと倉田は察した。彼自身がそうだったからだ。

すると突然立ち上がる者がいた。増淵英也だった。

「ありがとうございます。もしそうしてもらえたら、北月町は救われます」

「町思いなんだね」

日吉が目を細めていったが、英也は苦しげにかぶりを振った。

「そうじゃありません。俺があんな事故を起こさなきゃ、北月エリアのイメージだって悪くならなかったし、閉鎖の口実だって生まれなかった。せめて、事故を起こした後、逃げなかったら……」そういった後、彼は入江義之のほうを向き、床に膝をついた。

入江は眉根を寄せ、顔をそむけた。「やめてくれ。土下座はもういいよ」

「あ……すみません」しかし英也は立ち上がろうとはせずに続けた。「会長さんからも御要望があったことだし、今回の事件について、俺たちから警察に話すことはありません。でも去年の事故については、これから名乗り出るつもりです。本当に申し訳ありませんでした。まさかあんな大事故になっているなんて、あの時は気づかずに……。後になって、亡くなったとわかった時は、とにかく怖くて、名乗り出る勇気がなくて……。今回のことで北月町を守れれば、罪滅ぼしになるかなと虫のいいことも考えましたけど、やっぱりそんなのだめです。俺、自首します。何年かかってでも、

罪を償いたいと思います。　達樹君が立ち直るには、そんなことじゃだめかもしれない
けど」

桐林も彼の横に並んで膝をつき、黙ったままで頭を下げた。彼も一緒に出頭する気
なのだろう。

入江義之の妻に激突し、エッジで頸動脈を切断したことにも気づかずに逃げた二人
のスノーボーダー──それがこの二人だったという告白は、ここにいる全員がすでに
北月エリアで聞いていた。

「それは……そうすべきだろうね」入江は小声でいった。「警察には行くべきだと思
う。だけど、達樹のことはいいよ。あいつのことは、俺が何とかする。でも、とにか
く……名乗り出てくれてよかった。これで俺も、ゆっくり眠れそうだ」

増淵英也は顔を歪め、そのまま床にうずくまった。その背中が揺れている。桐林の
頰にも涙が伝い始めた。二人の嗚咽に、倉田も胸が熱くなった。

52

「さあ、ついにこの日がやってきました。命知らずのスピード狂たちの競演。世界中

から集まってきたトップライダーたちが、皆さんが見たことのないパフォーマンスを

披露してくれるはずです。どうか、熱い戦いに御期待ください。デッド・オア・アラ

イブ、生か死か、ダイナ・クロスのスタートですっ」

やや気合いが入りすぎているDJの声を聞きながら、根津はコース上部に設けられ

たエリアに足を踏み入れた。ここでは一般参加の選手たちが順番待ちをしている。

百人近くいる選手たちの中から一人を見つけだすのは難しい。しかも彼等はすでに

ヘルメットをかぶっている。ゼッケンだけを頼りに根津は探した。

するとどこからか、「こっちだよ」と聞き覚えのある声が飛んできた。急いで周囲

を見回す。ピンク色のウェア、ピンク色のヘルメットという出で立ちの選手が小さく

手を振っていた。近づき、ゴーグルの奥を覗いた。たしかに瀬利千晶だ。

「また、派手な衣装だな」

「今日はパトロールに見つかっても平気だからね」

「従兄弟たちは？　応援には来てないのか」

「東京に帰っちゃった。お金がなくなった上に、快人がふられたから」

「ふられた？　そうなのか」

「いいんだよ。あんな軟弱な奴」そういって笑った。「それよりさ、根津さんも出場

すればよかったのに」

「来年は出るよ。　優勝トロフィーを抱かせてやる」

「それはこっちの台詞。　後でパトロール小屋まで持っていくから。　そうしたら、何か奢ってね」

根津は苦笑し、がんばれよ、と声をかけてその場を離れた。

クロス大会は予定通りに開催の運びとなった。　コースは当初の計画通り、アタックコースに造られた。　倉田や辰巳たちが連日徹夜同様でがんばったと聞いている。　ある朝突如出現したコースに、根津は感嘆の声を上げた。　これなら国際大会で戦っている連中も納得するだろう、と思われる出来だった。

根津はスキーを付け、コースの横をゆっくりと下りていった。　大勢の観客たちが、並んで見物している。　いつもこれぐらいの賑わいがあれば、と経営者の気持ちになって考えた。

まだ正式には何も決まっていないが、倉田によれば、どうやら北月エリアを含めた形での売買契約がまとまりそうだという。　星雲興産は、今のスタッフをそのまま受け入れる姿勢を示しているらしい。

筧や二人の本部長たちは、すでに広世観光に戻っている。　代わりの者が来てはいる

が、殆ど形だけだ。現在、スキー場の最高責任者は倉田だった。

その倉田の姿があった。藤崎絵留と並んで観戦している。根津は後ろから近づいていった。だが声をかけようとして思い留まった。絵留の手が倉田の腕に絡んでいたからだ。

二人に気づかれぬうちにと滑り始めた。

いよいよレースが始まった。観客たちが大きな声援を送っている。コース上を選手たちが風のように駆け抜けていった。

From: Delphi@oracle.org
To: C_Evans@athena.edu
Re: negotiator, Lindsey Novak

Christine,

Congratulations to you and your team for recovering Lena Poole. I know her family was overjoyed at her safe return. However, I was devastated by your news that Teal Arnett is still in the hands of her kidnappers. This isn't the first time, or likely to be the last, that an Athena student's bravery has gotten her into trouble.

You asked about contacts in Europe. I have the woman you want. Lindsey Novak. She's a professional negotiator very experienced in taking back stolen goods, from art thieves or kidnappers. She'll have the contacts you need. I've attached her most recent info.

If there's anything else I can do, my resources are yours.

D.

Dear Reader,

I have loved writing every one of my Bombshell action-adventure/thriller books. I groove on the idea of powerful women who take charge of saving others, and maybe even saving themselves, while falling in love with a man who finds their moxie a turn-on. And so it was a delight to be invited to write *The Good Thief* as part of the Athena Force series, stories of truly fabulous women and their heroism. The added plus for me in this adventure was that Lindsey travels to beautiful, mysterious Prague, Czech Republic, in its winter wonderland time of year.

I'd love to hear from you. You can contact me and read about my other books at www.jhand.com.

Judith Leon

Judith Leon

THE GOOD THIEF

Silhouette®

ATHENA FORCE

Published by Silhouette Books

America's Publisher of Contemporary Romance

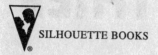

SILHOUETTE BOOKS

ISBN-13: 978-0-373-38973-5
ISBN-10:   0-373-38973-5

THE GOOD THIEF

JUDITH LEON

In July 2004 Silhouette Books showcased Judith's women's action-adventure, *Code Name: Dove*, to launch their new Bombshell line, and the book made the Waldenbooks bestseller list. The second and third books in the series, *Iron Dove* and *Captive Dove*, were released soon after.

Her epic historical *Voice of the Goddess*, a love story about a Bronze Age heroine, written under the name Judith Hand, won numerous awards, and her second epic historical, *The Amazon and the Warrior*, was published by Tor/Forge as a tie-in with the Brad Pitt movie *Troy*. Her book won the San Diego Book Award in 2005 for best historical novel. With friend and colleague Peggy Lang, Judith has completed a political suspense novel about a woman who runs for the U.S. presidency.

Her great passions now are promoting her two non-fiction books, *Women, Power, and the Biology of Peace* and *A Future Without War*, and her Web site about ending war, www.AFutureWithoutWar.org.

To Hal, the Marko of my life.

Acknowledgments

There are many friends and colleagues
to whom I owe profound thanks. I created this story
with my friend and writing partner, Peggy Lang.
She is a brilliant story editor, and we have begun
to write novels together. She helped me to envision
and compose *The Good Thief*. I am also profoundly
indebted to my long-standing writers groups
for their always-honest reviews: A. B. Curtis,
Donna Erickson, Pete Johnson and Judith Levine,
the Friday team; and Chet Cunningham, Al Kramer,
Bev Miller, Tom Utts and others of the Monday
faithful. And for their story input and editing, I have
two delightful editors to thank at Silhouette Books:
Tara Parsons and Stacy Boyd.

Prologue

Lindsey Novak fought a rising sense of panic, fought an image of standing before her father having failed. She couldn't let that happen.

A waning moon, still nearly full, shone above the White Tank Mountains northwest of Phoenix on the last Thursday night in March. The mild night air made conditions perfect for the final event of the Athena Academy's unique senior triathlon. Seventeen-year-old Lindsey checked the glowing display on her watch: 3:32 a.m.

She stifled an urge to shout at Gloria Muñoz, the current leader, that they needed to move faster—shouting would do no good whatsoever.

With her five teammates, Lindsey had been hiking and jogging for exactly four hours and thirty-two minutes, working their way southwest from their original helicopter drop-

off at an elevation of 2,800 feet in the northernmost ridge of the regional preserve.

She heard the whump-whump of the helicopter first. "Down!" she said in a hushed voice to the others. "The chopper!"

Their single-file lane instantly broke, each girl diving toward the nearest mesquite bush or darting into a moon shadow cast by a boulder. Lindsey's shoulder hit a rock. The nearest bush snapped. She winced in pain and inhaled the pungent scent of sage. Gloria killed the light of the one allotted flashlight.

Damn. Even if they weren't spotted, hiding would cost them precious minutes. At sundown, Lindsey's team, the Dianas, won the horseback relay on the Sonoran Loop of the competitive track. By 10:30, they had come in second on the bicycle course. This put them in a close second overall with the Persephones, their most serious competition. With a bit harder push, they could capture the lead. All girls at the Athena Academy for the Advancement of Women were assigned upon admission to a support group—a sort of team or coven or sisterhood—and each group picked their name from a character in Greek or Roman mythology.

The Dianas were tired but pumped, and Lindsey needed the big win as much as she'd ever needed anything. Her dad would be waiting in the park's amphitheater along with the other girls' parents. Mom would be there, too, of course, but Dad would be so incredibly proud of Lindsey if—no, when—the Dianas won this major test. His high expectations for her were the main reason he'd sent her to Athena, the extremely low-profile, highly selective, and premier high school for girls in America, really in the whole world, and Lindsey simply couldn't bear the thought of disappointing him. Not even once since she was twelve and she'd lost her nerve and

didn't even place in a skiing race had she disappointed her stern but loving dad.

She felt something, looked down, and realized that her legs were exposed—and that a scorpion had crawled up onto her boot, tail raised. Lindsey froze.

The searchlight of the chopper sliced back and forth through the darkness, approaching them and driving critters skittering in the brush toward them. If the scout in the chopper ID'd the Dianas, they'd be penalized fifteen minutes. The Academy, partially supported by secret Department of Defense funding and from such government agencies as the CIA, NSA and FBI, also had close ties to nearby Luke Air Force base. The men there enjoyed helping out in the annual event.

Rachel Stein gasped and swatted at Lindsey's shoulder. "Your legs."

"Freeze, chicas!" Gloria commanded, just before the beam missed Rachel by inches.

They wore desert camouflage hats with leafy twigs stuck into the band, black turtleneck shirts, camo pants, fingerless black gloves and hiking boots. Each carried a two-liter water bottle, Lindsey's now less than half full, ChapStick and simple food items. The team also carried water-based paint balloons for tagging, one knife, one pen flare and one simple first-aid kit. The designated leader always held the flashlight and the rappelling line and pitons, which had come in handy twice so far.

When the chopper finally passed, Lindsey flicked the scorpion off. She started to stand, but what felt like claws tore through her shirt. She swore. A cluster of razor-sharp thorns from a scrubby cat's claw acacia had shredded her forearm. Man, oh, man, she hated this plant. Ecologist Edward Abbey had said that everything in the desert either "bites, stabs, sticks, stings or stinks." He was right.

The way her classes had combined concepts, like biological adaptations and survivalist training, constantly amazed Lindsey. If women were to make things better, they had to hone every asset, every ability. Be all they could be, as her dad, a former army special forces commander, would say. Principal Christine Evans even brought in accomplished instructors to teach Lindsey's favorite subject, art. Her dad, however, encouraged art studies only as a hobby. Mom's income as a textbook illustrator hadn't brought in much money and so didn't measure up to what Dad believed Lindsey could achieve.

"Water break and alpha change," Gloria said. "Lindsey, take us in."

"Right." A quick swig of water, a chunk of power bar and a handful of peanuts, and they were off again, Lindsey in the lead. "Okay, they almost caught us because we're in the wash. We need to bend south, anyway." She set a faster jogging pace.

The chopper followed trails and the long, meandering dry washes that gleamed white in the moonlight, the idea being to drive the five teams into challenging terrain. The White Tank Mountains were essentially a series of ridges running east and west. The Dianas had already crossed or skirted three main ridges. With one more to go, they'd soon be in the public area with its many trails. Before coming in, though, they had to find a "treasure" in Waterfall Canyon. Each team's prize would be in a different location and they would know it because it would bear the initial of their name.

The distant lights of Phoenix lay like a spill of diamonds to the southeast, and even in the ravines, gullies and canyons, the city's ambient light was obvious. The girls kept Polaris shining over their left shoulders. In this park, Lindsey knew where she

was, even at night. She hiked through it several times a year and had spent the previous evening poring over maps.

She risked sweeping the flashlight beam across a rocky stretch. From the other side of the ridge, coyotes suddenly yipped the way they did over a fresh kill. Chills ran up her back at the sound. She held up her hand for a stop signal, and listened hard. When the yips grew fainter, team members audibly breathed again.

Leaving the wash would slow them down but the chopper was a bigger problem. "Go!" Lindsey said, and they scrambled over the rocks toward a protected arroyo.

This was a good time for one of their cheers. In a low voice, she chanted, "Dianas know no fear!" The others responded, instantly and softly: "No way, Jose!"

Lindsey called, "Dianas persevere!"

The response: "You bet, Suzette!"

Then all together, "Go, Dianas!"

They normally screamed the last line, but now each spoke barely above a whisper. If they alerted other teams to their location they risked getting pelted with dye balloons. If yellow glow-in-the-dark paint splattered a team member's clothing, the team would suffer a ten-minute loss for each girl hit. The Dianas were definitely the team to beat. Pelting any of them would be a bragging-rights victory. All Athena girls wanted to be like the famous Cassandra team that graduated five years ago, and the Dianas were shaping up to match the Cassandras' exploits and achievements.

"Over rock and ridge, gully and gravel, the Daring Dianas trekked on," Crystal said softly in her exaggerated movie voice-over tone, "jogging with goat-footed precision, panting and sweating, moving ever closer to victory." She wanted to become a screenwriter.

Out of the inky silhouette of a stand of organ-pipe cactus, black blots seemed to spew toward them, emitting tiny screams and squeaks. Bats. Lindsey raised her arms around her head, and the high-pitched noise rose and then apparently stopped as the bats' echo-location went into an overdrive inaudible to humans. They veered off then, shy things that they were, perhaps scared up by a great horned owl.

She'd felt no panic, no pounding pulse. Lindsey had seen only one snake so far, a mildly venomous nocturnal lyre snake coiled in a rock crevice, its head raised. She'd not even blinked as she faced its stare and directed others to move back, and then, finally, moved away herself.

Athena and the desert had been good for her courage. Understanding the desert's creatures had erased a lot of blind fears. Snakes. Bats. Coyotes. Scorpions. She understood them now, knew how to act and so had conquered the terrors they had given her at first. She could rappel down cliffs that once would have paralyzed her. She could handle guns and knives and wield a bow and arrows. Athena girls were being prepared to protect and defend as well as change the world for the better. She did have a fear, though, that she hadn't admitted to anyone. Little eight-legged things. Even a picture of a spider sometimes gave her goose bumps. She'd been that way since childhood. But she loved it that the other girls considered her the most daring, so if this particular hang-up ever seriously threatened to freak her out, she would just use force of will to get past it.

She inhaled deeply. The pervasive sage and creosote smells had freshened with moisture. The team crossed what Lindsey was sure was Goat Canyon Trail. When they entered the wide wash of Dripping Spring Canyon, Lindsey knew her direction was true. If all went well, they were a mere hour from the am-

phitheater. By 4:00 a.m., they'd found the treasure underneath dried cactus wood beneath a park sign bearing the letter
D. Lindsey noted that the letter, unlike the sign, wasn't weath-
ered. It had been placed recently. The sign explained the formation of the "white tanks," natural stone cisterns sculpted by
flash floods. Underneath some dried cactus wood, they found
their treasure: chocolate bars and something shiny. The girls
gasped at the beautiful gold pendants cast with the image of
Athena.

Someone hissed, their secret sound for *stop.* Everyone
crouched and froze.

"Voices," Portia whispered, "eight o'clock." Heads turned
west. Nothing.

And then the chopper returned, following the bends of the
wash. They eased into shadows, pressed into bushes, again
losing time as the chopper whomped by.

The sounds gradually faded, the team heard voices more
clearly. Portia hand signaled where she thought their competitors' course lay. Lindsey calculated her options. Since, in true
Athena thinking, no points would be gained in paint-tagging
another team, only a point loss in getting tagged, she would
not let them be sucked into losing time in an ambush. She
signaled by pointing away from the voices and toward the
rocks.

Soon they were nearing the area with the most vegetation.
This would probably be a shorter route in the long run,
anyway. And wasn't there a cistern, up ahead, a "white tank"?

An image of the new sign posted above their treasure
flashed in her mind. Had that been a clue, the key to success
from that point? Lindsey felt a flush of certainty. Going
through this region of tanks *was* the fastest way.

Dropping down the rock face by rope took less than ten

minutes. They reached a passageway so narrow, only one girl at a time could go through.

"It's black as starless space down there," Crystal said.

Lindsey signaled the others to wait. She moved a limb of a paloverde tree, stepped into the passage, and switched on her flashlight. Left behind, the Dianas blended into shadows. Within ten paces she came upon a rock "tank" filled with water, a deep pool of ink. It would be cold, and no telling what things lurked in it, but they'd be heroes if they pushed through and down to the amphitheater in record time.

The edges gave no footing, so the only way out was through. She shined her light into the leafy gorge beyond and saw a sight that chilled her to the bone. The beam shimmered across dozens of giant gray spiderwebs. A scream rose in her. She bit her hand in time to keep the scream inside.

Above her shoulder, a spider dropped along the rocky wall from its line of sticky web, doing a little rappelling of its own. White speckles sprinkled its body. She scurried back to the team, grateful for the dark. Otherwise, they'd see a completely white face. Her hands were sweating and her heart's beating throbbed in her throat.

"Can't go that way. The…uh…water…something moving in it. Like a snake." She couldn't return her teammates' look of surprise, her lie forcing her gaze to the ground. She was the designated leader from this point. The decision was hers to make. Moaning quietly and sulkily complaining of lost time, the girls climbed their way back out, and when they nearly reached the top, the Persephone team popped up, whooping.

"Kowabunga!"

Paint balloons flew at the Dianas, Lindsey taking the first hit. Persephones scurried away before Dianas could reach the top and fire back. A clean getaway.

It was all Lindsey could do to keep from crying. They came in well behind the Persephones, and because of the paint splatters, their score put them at third in the overall triathlon.

"We're so proud of you, honey," Lindsey's mother gushed at the closing ceremony.

She stood there with some paint still caked in her hair, wanting to disappear.

"Third, huh?" Her dad patted her on the cheek. He swiped a finger over her bangs, noting the paint. "Let's talk about this later, before your mother and I leave. See what you could have done differently."

She'd failed. At the big party in the gym the other girls would talk. Her father would hear about the dark passageway and about her retreat.

For two days, Lindsey could scarcely eat, and her father's disappointed pat dug itself a nasty little spot in her memory to remind her of the costs of fear.

Chapter 1

*P*erfect pizza!

So many reasons to come to Naples, Lindsey thought as she finished off the final bite of a slice she'd ordered while waiting to meet her backup man. The fabulous view of Vesuvius and the bay; masterpieces at the Capodimonte Art Museum that took her right out of the here and now and into a different world; an exciting air of danger and intrigue from the city's long history with the Mafia; and, of course, the best pizza in the world.

Eager to get into action, she drummed her fingertips on her water glass. She was waiting for Marko Savin at a patio table in the restaurant across the street from the world-famous National Archaeological Museum where she loved to browse, on quieter days, the best finds from Pompeii and Herculaneum.

A sudden strong breeze stroked her neck. February winds off the bay could be quite chilly. Yesterday it had rained. She

flipped up the collar of her black leather jacket, guessing the air temperature probably hung around fifty-six degrees. Billowy, gray clouds raced across the sky.

She pushed the plate away and took a drink of bottled water. A sturdy Chianti, as the waiter had suggested, would make the wait easier, but she needed to be at her clearheaded best for today's buyback.

After a month of investigation and then wangling, wheeling and dealing with a thief, she would buy back a painting, a small masterpiece, for its rightful owner. She would purchase an exquisite work by Artemisia Gentileschi. The little-known oil—three feet by four feet—was entitled *Cleopatra at the Bath*.

Artemisia had painted this Cleopatra in 1650. Lindsey loved the artist because she was one of the few acknowledged women masters of the time. During WWII the Germans stole the painting from the parents of Lindsey's clients. Recently, the grandson of an ex-Nazi officer who'd gone into hiding after the war had apparently stolen the piece from his own grandfather and put it up for sale on the black market. Lindsey's underground contacts—which were extensive since she had carefully cultivated them after becoming a middle-woman in this business over five years ago—ranged from street sages to shady "fences" to auctioneers, cabdrivers and snooty museum buyers. One had not only been able to help her find the painting, but shared the rumor with her that the grandson, Heinie Gottschalk, wanted the money from the sale to take his little drug-running business to new highs. Or lows, depending on how you looked at it.

She sighed. Maybe that was true. Maybe not. She didn't allow herself to judge or guess at what people did with the money exchanged in the buys. Her job was to serve clients

who could not get justice through the legal system. Insurance companies, private businesses and individuals—at one time or another, she'd negotiated a deal for them all. The black-market buybacks sometimes felt a little shady. After all, her clients didn't like paying for items they rightfully owned. But if her fees sometimes felt like thievery, she at least had the consolation of knowing she was a good thief, on the side of justice.

A man at a nearby table cleared his throat and stared at Lindsey's hand. She stopped drumming. Why hadn't she at least ordered coffee? She recalculated the time to reach Capodimonte Park, the site of the exchange. She'd set up the buyback there not just because the location was convenient and public, but also because of the poetic justice involved. The Capodimonte Palace, built in the late 1700s and now the site of the art museum, displayed what was perhaps Artemisia's best-known piece, done in the chiaroscuro style of the more famous, but in Lindsey's opinion not more talented, Caravaggio, and entitled *Judith Slaying Holophernes*. Lindsey would buy back a piece of stolen art under the caring eye, so to speak, of the artist herself in the sense that Artemisia lived on in her work.

Lindsey checked her watch. 12:56. Still early. But Savin obviously wasn't. Maybe he'd had a hard time renting a motorcycle on such short notice? She hated last-minute changes.

If she were meeting a friend or even doing business for NSI—Novak Sicurezza Internazionale, her father's security company—time could be experienced Italian style…casual. She had, however, never worked with Marko Savin before, and today's exchange, like all buys, was potentially dangerous. Everything had to be executed with care. That included timing.

When Lindsey, in a rush early this morning, had called her father from the Florence airport, explaining that a motorcycle accident resulting in a seriously pulled muscle had put her usual backup, Tito, temporarily out of commission, her dad, former Colonel Anton "K-bar" Novak, had highly recommended Marko Savin. "They don't come better," K-bar had said. "I can get him down to Naples for you quickly, no problem."

She crossed her long legs the other direction, black leather pants creaking with the motion. All five-foot-nine of her was in black: black leather, a black turtleneck cashmere sweater under the jacket, black boots. She'd secured her long, dark-red hair in a French braid at the back of her head, pulling it severely away from her face and slicking her bangs away from her forehead. No gentle femininity when dealing with thieves.

Art thieves as a rule didn't engage in violence. She didn't anticipate any problems today, but an unbreakable rule was to show strength—and be prepared for anything. More than once, a seller had tried to double-cross her, taking the money and then attempting to flee with the art. Instant wire transfers were not as common even five years ago and unmarked cash was a terrible temptation. Twice she had barely escaped from attempts by third parties to kill both her and the seller and steal the art. You just never knew. She worked carefully. She did not take unnecessary risks.

12:58. She watched the traffic streaming past the museum, the tourists strolling in and out, and finished off her water. Some of Lindsey's own handiwork could be seen in the museum, which gave her a thrill. Between her junior and senior years at the Athena Academy, she had volunteered as a gofer and assistant for an art restorer in Pompeii, and two pieces Lindsey had researched and assisted in restoring were displayed right across the street. How cool was that!

Athena Academy. Memories rushed her. The Dianas. The painful shame of losing the senior triathlon. The Dianas had, of course, eventually forgiven her for that awful blunder. She'd even been reinstated as "head daredevil." But her ten-year reunion was this year, and part of her dreaded going, knowing she'd take terrible teasing. *Oh, Lindsey, I'll never forget how you looked with all that glow-in-the-dark paint splattered over your head. Ha-ha-ha.*

She shook her head. Was it ever possible to fully escape shames of the past?

Time? 1:02.

A motorcycle zipped into a spot two doors down from the restaurant. A man she judged to be a couple of years older than she, shut it off and dismounted. He looked toward the restaurant, and Lindsey figured he had to be Marko Savin. She'd not only picked this time and place, she'd told her dad that she wanted Savin to rent a motorcycle, not a car. "I drive a car," she had explained to K-bar. "Tito is always on a bike."

Good-looking, she thought as Savin strode toward her. Confident. Maybe even cocky. That could also mean excessive risk-taker, but she would keep an open mind.

He walked straight to her, pulled out the chair opposite, and sat.

"You're late," she said before she could stop herself. Now why had that popped out? She hadn't meant to launch their day with criticism.

"No, I'm not," he countered, grinning.

Maybe she'd been thrown off stride by his looks. She took in the short-cropped dark brown hair, deep blue eyes, ever-so-male five o'clock shadow and an intriguing scar under his left eye that she immediately wanted to touch, if not kiss.

I've been without sex way too long.

She stuck out her wrist, displaying her black watch's neon-blue time display, at the same moment he stuck out his wrist, displaying his silver watch's black numerals. They both checked the time, and laughed. His watch said 1:00, hers, 1:02.

"It's nice we're both right," she said, happy for a chance to get back on a positive track.

The waiter arrived. "I'm not ordering," Marko Savin said. He had one of the most beautiful baritone voices she'd ever heard. His English had a mild Italian accent. K-bar had explained that Savin was born and raised in Venice but had traveled widely.

"We don't have a lot of time," she hurried on as the waiter sauntered away. "I appreciate your stepping in at the last moment."

"When your father calls, I come. I owe him a great deal."

"He said he found you serving in Kosovo, in the French Foreign Legion."

He nodded. "The Legion taught me a lot, but it's a rough crew. Working for your father's security business is more to my taste. And it let me return to Italy."

"What we're doing today should be an easy job. I don't know if Dad told you what I do as a side venture, when I'm not selling for and promoting NSI business."

Marko Savin angled the free chair at their table and propped one booted foot on it. He wore a black leather jacket with black jeans. "He says you buy back stolen goods for their rightful owners."

"Correct. Today I'm purchasing a painting for a million and a half American dollars." While thinking again how wonderfully deep blue his eyes were, she nodded to the bulky white cotton satchel at her feet. It held a four-foot-long tube which, in turn, held a quality reproduction of the painting.

"I'll trade the tube in this satchel for the tube that has the original. There's a minor difference in their labels that only I would notice." On at least four occasions this little bit of confused identification between the original and the copy had worked to good effect for her. A way for her "steal" the painting back if the deal went bad. It might not be needed, but again, better to be prepared for all eventualities than sorry for assuming all would go well.

She explained the history of the Nazi theft of the painting.

Savin frowned. "I don't get it. You're paying off a thief, an ex-Nazi, for a painting he stole. Owners shouldn't have to buy back their own stuff."

"The owners just want their painting back."

"Seems to me that's a job for the authorities. They catch the bad guys, retrieve the art, return it, and punish the crooks."

"I'm hired when owners discover that the authorities aren't going to be able to retrieve something the owners very much want returned."

"Isn't that sort of interfering with a criminal investigation—for money?"

His questions were starting to annoy her. "When the authorities can't deliver, people hire me. They're willing to pay a substantial retrieval fee. The fee is, of course, gratifying, but the real satisfaction—the reason I take the risks—is because I get to see the joy on my client's faces when I return what they loved and thought they had lost forever. I can assure you that I only work for legitimate owners or their representatives."

"You said the guy is a Nazi! Pretty much scum."

She glared at him. "The seller isn't a Nazi. His grandfather was. But, yeah, I'd deal with a Nazi. I deal with whoever has what owners want returned. And that's why you're here. Sometimes things can go sour. So, you in or no?"

Savin stared right back, then shrugged. "Sure."

"Okay. Here's the action," she continued. "You and I go to the meet, you on the bike, me in my rental car. We arrive a minute apart—you first—and we make no connection. They aren't to know I have muscle behind me. I've made my reputation—I am the best and intend to stay that way—by never coming armed and making certain that buyers and sellers get what they expect. I presume you're carrying."

He patted his chest where under the leather jacket she assumed he had a gun. She'd already figured out from the bulge on the calf of the leg propped on the chair that he carried a knife.

"That's fine," she continued. "But there's to be no use of weapons unless it looks like someone is going to kill me. Okay?"

"Got it."

"What I do, and my reputation, depends on being clever, not violent, but I *will* get the painting back, and I will not get killed doing it."

He smiled. It made his blue eyes twinkle.

From the white satchel she pulled out a map of the Capodimonte Park grounds. She explained where he would park and where Gottschalk was supposed to meet her—on an access road about a hundred and fifty yards away.

"If I need help, I'll jab my fist into the air. Or," she slid a small black box to Savin across the table and as he reached for it, his finger brushed the back of her hand. She felt a quick spurt of warmth to her face, her body's response to a profound sense of pleasure at his touch.

Stunned, she drew in a slow breath, then, "If I press this," she touched the center of a silver moon pendant, "the green light on your box will go red." The slim moon disk contained a built-in transponder, activated by a three-second touch.

"Don't come in unless I signal, okay? Any questions?"

He shook his head, then said, "I like your earrings. They're exactly the color of your eyes."

For a moment she couldn't find words, surprised at the sudden shift of topic and tone. Her earrings, a gift from K-bar and her mom when she graduated from the Academy, were half-inch, oval studs set in silver. "They're gray star sapphires. From India."

"Very beautiful."

She felt herself warming, knew that her face was reddening. How embarrassing.

She checked her watch. "It's time to go." She lay ample euros on the table, grabbed the satchel and, keeping her eyes off of Marko Savin, headed for the street.

Chapter 2

Lindsey drove the rented red Fiat uphill from the center of Naples through heavy traffic. The city spread across hills that allowed those spectacular vistas of Vesuvius rising in all its imposing splendor, an ancient sentinel watching over the bay, its peak shrouded in clouds. Everything was going well, even on schedule.

She kept Marko Savin in sight all the way to Capodimonte Park. With Tito, she stayed focused on the deal, but thoughts of the surprising rush of pleasure she'd felt at Marko Savin's touch kept intruding.

K-bar had said Savin wasn't married. She couldn't resist wondering what his "type" might be. She had always wanted to share her passions and joys and hardships with a special companion. So far, however, the only man she'd ever had a serious relationship with wanted her to quit taking the risks involved in her art buybacks. And he hadn't

even known about the sometimes extremely dangerous courier jobs she did, in secret, for the U.S. government as an Oracle agent.

She knew other Athena women who had sacrificed their lives of high risk for family, but that would never be Lindsey. Retrieving art, sometimes masterpieces, stolen and precious to their owners, gave her life meaning. Most of her assignments as a courier were important, some critical to U.S. security, and that also gave her life substance. This was who she was.

Saying no to the possibility of love and a family of her own had been the hardest thing she'd ever done. Sometimes, alone at night, she would get the blues and think she'd made a mistake, but, she'd inherited her mother's cheerfulness, and in the morning she'd look forward to the day's action.

No one in this life gets everything.

She pulled over and waited, carefully watching for one minute. Maybe she could risk some fun and adventure with this man. No ties. She would very much like that—if he showed any interest. He had seemed to. Why else comment on her earrings and her eyes with a look that said he couldn't stop mentally undressing her?

When the sixty seconds had passed, she drove through the entry and through extensive grounds with spacious lawns, now brown with winter, passing groves of leafless trees and a number of old buildings, including the palace that was now a museum, all of them tied together by looping access roads.

Heinie Gottschalk was waiting at the prearranged spot, seated in the back of a black Alfa Romeo sedan, parked as directed and accompanied only by his driver. She'd agreed that Heinie could bring one man with him and had said, "Sure, he can be armed." Her main line of defense against treachery by Heinie, or any seller, didn't rest on strong-arm measures.

She could be counted on by both sides to be an honest broker, no violence, no treachery and total discretion.

She parked the Fiat in front of the Alfa Romeo and turned off the motor. A hundred and fifty yards away, Marko sat on his bike, apparently studying a map or newspaper.

Carrying the white satchel with its slightly protruding tube, she strode to the Alfa. The driver stepped out and opened the rear door behind the driver's seat. Lindsey slid inside, sharing the seat with Heinie. He was perhaps twenty-five with neat shoulder-length blond hair and a flashy pinstripe suit. The diamond stud in his ear had to be at least a carat and a half.

Heinie spoke English, in which he was fluent. "So, we're ready to trade?"

"Let me see the painting," she countered. As he reached for it, she slipped her hand into her jacket pocket and palmed the tiny GPS transponder, the size of a dime. She had to slip it into the tube with the genuine painting and quickly because in the end, he might refuse to leave her alone with *Cleopatra*.

He handed her the tube she had supplied to him. "I need to have a few moments in private to inspect it," she said.

"Why the fuck would you need to inspect it? You think I try to cheat you? I know your reputation and I deal in good faith."

"Others have tried to cheat. Before we part, you will be able to verify that the wire transfer has been made. Right now I verify the painting's authenticity. It's all part of keeping everyone honest."

"What's in your tube there?"

"The tube has an accurate copy of the painting, in case I need to check any details. You may search it if you'd like."

Heinie didn't move, as rigid as if he were made of stone.

"If I can't inspect the painting in private, Heinie, I won't

wire the money. You need to let me do my job. You and your man should stand at the front of the car."

Finally he opened his door and hauled himself out. He signaled and the two of them moved to the front of the car, looking across the grounds. Looking toward Marko, actually.

Lindsey had studied art and art forgery. She knew all the techniques used to establish whether a statue, painting, lithograph, or other work, was the genuine article: pigment analysis, infrared analysis, or X-ray fluorescence to determine the age of the canvas or if metals in a sculpture were too pure. Sometimes these methods could pick up the artist's fingerprints left in the paint. "Craquelure" was the study of the distinctive network of fine cracks on very old pieces that were virtually impossible to replicate. She could even identify unique brushwork and perspectives to see if these were consistent with known genuine pieces. The problem with this was that forgers made the same analysis, and great forgers were able to re-create them. Even experts could be fooled. But none of these fancy techniques were needed for the Artemisia.

She opened the tube he'd given her, tilted it, and the painting slid into her hands. As she set the base of the tube on the floor, she dropped the GPS into it and heard it hit with a quiet thunk on the bottom.

She unrolled the painting just enough to expose the back side, lower right corner. From her pocket she took a small lighter, and held it close to the painting. Her client had informed her that only the family knew the painting had been signed on the back using urine with the three words, *Owned by Genovesa*.

Invisible writing had a long history. Milk, vinegar, fruit juices and urine, all had been used and all darkened when heated. The words soon appeared.

"Hello, honey," she said, longing to pull it out and gaze. She put away the lighter, returned the painting to its tube and knocked on her window.

Heinie returned to her. "Satisfied?" he asked in a sulky tone.

Gee, might he have been raised as a spoiled brat? She ignored him and pulled out her BlackBerry. He watched her intently as she keyed in the information that would transfer one and a half million American dollars to a bank in the Cayman Islands. She waited. Finally she read aloud, "Transfer complete."

It was his turn to verify. He started to punch keys in his own communicator but the driver, looking behind them, yelled, and as he fumbled to pull his gun, a hulking figure in black rushed him. The door beside her flew open and a big hand yanked her out of the car. Another grabbed Heinie. She stared into the black barrel of a Beretta semiautomatic pistol. The hulk in black slugged Heinie's driver. He dropped to the ground. In the distance a motorcycle roared to life.

"*Du verdammten schwein,*" a gray-haired old man screeched at Heinie.

A dark-gray Daimler now blocked the Alfa Romeo. There were four of them, including the old man. She figured the old guy had to be Heinie's granddad.

Hellfire and damnation!

Two of the old Nazi's goons grabbed both tubes and her satchel. Another clubbed Heinie with the butt of his own gun. Heinie's yowl was earsplitting and he fell to his knees.

Clearly the old man intended to steal the painting back from his grandson. She pointed to the tube holding the original and shouted, "*Sie konnen nicht mit dem Bild—*"

She was going to tell them that she had placed an incen-

diary in the container, and she would incinerate the picture rather than let them take it again. Not true, of course, but she'd used the ploy before to get the upper hand. The key, after she calmed everyone down, was to offer more money.

Instead, Marko Savin, racing in a loud roar across the lawn, distracted everyone. Heinie's driver, having regained his senses, pulled his gun and blew a hole right between the eyes of one of the old Nazi's men.

Chaos! The old man and his remaining two guards sprinted to their car, each clutching a tube, as Heinie staggered to his feet. Lindsey ran after them, but had to duck behind the Alfa Romeo when both goons turned and started firing.

Marko brought the motorcycle to a sliding stop on its side with the motor still roaring. Ducking bullets, he dived behind her Fiat. The old Nazi and his goons made a U-turn, running up onto the lawn on the other side of the access road, and burned rubber as they headed toward the park's exit. Both tubes were gone. Artemisia's *Cleopatra*. Gone.

Chapter 3

Lindsey stood dumbstruck for a second and then turned to Marko, furious. "I didn't give you the signal."

"I consider drawn guns a signal."

"They wouldn't have hurt me."

"How the hell can you know that?"

"Later! We have to catch them. Take the bike."

He had the good sense not to argue. She leaped on behind him and hugged his waist. They reached the exit. No sign of the gray Daimler. They could go right, left, or straight ahead, heavy traffic in all three directions.

"What now?" he called back to her over the motorcycle's noise.

She pulled out the BlackBerry, pushed three buttons, and picked up the signal from the GPS. "Left," she said. "And hit it. Go through stops when you can."

Her pulse raced as he wove in and out around cars,

bicycles, pedestrians and buses. They started south on the Corso Amadeo Di Savola, but soon the GPS signal indicated that the Daimler turned west. She pointed right, toward the next cross street.

"I see them," he called out. "Two blocks ahead."

For agonizing minutes, they made headway, then traffic would interfere and they'd drop behind only to gain again. After fifteen minutes they reached the section of Naples called Vomero, an elevated area filled with views in all directions where they kept up the crazy cat and mouse in a heavily commercial area with all sorts of offices and pedestrians.

They sat waiting at a red light, the Daimler only a block ahead. "Hang on," Marko called to her.

He gunned the bike and they blasted straight through the cross traffic, barely avoiding a truck.

The light turned green for the Daimler; it moved ahead. Marko skimmed the outside of their lane and then swung into oncoming traffic to go around two trucks blocking their way. She looked forward over his shoulder, right into the grill of an oncoming van whose driver was frantically honking his horn. She sucked in her breath as they zipped back into their own lane. She could hear the van's driver cursing.

They were within a limousine's length of the Daimler. "I'm going to stop their car," Marko yelled, and she sensed he'd drawn his gun.

"It's too dangerous for pedes—"

She heard the shot. The Daimler's left rear tire blew, and the car jerked left and then back to the right. Normal traffic parted to flow around it. The driver pulled the Daimler to the curb and everyone bailed out, including the old man.

The three thieves ran into the cross street. Marko stopped the bike. Lindsey jumped off. Together they dogged the three

men who suddenly veered left. The men ran past the ticket booth to the Via Toledo Funicular, and shoved their way into a car. Lindsey watched in horror as the door closed behind the three men, and the funicular began to descend. Another cable car would not arrive and then begin the steep descent, she knew, for at least ten minutes. All three men grinned back at her. One held up one of the tubes.

We're going to lose them! I'm going to lose the Artemisia! Her stomach twisted.

"Shit!" Marko said.

Lindsey scanned their surroundings, fighting disappointment, and saw that a long flight of stairs descended alongside the funicular. She pointed.

"The bike," Marco exclaimed.

They ran back to the bike, and Marko drove them to the head of the sidewalk. "Hold on tight," he said, stating the obvious.

They bumped their way down the stairs, which thankfully had few people coming up. Almost all the foot traffic was heading down and Marko stayed well to the left, yelling in Italian for them to clear out of the way.

She ignored the shocked stares of the people they passed. She accidentally bit her tongue, tasted salty blood. Too soon they had to detour to a side street, then an alley, but they didn't lose sight of the funicular. Finally they caught up and as they passed the cable car, she took perverse pleasure in the amazed looks on the faces of the three men. She prepared herself for one hell of a fight.

"No gun," she said to Marko, thinking of the hordes of people who would be waiting at the bottom to board.

Marko nodded.

When the three thugs entered the street, Lindsey and Marko sprang after them. The old man didn't even try to run. She

singled out the smaller thug, and Marko headed for the larger one. They were, apparently, woefully out of shape. Her man turned and charged her. She landed a forward kick to his diaphragm and he went down with the follow-up chop to the back of his neck. She kicked him over onto his side and, as he gasped for air, she grabbed the tube he carried, and took his gun.

Marko dispatched the man with the other tube, apparently with the same ease. He mounted the bike. Panting, laughing and flushed with a sense of triumph, Lindsey hopped on behind, clutched both tubes fiercely, and they took off. Hot damn, she'd done it again.

"Ooo-rah!" she whooped as they passed a row of plump elderly women in black dresses waiting in line at the funicular.

Given all the havoc they had left in their path, perhaps including a dead body in the park, witnesses might be describing a woman in black leather and red hair and a man also in black and looking like a criminal. The authorities might very well be watching all transport stations, so they ruled out getting onto a plane dressed as they were. She had used a fake ID and paid cash for the Fiat so she left it to the police to return it. She and Marko picked out a small, no-name store that sold men's and women's Levi's jeans and sweatshirts. At another store they bought new clothes and duffel bags for their leather ones. She bought a cheap black wig and black eyebrow pencil and he bought reading glasses. At 4:30 p.m. they caught a flight back to Florence.

On the plane, with her treasure secure in the bin overhead, Lindsey ordered that Chianti she'd missed with her pizza, and Marko joined her. She explained what she had intended to do in case of trouble—threaten to incinerate the painting if the

old Nazi and his gang thought they could take it from her, and offer them more money instead. "It's worked for me before."

"Tell you what. I apologize. I acted from the gut when I saw the gun."

"Well, I admit that you saved my client any extra money." She smiled. She liked a man who felt strong enough in his masculinity to actually apologize. She sipped the wine, thinking that Marko was earning points rapidly. He'd shown himself to be bold. Smart. Courageous. And a damn good fighter.

"Your dad told me you were tough," he said and then laughed, that beautiful baritone. "I don't know what I expected, but it wasn't that karate kick."

She shrugged with a smile. Like K-bar, he was impressed with her daring.

"I'd like to see you again, Lindsey. Would you like to go skydiving tomorrow? I have a buddy, a hotdog instructor."

Her hand froze in midair. She slowly lowered the wineglass. She'd never been skydiving. The idea was…pretty intimidating. She felt her chest tightening, a sure sign her body didn't really like the idea. Why had he picked skydiving, for heaven's sake?

"According to K-bar you're a real risk-taker," Marko added. "Ever been skydiving?"

She shook her head. Of course, her father would describe her as a risk-taker. Wasn't that the image she always projected to him? Part of what he admired about her?

"Okay. Skydiving sounds fine. Let's do it."

Marko explained what she ought to wear and that he'd pick her up at 10:00. For the rest of the trip, they talked about his joining the French Foreign Legion, the action he'd seen in Afghanistan, the Ivory Coast and Kosovo.

"Why did you join?"

"Oh…" His jaws flexed, as if gritting his teeth. "My family background is a little on the shady side. I…wanted to break away." He smiled with a hint of mischief. "And I wanted to see the world."

And he wants to keep things vague, she thought as the plane began its descent, so she asked no more questions, and he didn't offer any more information about himself. He'd left his car, a very sexy black Maserati GranSport Spyder with a red-and-black interior, at the airport in a high security lot. Whatever he did for K-bar must pay very well, or else he'd lied about separating himself from his family background. You didn't make that kind of money in the FFL.

Lindsey used a motorbike or taxis for transport in Florence and had taken a taxi to the airport. Who could resist a ride with a handsome man in a fantastic car?

They drove in quiet, comfortable silence. She also liked a man who didn't feel that he—or she—had to talk all the time.

It was still dusk when they stood at the door to her apartment. Her six-room spread on the top floor of a six-story building on the south side of the River Arno nestled below the hilltop where the Piazza Michelangelo offered thousands of tourists one-eighty-degree views. From her dining room window, she could see the Ponte Vecchio. She was tempted to show Marko her view.

He hesitated, body language betraying his desire to be invited in. He looked past her at her painting hanging in the entry. "That's quite a work of art."

Nice try. She smiled. "Thanks."

"You didn't…did *you* paint it?"

She nodded and they shared a long moment. But she wasn't ready to take things to the next step. Not yet. "A long day," she said, smiling. "I look forward to tomorrow."

He pulled her to him and kissed her, a long, delicious, hungry kiss that sent waves of heat through her body. He didn't move his hands over her, just held her gently.

"See you tomorrow, then." He turned and walked away with Lindsey still savoring his kiss.

Right. They'd be jumping out of a plane together. Was she beyond insane?

Still thinking of Marko, she pulled some leftovers from her refrigerator and turned on the TV while finishing the last of the pasta salad. An Italian sitcom. She made a point of watching these to hone her ability to understand Italian humor. A glass of wine and more thoughts of Marko. She switched to CNN, and as she rinsed her plate in the kitchen, the television's commentary riveted her.

"...students from an exclusive high school near Phoenix, Arizona, Athena Academy, were abducted and have been missing for more than twenty-four hours."

Athena girls? She raced back toward the TV. The screen showed photos of two smiling teenagers. "It is now believed that the girls were taken to Colombia. The abductor hasn't demanded any ransom, Academy principal Christine Evans reported." And that was the end of the report.

Christine being quoted on CNN! Dear God.

Christine Evans had been the Athena Academy's principal since the school opened. She'd accepted the position after retiring as a captain from the army, having been blinded in one eye by a training accident. She not only had the job of hiring staff and running the school; Christine was in charge of assessing the students for potential work in government security agencies after their graduation. The Academy had been partially funded from the "discretionary" (unlisted and unexplained portions) of the budget of the DoD from the be-

ginning. One pivotal Academy founder had actually been the head of the CIA. He realized the potential value to the United States of a military-type prep academy for women. Many Athena graduates worked for various government agencies. Lindsey, herself, was now a courier for Oracle because Christine Evans had singled Lindsey out as a potential recruit.

The news report had said Colombia. That didn't sound like a simple kidnapping, Lindsey decided as she walked into the home office where she spent so many of her waking hours. Her computer suite offered three oversize, linked monitors. She could drag her mouse from the left, continue through the center screen and end all the way over on the right screen. One of her art projects could be going on one screen, the Internet or television on another and documents on the last.

She immediately logged onto AA.gov. This Web site linked Athena grads to each other, ran a terrific, newsy blog and offered a host of services like links to articles on up-to-date equipment and weapons, or even where to get the best health insurance.

The featured item on the home page offered a new video of Christine. She looked tired, making her eyelid droop a little over her blind eye. In her early sixties, she was still an attractive and healthy-looking woman, barely changed over the last ten years. Lindsey clicked on the feed and watched her former principal express her sorrow and then reveal more details of the kidnapping.

"You all know how hard the Academy works to keep a low profile. Shannon Connor's dogged pursuit of us on the ABS network is quite regrettable."

The Web site wasn't secure. Lindsey wouldn't learn much more there. She checked her e-mail and sure enough, she had one from Christine. The time in Phoenix, at the Academy, would be just after 10:00 a.m. "Call—private," was all the

e-mail said, the code instructions for using her secure cell phone and the secure satellite connection. Lindsey placed the call and Christine's secretary answered.

"We're putting out an alert to a special list of Athena grads, Lindsey. Hold this line and I'll transmit Christine's message. It's all the information we have so far."

"Holding," Lindsey said. Then she listened as an obviously prerecorded message created for this secure line came on.

"I fear," the Athena leader said, "that there is a drastic breach of security in this kidnapping. Those of you who have followed the tragic and bizarre story of Athena graduate Lorraine 'Rainy' Miller Carrington and her 'egg babies' will understand why."

Lindsey had indeed followed the story of the ova that had been stolen years ago during a clandestine operation from a very young Athena student, Lorraine "Rainy" Carrington. She'd been only twelve. Much later, events revealed that a perverse scientist had genetically manipulated the stolen "eggs" in a way intended to enhance the resulting children with special talents. He'd then implanted the modified eggs in unsuspecting surrogate mothers. The insider term for these girls was "egg babies." The full extent and results of these experiments were still largely unknown, although the girls that were known to have resulted from them were indeed gifted with some extraordinary abilities. The genetic modification process apparently only worked on eggs with two X chromosomes.

"The abductor," the recorded message continued, "attempted to take three of our girls—Kayla Ryan's daughter, Jazz, and two others, Teal Arnett and Lena Poole. Jazz is fourteen. Lena is fifteen, and Teal is seventeen. They'd gone together to the movies when someone abducted them." For a

moment Christine's voice rose. Then, "Thank God, Jazz escaped. This is perhaps the only fortunate thing to happen so far."

Lindsey clicked through the Athena Academy Web site, searching out the girls' pictures as the recording continued.

"I'm especially concerned about the lack of a ransom demand, deeply troubled. I'll provide updates on this secure connection as soon as possible. We're asking you to keep your antennae tuned for any clue as to the perpetrators and the whereabouts of the captives.

"As this kidnapping demonstrates, our days of keeping an extremely low profile may be waning. You wonderful young women are becoming a force to be reckoned with around the world. One final thought. The good guys and the bad guys are taking note of the increasing numbers of Athena alumni in positions of power and influence. Allison Gracelyn of the National Security Agency is here with us. Katie Rush, who is with the FBI and an expert on missing persons, has made extraordinary progress and is now in Colombia. Together with our 'Athena Force,' we're going to get our girls back."

The recording ended. Lindsey hung up. She studied the faces of the three girls in their class pictures and bookmarked the sites.

What a mess. Lindsey knew that Rainy's eggs had been harvested in secret. They lied to her, told her that she'd had an appendectomy. She never found out, before she was killed, that she had three daughters. The scientist at Lab 33—what was his name? Aldrich something. But the "egg babies" controversy was over and done with. A year ago they shut the lab down. What in heaven's name was going on?

Lindsey wanted to do follow-up research immediately, but a wave of fatigue leached away her concentration. And tomor-

row she would jump into the sky. Of course, she wanted to look good on her way down—before she splattered.

Marko had already seen her hair sleeked back, which made her look almost brunette. She'd do the French braid but let wisps fall at the hairline. She was tired. Nevertheless, she exfoliated her face. Then her whole body. God, her nails were a mess. She did a quick sport manicure. And touched up her pedicure.

It was 11:30. She sighed. Time to crash.

Ooooh. Bad choice of words.

In her sleep that night, she dreamed of falling.

Chapter 4

Gesù Cristo e mamma-goddamn-mia, Marko thought as he drove to his place.

Lindsey...

He absolutely shouldn't mess with the boss's daughter. He loved women and plunged wholeheartedly into passionate relationships that burned out in disappointingly short times. If that happened with Lindsey, K-bar would never again give him the *primo* clients, let alone hire him to head up the new private extraction team. Hell, he'd probably fire him, and blacklist him from the personal security business. Actually, K-bar was capable of much worse.

The tires of the Maserati screeched as Marko took a corner too fast. He paid little attention. His mind was on other things.

Okay, say the passion didn't burn out, he said to himself. K-bar would do almost anything to protect Lindsey from

winding up with the wrong man. He probably had her lined up to meet rich sons of diplomats, or some of his wealthy clients.

Marko was pretty sure he wasn't the right long-term guy for Lindsey. Yeah, they had the adrenaline rush thing going. But she was so well educated, classy. The final shock had been her painting. She was an artist, too. That painting…he kept picturing the way she'd captured the moon through branches….

At least he'd impressed her with the skydiving idea. How many sons of diplomats could offer that?

He pulled into the garage he rented and walked three blocks to his tiny second-floor apartment overlooking an alley. He'd put all his money into the car. Such pleasure it gave him to send his mama a picture of himself beside it and tell her he'd earned it. She alone in his family would be proud of him. The rest of the lot were exactly the kind of people Lindsey dealt with in buybacks—the thieves, not the clients.

Marko came from immigrant trash, though his great-great-grandfather had been part of the Russian aristocracy before WWI. Lindsey's draw was more than skin-deep. She was everything he admired, maybe even what he wanted to be. Marko had been a poor soldier just out of the FFL when K-bar hired him six years ago. For the last three years, he'd been earning real money. He could speak the untutored Russian of his family, Italian, of course, French and English. He knew he could advance in a business like K-bar's. He just had to get rid of his rough edges.

He called his friend Claudio who said there was a jump tomorrow and Marko and his girl were welcome. Marko hung up and stared down at the shabby tan carpet and then out into the night sky above the neighboring building. By what mysterious process had he looked at Lindsey and seen his own ambition and potential?

* * *

Lindsey looked a bit pale and didn't say much on the forty-minute drive down *al autostrada* except to ask how many jumps he'd made.

"The next will be my 578th," Marko said before reviewing safety issues and explaining about the drop zone. "You're going to love it."

They reached the little airport at Arezzo for an adventure in *paracadutismo,* parachuting, at 10:45 a.m. He and Claudio personally packed the chute for the tandem jump he and Lindsey would make.

Marko said, "A certified parachute rigger put in an altitude-sensitive device that opens automatically if for any reason we're both unable to pull the cords."

Lindsey looked even paler.

"But we will both be acutely conscious and loving it," Marko said.

Lindsey laughed nervously. She pulled a bright yellow nylon suit over her tight but stretchy black ski clothes. Marko stepped into his orange suit. Several divers were boarding the small plane, whooping and laughing in their wild bicolor jumpsuits of turquoise and white, red and purple.

"They'll jump ahead of us," Marko said. He attached the tandem harness straps to Lindsey around the tops of each thigh and over each shoulder and under her arms. The tight shoulder straps emphasized her breasts, which he'd already surveyed more than once.

After a few more instructions, their plane was in the air, climbing and making a wide loop to the south, passing by the northern shore of Lake Trasimeno, a blue mirror of the sky. He pointed to Isola Maggiore, Major Island. "Not a very imaginative name."

"In Italian, everything sounds romantic. It doesn't have to sound imaginative," Lindsey said.

At an altitude of six thousand meters, Marko attached Lindsey's clips to his own straps in four places, powerfully connecting the two of them. He stood beside her as the others were lining up beside the transport door. One of the jumpers accidentally bumped Lindsey backward, thrusting her body against Marko. He was surprised to feel her shaking. Could the female daredevil be frightened?

He spoke softly into her ear, "Would you like to just watch this first time?"

She looked at him over her shoulder. "Of course not! I'm making this jump." She shoved her goggles down over her eyes.

He did likewise. The door opened and the formation divers leaped from the plane, yelling and whooping. The plane began dropping and quickly reached five thousand meters.

"Okay, your turn," Claudio yelled.

"Jump," Marko said.

They made a paired spring into the sky. Arms like wings, they leaped into icy wind. In belly-to-earth position, they would drop for sixty seconds. Strands of her hair slipped out and lashed at his face a little. Her legs spread apart, and he hovered over her as if about to mount her in their free fall over the patchwork terrain below. They kept touching in places, her backside bumping at his groin. It was both erotic and exhilarating.

To the south, puffy arcs of color opened. The formation flyers. Marko yanked their cord also. With a jerk, their canopy wing chute opened. He held Lindsey around the waist to guide her upright. They floated gloriously as the earth approached, bumped down only a few feet off the assigned target.

Lindsey came alive, screaming with delight and laughing. After he'd gathered the chute, she grabbed him and planted an amazing kiss on his lips. No tongue, but full of passion.

When she pulled back they both grinned, a distinct sense of shared awareness in the moment of pleasure.

Back in Florence in the late afternoon, she didn't invite him in. She took his hand and tugged him in. They flew at each other the second the door closed. He moved his hands over her slim waistline, her hips, her firm breasts. He was about to take her sweater off when the phone rang. She kept kissing him, but after the fourth ring, she pulled away.

"I guess I'd better get that," she said.

He laid his head back on the sofa in frustration as she answered and then watched as she grew more and more focused. "I'll call you right back."

"Marko, something has come up. I have to take this call and then get to work."

He looked at her, groggy with lust. "This is American humor, right?"

She shook her head, leaned over and kissed him, a thorough *hello* kiss, not a *goodbye* buss. "I can't thank you enough for today."

"That seems to be true," he said with mock sadness. "When can I see you again?"

"Soon. I hope."

His Maserati was inadequate comfort on the cold ride home. What could be more important to her than making love to him at that moment? *Mamma goddamn mia.*

Chapter 5

Lindsey closed the door and sagged against it. *I was scarily close to hopping into bed with Marko Savin. I must be out of my mind!*

She'd been on the verge of doing something she would have surely regretted. It was way too soon for that much intimacy. Maybe it was the intoxication of the day that had her close to losing herself with him. She'd sipped the old adrenaline cocktail and loved it. "Adrenaline fright" was definitely an acquired taste. She'd almost wet her pants with relief after they landed and had forced herself to jump again to banish any remaining doubts about her nerve. What a thrill! That's what happened when you conquered your weaknesses. Just like K-bar said.

Thank heavens Allison Gracelyn had interrupted before Marko had slipped her sweater over her head. Stopping at that point was sensible. Sane.

With Marko's taste, like an especially sweet orange, still lingering, the feeling of his touch still fresh in her memory, Lindsey dialed the secure number Allison had given her some time ago. The gifted computer programmer worked as a code-breaker at the National Security Agency in Ft. Meade, Maryland, and lived in Chevy Chase. There was only a six-hour difference between Florence and Maryland.

They exchanged quick hellos. "Are you still with Christine in Phoenix?" Lindsey asked. Lindsey pictured Allison and her straight, shoulder-length hair, the soft yet keenly intelligent eyes.

"Yes. I'd appreciate your attention on this, Lindsey. Have you followed the kidnapping?"

"Yes. I called the Academy and listened to the recording by Christine. What's the latest?"

Lindsey grabbed a diet soda and headed into her office.

"FBI Agent Katie Rush traced Teal Arnett and Lena Poole to a gang of Colombian lowlifes."

Lindsey typed in her AA.gov password and then brought up the photos of the girls, their names listed below their photos.

"The short version," Allison said, "is that Katie went to Colombia and helped to free Lena, but Teal stayed with her kidnappers on purpose."

"A seventeen-year-old girl didn't escape when she had the chance?" Lindsey studied Teal's image. She looked like a normal teenager. Blond-streaked chestnut hair pulled back in a ponytail, clear hazel eyes, vivacious. And yet, those cheekbones… There was some American Indian blood in this girl somewhere. "She looks like the kind of person people call an 'old soul.' Is she…?"

"Teal is definitely special. I'll get to that in a minute. Lena says Teal thinks there is something much bigger going on. Something…well, strange and terrifying was how she put it.

The good news is that we know that Teal is on a plane from Colombia to London. I've contacted the British SAS and called in some favors. They'll have a team waiting when the plane lands, rescue Teal, and arrest the kidnappers. I've also twisted the arm of an NSA friend and we've got a secure satellite that will be able to pick up the plane's arrival at Heathrow."

"It looks like things will be okay, then. If you have the kidnappers, you can get to the bottom of this." Lindsey sat back, swigged her soda, and wondered where she fit in.

"Yes, and no. Teal has proven psychic abilities."

Wow. She picked up a pencil. "Okay."

"And, Teal, like Lena, is an amazingly fast runner. Amazingly fast."

Now tapping the pencil, Lindsey suddenly felt the conversation wasn't going in a direction she'd anticipated.

"Jazz was the third girl. Like all Athena girls, Jazz is very bright and has her own special gifts, but nothing beyond the ordinary. We think the attempt to take her was accidental. The kidnappers wanted Teal and Lena. The girls were lured to a pickup location. And Teal and Lena share something else. In addition to having these standout abilities, there is this profoundly disturbing fact: Their mothers underwent fertility treatments—at the very same clinic, the Women's Fertility Center in Zuni, New Mexico."

"It's unusual. Seems a rather large coincidence. But why so disturbing?"

"Lindsey, the clinic may have connections to Lab 33. We're starting to think that they may be Lab 33 babies."

"Oh, good God." Lindsey leaned forward in the chair and tossed the pencil onto the desk. "More egg babies?"

"Exactly. An Athena grad, Kim Valenti, is working with Lynn White to decipher the files that were rescued when we

took down Lab 33 a year and a half ago." Rage and disgust boiled in Allison's voice. "There's still much that we don't know about Aldrich Peters' genetic research. The encryption is difficult to break. Very frustrating for Kim and Lynn. Also, a lot of the data was destroyed. But, yes, it appears that Peters didn't just harvest Rainy's eggs. He took and then secretly manipulated the eggs of other women, as well."

"That's sick. Disgusting." Lindsey felt a chill on the back of her neck. "Isn't Lynn one of Rainy's 'daughters'?"

"Yes. It's a mess. If you knew Rainy's daughters, or Teal and Lena, you'd say it's a wonderful thing that they were born. But the method, if it's true that they are genetically modified egg babies created by Peters, is absolutely abhorrent." Allison's anger shifted to sadness. "If Rainy were alive, she'd be utterly confounded."

Lindsey recalled something that might explain Allison's deep passions. "Weren't you especially close to Rainy?"

"She was my best friend. She was the senior mentor to the Cassandras and every one of them will tell you that she made them the tight-knit, formidable group they became. A most extraordinary woman." She paused, sighed. "Rainy's murder—I still can't talk about it."

Last year, when the new science building was dedicated to Rainy, Lindsey had attended the ceremony. "At the dedication, I actually met Lynn. She seemed normal…but she's—" It seemed somehow rude to call Lynn genetically modified. "Enhanced in what way?"

"All three of Rainy's daughters, Lynn, Faith and Dawn, are a continual amazement. It's mind-blowing. Lynn is blindingly fast. Faith is psychic. But Dawn's abilities to heal herself are astonishing."

"How do I fit in?"

"We're beginning to worry that somehow, someone from the outside has learned of Teal and Lena's talents, and that's why they were taken. Katie is working with a psychic who is occasionally in contact with Teal. That's how they located the plane."

Lindsey still couldn't see a way to help.

"Katie thinks the kidnappers are middlemen," Allison continued, "and that they very likely don't know the real value of the girls or who is really behind the kidnapping."

"Ah!"

"Yes. That's why I've called you."

"You want me to scour my European underground contacts and see what's up?"

"They *are* going to London. That suggests that a British, or possibly other European party, is behind the whole thing. See what you can find out. Particularly anything with a whiff of genetics involved. I've set up a site here at the NSA that holds everything we have about Lab 33. I'll be updating it regularly about the kidnapping, as well. I'll have some photos of and files on the few individuals we know who worked with Peters and escaped the lab bust. We've also been able to decipher scraps of information on the genetic manipulation process. We know what was done, but not how. If you have any questions, call me. Katie and I watched from a satellite when the private jet carrying Teal took off from Bogotá. As I said already, we know the flight plan they filed said London's Heathrow as the final destination. Do you want to watch the arrival when the SAS guys pick her up in London? The plane is due to land around six this evening London time, seven your time."

"Absolutely."

Allison provided a Web address and two passwords that would give Lindsey access to the data on Lab 33, the kidnapping and the feeds from the NSA satellite. Lindsey checked

the clock on her computer screen. The plane would reach its destination in about twenty minutes.

"By the way," Allison added, "Lena said the kidnappers videotaped her and Teal using their abilities during staged escape attempts. This makes me think they wanted proof of what the girls could do."

Lindsey shook off another chill on her neck. "I understand."

They exchanged farewells and Allison hung up. Lindsey stood and stretched. She felt exhausted. The adrenaline rush from the skydiving, and from all that lovely physical contact with Marko, must have expended itself. She needed a caffeine hit before she spent time with the Lab 33 file.

As she made her way to the kitchen, a sad weight pressed on her heart for Teal, who would probably never know who her real father was. And who, if she was ever told the manner of her conception, would surely have some psychological hurdles to conquer.

Alternately sipping the strong cappuccino and scrolling through the kidnapping file, Lindsey learned a bit more. Most interesting, the psychic who'd worked with Katie Rush, Stefan Blackman, was pretty certain Teal could only make that kind of strong contact with someone like him, or like Teal herself.

She opened the file on Lab 33 and started to read about Aldrich Peters and his egg babies. At ten to seven, she put the NSA satellite feed onto one of her side screens and monitored the London airport as she continued to skim the egg baby file. The plane was late, but finally it landed and the SAS, fully armed, swarmed inside.

Ten minutes crawled by. After fifteen minutes of total in-activity, a handful of SAS men left the plane with three men, doubtless the cockpit crew, given their uniforms. Lindsey sat

up and leaned toward the screen. This didn't at all fit with what she'd anticipated. Where was the girl? The SAS men walked out with the crew, went to the cars, got in, and drove off.

Something was wrong.

Chapter 6

Lindsey continued to stare at the scene on her computer monitor. Clearly, Teal was not on the plane the SAS had just searched. Could Allison have gotten her information wrong?

Lindsey's secure cell phone rang. "Did you just see that?" Allison asked without preamble.

"Teal is not on the plane, right?"

"I know absolutely that she boarded their private jet in Bogotá and the flight plan called for the trip to be nonstop. When I learn more, I'll contact you."

"I'll be here. I'll be checking my contacts who may have information about this kidnapping or about genetic engineering."

"This changes everything. We thought we had her safe." Allison's voice held an edge of urgency.

Allison, who Lindsey had never known to be anything but amiable and polite, hung up without formalities, clearly terribly worried. Lindsey didn't just need information about

who was involved and why, she now needed to find where Teal might be. Assuming Teal was still alive.

Well, put that thought right out of your mind, Lindsey Novak! You will operate on the assumption that Teal is alive.

She kept two separate files for her information contacts: legit and shady. She opened up the legit file on her hard drive and scanned names: media contacts, private investigators and professionals in a wide range of disciplines that mostly related to art, archeology or anthropology. But there was one contact in genetics. Beatrix Riegler in Geneva of World Care Watchdogs International. WCWI exposed illegal traffickers in medical or scientific areas the way Amnesty International exposed tyrants who imprisoned people unjustly.

Lindsey combed through the file. Beatrix had sources for information about the sale of expired drugs sold on the black market. She monitored sales of untested drugs—like antiaging and cancer treatments. She dogged global traffickers of body organs for transplants and blocked sales to corporations or insurance companies of the medical files of private citizens. The latest scam Lindsey had discussed with Beatrix was the black market in stem cell lines stolen from legitimate laboratories. Unsuspecting buyers had no real way to know if the lines were contaminated.

The phrase *human genomes* grabbed Lindsey's attention. WCWI monitored the ongoing DNA project in Maldovia, a massive database of human genomes second only to the original one set up in Iceland. Every citizen gave a sample of their DNA and answered an extensive questionnaire about their medical and psychological history. This information was matched to the surprisingly complete birth and death records kept in the country for nearly two hundred years. WCWI made sure that the data collected on the population

wasn't sold to anyone except licensed users/researchers—medical, genetic, or historical—and under strict conditions. If someone were seeking illegal information on genetics, WCWI might hear of it.

Lindsey checked the clock—it was not too late to call. No one beyond her contacts must know what she was searching for, and even then, this kind of information wasn't something to be discussed via easily compromised phones or e-mails. For this she'd have to make contact in person.

Using her landline, she dialed the number. Beatrix had a sweet voice, and she answered at once with a cheery, "Beatrix *hier.*" The strains of Brahms played in the background mixed with sounds of laughter.

Lindsey's German was much worse than Beatrix's English. In English Lindsey explained that she needed to meet with Beatrix tomorrow.

"This is rather sudden, Lindsey."

"It's urgent."

Lindsey heard a long sigh. Beatrix owed Lindsey, but knew she was going to be asked for information. After a moment's silent pause, Beatrix said, "I'm swamped at work. What have you in mind?"

"I can take an early flight and meet you in the WCWI lobby at twelve-thirty."

"A bit later, please, I have a lunch meeting. One o'clock."

"I'll be there."

Satisfied, Lindsey hung up. This was the source most likely to pay off. She faxed a message to the charter company for the Learjets her father's business leased, telling them she'd need a 7:30 a.m. flight for the four-and-a-half-hour trip. Then she made a tuna sandwich and returned to the computer, eating as she pored over the legit files.

After forty minutes, she closed the files, discouraged. From a baggie in the freezer, she retrieved the key to a locked jewelry box in a bathroom drawer. In the box, under some fake jewelry and the bottom lining, lay the flash drive with the file of all her contacts that were not so legitimate. Of course, most of them did have some legitimate cover, but it was their contact with the darker world that put them on this list.

She inserted the flash drive into the computer and starting at the top, analyzed each entry. Although her eyelids grew heavy and her eyes burned, she didn't skip anyone.

The annoying ring of her landline phone shocked her awake. She lurched upright, her hand knocking her empty cup onto the Oriental carpet.

What time is it? The last time she remembered looking at the clock it had been eleven-thirty. It was now one-thirty in the morning.

She snatched up the phone receiver. Allison was again at the other end. "I know it's very early for you," Allison said. "I apologize."

"No problem, Allison."

"We have new information. Do you know Samantha St. John?"

"Athena alum?"

"Yes. She works for the CIA. Sam's been on this mess from the beginning. She accessed CIA satellite intel tracking the plane carrying Teal. The plane lost altitude and three people parachuted from it well before landing in Britain."

Lindsey sucked in a sharp breath. She saw herself only a day ago terrified as she stood at the open door of the plane with Marko holding her. Her heart went out to Teal. The poor girl, young and frightened and forced to leap from a plane.

"Obviously," Allison continued, "one of the three had to be Teal. They were likely picked up in the ocean south of Ireland. Authorities are searching, Lindsey, but you need to put this information into your calculations. I didn't want to wait until morning."

"I agree. I want to be in the loop at all times."

They hung up, but Lindsey was too awake now to go back to sleep. She returned to her list of possible sources. Ten names. Ten chances to find Teal, each less promising than the one before it. Her references were geared for art, not human trafficking. Beatrix just had to come through.

She went to the bedroom closet. To each of her contacts, she presented different but appropriate personas. For Beatrix it would be tailored and professional. And it was cold in Geneva. She started sorting through her outfits.

With her strategy in place, she set the alarm for 5:45. She needed to be at Novak Sicurezza Internazionale by seven in the morning to explain to K-bar, who was always at work before anyone else, that she needed a couple of days off.

Novak Sicurezza Internazionale, or NSI, occupied the two top floors of a lovingly renovated four-story building four winding blocks from the Uffizi Gallery. Views from K-bar's fourth-floor office were of the Ponte Vecchio, the river Arno, and the city's red-tile roofline. Other NSI offices looked onto the Campanile di Giotto in the Piazza Duomo.

Her father allowed her to kiss his cheek. He smelled of expensive cologne—like nutmeg—and was dressed, as always, in an impeccable Italian suit, this one a charcoal gray that complemented the white streaks in his dark-red hair. His eyes, like hers, were also gray. She only resembled her mother, Lindsey often thought, in personality: artistic, empa-

thetic and enthusiastic, not the natural daredevil that K-bar was. Loretta Novak had been a textbook illustrator. She'd died in an auto accident seven years ago, when Lindsey was twenty-one. The shocking loss had made Lindsey's relationship with her father even more complicated. And the emptiness still sometimes felt unbearable.

"So you are back safely and soundly from Naples," he grumbled.

"*And* with the recovered Artemisia on its way by special courier to its rightful owners."

K-bar dropped into the brown Italian leather swivel chair behind his desk and leaned back, making the leather creak. *K-bar Novak* was engraved on his gold nameplate. His employees might be surprised to know his name was Anton, but they all knew the story of how a young Special Forces commander with a few too many beers in his belly had chased a man out of a house of prostitution wielding his KA-BAR knife. Big-screen hero, her father. When she was young, she'd called him both "Daddy" and "K-bar," but the latter had stuck at some point.

"So. To what do I owe the honor of your appearance this early on a Monday morning?" he asked.

"I need to take a couple of days off."

"More art business? You know, I was counting on you to bring in the Berlin telecom account. They'll need advice and staffing for all their operations in Guatemala and Honduras. I don't have anyone as persuasive as you, Lindsey."

"Damiano can handle it."

Her father said nothing. She loved working for NSI and knew K-bar expected that one day she would take over the entire security business. But for now, he also accepted that she had another passion and never interfered when she asked

for time off. She would let him think it was another art recovery deal. He had no idea she took on operations for Athena or served now and then as a courier for the U.S. government.

"Okay. But keep me informed. By the way, how did Savin work out?"

"Marko's very…take-charge. But it all ended well. I actually went skydiving with him yesterday."

K-bar's eyebrows shot up. "Marko, huh? He's a good man on assignment, Linds. I've never employed better. But skydiving with him? I never can figure why women can't see when a man is just on the make."

Lindsey took a deep breath to keep from blushing. "It's not a problem. Really."

"Easy to say. Marko is a typical Italian male. New woman every month. Then when it doesn't work out for one reason or another, he's off again. Women are attracted to Marko Savin like barflies to beer."

She laughed but felt even luckier that she hadn't gone to bed with Marko. On some level, she'd sensed what K-bar was saying. "I agree that a woman would have to be nuts to get involved with him. Don't worry. I just considered it a chance to do something exciting that I'd never done before."

"You liked the skydiving?" He gave her a challenging look. It was always a question, always a test for him.

"Fabulous," she said, her voice firm.

"Sure you'd like it. Nothing after the Athena Academy would be too much. I've always been glad your mother and I sent you. It made you tough. You've always managed affairs of the heart just fine."

"Right. I'm a 'no tears' kind of woman." She was skilled

at walking away from anything sticky. Distancing herself. She was good at that.

He frowned and leaned forward, arms on the desk. "You sure this is just an art thing you're doing, Linds?"

She laughed. "If I told you what it was about, I'd hafta kill ya."

She stood, wanting to kiss him on the cheek again, but knowing the gesture would only make him uncomfortable, she left.

Chapter 7

Lindsey resisted the urge to tell the cabdriver once more how urgently she needed to be on time for a meeting at the *Place des Nations*. Beatrix expected her in five minutes, but they were stuck in traffic on Geneva's Pont du Mont Blanc. The cabbie couldn't change that miserable fact.

At 8:00 a.m., a half hour later than planned, she'd hurried aboard the private jet in Florence. In Geneva, she spent another fifteen precious minutes connecting with a taxi. It was now 12:55. If she didn't make it on time, Beatrix could use that as an excuse to avoid seeing her.

A young girl's life shouldn't depend on making transportation connections, Lindsey thought as the taxi burned fuel going nowhere fast.

The bridge spanned the southern tip of Lake Geneva where the lake flowed into the Rhone River. A thick layer of ice created by winds gusting off the lake covered benches on the

quay on the north shore in white. The famous Jet d'Eau geyser was, of course, turned off for the winter. Everything seemed pewter-colored, the buildings, the lake, the sky, the peaks of the Savoy Alps beyond Geneva. Despite the warmth of the cab and her black Cossack-style coat and boots, Lindsey shivered. The gray, cold day mirrored her mood.

Her cell phone rang. Beatrix. Lindsey explained the traffic mess and added, "I'll be no more than ten minutes late if I have to get out and run."

"You still wouldn't make it. But I was calling because I must cancel. My lunch appointment is lasting longer than anticipated."

Lindsey clutched the telephone, her pulse accelerating. *Remain calm.* "Just tell me where you are, and I'll meet you there afterward. I only need a few minutes, Beatrix."

"Do you realize that I could be fired just for being seen with you, if your line of work were discovered?"

Beatrix was overreacting. Probably. "I'll wait till your lunch meeting is over and—"

"No, Lindsey, I'm sorry. It's just impossible. I have to prepare for an—"

"Beatrix, when you hear how important this is—"

"Dear girl, I have all the high-priority crises I can handle, thank you very—"

"R-JUV-8."

The connection between them fell silent. Last year, Lindsey, in a dicey contact, had stumbled onto a shipment of an antiaging serum claiming to be chock-full of human growth hormone but being instead a mix of herbal derivatives and an illegal new, and very dangerous, stimulant. She'd involved Beatrix, who then received credit for the confiscation of six million dollars' worth of the product. Beatrix owed

Lindsey a favor or three. Since Lindsey worked outside of legal channels, Beatrix was extremely nervous about dealing with Lindsey.

"Are you there, Beatrix?"

Beatrix sighed. She gave Lindsey an address in the Paquis district, one of the few interesting areas in this city, which was, for such an international population, pizzazz-challenged. Behind practical gray stone walls, powerful people met and conducted world affairs. World Council of Churches. World Intellectual Property Organization. Eurovision. All those banks. Virtually every major NGO, and, of course, the diplomats. Geneva was unofficially the world capital of bureaucracies. "We can meet there. No one I know eats there and I can return to work quickly."

The menu outside indicated that the steamy restaurant, Bistro Eidelweiss, offered typical Swiss and French food. The tiny lobby was crowded. Lindsey immediately spotted Beatrix's brown chignon and on her way to Beatrix's table she passed hot fondues and soups, onion tarts, crepes with all kinds of fillings. Her stomach growled. All she'd eaten on the jet was a health bar topped off with coffee.

By the time an obviously overworked waiter signaled he'd soon be there to take Lindsey's order, Beatrix had already listened to Lindsey's story about the possibility of trafficking in genetically modified human embryos. She checked her BlackBerry, then shook her head.

"Whatever it is, it's monstrous," Beatrix said. "I'm sorry I avoided you. I'll help. We'll just have to work around your…fascinating connections—even if it means I lose my job." Her blue eyes sparkled with what looked like determination. "Kestonians are looking to develop human supersoldiers. Their new dictator, Vlados Zelasko, is a nut. The idea

is outrageous and impossible. We log the movements and actions of Kestonians wherever they turn up. I can provide you with the names of all the labs we're watching, but that's all I have that could be relevant."

Human supersoldiers. Extra strong. Extra fast. Superhuman eyesight and hearing. Human weapons. Exactly the kind of thing that would bring a huge black-market price. And maybe no longer an impossible idea at all. "That's exactly what I'm after—"

"Oh, my God!" Beatrix blurted out as she hid her face with her purse.

"What?" Lindsey said.

"The man that just came in, he works with me."

"Shall I—"

"Just leave, okay?"

Lindsey reached across the table and squeezed Beatrix's arm. "Done. You take care. And thank you."

No specific leads. No crepes. No fondue. She rose and made her way back to her coat and hat, her stomach demanding that she eat a mountain of pasta very soon.

Chapter 8

His name was Iacapo Donato, but Lindsey called him Jake. Known publicly as a highly respectable antiquities dealer, his various and nefarious ties extended far beyond the world of thousand-year-old *kraters,* coins, or marble busts—things that were occasionally reasons for Lindsey to contact him about underground rumblings. Jake had also helped her father find the son of a billionaire Moroccan, kidnapped despite her father's security team. Jake had learned of a shipment of illegals from Morocco into France. The smugglers of cheap labor also had the boy. NSI had successfully returned the boy to his family.

It was quite possible that Jake may have heard of something involving a kidnapping, maybe even specifically about the high-profile kidnapping of two American girls from Phoenix, Arizona. Checking AA.org, Lindsey saw that Shannon Connor, a former Athena Force student with no love for

her alma mater, had also been on international broadcasts of BBC and CNN, continuing her negative spotlight on the Athena Academy.

When Lindsey had called Jake from the jet to make sure he'd be at his private club in Florence tonight, he'd invited her instead to his villa for the evening. "I'll be showing off my latest acquisitions—and more," he said in his affected British accent. "Wear that marvelous jade gown."

So. Formal attire instead of cocktail. The dress was actually sage-green, but definitely the sexiest thing she'd ever owned. Stretch satin and nearly backless, its modest neckline set off a faux emerald necklace while the daring cut of the sides displayed more of her breasts than an unescorted woman in Italy should reveal. The floor-length sheath was slit only to midthigh level, but the back plunge and clinging fabric made underwear impossible.

Dress and heels. Nothing else, except necklace and earrings and her fluffy hunter-green mohair shawl.

Jake's villa lay sixteen kilometers from Florence. She pushed her Alfa Spider above the speed limit through the village of Malmantile, which had grown around an old Tuscan fortification on the road to Pisa. The villa, perched on the side of a shallow canyon, had been added onto a centuries-old square tower. Five stories tall, its crenellated top had been roofed and glassed in. The four-story front section and the three-story wings featured romantic balconies and rows of narrow arches. The place was architecturally stunning and filled with pricey antiques—all watched over by Jake's staff and all for sale.

Inside, she checked her shawl, ascended a broad staircase to the second floor, and worked her way through elegantly attired guests toward a buffet table without spotting Jake. He

was probably in the gaming room in the back where high-stakes, illegal baccarat and roulette were played. Jake's payoff from her for his efforts was always two things: five percent of her finder's fee and that, every time she came to him soliciting information, she spend at least two hours in the back room schmoozing with his gamblers and looking her most alluring.

Before she could select any of the gorgeous morsels on the buffet, a man's hand clapped her bare back and swept her from the table. Beppo, a glorified fence for stolen goods, whisked her onto a balcony into the shock of cold air and thrust her backward in a motion so smooth and sudden, she had no immediate defense. Smelling of stale tobacco, he leaned on top of her like a tango dancer bending over his partner, and the rail pressed painfully into her spine and kidneys.

Potted palms and heavy drapes prevented onlookers from inside the party witnessing what they'd assume were eager lovers if they did catch a glimpse. With one hand he clamped her throat, fingers digging in. She could barely breathe.

"No one will hear you scream over Iacapo's pretentious chamber music," he said.

She struggled, but with his other hand, he forced one of her arms behind her.

"Because of you," he snarled, "I had Interpol breathing down my back for weeks, *carabinieri* and private detectives, too." He pushed her head farther back as she thrashed. "Double-crossers get what they deserve."

Her hair clip loosened and fell into the canyon below—where she just might fall if she didn't do something. Her throat and back in agony, she still clutched her purse in her free hand. She tried to push him back. Failed. She screamed,

though weakly, to distract him. With her thumb, she flicked the clasp open, hooked fingers around the small container, let the bag drop, flipped the release and sprayed him full in the face with superstrength mace/pepper foam.

He screamed Italian swearwords, or tried to, and dropped to his knees.

"I don't think anyone can hear you over Iacapo's pretentious chamber music," she said as she picked up her purse. "And if guys leaned on you, Beppo, it wasn't because of me. Pieces looted from the Baghdad Museum are still too hot." Through Beppo and extremely discreetly, Lindsey had helped a benefactor of the museum return a Persian golden lion to the curators.

Shivering, she left him writhing on the balcony, shut the double doors, locked them and closed the heavy damask ivory drapes.

Jake, delighted to see her, joined her and squired her into the gaming room. She complied, inwardly seething with impatience. *This better pay off.* Every minute she played hostess, Teal Arnett might be gasping a last breath.

"I like your hair flying loose that way," Jake said. He was in his early fifties, pudgy and bearded, black hair shot through with gray. She stepped back a little. He said, "Did you know that musk from the male musk deer is worth three times more per ounce than gold on the black market? One of my many friends here—"

"Jake, I hate to interrupt but I have two urgent situations." She quickly explained, as if she were dealing with separate cases, a kidnapping of an American girl and any news of trafficking in human genetics, in any form.

"I have nothing for you." He frowned. "Do you hear banging?"

"That will be Beppo. We had…a little disagreement. I locked him onto the downstairs balcony."

Jake looked genuinely distressed. *"Il figlio di putana!* I'll have the bastard thrown out, Lindsey."

She put in her two hours as hostess, and when he finally returned to her as she was preparing to leave, he looked sad. "If I hear anything—"

"Time is critical, Jake. Wake me up if necessary."

Her secure cell phone rang as she opened the door to her apartment just before 1:00 a.m. Lindsey fetched it from her purse.

"Lindsey? It's Allison."

"Any news?" Lindsey felt suddenly breathless.

"I think so. Katie Rush's friend, Stefan, the psychic. He's receiving powerful mental impressions that he's sure come from Teal."

"Oh, thank God. She's still alive and okay, then?"

"The communication is more in images, not words. We can't be sure of much."

Lindsey grabbed a pen and paper. "Okay, I'm ready."

"He says he has an image of a city that looks old and European with drifts of snow on red-tile roofs, domes poking out of the snow, and spires. Lots of tall spires."

Lindsey scribbled—old, Europe, snow, spires. "That sounds like a hundred European cities this time of year."

"No kidding. Sam cross-referenced satellite visuals of snow across Europe with architecture and cities of over a hundred thousand and came up with over 250 cities."

Lindsey sighed. "Why didn't Stefan send messages sooner?"

Allison sighed, as well. "I feel sorry for this young man. He admitted to, at one point, seeing only blackness around

Teal. He secretly feared she'd died. Now he thinks she may have been drugged. Maybe they drug her off and on."

"I have a few more leads, but all I've turned up is that the Kestonians are interested in creating an army of genetically enhanced soldiers."

"Ye gods... Well, then the Kestonians would certainly be interested in any Lab 33 info that might be for sale."

Lindsey ended the call. "Lots of tall spires." God, she was tired. She couldn't think. *But that's why we have computer searches.*

She brought up the Web browser on her computer and entered *Europe city spires* and immediately found what she was struggling to remember. The first entry of hundreds of thousands of hits. "Golden city of spires." "City of a hundred spires." Prague.

Nothing was that easy. She knew better than to jump to the conclusion that she'd found the answer, but it was nice to have a name at the top of the list. Fatigue took possession of her body. She stared blankly, as if her mind was like the static of "snow" on a TV screen. She had to eat something.

She stumbled into her bedroom instead and took her shoes and gown off. Naked, she threw the covers back and focused on setting her alarm. Too tired to even wiggle into a night-shirt, she crashed onto her pillow.

To her amazement, she thought of Marko, picturing his arms around her, imagining the warmth of lying together.

No...

No.

Chapter 9

She woke after six hours, feeling desperate. In the shower, Lindsey remembered she'd had a disturbing nightmare of parachuting and landing in a cold, black sea. Like Teal must have done. The sea...

Of course!

Someone she'd only worked with indirectly was in her files. She threw on sweats, made peanut butter and jelly on toast and opened her file on a man who specialized in sea traffic in the Mediterranean and eastern Atlantic—including modern-day piracy and human smuggling. He lived in Pisa but choppered daily to the port of Livorno for his business. Anything coming in through a port, especially in cargo containers, came to his attention sooner or later. He paid hundreds of miscellaneous crew members, private and military. He knew the strictest ports in Europe, as well as the leakiest. She e-mailed him asking for any knowledge of a rescue at sea in

the Atlantic south of Ireland, along with where the ship may have docked and any subsequent destination, and left her cell phone number, urgently requesting a call.

Maybe finding Teal would require putting bits and pieces together instead of making one right connection. Her next contact, Cesare Fumagalli, required another shift in persona. He'd originally met her at one of his wild parties where she'd cornered a drugged-out thief from a tapestry buyback gone south. She'd caught the thief stealing one of Cesare's heirloom pinkie rings worth several thousand dollars—which proved the power of drugs, since no one sober would consider pulling such a stunt. Word was, the creep was never seen again. Ever. Lake Como was the deepest lake in Italy.

Cesare was the son of a bona fide Mafia don—whom he had, he bragged, badly disappointed. He wanted people to think he was legit but didn't even bother with a front to account for his lavish spending and fabulous villa on Lake Como. Still, Cesare had plenty of money and nobody messed with him. And he had amazing black-market contacts, buying and selling South African Krugerrands and diamonds, pharmaceuticals, legal and otherwise, religious icons, weapons, "black gold," which was not oil but caviar, regular gold and anything else of value.

He thought of Lindsey as hot and wild. It was cold up there now in the lake district, and she could wear her Cossack coat and boots, but after that, she'd look nothing like she had in Geneva. She pulled on purple tights. Then the spandex micromini. Sheer teal knit top—no bra. Gray silk shirt unbuttoned. Shabby-chic iridescent black wool scarf. Hair gelled, twisted up and clipped, teased and sprayed. Makeup. Layers of it around the eyes.

Ready.

With desperation snapping at her heels, she caught a train to Milan and another to Como, where she rented an Alfa Romeo and drove to the grand hotel in Bellagio for lunch at one, a three-hour trip, one-way.

Cesare was handsome and amusing, midthirties, very Latin with dark eyes and lashes any woman might covet. Their table overlooked the lake, everything in view lightly dusted with snow. Her Eurotrash persona attracted stares from the hotel's sedate clientele. Cesare wouldn't mind. He loved flaunting his outrageous lifestyle.

"You know," he said after he'd ordered, "I always thought my ancestors were cooks who smoked chickens."

"Oh? Let's see, fuma is smoke and galli, yeah, chicken. So what were they really?"

"I just learned that they smoked henhouses to keep chickens from squawking when they were being stolen. So, chicken thieves!"

They both laughed.

"Not cooks but crooks," she joked.

He stopped laughing.

My God, Lindsey, watch it. This Mafioso can make people who tell jokes at his expense disappear.

They chitchatted. He seemed interested in what she knew about musk from male musk deer and about Dacian coins. While eating eggplant parmesan, she spoke to him of the kidnapping. Almost as an afterthought she also explained she had another client interested in anything about genetic tampering with humans. Of all the things Cesare would be least likely to know about it was genetic engineering.

He held his hand out, indicating she should put her hand in his. She did. A passing busboy gawked and dropped a dish off his tray. Ignoring the boy completely, Cesare pulled her

hand up to his lips and kissed slowly, never taking his eyes off hers.

Still holding her hand, he said, "You found my ring, and I retrieved your tapestry. Mutual reciprocity is a wonderful thing." His gaze traveled to her breasts and then back to her eyes. "If I find information on this matter for you, the debt will again pass to you." He kissed her hand again. "And I'm sure we'll think of something mutually gratifying."

She drew a deep breath, and then laughed, as though thinking his comment was intended to be one of his fake Mafia jokes. "Right. I'd owe you one."

He smiled slightly, staring at her as if he knew something she didn't. Then from the inside pocket of his soft black leather jacket he pulled out something she never expected a playboy like Cesare to even know about, let alone own—a BlackBerry. "Let's check out the latest on the black-market eBay."

He clicked several times, frowned, began another series of clicks and smiled. "What do you think of this? 'Private auction. Anyone interested in genetic engineering of humans for medical or other uses would be interested in this sale item. Seven-figure bids only. Prospective buyers will be screened. Personal contact required.'" Another smile, one of victory. "It is to be in two days in Prague and there is a Prague contact number."

Oh, my God! Prague!

"This source is dated. It's been circulating for nearly four weeks. But it's big-time black market stuff."

Not surprising. Whoever had planned the kidnapping would have wanted to line up potential buyers. She stood, giving him a warm smile but feeling more than a bit displeased. Lots of competition would already have had this information for four weeks.

"You owe me, Lindsey."

* * *

Using her cell phone on the return train trips, Lindsey made flight reservations to Prague for the next morning. A call came in from her shipping contact in Lovorno, saying he'd traced an arrival in a charter ship under circumstances like those she'd described into the French port of St. Nazaire on the Bay of Biscay near Nantes, but he had no further information. But it didn't matter. No more contacts needed. Cesare had come through.

She punched another number and was connected to her dad's voice mail. "K-bar, it's me. Sorry I missed you. I'm leaving for Prague on a ten o'clock flight out of Rome in the morning. Czech Airlines. It's another…this art deal is more complex than I'd thought. Back in two or three days. Kisses. Bye."

Finally a call to Christine at the Academy.

"You did it! Excellent work, Lindsey," she said after listening to Lindsey's news. "Stefan has been bombarded again with images and feelings from Teal. She's in a place Stefan describes as a dungeon, and she's anxious, freaked out but not terrified. They must still be taking relatively good care of her. He senses her powerful loathing for a slender man with slicked-down hair. Mediterranean-looking."

"I'll need cover." She gave Christine her flight number and departure time.

"I'll put people on it immediately. You'll have a packet waiting at the Florence airport tomorrow morning. What we can't have ready for you by then will be waiting at the CIA safe house in Prague. I'm virtually certain I have the pull needed to arrange for the safe house to be your base. If not, I'll arrange something else."

"We're going to get Teal back," Lindsey said.

"Be careful, Lindsey. We don't want to lose you, too. The sense here is that something far more sinister than a kidnapping seems to be going on, we just don't know what."

Chapter 10

"I don't understand," Marko said to K-bar. K-bar sat behind that massive, virtually bare walnut desk playing with a silver letter opener that always reminded Marko of a dagger. "What is it you want me to do?"

"I think Lindsey may be into something more dangerous than she fully understands. I want you to follow her. She's not to know it, but I want you to keep on her tail. And should it become necessary, protect her."

Marko could not suppress a smile. The memory of Lindsey's body trembling against his rose in his mind, and he imagined the touch and taste of her lips and mouth. He also remembered that she'd tossed him out after setting him on fire. The woman was danger personified. "Mr. Novak, with all due respect, I've seen Lindsey in action. That is one woman who can take care of herself."

K-bar laughed. He tossed the letter opener onto the desk.

"Actually, you don't know the half of it. My daughter had training at a very special high school. A kind of military, survival, and spy academy for women. I sent her there so that she'd be able to handle herself."

"Then—"

K-bar held up a restraining hand. "You know about her art retrieval enterprises. She's told me she is taking off for Prague on another one, but I don't believe her. I can't explain why this one feels different. Maybe because she's never gone as far afield before. But there's also the fact that I have, for some time, suspected that she's involved with a government agency. Something she hasn't told me about. Officially can't."

"You think she's been spying?"

"Maybe. Many Athena Academy graduates go into government service. Often quite openly. Analysts for the NSA or CIA or FBI, for example. But I know some of them must be recruited for secret service. I'm worried that this is true for Lindsey."

"Still, you've said she's capable and I've seen it myself."

"Marko, this isn't a request. You work for me. This is your assignment. You follow her. To Prague or to hell if necessary. I want to know what she is doing. And most of all, I want to know someone I trust has her back. What I understand—and I doubt that Lindsey does—is that these agencies see their people as soldiers, unfortunately but necessarily disposable. My daughter is not disposable."

They lapsed into silence, K-bar's gaze boring right into Marko's skull. Sweat trickled at his neck. Following Lindsey Novak would be about the last thing in the world he'd want to do. If anything happened to her, Marko would be skewered and barbecued over the flame of K-bar's anger. And then

there was the fact that being around Lindsey sent Marko's hormones into overdrive.

K-bar broke the silence. "Aren't you going to ask me when and where?"

Early the next morning, Wednesday, as he settled into his coach-class seat on the commuter plane that would take him and Lindsey into Rome, Marko reminded himself again of his obligation to K-bar. The man had rescued him from the pit of the French Foreign Legion and given him the best job he'd ever had or ever dreamed of. Action. Adventure. Women. Interesting places. He loved working for NSI. He would do his damnedest to protect K-bar's daughter.

And he wouldn't actually have to *be* with Lindsey, just shadow her. Surely he could manage that. Couldn't he?

From Rome they would fly direct on Czech Airlines into Prague. K-bar had used his resources to find her schedule and had tickets waiting in Florence. Marko wore sunglasses, a heavy black winter overcoat and a black, shearling lamb Russian Ambassador's winter hat; Prague was going to be colder than Mont Blanc in a blizzard. About the only part of him not covered were his cheeks. Marko had boarded the plane after she had, and she never even looked up when he walked past.

He still wore the sunglasses and hat, although he had shed the coat. He'd chosen plain black wool slacks, black shoes and a brown, heavy knit sweater layered over a black shirt. He would pretty much blend into any Prague crowd. He leaned into the aisle and looked forward into business class. Lindsey was also sitting in an aisle seat. God, she looked gorgeous. A pale-blue turtleneck sweater set off her long, dark-red hair. In Naples he'd tagged her as tough. For sky-

diving she'd seemed sporty. This was an entirely different look—soft, feminine.

Yes, he wanted something better out of life. But it couldn't be with Lindsey Novak. She was a perfectionist, methodical, punctual. His thing was spontaneity. He'd grown up by his wits, *alla giornata,* hand to mouth, among the criminal elements along the canals of Venice. She was high-class with a first-rate education. They couldn't be more unsuited for anything permanent. He was far too quick to imagine himself struck by *il colpo di fulmine,* the thunderbolt of love. He could maybe have a better future life, but not with K-bar's daughter.

He'd brought a new Dan Brown novel. He pulled it from the magazine pocket in front of him, opened it, and forced his eyes to the first page of text.

Chapter 11

Lindsey spent the flight to Prague prepping for her identity as a Griffin Pharmaceuticals representative with the information provided just before the flight out of Rome by someone she presumed was CIA. Boring stuff but critical to staying alive.

She had the creepy feeling of being watched, but couldn't tell who her watcher might be. She'd glimpsed a man in the kind of black lamb hat seen all over Prague who made her nervous, but he seemed oblivious of her presence. Still, those sunglasses…

Had Cesare tipped off someone? Had her contact sent someone to follow her?

Inside the Ruzyne International Airport, the new portion of the North Terminal was ultramodern, shining with porcelain and marble tile. Shafts of cold winter sunlight brightened huge windows. After a casual glance, directly and in her cosmetic mirror, to make sure no one watched her, she found

phones and covered her free ear to block out human babble as she dialed the number provided in the notice on Cesare's BlackBerry.

"Speak," a male voice said in English. Given that news of the impending sale had been in English, she wasn't surprised. Potential buyers from many countries would be involved, and the language they would all be most likely to share was English.

"My name is Sylvia Platt. I am interested in the property for sale."

"What is your business and what is your country?" The man's voice was cultivated, his accent American.

"I represent a pharmaceutical company. If we meet, I'll provide more details. I'm an American, but my company is headquartered in Milan."

"A personal meeting is required. Where are you staying?"

"I have a reservation at the Grand Hotel Wenceslas, but I have some business before I go there." Her watch said ten minutes after eleven local time. "I should be able to check in by one o'clock and be available afterward."

"I shall meet you in the bar at fourteen-thirty. How will I recognize you?"

"Dark-red hair and wearing a black suit with a green stone pendant at the neck."

They broke off, and she strode out of the terminal into a stiff, cold February wind. Gray wisps of exhaled air curled up from the cold lips of people making ground connections. Fresh snow blanketed the distant roofs and fields. She gave a taxi driver the address of the CIA safe house, located in the Old Town section, the Stare Mesto. Christine clearly had come through with the CIA.

And then, magic. The city had escaped the ravages of the

Second World War and she'd expected something beautiful, but the dazzling sight of this jewel of a medieval city draped in winter white, set among pincushion hills, studded with the needle-pointed church spires, exceeded all of her expectations.

The massive gray Prague Castle and its towers surrounded the famous St. Vitus Cathedral, and together they dominated the city. Its four main spires reminded Lindsey of the sand castles of her childhood, carefully dripped into tall delicate points. What powerful kings and bishops must have ruled from here during the Middle Ages, Lindsey mused. One day, she would return to Prague for pleasure.

The taxi crossed a bridge over the Vltava River, which was frozen over, into Old Town. Built over hundreds of years of occupation, its architecture consisted of layers and facades, combining structures and styles.

As they swept through Old Town Square, across the Charles Bridge from the Prague Castle, the cabbie, clearly pleased to practice his English, said, "Buildings are Gothic, Renaissance and Baroque. You come back to see the famous clock. Astronomical. Every hour Twelve Apostles comes out."

He let her out in front of a tobacco shop on one of the narrow, cobbled streets radiating out from the square. Once inside, surrounded by the pungent smell of raw tobacco, which she actually loved and which reminded her of K-bar, she gave the password to the vendor. He directed her to a door at the rear of the shop.

A man reading a comic book asked for ID, then directed her into an elevator that took her down. She stepped out into familiar surroundings of desks, computers, phones and maps. "Welcome," said the thin, gray-haired man who greeted her. "My name is Bendrich. Your things are waiting."

"How did they build an underground complex like this without attracting a lot of attention in this quaint old part of the city?" Lindsey asked.

"Very astute question," Bendrich said, smiling for the first time. "The ground level used to be much lower when the original city was built over six hundred years ago. The Vltava River banks had no walls, and flooding over four hundred years left new soil. With all the invasions, looting and sacking, people just built on top of what was already there. Now everybody in Stare Mesto has Romanesque ruins in their cellars, and those original foundations had cellars, too. This building was bought because it went down twenty feet."

Lindsey found this both charming and unsettling, like building on top of a graveyard.

He handed her another packet that she presumed would have the appropriate passport and other papers for Sylvia Platt, Assistant Director of Marketing of Griffin Pharmaceuticals. "Currency?" she asked.

"You'll find it in the packet."

Only one other man and a young girl were present. Both had turned and smiled as she came in. They were now back to their work.

"Will you need a weapon?"

"No."

"I have been told to give you every assistance I can. I regret to say that, as you can see, we are a very small operation."

She filed the information away. Since her mission was information gathering, their short staffing shouldn't be a problem, but you never knew how an op might go.

Bendrich gave her a work area, and she combed through the information in the new packet. It turned out that Sam—

Samantha St. John, a fellow Athena alum—had been responsible for assembling it, and Lindsey was directed to contact Sam on her secure phone for any needed assistance. Lindsey needed more time to do homework before the meeting, but she needed to hurry if she didn't want to keep the man waiting. She had everything she could anticipate needing. Sam had done an excellent job. She thanked Bendrich, waved goodbye to the two others, and returned to the store level.

The Grand Hotel Wenceslas sat on a boulevard in the shopping and business heart of Prague, Wenceslas Square. The taxi driver pointed out the massive statue of a mounted Czech prince, St. Wenceslas. The bronze prince rode through the years, carrying his banner in the shadow of the grand Neo-Renaissance National Museum.

Her suite, a sitting room and bedroom, overlooked the street with a broad promenade down its center. She glanced out a window. Along the promenade, planters now covered in snow would, she imagined, come alive with blossoms in spring and summer. Warmly bundled shoppers and business-people hurried past, hunched against the biting chill of the wind. A sinking feeling settled in her gut. Lindsey was ensconced in luxury. Where was Teal? She had to be terrified. Why had the foolish girl chosen to stay with her captors? *Would I, at her age, have been so brave? Or foolhardy?*

Lindsey touched up her makeup for a colder look and smoothed her hair into a no-nonsense twist as she thought about the real nature of this mission. Now that genes could be easily manipulated—apparently snipped and pasted together at will—there was probably nothing that could stop the urge to tinker with humans. Bacteria could be made that secreted human insulin. Someone had created tobacco plants that glowed in the dark, able to synthesize an enzyme that

nature produced only in fireflies. Genetically manipulated pigs had meat with more fish oil than pig oil—something presumed to be healthier for the human diet. Why not zap a little gene into a woman's egg to make sure her son grew tall enough to be a pro basketball player? Or fast, like Teal was said to be? Or even able to read minds?

How could a man of science have no moral qualms about where he might be taking the human race?

She looked at herself in the mirror, armed with her appearance of cold, sophisticated competence, ready for battle.

Chapter 12

Marko slung his overnighter onto a queen-size bed in the Grand Hotel Wenceslas in a room on the same floor as Lindsey's. Whatever she was doing, it felt like a sting. He'd followed her to a tobacco shop, into which she'd disappeared for over an hour. The place clearly could not be just a tobacco shop. Now she'd registered at this expensive hotel.

Marko had bribed the bellman who'd taken her bag and knew she'd taken a suite on the top floor, room 602. She'd tipped extremely generously. Conclusion: The sting involved looking plush with money.

He stepped to the phone and punched the number for the registration desk. "I'm joining my friend here in the bar. Lindsey Novak. Could you ring her number please?"

"Certainly, sir." A pause followed, then "I'm sorry. We have no one registered by that name."

"Thank you." More confirmation that Lindsey wasn't acting as Lindsey.

Leaving his bag, he returned to the lobby. At the airport he'd bought a copy of the *London Times*. Now he found an unobtrusive spot where he could watch the bank of elevators. He removed his outer coat, but still wearing his hat and sunglasses, he settled in to wait.

At 2:20 he asked a bellman for coffee. A waitress appeared promptly; the coffee was strong and excellent.

At 2:28 a stunningly transformed Lindsey stepped out of an elevator and strode directly to the bar. Instead of the comfortable black slacks and soft blue sweater she'd worn on the plane, she wore a classy black suit, its skirt showing long, slender and impressively firm legs.

She'd pulled her hair severely away from her face, the effect bringing out her full lips, large gray eyes and high cheekbones. That artsy green stone at her neck and especially the bright red lipstick gave her a very you-don't-want-to-mess-with-me image. The words that came to his mind were *rich, cold* and *bad*.

He folded his paper, donned the heavy coat and followed her, hanging well back. Inside the bar she hesitated, presumably letting her eyes adjust to the dimmer light, then picked a booth near the back. He waited a moment, stepped inside, and slid onto a stool at the circular bar.

"Stoli, on ice," he said to the somber bartender.

A waiter had just delivered Lindsey her drink when a man still wearing his heavy winter topcoat joined her. Forty-fiveish, brown hair, five-ten or -eleven, goatee. Lindsey gestured for him to sit. He shrugged out of his coat and then slid into the booth opposite her.

Marko had expected to follow her out of the hotel, but now he had a chance to find out what name she was using. That

could be useful. He had to risk that she and the man would talk for at least ten minutes, possibly fifteen.

The man also ordered a drink. Excellent. Presumably he intended to take sufficient time to drink it. Marko stood and signaled the bartender. "I'll be back," he said, indicating with an open palm that the bartender wasn't to remove the drink.

The elevator, old and slow, returned him to the sixth floor. Using the phone in his room, he reached housekeeping. "We need two more towels in room 602, right away."

"I'll take care of it immediately," said the woman on the other end of the line.

"Immediately" turned out to be a wait of eight minutes. He picked an alcove from which he could watch the hallway leading to Lindsey's door, and he passed each second, praying that Lindsey was still in the bar. Finally the maid appeared with two towels draped over her arm.

He followed her down the hall, leaving enough time for her to knock, knock again, and then enter the room just before he arrived at the door. As she crossed a sitting room and entered the bathroom, he sped inside, scanning for any papers on the desk that might have Lindsey's name on them—nothing.

He crossed the sitting room and went into the bedroom, closing the door halfway. He waited quietly until the maid reappeared and left. It took only moments to check the luggage tags. The name on her bag was Sylvia Platt.

Back at the bar in just under twelve minutes, he sipped his drink as his heart rate dropped to normal. Lindsey was still talking to Mr. Goatee.

When her contact had introduced himself, he said she could call him James. Lindsey recognized him at once as the

man in the photos of Teal getting on the plane in Colombia. James was, in fact, the infamous Jeremy Loschetter, the scientist who had worked at Lab 33 and escaped, apparently taking with him an undetermined number of Lab 33 files or copies thereof. She'd taken a nice long drink of her white wine to give her a chance to hide her excitement.

For ten minutes now she had answered extremely pointless questions about her work at Griffin, put to her as though they were somehow profoundly significant: How long had she worked there? Did she like the company? Did she like her boss? What was her boss's name? How long had she lived in Milan? Had she been to Prague before?

Without being obvious, she checked her watch. Ten minutes of this drivel was long enough. "I'm sure your time is as valuable as mine. I'm here to learn more about a property you have for sale. Our company, of course, not only produces drugs, we produce a variety of chemical agents for the medical profession. We are specifically interested in cutting-edge work on fertility treatments and genetic modification of embryos. Particularly, as your information stated, genetic modifications of human embryos."

Loschetter gave her a cold stare. Ice-blue eyes gave his look an added chill. She loathed the vibes coming off him. His verbosity reeked of arrogance, and she knew he had been a collaborator in the sickening plan to steal and modify Rainy's eggs.

"I must, of course, check out your credentials, Ms. Platt. I will contact you tomorrow to let you know more details. There will be a demonstration of the sale items tomorrow evening. Attendance is required. You will be picked up."

"Fine." She wanted to ask specifically what he meant by sale items, but sensed the question might make him suspicious. If he wanted her to know, he would have told her.

Was Teal one of the sale items? Loschetter, with his cold blue eyes and condescending talk, felt utterly creepy, even if she hadn't known his slimy history. Teal shouldn't be in the clutches of such a man...no one should.

"There is something else," he continued. "Something I will explain when I contact you later." He leaned toward her and lowered his voice. Not to the point of whispering or actually sharing a secret, but a slight gesture that signaled that he considered the information special. Again she felt a rush of loathing for him. "Be prepared to make a rather unusual arrangement for the demonstration."

Chapter 13

On the edge of panic after meeting with the Platt woman, if that was her name, Jeremy Loschetter returned to his Opel sedan where Pietro waited, leaning against the hood and smoking a disgustingly sweet-smelling French cigarette. The urge to dismiss the slick-haired Italian crook from his service struck Jeremy again, but Pietro was useful and far too knowledgeable now to be dismissed. The only way Jeremy would allow Pietro to leave his service was via the grave.

Furious and frustrated, he recalled the day a year ago when Pietro entered his life. Slender and an inch shorter than Jeremy's five foot ten, Pietro confronted Jeremy about his illegal sales of stolen crucifixes and candlesticks from medieval artisans. Jeremy's legitimate research was, unfortunately, always starved for money, thus his need to stoop to black-market dealings. And his vulnerability to Pietro.

Pietro had refused to divulge how he had come by the in-

formation he'd used to blackmail Jeremy. For Pietro's silence he demanded a cut on the sales. Their arrangement had grown over time. At first Pietro extended their dealings to include triptychs and occasional small paintings, but now he was in on the kidnapping and knew the reason for it. Pietro had even offered to line up the men required, claiming they were absolutely trustworthy and would do whatever was necessary.

Jeremy had asked Pietro if he was up to something that might get physical, maybe involve some killing. He'd been stunned when Pietro said, "Whatever needs doing, I'm the man." He'd said it totally without expression. Jeremy considered himself a scientist, forced by circumstances to do some unfortunate things. He was, of course, not a brute. Jeremy had, for the first time, felt a bit afraid of Pietro.

Jeremy opened the door to the passenger side and took a seat. "Take me to the laboratory."

Taking what Jeremy felt was a glacially slow time putting out his cigarette—slow enough to be insolent—Pietro finally climbed in and started the motor. The drive to the Loschetter Laboratory would take no more than twenty minutes, traffic still being relatively light.

After a meeting with his development team for the reproductive technologies he'd dubbed Fertilizen, which should take no more than thirty minutes, Jeremy would taxi to meet the last representative for his potential buyers, a man from Hong Kong. After that, he could return, by taxi, to the chateau, an expensive but necessary cost.

Jeremy considered again his nervous reaction to Sylvia Platt. Beautiful. Lusciously so. But cold. What was it about her confident speech or demeanor that had set off alarm bells? He'd probed her, asked her questions ostensibly about her work, but he didn't buy it.

"I have a bad feeling about this Platt woman."

Pietro waited, judiciously letting Jeremy further collect his thoughts.

"She's about the same age as the agent in Colombia, that Katie Rush, who very nearly ruined this whole operation. And confident. Tough. Rush is an Athena Academy graduate. This woman gives me the same impression."

Pietro cast him a surprised look. "How can that be?"

"I don't know. But I have a gut feeling."

Jeremy felt himself sweating. It wasn't that the car was overheated. It was the goddamn woman, Platt. And A. In truth, A was really running this operation, and if Jeremy blew it, he had no doubt that A would make him pay dearly. Perhaps even have him killed.

When the first girl got away, someone had tried to kill him. He suspected A. Who else could know about his role in the kidnapping?

In the end, A had arranged for Colombians to do the job. Jeremy hadn't needed Pietro. The kidnapping of the girls produced from Lab 33 had, in fact, been the sole idea of the mysterious A. Even the Colombian, Tulio, had admitted to Jeremy that A had blackmailed him into doing the kidnapping, and he swore he didn't know who his blackmailer was, only that A had proven to have enough on Tulio's drug operation to shut him down cold.

Since A was blackmailing Jeremy—able to turn him in to the American authorities at any time as the sole possessor of papers and data he'd taken with him about Lab 33's genetic enhancement techniques—Jeremy had no choice but to execute A's demand. Moreover, he'd repeatedly been given extremely knowledgeable assistance by A during the planning of the girls' capture. His blackmailer with the spidery hand-

writing had sources of information that, on occasion, had left Jeremy dazzled.

But A didn't know everything, and when Fertilizen finally paid off and went into production, Jeremy would at last become independently wealthy. Maybe he could find a way, then, to buy himself away from the bastard with the spidery script. Until then, however, there was a need to protect himself and find research money in this black-market backwater of the research world.

It was risky—even frightening sometimes—to think of double-dealing A, but it was necessary. Hadn't A tried to kill him? He was fully justified cutting a slice off the bacon here and there. These sales would bring in fabulous sums.

"What if Platt isn't from Athena?" Pietro asked. "She claimed to be from a pharmaceutical company. Pharmaceutical companies have big money."

Pietro was obviously concerned about any potential loss of profit. And it was possible, just possible, that Jeremy might be overreacting.

They turned into the street housing the laboratory. Pietro braked, waiting until a horse-drawn cart, some hick from the sticks, moved out of the way. When they could move again, Pietro asked, "So what do you want me to do?"

"I can't afford to take risks. I want her removed from the picture."

"Permanently?"

"Yes. As soon as you can. I want it done before I go to sleep tonight. Make it look like a robbery gone bad."

They stopped at the front of the laboratory, a fully renovated eighteenth-century building with a restored original facade. Pietro gave him that emotionless, cold stare. "Did you get a bug on her?"

"Yes."

"Then consider it done."

It was a shame, Jeremy thought. Sylvia Platt was intelligent and beautiful. He would rather make a mistress of such a woman, but if she was from Athena, or even from some official government or law enforcement agency, she had to be eliminated—and swiftly.

He stepped out of the car into welcome cool air but leaned back down, holding the door open. "Tomorrow is critical. Will the Arnett girl be...cooperative?"

"Don't worry. By tomorrow night the little telepath will be dying to cooperate." Apparently amused by his lame pun, Pietro offered a stiff smile that failed to reach his cold eyes.

In time I will eliminate Pietro.

Chapter 14

When Lindsey and her goateed contact left the hotel's lounge and headed into the lobby, Marko laid cash on the bar to cover his drink, grabbed his coat and followed them. Without speaking again to the man, Lindsey took the elevator.

Marko followed Goatee outside and watched him stop twenty yards away where another man, slightly shorter and smoking, leaned against a car. By pretending to look into a display window, Marko could watch them in the glass reflection.

The smoker, he thought, had a familiar look. Growing up in *la malavita di Venice* among a family of thieves, Marko had encountered more than a few really bad types, even a man his father assured him was a contract killer. The FFL had been home to other rough men. The smoker gave off that same aura. Mean.

As they drove off, Marko entered the license plate number into his cell phone's data bank. The smell of something meaty turned his head and his stomach growled. Across the street

from the hotel, on the promenade, a vendor was peddling wurst. Marko sent the license number to K-bar with a message explaining that Lindsey had met this man. Marko would send more information later.

Excited to be able to tell Sam that she'd actually met Jeremy Loschetter, Lindsey hurried to her room. One of the big plusses of staying in a five-star hotel pretty much anywhere in the world was that they provided WiFi access to the Internet. Lindsey accessed AA.gov. Before calling Sam, she wanted a visual image of her contact and the site provided graduation photos of all the Athena girls.

While she waited for the site to load, she checked her purse and smiled when she discovered a tiny slit in the lining through which Jeremy had slipped a slim transmitter. Fortunately, the device didn't include a microphone; she wouldn't have to guard her every spoken word.

The face of a younger Samantha St. John appeared on Lindsey's laptop screen. At once she placed Sam. Lindsey had met and talked briefly with her at the Athena Academy science building dedication. No question but that Sam had a beautiful face in a Slavic mold. Strong cheekbones and large, ice-blue eyes were framed by shoulder-length white-blond hair. She had worn just a touch of pink lipstick for the photo.

Lindsey also checked Sam out on the AA.gov section that profiled Athena graduates. She was a certified genius and computer whiz, a master of languages and a CIA linguist.

She dialed Sam's line and when they connected Lindsey said, "I have my papers. I've made contact, and Jeremy Loschetter came in person. This is absolutely Lab 33 related and he's at the heart of whatever is going down."

"That's huge progress. I'll pass everything to Christine.

Allison is also keeping tabs as best she can at the NSA. She has pretty highly placed friends there."

Lindsey described their meeting and told Sam about the demonstration of the sale items that would take place tomorrow. "I gave him the chance to bug me, and he did. I spilled my drink, went to get a napkin and left my purse."

"Perfect."

"My guess is that he's bugging the representatives of every potential buyer. He's going to want to know where I go, and I'm sure he'll be checking out everything I told him about Griffin Pharmaceutical."

"Don't fret. We have you totally covered at the pharmaceutical, your passport…everything."

"I plan to kill time waiting the way any woman who has a fondness for art would do in Prague. And I need to get out of this room, make myself available to them."

"I checked with Bendrich at the safe house. He says he can't spare anyone to back you up. So you're pretty much on your own."

"I can take care of myself."

"Please be extra careful, Lindsey."

Marko watched the hotel entrance. He'd taken his time consuming the hot spicy wurst on a stick. *Delizioso.* The lobby would be warm, but he'd already spent a lot of time there. It might arouse suspicion. On the other hand, he was damn cold. He'd been outside for fifteen minutes, stomping his feet to keep them from freezing. The sky was dark gray. Maybe it would snow. If she didn't come out soon, he'd have to go back inside.

After breaking off with Sam, Lindsey checked her e-mail, looking for anything from delphi@oracle.org. For three years

Lindsey had been an Oracle agent, recruited by a mysterious person she knew only as Delphi. She had been contacted, she was told, because of the skills she had honed at Athena and because of her access to the black market. Her assignments would come only from Delphi. She would report only to Delphi. She would never know the identity of any other Oracle agent.

Every assignment so far had been as a courier. Today, there was no message.

She then brought up her own personal Web site, www.adiana.net. Here she had created several secure pages of information she found useful when traveling: great restaurants where she'd eaten or where she'd like to eat and similar lists for things like hotels, art museums and art dealers.

After taking down three addresses—one of the art dealers was apparently located right here on Wenceslas Plaza—she changed back into her slacks, sweater and warm boots, grabbed her coat, gloves, purse and woolen hat and headed out for some fun.

She spent forty minutes in the gallery shop of Ctirad Hruza. He carried several pieces by Nikola Savic, whose colorful acrylics—always an explosion of shapes and movement—Lindsey admired. Lindsey's business dealt mostly with old art, but she painted modern and felt most joyful when losing herself in great modern works, Jackson Pollock and Georgia O'Keeffe being her favorites.

A taxi spirited her across the river to Malá Strana, or Little Town, a beautiful baroque sector where the gallery of Vavrinec Nejezchleb was located, not far from the famous Charles Bridge. Malá Strana nestled around the base of Prague Castle. What had once been homes of burghers had been converted into quaint shops, restaurants and pubs.

For a moment, before she stepped into the shop, Lindsey

felt that sixth-sense itch of being followed. She whirled around. No more than a handful of people walked the snow-covered street. A figure disappeared into a shop. Could have been following her. Maybe not.

For half an hour Vavrinec Nejezchleb delighted in showing her his wares, including several of Jiri Borsky's strong figurative works, like Picassos but with a gentler spirit. At one point the tinkle of a bell over the door preceded a slender man with slicked-down hair. He caught her attention because he didn't wear a hat and didn't stay long. Jeremy himself wouldn't be following her, so maybe this was his man, checking her out. A chill moved down her spine. Jeremy's looks were creepy, but not especially menacing. This man looked cruel.

Watch your back, Lindsey!

She'd already decided that if someone jumped her, she would not go into aikido mode. She was to be strictly a businessperson. If necessary, she'd have to take a beating to stay in character.

It was now nearly five o'clock. A travel brochure had said that the Charles Bridge was a must-see, and that sunset was a good time to visit because one could view the fully lighted Prague castle against the evening sky. She asked Vavrinec for the best place to have a cup of coffee until sunset.

His directions sent her down a narrow, cobbled side street. Converted burgher homes with red-tiled roofs, four and five stories high, created a canyon of city walls on either side. Pedestrian traffic was steady but light.

She'd nearly reached the coffee shop when a black sedan braked beside her. Two men wearing black ski masks leaped out from the passenger side.

Loschetter! She hunched, prepared to fight, but caught herself in time. *Stay in cover!* This was a move to test her.

She faked an ear-shattering shriek and swung her purse, spinning and slipping awkwardly, as though unable to get footing in the snow. The purse slid harmlessly off the bigger man.

The second man grabbed her from the rear around the neck and pulled her against his chest. She shrieked again and shouted, "Help!" as she resisted her trained response to bite his hand, whirl and kick his balls.

She pushed against him and they staggered backward a couple of steps. The taller creep was closing in when a man in black wearing dark sunglasses crashed into him.

The man holding her spun them both around and threw Lindsey against the building, into the front of a bookstore. She slid to the ground, striking a wooden book rack as she fell. She ignored a sudden, sharp burning sensation on her neck, scrambling to regain her footing.

Chapter 15

Marko made a flying tackle into the hooded goon with the knife, sunglasses falling off on impact. At the corner of his vision he saw Lindsey fall. How could Lindsey be so foolish as to be out alone on the lightly trafficked street? How could this woman, who was so extremely capable when dealing with criminals, be so clumsy in her own defense?

He and his opponent scrambled to their feet. The man had lost the knife in the snow. He took a swing and planted a solid right to Marko's cheek. Marko returned the blow with one of his own to the man's stomach.

The man doubled over, at the same time yelling something in strangled Czech and waving a hand toward the car. Lindsey stumbled into Marko's arms. She grabbed him as though terrified, but when she spoke she whispered, "Let them go."

The two men jumped into the car, which squealed with the sound of tires burning rubber as they took off.

Still in Marko's arms, Lindsey looked up at him. She had a cut on her neck, and her pulse pounded in the crook of her throat. She looked angry, but safe. A wild, crazed urge to kiss her welled up in him.

She pushed herself out of his arms as an elderly Czech couple and a pair of Anglo girls rushed up. "Are you all right?" one of the girls asked with an American accent. The bookstore owner stepped outside his door, taking in the scene.

Lindsey smiled and assured everyone, first in Italian and then English, that she was fine. The older woman pointed to Lindsey's neck and handed her a handkerchief. After more reassuring gestures from Lindsey, the owner returned to the comfort of his store and the concerned citizens went their ways.

Her face flushed, pressing the handkerchief to the wound, Lindsey turned to Marko. He flashed on the arousing thought that the earlier fake hug of terror might be followed by a hug of gratitude.

"You idiot!" she said quietly, but with force. "What are you doing here?"

Idiot! Some gratitude!

Furious, he countered. "What are *you* doing here, *Sylvia?*"

Chapter 16

If Marko had slapped her, Lindsey could not have been more stunned. "Sylvia?" she said, repeating him.

"Right. Sylvia Platt."

"Damn it! You've been following me."

"Since you—we—left Florence."

"You have no right—"

"It wasn't my choice. K-bar is worried about you."

"My father sent you?"

"Sounds harsh when you put it that way. But true."

So much anger was boiling inside that she couldn't find words to express it. A young girl's life was on the line, and her father's meddling and Marko's interference may have compromised her entire mission. She stared at him, wanting to scream, *You may have killed her!* But she choked it back.

She clenched a fist, fighting for control of whirling emotions. When he'd held her in his arms, she had looked up

at him, furious, her heart racing. But she'd had the insane thought that he was going to kiss her, and more insane still, she wanted him to in spite of the fact that he'd ruined everything. "I'm here for a purpose. I know exactly what I'm doing. And you have probably messed up something very important."

"Messed up? The guy was going to kill you."

"It was a test, Marko. At worst they might have taken me with them, and that would have served my purpose fine. Now you've botched that."

"He wasn't taking you anywhere. What about the knife?"

"Knife?"

Marko snorted. "The knife he was going to stick into your guts."

"There was no knife."

Marko grabbed her gloved hand and tugged her toward snow piled beside the bookstore doorway. Bending down, he brushed a few inches of white fluff aside and then, saying nothing, held out a serrated knife with an open five-inch switchblade.

A shiver swept through her, head to toe. Had Loschetter sent the men to kill her? It was possible, and it would mean that he didn't buy her cover story and suspected she was some sort of agent. On the other hand, maybe the knife was simply to be used to persuade her to come with them. There was no way to know. And she could certainly understand, now, why Marko had felt the need to barge in.

She looked around for her purse. Gone. That was a plus. She was free of the tracking device and her faked credentials would soon be in Loschetter's hands. Maybe they would convince him of her authenticity.

"Okay." She felt herself relaxing. "I'll concede you may have thought they were going to harm me."

"Well, that's a crazy thing to say. Two hooded men leap at you. What else would I think? That they were going to ask if you wanted a tour? Even if he hadn't had a knife."

Again she felt a chill. "Let's walk. I'm getting cold just standing here." He retrieved his dark glasses, and then she led them toward the Charles Bridge where they could easily find taxis. "I have a room in a hotel."

"I know. I also took a room there."

"In my hotel! Unbelievable! I'm furious with myself that I didn't spot you."

"Your dad employs me because I'm good at what I do. So what's going on, Lindsey?"

"I can't say. And it's a damn shame that K-bar has interfered."

"He's a father. He thinks you may be into something more dangerous than an art buyback."

"Marko, I can't tell you what I'm doing. But I believe this was just a test. To see how I would respond. Basically to see if I'm who I'm pretending to be, a representative of a pharmaceutical company."

"Well, if that was your intention, you fooled me." He chuckled. "K-bar told me you attended a school for girl spies that taught you everything from survival techniques to martial arts to bomb-making, but it looked to me from that flaky swing of your purse that you were in big trouble."

"Well, let's hope they think so, too. The problem is, they need to think I'm alone, not with a partner."

They trekked down narrow old streets, snow piled in banks beside barren trees. The arched spans of the Gothic bridge came into view. Built in the middle ages, Charles Bridge no longer carried vehicles, only foot traffic. Even on a thirty-degree winter day, a few artists, musicians, vendors and tour-

ists sold wares or milled about. The towers on both ends offered climbers great views of the beautiful old city.

"They can just as well think I'm some guy on the street who barged in to rescue a stranger and is now escorting the frightened lady with no money and no papers back to her hotel."

They reached the entry to the bridge and the clusters of people crossing it. She turned and looked up at the massive castle, the largest castle complex in Europe, maybe the world, now lighted for the night as the sun was setting. "They say the view from the bridge is spectacular. Let's walk across. There will be cabs on the other side."

They started across, and he took her arm, as though they were friends on a stroll, pulling her close against him. She liked the feel of being beside Marko, a man of action. Half an hour had passed since that look in his eyes when she thought he might kiss her. And she'd wanted him to, hadn't she? She could feel his attentiveness as they moved side by side, making their steps match. If she smiled at him in this moment, she was pretty certain that he'd melt. This thought warmed her, despite the cold and the shivers from the adrenaline letdown. Suddenly she felt gratitude. He had risked himself to save her. "I'm calming down. I need to thank you for trying to help me."

"Thanks gratefully accepted. In return, will you tell me what's going on?"

She shook her head, and he didn't press further.

An old man bundled in dark gray was roasting chestnuts the old-fashioned way over heated sand with added sugar. The nuts absorbed the sugar from the sand while they toasted, making the sweet chestnuts even sweeter. She heard the "popo-popo" sounds the nuts emitted when the shells turned

brown, indicating that the toasting was done. The vendor handed Marko a bag, and Lindsey savored the taste of her first golden bite.

For a while they enjoyed the chestnuts and the stunning view of a fairy-tale castle covered in white snow and cast against a pastel mauve-and-purple sunset. Her reverie was abruptly broken when Marko said, "I should get you to the hotel. You should clean the wound on your neck."

What was wrong with her? Falling into a fairy tale when lives were at stake!

Several imposing statues lined both sides of the bridge, and as they passed one, a patch on the statue's dark patina caught Lindsey's attention. "Wait, Marko," she said, and took his hand, drawing him to the statue. The shiny spot covered a woman and a dog on a relief scene near the statue's base. "Legend has it," she said, "that if you rub the dog's nose, a secret will be revealed."

She took off her glove. The secret she wanted to know—where Teal was being kept. She rubbed the dog's nose. But she gave the nose a second burnishing because she also wanted Marko to somehow know about the secret side of herself. Despite what she knew had to be, she would love to confide in Marko.

"You want to have a secret revealed?" she asked, waiting to see if he'd join in the fun with her.

"Sure," he said. He took off his glove and gave the dog's nose a vigorous polishing.

"So can I tell you my wish?" he asked as he took her arm and drew her close again, "or will that cancel the spell?"

She leaned into him and looked up at his face. "I don't know. The brochure I read didn't say."

He grinned, a lovely smile with straight, white teeth and

lips edged by corners that turned up. "Then we better not take a chance. Better keep our wishes to ourselves. I definitely want mine to come true."

Snow started falling when they reached the other end of the bridge. They found a taxi stand and were soon back at the hotel.

At the elevators she said, "I'm on the sixth floor."

"So am I."

"Jeez, Marko."

They rode up in silence, but when they stepped out, he said, "I have a small emergency travel kit with antiseptic. I could go get it."

Marko. In her room with her. The two of them alone. She should say no.

"Sure. That would be fine."

Chapter 17

The more Jeremy Loschetter obsessed over the possibility that an Athena woman had discovered his whereabouts, the more he felt as though something had him by the throat. Darkness had settled in on the old chateau. The place had proved difficult to light. No matter how much wattage burned, the angles of the vaulted ceilings, beams, nooks and crannies all cast black shadows.

He sat near the fire in the den with his latest missive from A in his hand, the one that had explained exactly how, where and when to hook up with Tulio for the Colombian connection of the kidnapping. He stared at the letterhead, a spider's web. He was frequently drawn to these letters and studied them for style, trying to figure out who A could be. What age? What nationality?

He could tell nothing. "May you be skinned and burned alive!"

His predicament was his own fault, which made it all the more maddening. Knowing that before his death, Aldrich Peters had been dealing with this A, after fleeing the lab, Jeremy had used information he'd stolen to contact A, thinking he could do the same business as Peters. What a stupid, stupid move that had been. All for love of excellence in science, for the chance at the recognition he deserved, the chance to stagger the smug geneticists of the world with his own brilliance. But now A called the shots. A knew too much about him, would sabotage him at every turn if he didn't play ball. Tomorrow night's auction could change all that. The future of his new fertility company depended on it.

He returned the letter to the safe, closed its door, and threw himself in anguish and disgust into the swivel chair.

When will Pietro show? I must know that the new woman is no longer a threat.

The auction of genetic secrets seemed to be veering out of control. First, the Platt woman, a new bidder at the last moment. Then the meeting with Foo Hai, the representative from Hong Kong, had taken place in the bar of the Hotel Vlensk, in the middle of Old Town. It had gone well, although he found the man even more menacing in his silence than Pietro could sometimes be. Jeremy had returned to the chateau at five-thirty. It was now approaching six o'clock.

His gut was in knots. He pictured angry ulcerous lesions just where his stomach joined his duodenum, undefended against the hot baths of hydrochloric acid and pepsin ever since he'd started this project. *Take a deep breath!*

He pictured the black, poisonous spider in his shoe. That was surely no accident. Had A punished him for losing the second girl? Hired one of the Colombians to try and kill him? The knot at his duodenum squeezed tighter.

He would like to think of himself as fearless in the pursuit of science, but his body seemed to think otherwise. There was no going back, though. He could see no other route of escape from A's hold on him. And yet, he had the Arnett girl. He had the Lab 33 files. He, and he alone, knew all aspects of the procedures. He would not back down from his plan to cut A out of his profit.

Still, so much could go wrong.

The woman he hired for cleaning and making evening meals had set a fire in the fireplace. He rose and stood with his back to the cedar-scented blaze, thinking of the strange taste of his tea at dinner. Could A have sent someone here to poison him? A knock on the door caused him to flinch. "Enter!" he called out.

The very sight of Pietro caused that miserable fist in his stomach to clamp down again. "Is she dead?" Jeremy asked.

In his hand, Pietro held a woman's black purse. "You got this woman wrong."

"What the hell do you mean?"

"She is not an Athena woman, that is certain."

"Is she dead?" Jeremy repeated.

"No. But not because we had any trouble with her. A man from the street tried to be a hero."

For a moment, anger and fear choked off his breath, then he exploded. "You didn't kill her?"

"Cool down. This is no problem. She was a screaming, hysterical woman. If the man had not interfered, I could have killed her easy. Now we have her papers. We can check her out."

"Maybe the man was with her. A partner."

"No. He just came running down the street."

"Hmmm." Certainly he would not expect a woman who was spying for Athena in this kind of undercover operation

to have a partner backing her up in the way Pietro had described. Athena women were famous for being able to handle a man like Pietro on their own, the reason Jeremy had insisted that Pietro take Hudak along.

Pietro continued. "We should not panic. We check out her papers. There is a passport. Credit cards. An international driver's license. There's a bank debit card from an Italian bank. I can handle most of it."

Jeremy hated to turn to A's astonishing resources, but A had ways of checking out information and accounts. He refused to deal with A directly, though—Pietro would handle it. "All right. Contact A. I already called the woman's company. Griffin Pharmaceuticals. They confirmed that Sylvia Platt works for them."

Jeremy felt stymied, but the knot in his stomach slowly uncoiled. He moved from the fire, which now felt too warm, and sat again at the desk. If A found out that Jeremy had rejected a legitimate bidder, and a possibly very high bidder at that, there could be serious and unpleasant repercussions. It might have been disastrous to have killed her. Perhaps it was good fortune that Pietro had failed.

Pietro approached the desk, and leaning down with both hands on it, said, "The transmitter is off the Platt woman. Send Hudak to the hotel. See if we can pick her up. He is a good shadow."

Jeremy said nothing. Pietro, as always, was pushing him, the meat-brained sleaze. As Pietro turned to leave, Jeremy glimpsed what looked like a small tattoo of a spiderweb hidden beneath Pietro's collar-length hair. He'd had no reason to connect A with Pietro before, but a chill wiggled down Jeremy's spine. "What is the significance of the tattoo you have on your neck?"

Pietro slowly turned to face him. "Why the fuck you ask that?"

"I don't know exactly."

"Well, there is no significance. I just liked it. Why you always wear that ring?"

"The ring stands for excellence in learning."

"Well, my tattoo stands for time in jail."

They were at a draw, but the images of a spider's web on A's letter and on Pietro's neck… Jeremy hated this kind of coincidence.

For the moment he must let it go. "Do as you say. Check out everything and have Hudak tail her."

If the beautiful Sylvia Platt could not pass inspection, he could send Pietro again. Surely Pietro would not screw up twice.

Pietro left and Jeremy returned to the fire, a chill in his bones despite the heat.

Chapter 18

Marko knocked on the door to Lindsey's hotel room with his emergency travel kit in hand, still wearing his coat. Keep the coat on, he advised himself. Lindsey would understand that he didn't intend to be invited in.

She's K-bar's daughter. You will keep your damn hands off.

She opened the door and smiled. The black suit, the slicked-back dark-red hair, everything about her still said *dangerous,* but sweet Madonna, she was beautiful.

"Come in," she said. "You must see this exquisite stove."

He knew what she meant about the stove. The hotel receptionist had explained when Marko registered that one of the hotel's features was that the suites were not only decorated with authentic reproductions of period furniture, each was warmed by an antique, wood-burning ceramic tile stove.

A little voice at the back of his mind whispered, "Say no." But hadn't K-bar sent him here to find out what she was

doing? Wasn't this the perfect time to squeeze out the juice, while she was relieved, recovering from stress?

He went in, for the second time today, but now the room was toasty. Apparently staff fired up the stove early in the evening so that guests did not return to a cold suite. His single room provided no such luxury.

"Let me take your coat," Lindsey said.

She moved close to him and he smelled just the hint of a perfume that reminded him of...of a ripe peach. He watched the sway of her hips as she carried the coat to an entry closet in the sitting room. *You* will *keep your damn hands off.*

When he'd dashed into the room behind the maid, he'd paid little attention to its details. The space was small but the furnishings shouted money. The antique stove stood in the far corner, the flickering light of the burning wood shining out through the glass fire door. The stove's enameled color was a pale green that matched the forest green of the furniture. Like virtually all of these classic old stoves, it was decorated with crenellations studded with many colors of tiles, in this instance mostly red and gold. The tiles along the top created flower patterns.

A red Oriental rug covered a parquet floor. From the center of the stark white ceiling hung a crystal chandelier, and on the plaster someone had painted a mural of a forest scene with scantily clad nymphs. A desk stood in another corner with Lindsey's laptop sitting open on it. A comfortable sofa and two chairs had been arranged so that occupants could enjoy the stove or a TV. There was an armoire that, if opened, probably held a minibar. And in the room's center, under the mural, was a table of finely inlaid woods on which sat a vase of white roses and a bowl of fruit.

He helped himself to a red-skinned apple, following Lind-

sey to the stove. "It's a Gyula Kovacs," she said of the stove. "He was a Hungarian master. Nearly a hundred years old and still working beautifully."

He bit into the apple's sharp sweetness, set it down and held out the kit. "Let's get you cleaned up."

She started to touch the wound, and he grabbed her hand. She didn't immediately pull her hand away from him.

Why not just pull her into my arms and kiss her? That's what I want.

"Okay," she said, as if in response to his thought and not his words. He let go. She took the kit from him and turned toward the bathroom.

He followed her.

"Fortunately," she said, smiling and using the mirror to examine where she'd been cut, "blood won't show up against black."

"Sit and I'll clean it."

She gazed into his eyes a moment and then sat, and he felt his pulse rise a notch.

The bathroom floor was tiled in a black-and-white checkerboard pattern. The tub, sink, toilet and bidet were virgin white, and all the fixtures gleamed like gold. He wet a fluffy white washcloth as she tilted her head, exposing the wound, which had bled a lot but was shallow.

"A cut at the neck is very dangerous. You're lucky it was just a nick."

She touched the scar under his left eye. A jolt of fire flashed over his chest and down his belly. *Madre di Dio,* did this woman have any idea what she was doing to him? What the hell was she thinking? *And what the hell was he doing?*

"How did you get this?" she asked.

He took a long, deep breath. "I took a crazy dare when I

was fifteen. I was raised in Venice, and I jumped off a balcony into a canal. I hit a boat."

She smiled. "I have no trouble imagining you taking a lot of crazy dares."

"What about you? K-bar says the school you went to was full of girls who learned to meet any challenge. I suppose you did your share of risky things."

"The years in Phoenix were wonderful. I met friends with whom I'm still close."

"It's clean now." He reached for the tube of antiseptic.

"I learned how to take care of myself in a lot of situations, but I also have memories of being very scared."

He remembered her trembling against him on the plane, the stiffness of her body, the paleness. It hadn't been the excitement. She'd been terrified of the jump. He had another thought, given her risky side business and what she was doing now. "Did you ever tell your dad it was scary?"

She stiffened and shook her head. "No. Of course not. Scary would be the wrong word with K-bar." She relaxed again as he put the cap back on the antiseptic tube. "I just meant challenging. I wanted to make K-bar proud." Her lips thinned. "That wasn't—isn't—always easy to do. He has very high standards."

He recalled her apartment—her paintings—her apparent preference for art and history rather than martial arts and weapons. Was it possible that Lindsey was caught up in continually pushing herself to impress her father? Unlike Marko's by-the-gut way of working, Lindsey was methodical, maybe a reflection of essential cautiousness. "I can tell you that he *is* proud of you. I'd say he adores you."

She looked up at him with those huge, dove-gray eyes. His gaze traveled from her eyes to her lips. Luscious. Would she

taste faintly of peach, like the scent of her perfume? "Why do you do this…dangerous stuff? You could have been killed this afternoon. If your father dared you to plant yourself in front of a high-speed locomotive and only jump away at the last minute, would you do it?"

"What kind of question is that? Of course not. He'd never ask such a thing."

The uneasy look in her eyes suggested that she wasn't all that sure of what K-bar might expect of her. "What the hell are you doing here in Prague? Tell me, Lindsey. I could help you."

She stood. The urge to kiss her shook him so hard that he stepped backward quickly. Was he imagining it, or had she seemed to hesitate for a moment, as if expecting a kiss, maybe wanting a kiss?

She led him out of the bathroom. "I've already called K-bar," she said. "While you were fetching the antiseptic. I couldn't reach him, but I left a message telling him that I'm sending you home. First thing tomorrow, you should fly back."

"*Cristo!*" He grabbed both her arms. "K-bar will be furious with me. I wasn't to let you know I'm here." She twisted from his grip. He shouldn't have touched her.

"I can't help that. I expect he'll understand when you explain why you barged in. But the bottom line is that I have to be here, and I have to be here alone." She licked her lips. "I need to concentrate on what I have to do. I can't have any…distractions."

He felt like pounding his fist in frustration, and stopped himself by turning away abruptly to cut loose from the aura of sex and conflict sizzling between them.

Patience, Marko, he cautioned himself. He grasped at the only exit that popped into his head. "Are you hungry? I think we need to go to dinner. Get a taxi and get away from here."

She drew in a long, raspy breath. "We definitely need to go to dinner." She snatched at the distraction he'd offered, then quickly added, "But it must look like I'm simply thanking you for saving me."

No way would he leave Lindsey alone in Prague now, not even if K-bar ordered it.

Chapter 19

A single loud knock sounded on the door to Jeremy's den. Pietro strode in without waiting for Jeremy to say *enter*. The old-fashioned brass hands of Jeremy's desk clock read 10:33. Normally he would have gone to bed by now. Too nervous, unable to sleep until the matter of Sylvia Platt was resolved satisfactorily, Jeremy had brewed a concoction of calcium and mucosal protective agents to soothe the raw pain in his stomach. He sat in his night clothes, sipping it.

"What do you have?" he asked Pietro.

"Everything I could check out seems in order."

"And from A?"

"A fax came in only minutes ago. All items on Platt came back clean. We wait only for results on the woman's phone records."

"Fine." Jeremy should feel better. He didn't.

Pietro pulled an armchair close to the fire, dropped into the chair and propped his heels on the brass fender.

"What about the Arnett girl?" Jeremy asked.

"As you ordered, I stopped feeding her two days ago. She has stopped yelling and banging. I still hear her weeping once in a while. She will be ready." Pietro folded his hands behind his head and stared at the fire. "So who do you think will come up with the high bid?"

All the bidders had gathered in Prague now. Jeremy swallowed the last of the potion and the duodenal pain dulled a bit. All but the Platt woman had instructions for where and when they would be picked up for tomorrow's demonstration. He fingered the printout of the assets of Griffin Pharmaceuticals. "Assuming Platt is genuine, I'd say Griffin Pharmaceuticals might pay the most." He pictured the other potential bidders. "It isn't likely to be the scar-faced martinet who represents the Kestonians' new dictator. Vlados Zelasko is a third-rate petty tyrant. Certifiably insane in my opinion. He and the North Koreans are perfect examples of terrorists who fear the power of the United States and know they can't fight with conventional weapons. Zelasko's mouthpiece will, unless I am much in error, try to buy with unstable currency, even though I made it clear to Zelasko that it had to be euros, dollars, or pounds sterling."

"I think our high bidder will be the Russian woman," Pietro said, helping himself to the brandy Jeremy wanted to drink but couldn't. "A is sure her backer isn't the research geneticist at Moscow University but the Russian defense laboratory the professor works for. That means government money. Big money. The woman is an expendable front. The bitch probably doesn't even know who she represents."

"Possibly. But even if it is the Russian government, can

Russian money compete with a big international pharmaceutical like Griffin if Griffin really wants the buy?"

Pietro made no comment to that and they sat in silence, listening to the crackling of the fire.

Finally Jeremy said, "I do not like Foo Hai."

Pietro's lips twisted into a sneer. "Why? Because he's tall and handsome?"

Insulting little bastard! "I don't like him, you miscreant, because I don't understand his motivation. He doesn't represent a government, like the Russian woman or the little North Korean or the Kestonian. And he's not affiliated with a business, like the Platt woman. I couldn't get him to say anything beyond the fact that his buyer is extremely wealthy, will be outbid by no one, and is interested in genetic engineering of humans. If they don't want the buy for business or for some military, then for what? And all that black clothing." Jeremy snorted his disgust. "It's very affected."

"Guess he figures he doesn't need to talk. His money will talk for him." Pietro's gaze had been steady and smug, but now it darted from the fire to Jeremy's face and back.

Pietro seemed to know something. Jeremy probed. "What did A's sources say about the pendant?"

The menacing Asian with the ponytail had worn a pendant around his neck with symbols in gold against a hexagon of black onyx. Pietro had, of course, surreptitiously taken several dozen photos of Foo Hai when Foo Hai came out of the meeting with Jeremy. They'd sent a blowup of the pendant to A.

"Chinese symbols. They stand for the female name, Kwansook. Impossible to know why he would wear a woman's name. His mother's? His mistress's? Maybe it is a business named after a woman. Ask him."

Jeremy had started to ask the meaning of the pendant during his meeting with Foo Hai but a sense that he did not want to anger Foo had clamped his mouth shut. "If it's a business big enough to bid for what I'm selling, why could neither you nor A find any information about it?" A little chill tickled the hairs on the back of his neck just thinking about Foo.

At a knock on the door, Jeremy called out, "Enter."

A young boy Pietro used to run errands entered carrying a fax. He looked from Pietro to Jeremy, then back to Pietro, who gestured that he should take the fax to Jeremy.

At the top was the familiar spider's web. The message read:

Platt phone records check out. This woman is a legitimate buyer. Act accordingly.

Jeremy drew in a long breath and exhaled. Everything was now in place. Noting that he was now rather looking forward to seeing the sultry Sylvia again, he picked up the receiver to his landline.

Chapter 20

The snow steadily fluttered down in nickel-sized flakes outside the restaurant window all during Lindsey's dinner with Marko. She had joined him in sharing a pot of traditional potato soup, but their tastes separated over the main course. He went for pork roast with dumplings and sauerkraut, she for salmon and rice.

He also insisted on dessert—delicate crepes stuffed with strawberry jam—and he didn't mind when she wanted to share just a bite, a plus on the scorecard she realized she was keeping in spite of the fact that she had absolutely no reason to be keeping score.

When they stepped out into the snow, he took her arm and with matching steps they waded through new-fallen powder that glistened in the streetlights.

Marko said softly, "We're being followed."

"I know." She didn't add any explanation and decided that

when they reached the hotel she would insist that he make no further contact with her and return to Florence ASAP.

Their hotel lay only half a block from the restaurant, and they were walking up the entry steps when her new cell phone rang, a backup that had also been in the package prepared for her by Sam.

She stopped. It was late. "I need to take this call, Marko. Please go on in without me. And please do not contact me further. I'll see you again when I return to Florence."

It wasn't a request and he knew it. His lips thinned. "You're making a damn big mistake, Lindsey. I could help you." When she said nothing, he spun around and continued into the lobby.

The phone's LCD display indicated that the incoming call was not encrypted. "Sylvia Platt," she said, keeping her voice hard and in charge. She stepped away from the door and to one side.

"I hope I am not disturbing your sleep," Jeremy Loschetter said.

"Not at all. I'm just returning from dinner."

"You are dining so late alone?"

"Actually, no. I had a…a bit of a problem today, and a very capable man came to my assistance. We shared a dinner before he leaves Prague."

"I hope your problem wasn't serious."

"I'd rather not talk about it. I'd rather talk about the buy."

"I look forward to meeting you again. I'm sure you will understand that I require a certain amount of secrecy. You will be picked up tomorrow evening in front of Betlem Chapel at 6:00 p.m. Your hotel concierge can direct you. It is not far from your own hotel but in a quieter, more private, neighborhood. Please do not be distressed, but my man will blindfold you."

He needed to feel she was no pushover. With sarcasm she said, "I'm already *distressed*," with heavy emphasis on the *distressed*. "Is that really necessary?"

"I set the terms for this sale."

"Yes. I suppose you do."

"There is something else. You will experience a firsthand demonstration of psychic ability."

She inhaled deeply, flushed with a surge of triumph that she struggled to keep in control. A firsthand demonstration could only mean that Teal would be present at the demonstration. "I have no problem with that."

"If you wish, you may bring one other person with you. I would suggest someone who is psychic. Someone, obviously, whom you trust completely."

"What the hell! How can I fetch a psychic here in time?"

"It's the best that I can offer. You have joined us very late. Perhaps you don't have sufficient resources to make this purchase. That is your problem, not mine."

"Then let's finish this conversation. I have to make inquiries immediately."

"You will recognize my man because he will have a red-and-black checkered scarf at his neck."

She hung up. A psychic? Did she really need one? She hurried into the lobby and fidgeted during a much-too-long wait for the elevator. In her room, she immediately called Sam.

"What else can it mean," Sam said, "but that he has Teal and he will show her off? This is fantastically good news. I'll pass it along immediately. Now about this psychic thing?"

"Do I need one?"

"I'll check that out with Christine, but I'm going to say yes for now. If she also feels it's essential, I'm sure she can use her influence to scramble up such a person. Believe it or not,

there was a time when the Eastern European secret services thought that having a psychic on hand would solve their intelligence problems. Our government even spent a lot of money to determine the potential. Turned out, in most instances, the gift was too hit-and-miss to work for espionage."

"Maybe that will change. Girls like Teal may be the future."

"Maybe so. For now, I'll talk to Christine. Other European stations might have someone who could reach Prague in time. The genuine benefit would be that you'd have company. I hate to think of you alone with Jeremy in his nasty little den of thieves. And if we could actually find a trained operative, all the better."

"I was certainly hoping for some backup. If it turns out that this is, in fact, where they have Teal, I'm going to need an extraction team immediately."

"I doubt CIA can be any help there. But I asked for and received time off. Christine and Allison both anticipated that you'd need some backup. So, I'll be coming myself. I hope to reach Prague before the demonstration, but to be honest, it's a long shot. For the demonstration you will likely be on your own."

"It is what it is. I can handle it, but I'll be extremely happy to have you here." She checked the clock on the computer. "It's now after eleven my time, and I'm exhausted."

"Go to bed. Get what rest you can. I'll be on my way shortly."

Lindsey thought of something else. "I have a man following me. Probably one of Jeremy's henchmen. I'll have to ditch him tomorrow early."

Sam paused.

"'Night, Sam."

"Anything else I need to know?"

She thought about confessing that her father had put Marko onto her but decided there was no need to mention it. He was now out of the picture. "No. Nothing."

Her body craved sleep, but first she must make one more call. She dialed.

"*Pronto,*" she heard Tito growl.

She'd met Tito eight years ago when Tito still worked for K-bar. The burly muscleman was one of NSI's best security enforcers, a tough talker with a sapphire stud in one pierced ear. Lindsey had discovered he was, in secret, an art lover and amateur painter. After that, they hit it off famously. Then six years ago Tito left NSI to start his own private company. NSI took on security for corporate clients. Tito provided crack security teams for rich private parties who needed someone top-notch to guard an expensive transport or to find and rescue a kidnapped loved one. Most of Tito's business was in Africa, with occasional jobs in the Middle East. He helped Lindsey with the art buybacks out of friendship, not for the money.

"Are you in bed?" she asked.

"Lindsey?"

"I need help, Tito. Big time. And it has to be kept ultrasecret."

Chapter 21

Old Prague in the morning, when Lindsey stepped out of her hotel, was a city of Romanesque red-tile roofs, steep Gothic gables, towers and, of course, spires, a city awakening under a crystal-clear sky and a blanket of fresh snow. She again wore the simple blue sweater and black slacks. The doorman greeted her, and, encouraged by the strong possibility that by this evening she might actually have found Teal, she gave him a warm smile.

She had called the concierge earlier and asked that a taxi be waiting and that the driver must speak English or Italian. As the doorman held open the rear passenger door, Lindsey knocked on the cabbie's window. He rolled it down. "Yes, madam," he said in English.

"Just checking." She climbed in.

She had glanced around to see if she could spy Jeremy's

man, but if he was still on her, it wasn't immediately obvious. The doorman closed the door.

Her driver asked, "Where do you wish to go?"

"I have a destination in mind. I want to purchase something for my husband. But a man, an ex-boyfriend, has been following me. Do you think you could lose him? I will pay you extra."

The man turned and smiled broadly. She guessed him to be in his late fifties and one front tooth had been capped with silver. "You are a beautiful woman. It does not surprise me that a man would hate to lose you."

"Can you help me?"

"Just you watch. And no need to pay extra. Only what the meter says." He flipped up a flag on the taxi's meter, checked his rearview and side mirrors, and briskly pulled away from the hotel into the business traffic on Vaclavské Boulevard.

Claire turned around to watch behind. The first vehicle to join the stream of traffic was a truck, obviously not the transport choice of a shadow. The next to pull into the traffic was a dull brown Opel, and behind the Opel, a Silver Renault Clio. Her driver made a left turn.

He maneuvered skillfully west toward the Vltava River. Again she looked behind to find that all three vehicles were still behind them. Shortly they passed the Betlem Chapel, the place where Jeremy's man would pick her up this evening, and as she checked behind again, the truck turned off. Both the Opel and Renault hung with them. The Renault was too far back to get a good look at the driver, but the man in the Opel was covered much as Marko had been, with a fur hat, sunglasses, and a coat pulled up around his neck.

"Two cars I have seen to follow," the driver said. "I test them now."

They turned off the main street into a quiet side street behind the Betlem Chapel. Both cars followed.

"More than one man follows you?" the driver asked.

"No. Just my ex." She did not want this helpful man to think she'd lied to him. Escaping one man could fit into his view of life. Running from two would trigger doubts and questions.

They made two more turns, and both cars hung with them. She had the irritating thought that maybe Marko had not followed her instructions and left Prague. That thought was followed by another, equally irritating because it suggested she had possibly made a miscalculation. Perhaps she'd acted too hastily when she insisted he go home.

"Now I lose them both," the driver said. He gunned the motor and they shot forward into the southbound traffic on the main boulevard running north and south along the east side of the river.

He zigged and zagged through the traffic with impressive skill and turned right onto a bridge that took them flying across the river. Once on the other side, she looked behind. She saw only the Opel, and it was well behind them, boxed in by two large vans.

"I think you're doing it," she said.

The driver checked his rearview. "I make sure."

Coming off the bridge they turned left and then soon right and then another right. They were heading north, toward Lesser Town. For perhaps ten minutes they threaded their way through narrow streets with no sign of any car behind them while she considered her situation vis-à-vis backup for the demonstration tonight. Perhaps Marko had not left Prague. And maybe that was a good thing. Tito was assembling a team and equipment, but he couldn't possibly be here by this

evening. He hadn't been certain at all when he would arrive. She could not, however, risk calling Marko on her unsecured cell phone.

They emerged onto Nerudova street. At the sight of the white exterior of the baroque gem, St. Nicholas Church, she knew where she was again and she felt confident she had lost both tails, assuming that the Renault had actually been following.

"You are a driving genius," she said.

He looked at her in his rearview mirror and grinned with satisfaction, his silver tooth shining brightly. "Now where does the lady wish to go?"

She gave him the address of the tobacco shop in Old Town. When she walked inside, she was stunned to see Marko. She quickly recovered, however. He must have tailed her there yesterday from the airport when she'd not been on guard. He looked up from a pipe stand he'd been checking out and glowered at her. She smiled, quite pleased, and drew him to the back of the shop where they would not be overheard.

"If you don't tell me what the hell is going on," he said, all bristly, "I'm going to inform your father that his worst fears are right."

"You followed me from the hotel."

"Damn right. And so did someone else."

"I lost you both." She grinned, rubbing it in.

"That's not the point."

"It's okay, Marko." She gave his arm a friendly squeeze. "I'm actually glad you're here."

His jaw dropped.

She continued. "The taxi chase gave me time to think, and I'll concede that you are right. You can help me. At the moment this op is essentially just me and some paperwork types. I need someone like you now."

He gave her a slow grin, as though she were talking about something other than work, and the anger in his eyes softened. "*Bene.* I salute your ability to admit when you are wrong."

She let the small criticism slide. "Come with me."

He followed her into the back room and into the elevator. He said nothing but gave her a strange look as they dropped downward.

At first Bendrich protested that she'd brought an outsider into the safe house without first getting an okay. He protested louder still when she said Marko was going to be her backup for the demonstration. But his protests were weak. Since Bendrich could not help her himself, it was perfectly reasonable for her to want cover, and he had instructions to give Lindsey Novak any reasonable assistance.

When she explained that Marko worked for her father's security company, he'd been fully vetted by NSI, and she could personally vouch for Marko's competence, Bendrich conceded and introduced him to the other two agents. The woman, Lindsey noted, paid Marko rapt attention with dancing eyes.

Bendrich ushered them into a second room and to a well-equipped desk. "I set this up for you, Lindsey. I'll fetch another chair." He looked to Marko. "Sorry, but our space here is rather tight."

"No problem," Marko assured him.

Lindsey pulled out her laptop and opened it. "I need to check a couple of things before I start filling you in. Can I trouble you for a couple of coffees first? Black for me."

He nodded and left her.

She used a secure line to call Sam, who came on almost immediately. She was somewhere over the Atlantic Ocean. With some embarrassment, Lindsey explained Marko's presence, but Sam accepted Lindsey's decision to recruit Marko.

"I'm glad you'll have some backup, Lindsey, because, well, I have some good news and some bad news."

"Give me the good news first."

"Before I left, my friends here located a psychic. She's a Czech woman born and raised in Prague but living for the last five years in Vienna. She'll be at the safe house soon."

"And the bad news?"

"Stefan has been flooded with images and feelings from Teal. The girl is being kept in a dark, cold place. Maybe something underground. Like a small cellar. Stefan said he saw a spider crawling on her face. She's panicked. Terribly frightened for the first time. They apparently haven't fed her for three days. Only water. Stefan is nearly overwhelmed with feelings of terror from her."

The hair in every follicle on Lindsey's skin rose. Lindsey thought of Jeremy and how she'd like to force him to trade places with Teal.

"Of course, they have no intention of killing her," Sam said.

"Does she know that? Can Stefan assure her that we're coming? To hang on?"

"So far, their communication hasn't worked two ways. Stefan is a powerful receiver and obviously Teal is a powerful sender. But try as he might, he can't seem to reach her with anything other than the vague sense that someone out here seems to be listening to her. We're figuring that she can't read their specific intentions about her."

"Well, we know she has guts, or she wouldn't have stayed with them in the first place." Lindsey struggled to keep her own frustration and fear for Teal from paralyzing her. She must stay sharp and positive. She envisioned Teal's face turning toward light, no matter how faint, just seeing light and knowing someone was coming for her.

"I have more bad news," Sam added. "I won't be able to reach you until very early tomorrow morning, your time."

"All the more reason for me to keep Marko. I also have some other help coming, Sam. Very experienced help. The best."

"Excellent. Get to Teal tonight, Lindsey. Let her know she's not alone."

They signed off. Marko sat leaning back in a chair on the other side of the desk, waiting patiently, staring at her with his arms crossed. A steaming cup of coffee sat before her.

"This is a CIA safe house," she said as she began to explain. "I'm not with the company, but I have colleagues who are. I'm here to rescue a young girl who has been kidnapped, and who, I've just learned, hasn't been fed for three days."

Chapter 22

Lindsey waited for Marko's response. He finally said, "Looks like K-bar's intuition is dead-on. Working undercover for the CIA is exactly what your father feared."

"This is actually me working on behalf of my alma mater, Athena Academy. An extraction team, some acquaintances of a close friend of mine, will arrive sometime tonight to help me free the girl. If we can find her."

He shook his head, tipped the chair back to the floor, took up his own coffee cup, and waited for more.

She explained about the kidnapping, that one girl was rescued while the other had voluntarily stayed with her captor for reasons not altogether clear.

He frowned. "How can you know this Teal stayed voluntarily?"

She sipped coffee while she debated how much she could reveal. If she even hinted at the extraordinary history behind

a girl like Teal or anything about Teal's exceptional speed or psychic abilities, Marko would pester her to reveal all. The existence of and the nature of the egg babies was a very tight secret. "On that you'll just have to trust me."

"I do trust you," he said.

His tone was loaded with double meaning, and he held her gaze as though he were holding her by her arms and drawing her close. He smiled softly, and she felt the strangest sensation ripple like a warm, soothing liquid through her chest. She wanted to be in his arms, to be held by him. Hearing sweet things from him, caresses, joking together—she could imagine it all. But she'd been over this terrain before and no prior relationships had worked. There was no reason to think Marko would be different. She would just end up embroiled in an emotional mess again.

When she didn't say anything, he said, "So it seems that the Athena Academy is much more than just a finishing high school for gifted girls."

"No. That's exactly what it is. But many Athena grads, like me, end up in government service. Samantha St. John is coming. She's one of the Academy's original graduates and CIA. Of the other four who will arrive, I know only Tito. He works with me. You filled in for him in Naples."

"So why me?"

She explained about the demonstration of whatever Jeremy Loschetter was selling.

Marko asked the obvious. "What is he selling?"

She struggled again with the problem of how much to divulge. "For now I'd prefer not to speculate. We'll know after the demonstration."

He finished his coffee and stood as Bendrich entered their small room with a chubby woman, about fifty years old, at

his side. "This is Zuza," he said, introducing everyone all around.

"I am psychic for you," Zuza said, smiling sweetly as she took off her outer coat and woolen cap and hung them on a coat peg. Zuza was stout but not from fat. She wore a soft pink shaggy sweater over a long black skirt and both her forearms and calves suggested she was solid. Her features were heavy but her expression was kind and her demeanor calm. Graying blond hair, soft and short, framed her face.

Bendrich left and Marko returned with coffee. Zuza beamed a huge smile at him, a motherly one.

Bendrich returned with another chair and coffee for their new arrival and disappeared.

"I'm glad to have you join us, Zuza. You're from Prague?"

"Originally. I live now in Vienna."

"Do you know why we need you?"

"Yes. I am psychic. I was told is good I am black belt, too. I understand this is government business. I am to keep all secret."

"Yes. Everything you do and see can be told to no one."

Zuza's light blue eyes twinkled. "I keep secrets as well as tell them."

Lindsey stole a glance at Marko, who was frowning, studying Zuza. He must be near boiling over with speculation. To his credit, he didn't ask even one question. But then, he had been trained by the FFL and K-bar to know that if someone running an operation wanted him to know things, they would tell him.

"Zuza is an interesting name," Lindsey said.

"It means graceful lily." Zuza giggled. The name didn't exactly fit this stout matron now, although perhaps it would have when she was young. She wagged her finger between Lindsey and Marko. "You are lovers?"

Lindsey felt her neck burning under the turtleneck sweater.

"No," she said, at the same moment that Marko, grinning, said, "You really are psychic."

Zuza frowned, puzzled, then smiled again. "Some t'inks I see I keep to myself. Partners, then. Good workink together."

Lindsey laughed, thinking how very different she and Marko were; she cautious, he impetuous. "We have worked together and everything went okay in the end."

Clearly satisfied that she had correctly pegged Lindsey and Marko, Zuza crossed her legs. She now was waiting for information and directions.

Marko asked, "How do you intend to get to this demonstration?"

Lindsey took a few minutes to explain to Zuza that Teal was being held captive, that she and Zuza were to be picked up that evening, and that they would be blindfolded. Lindsey wondered for a moment at Zuza's motivation: money, past work with the CIA, past work for Athena, hooked on thrills, proud to show off her psychic skill? Whatever it was, she seemed quite at peace to be involved.

Marko said, "I can try to follow the pickup car, but what if I lose you?"

"We do have to do something about that." From the doorway, she signaled Bendrich in the next room to join them.

"A 310 Rolly Finder Recorder would be perfect," Marko said.

Lindsey described it to Bendrich. "A combination GPS and recording device about the size of a kidney bean. It can be sewn into the lining of a purse or into clothing or stuck behind a lapel."

Bendrich shook his head sadly. "I don't have one. We are not well equipped."

"Please, Bendrich. See what you can do." She checked her watch. 11:30. "We have six hours to have a Rolly here in time."

He left, and she said, "I'm going to need clothing that looks the part and that will accommodate a Rolly. I spotted something at a department store earlier. You two wait for me here, please."

They both frowned, but let her go. The department store was only a few blocks from the tobacco shop. She loved cashmere, and when she worked an Athena job, whatever she bought in the way of clothing as part of the op she was allowed to keep. She found a stylish black-and-gray cashmere suit—thin, more like a skin-hugging skirt and top. Even under the thin wool, the Rolly would have excellent reception.

She purchased a modernistic black and silver necklace and earrings, a black half slip and camisole, and a pair of sophisticated yet also businesslike heels, and then returned to the safe house, where Bendrich announced, beaming happily, that he had found a Rolly in Vienna and that it should arrive in time.

At 5:00 the device had still not been delivered.

With growing alarm, Lindsey slipped into her new outfit. When she came out of the small bathroom, both Zuza and Marko said she looked terrific.

"I'll be on you all the time, Linds," Marko assured her.

"You can't be so worried for me that you come too close and they spot you. That would be even more dangerous for Zuza and me. Are you committed to making this op work, Marko?" She needed his full cooperation for this mission. It wouldn't be easy to steal Teal away from her captors.

"Yes, of course, Linds. I won't endanger you or your op. I promise."

Bendrich came into the room running. He stuck a small package into her hand. "It came, Lindsey."

She opened the package and the small brown box. She picked up the GPS unit. As she expected, one side was meant to adhere with an adhesive strip. She handed it to Zuza, saying, "Pull off the tape and secure the device into my belly button." She lifted the hem of the cashmere top and her camisole.

"Have you ever attached one of these?" Marko asked Zuza. Zuza shrugged. "No. Is not easy?"

"Only if you know what you're doing." Marko took the Rolly from Zuza and turned to Lindsey. "Let me do it."

She felt his warm hands on her belly like an electric shock and sucked in a surprised breath. Taking care, Marko aligned and inserted the small device into her navel and, putting the other hand into the small of her back, pressed it firmly into place. His focus had been professional, but with his hand still spread over her skin, he caught her gaze.

Zuza giggled.

Lindsey brushed his hand away and smoothed the cashmere top down again without taking her gaze from his. "Complicated process," she scoffed.

"I couldn't pass up an opportunity like that to lay hands on the boss."

Zuza patted Lindsey's arm. "We must go."

Lindsey warmed with a sense of inappropriate pleasure and irritation with Marko for such boldness. "Damn right, Zuza." She and Zuza had only twenty minutes to be in place, and it was peak traffic time. Bendrich had a taxi waiting outside the shop. She and Zuza arrived five minutes early at the front of the church where the reformist Jan Hus preached the gospel that got him burned at the stake in 1415.

Promptly at 6:00, a black Opel sedan pulled into the quiet of the cobbled street and two male passengers stepped out.

The older man, heavily coated in black and with bushy black eyebrows said, "You cannot take any electronic devices. Let me see what you carry."

Both she and Zuza had cell phones in their purses and she also had a BlackBerry. He lifted both and gave them to the other man, a boy really, eighteen or so. "The kid keeps them. You get back later. You," he said to Lindsey, "sit in back with me. You," he said to Zuza, "up front."

Zuza looked at Lindsey, an expression Lindsey interpreted as, *and so, into the void.*

They drove only a few blocks before the driver stopped and Mr. Bushy Brows thrust blindfolds at Lindsey and Zuza. They looked like sleeping eyeshades. She put hers on, and the world went black. Not a hint of light. Peeking out from under these would not be possible. She shivered. The darkness evoked her fear of close, confined, dark places. Thank heavens Marko would never be too far behind.

The driver again pulled them into the traffic.

Chapter 23

For a short time Lindsey estimated the direction the car was traveling, how many turns and the kinds of sounds, all the while trying to calm her heartbeat. The blindfold tricked her into imagining that swerves were major curves and made her feel like a prisoner. Trying to sense direction quickly became hopelessly confusing. She didn't have sufficient training in the kinds of memory techniques needed to make the effort useful. Keeping track of where they were would be Marko's job.

Listening for sounds, she was certain they'd crossed the wide Vltava River, and she recognized the distinctive chime of church bells. After maybe fifteen minutes, they passed something that had the nasty reek of a cattle rendering plant. Since they hadn't recrossed the river, she guessed they might be driving west.

She made no effort to make casual chat with anyone. When

the car stopped and hands she assumed belonged to Bushy Brows pulled her out of the backseat, she made the mental note that after the first ten minutes or so, the drive had fewer twists and turns and had taken roughly half an hour.

Not nearly enough to nail the location. "Are you okay, Zuza?"

"Oh, yes. I am fine."

Brows, or whoever was gripping Lindsey's upper arm, held it so tight that it hurt and squeezed still harder as he steered her forward. "Let go! This is no way to treat a client, you idiot."

The grip lessened, but he didn't release her. *You can't take the brute out of a barbarian.* Maybe Jeremy was short on civilized staff.

Her steps shifted from the gravel of what was probably a driveway to solid footing, perhaps flat stone? Sound of a door opening immediately in front of her. So, no entry steps.

"This is very mysterious," Zuza said, her voice cheerful as if all this treatment were somehow normal. Zuza was a black belt, but also, apparently, an aspiring actress. Or maybe she drew some confidence, as Lindsey did, knowing that Marko wasn't far behind. "I have a strong image of a tree or trees," she said softly to Lindsey. "A tree will be important."

"We can use all the help we can get," Lindsey said. Even from kindly trees.

Immediately inside, a hollow sound, like a big room with high ceilings. The faint sounds of a piano in the background playing something soothing, perhaps Schubert. Lindsey reached for the blindfold.

"Not yet, please," Brows said. "Please give me your coat, hat and boots."

So, the man with the bone-crushing grip did know the word *please.*

She heard soft footsteps and smelled a lilac perfume. After relieving her of her outer wear, Brows said, "You need to let this lady search you." Lindsey's flesh crawled as gentle hands swept over her shoulders, across and under her breasts, and down her sides. In a few seconds, Zuza giggled.

Someone took Lindsey's arm roughly again, probably Brows, and moved her forward, then up a flight of stairs, and to the right. She had counted thirty paces when another door opened. They entered a room filled with the sounds of perhaps a dozen voices and what she guessed was recorded piano music.

"Take off the blindfold," Brows commanded.

Lindsey did; he took her blindfold and the one Zuza removed and then, without further comment, stepped into the corner and crossed his arms, now on silent guard. Lindsey searched the large, medieval-looking room for Jeremy. He emerged from a group of four and hurried toward her, stroking his goatee nervously.

His dark brown suit pants hung too low over shiny brown shoes and bagged around the crotch. His jacket, worn over a gray turtleneck wool sweater, was also badly cut. Jeremy was no fashion maven. His cold, light-blue eyes blinked rapidly. He didn't offer to shake her hand, which was fine by her.

"Good evening, Ms. Platt. You are the last to arrive. I apologize for the necessary security. I'm sure you understand my caution."

Unsmiling, she regarded him with the cold professionalism and focus of a woman used to making large, unscrupulous financial deals. "My companion is Tara."

He smiled at Zuza. "You, I believe, are going to have the experience of a lifetime tonight." Lindsey sensed something smugly sadistic in his look of satisfaction. Returning his at-

tention to Lindsey he continued, eyes gleaming, "Let me introduce you to your competitors."

Lindsey quickly sized up the room. Gothic arches vaulted the ceiling that curved down into the walls, all finished in clean white plaster. Massive long wooden table in the center. Curved-back Gothic chairs around it. Flickering candles in pewter candlesticks below the tiered gargoyle chandeliers, together casting shadows into the room's many corners and angles. Instinctively, Lindsey cringed at all the likely places for cobwebs. Was this why Stefan had seen a spider on Teal's face?

Along the wall to her right, heavy ruby damask drapes closed over a row of windows. Directly opposite Lindsey a small servant's door led from the room, and opposite the windows, two arched wooden doors undoubtedly also led into other rooms. *Always know your exits.*

Between the arched doors, a mural of an epic scene looked to be partially restored. It was not done in the Gothic style of the building. The building might be one of Prague's genuine Gothic structures. She would love to inspect it carefully, but this was not the time.

At the room's far end, next to the servant's door, stood the one anomaly: a rectangular box, like a big ice cube of clear plastic, about four feet wide and six feet tall. And in the middle of it, one of the Gothic chairs. Who would be sitting in the chair, visible but beyond the reach of bidders?

She could think of only one answer. These horrid people would be inspecting Teal as if she were a prize horse. Lindsey fought back a shudder.

Her fellow bidders, all presumably representing the true purchasers, now included five men and five women. They stood in clusters at small tables where food and drinks were

available, but every so often they looked at the ominous box. Except for the music the room was mostly silent as these somber-faced participants in this criminal auction studied each other. Jeremy's obvious calculation was that by thrusting all of them into a face-to-face competition it would stimulate higher bids.

Zuza took Lindsey's arm, drew her aside and whispered, "My skin creeps in this room. Very evil presences here. All of them. That one," Zuza indicated a barrel-chested man with a face so scarred it looked as if he'd survived an explosion. "He is very dangerous. Military. But most important that you look out for this tall man in black." Lindsey had already noted the coldly handsome Asian. "The silent one. He is violent. A killer. I am positive."

She squeezed Zuza's hand, squelching the urge to reply that it didn't take ESP to know that everything Zuza said was correct.

Jeremy led the way to the closest group, all of them Asian, and it included the tallest man in the room, the one Zuza feared most.

"We use only first names," Jeremy said. "Gentlemen, this is Sylvia and Tara." Jeremy was acting like this was some damn cocktail party—a friendly get-together and he the gracious host.

Another man in the group, shorter than Lindsey by six inches, hair cut in a Western style and wearing a dark expensive-looking suit, nodded in her direction. A long, thin mustache drooped on either side of his narrow lips. Thick-lensed, steel-rimmed glasses magnified heavy eye folds.

"This is Yun," Jeremy said. Yun did not offer to shake hands. Everyone in the room was surely as reluctant as she was to make physical contact. Yun. Might be Korean. And

probably North Korean, given the interest in military uses for genetics. The man looked like an accountant, not a wheeler-dealer, but the woman he was with was surely not the power broker of the two.

"And Haneul," Jeremy added, as if an afterthought. This woman was easily the smallest person present. Her gorgeous red *cheongsam* was elaborately embroidered with a dragon in green, gold and silver. The psychic, no doubt.

"Good evening," Lindsey said, cynically going along with Jeremy's party tone.

"And these gentlemen are," Jeremy continued, looking up at least four inches to the tall Asian man, "Foo Hai and Bing." Jeremy named the man next to Foo Hai, but his gaze never left that of Foo Hai.

So, Chinese names. Foo Hai probably had some Anglo ancestry. He could be around forty, but was well muscled and trim at the midsection. Complete with ponytail and dressed all in black, he reminded her of the actor in all those kung fu movies, Steven Segal, except that the man's features were strongly Asian. Only his height and the lack of an eye fold suggested Anglo genes. This man's dominating presence was impressive. He wore a black pendant with gold calligraphy, but the symbols were complex. One element looked slightly familiar, but if she had any chance of remembering it she must soon write it down.

Foo Hai—that wasn't likely his real name—simply stared impassively at her, a black, frightening cipher. She felt his gaze touch her throat, felt her skin there tighten.

Bing, probably the psychic, watched her. His gaze felt like it cut right under her skin. His hairline had receded severely, giving him a high, shiny forehead. Short, trimmed mustache. A black mole the size of a nickel on his left cheek sort of

pointed toward eyes that shifted and darted, taking in everything.

Lindsey nodded to him coolly and followed Jeremy to a second cluster of four. With Zuza sticking close to her side, Lindsey saw, to her amazement, that what she had thought was a very petite man was actually a boy of about thirteen years.

He had a gentle face, blond hair, cobalt-blue eyes and a noticeably hunched back. Hovering next to him, a stocky woman in her late fifties. Her angular face was made even more severe by dyed black hair cut in a pageboy with bangs. Gaudy red lipstick. Cheap but stylish dark-gray suit. Unfortunately, she looked like a lump and smelled too strongly of attar of roses. But her haughty composure suggested she felt certain of winning the bidding war.

Jeremy introduced them as Galina and Yegor. Their accents, when Galina said "Good evening" and the boy said "hello" confirmed that they were probably as Russian as the names they were using. If they were fronting for the Russian government, they might very well be able to outbid everyone else.

Lindsey's final set of competitors made up what was perhaps the strangest-looking pair of the whole bunch. The man calling himself Todor was clearly the bidder, and Petia, the tallest person in the room, his psychic. Thin as if recently out of Auschwitz, she had to be six feet three or four. She wore a long black baggy dress, a pewter pendant with a single green stone in it and her salt-and-pepper hair was pulled into a severe bun at the back of her head.

If Petia was extraordinary by her thinness and height, Todor was extraordinary by his ugliness. Burly. Slightly shorter than Jeremy with bulging greenish eyes that made

Lindsey think of sunless bogs and peat. His ginger-colored hair was his only asset, as far as she could tell. Big hands with fat fingers and two rings on either hand. Sweat trickled down into the lines of his many scars.

The two people in this room that she would least like to encounter in a dark alley were the big Asian and this pug-faced Todor. How horrid that Teal could fall into the hands of any of these people.

The small door at the far end of the room opened, and a new male joined the party, a slender, sharp dresser in black slacks with a red turtleneck and slick, greasy dark hair, long in back.

Jeremy stepped back from everyone a bit and cleared his throat. "If I may have your attention. I have two announcements. First, you were all relieved of your digital devices as a precaution. But in this day of nanotechnology, I find it necessary to take additional protective measures. I have in my bag of tricks an interference system that disrupts all electronic transmission within a seven-kilometer radius of this site."

He smiled that smug smile of his as Lindsey's heart dropped to her stomach. She and Zuza were cut off from Marko. They were totally alone in a den of thieves and cutthroats.

Jeremy continued. "So if any of you thought to detect this location using a GPS, you will be disappointed. The only way you will get from me what I have to offer tonight is by delivering the highest bid, paying, and waiting for me to arrange an exchange. Secondly, I must leave you briefly for something important, but my assistant—" he gestured to the mean-looking strong-arm type with slick hair "—will remain with you to see to your needs. Please continue to enjoy yourselves."

Enjoy! Lindsey swallowed back the urge to laugh in

contempt. She could see the bulge of a weapon under Slick Hair's sleek gray jacket. Something about this guy nagged at her. Rather than stare at him, she steered Zuza toward the mural. They looked at it until the man stopped watching them. When he turned to watch Foo Hai on the other side of the room, she saw a tattoo on Slick Hair's neck behind his right ear. Was that…? Yes, a spider's web!

A shiver ran along her sides, and the room suddenly felt like a trap. She imagined the spider arriving, ready to devour its victim. To devour her.

He snapped his head back toward her and she saw a colorless mole embedded in one of his eyebrows near the nose bridge. She hadn't noticed it earlier, but now she did. No longer bundled in his black coat she hadn't recognized him, but this was none other than the man who'd attacked her with the knife.

Lindsey retreated with Zuza back to the food as she absorbed the knowledge that Jeremy had, as she thought he might, tried to either kidnap her or test her. Clearly Marko's intervention hadn't blown her cover.

Zuza whispered, "That man is like a spider."

Maybe she'd seen the tattoo, or maybe her psychic sense was in high gear. Lindsey thought again of the image Stefan had of a spider on Teal's face. The heat of immediate loathing was so strong she forced herself to focus on the food lest detestation show in her face. Everyone had resumed drinking and eating silently as they waited for the real action. Todor stepped next to Lindsey, reached past her to a plate laid out with black caviar on crisp white crackers and plunked seven on his plate.

With his arm only inches from hers, she was struck by the heat coming off his body, as though he had a fever. Was he ill? Under intense pressure? Possibly on amphetamines?

Runnels of sweat rolled along the grooves of his scarred face. You'd have thought he was a pig roasting on a barbecue spit.

Zuza spoke softly, a nervous edge in her voice. "We are alone. No Marko. Right?"

"I'm afraid so."

Jeremy approached the ancient dungeon cubicle using a high-powered flashlight, juice and cup in the other hand. At the beginning he and the Colombians had treated the Arnett girl with care. She was, of course, valuable alive, not dead. He hadn't seen her for three days now. Time to observe the effect of starvation, darkness and total deprivation of human contact on his marvelous creation.

Holding the flashlight under his arm, he took the key from an ancient stone ring, used it to unlock her cellar door and stepped inside. The girl, seated on the floor, flinched and pulled herself into a tight ball, squinting up at first and then covering her eyes from the strong beam.

He switched on the cell's overhead light. She pulled into an even tighter ball.

"You will straighten yourself up. Comb your hair and wash your face. It's time now for you to show people what you are worth."

Hands over her eyes, she sat up straighter. "Please give me something to eat."

"In few minutes Pietro will fetch you." He set the pitcher of high-energy juice and the cup on the floor but stood between them and her. She looked so pathetic. Maybe this hadn't been the best strategy.

"What's happening?"

"You will do what I ask of you without question. If you do that, I'll let you live. If you fail to perform satisfactorily—"

"Perform? I'm starving. I won't—"

"You listen to me, you little bitch. If you fail to perform satisfactorily, you will be of no use to me. I'll remove you from the demonstration and have Pietro bind you and bury you alive in the snow."

She slowly lowered her hands from her face and squinted up at him.

"Do you understand? Do as I wish and live. Fail me and you die."

Chapter 24

All was darkness around Marko, a darkness freezing cold and silent, except for the roar of an occasional car or truck. No moon had risen yet to reflect its light on the surrounding fields of snow. Under patchy starlight, the fields appeared only slightly lighter than the blackness of the wooded hills beyond. He sat, fuming in the rented car, staring at the little receiver in his palm, willing it to come to life and blink again in the compass point crosshairs. It had remained dark for at least fifteen minutes. Something was screwing up this critical GPS link to Lindsey.

A car with two Asian men had also pulled over in the shelter of a stand of evergreens not far behind him. Why? Or rather, who? Whoever they were, it would be one hell of a strange coincidence if they just happened to decide to rest in the same isolated spot where Marko had stopped. The car's presence triggered all of his alarms, but he had decided

against confronting whoever was in it. His task was to keep track of Lindsey, not pick fights.

A black car that had passed at least ten minutes earlier whizzed by again going in the opposite direction. It must have turned around somewhere up the road and now was possibly returning to Prague. The driver had high cheekbones. Someone, scarcely visible, sat in the back.

Cristo! I can't just sit here doing nothing. He started the motor, left the parked car behind, and took a potholed road he hadn't tried earlier. As far as he could tell, the car didn't follow him. At least he couldn't see headlights.

He slowed at lighted houses and an occasional building, taking in everything he could but having no clue what kind of car might have picked up Lindsey. He repeatedly checked the Rolly but its screen remained ominously black.

When he heard a sound in the distance, he pulled over again and shut off the motor. The noise grew louder and then deafening as a chopper passed overhead, its course zigging and zagging. Damn odd, flying a copter at night.

A Rolly that wouldn't work, a mysterious car with Asians in it in the middle of Europe and a night-flying helicopter. A lot of things were damn odd.

Thinking maybe someone in the chopper was on the same kind of hunt he was, he followed it, but soon lost it and then couldn't find the main road again. He backtracked and approached foothills he hadn't seen before. He'd lost Lindsey and now he was lost.

Headlights flashed on behind him, as if someone had been following his taillights and then suddenly hit him with their brights. A bullet shattered his rear windshield and passed through the front. Instantly, Marko pulled over, braked hard, ducked down, grabbed his gun and returned fire. The ap-

proaching car braked to a halt behind him. Another bullet pinged into his car. Two more shots and his left rear tire lost air; he felt the car sink lower.

He went on the offensive, leaping out in a crouch, whirling to take shelter behind the open car door, then rising and firing six rounds into the black car's windshield. He fired again as the Asian bastards backed up, turned around, and left him there.

Back in the car, his pounding heartbeat slowing, he stared at the Rolly receiver that refused to blink. He let fly a stream of blistering Italian swearwords, ending with *stramaledetto*.

He was being irrational. It wasn't his fault the damn receiver wasn't working. But he felt a sick twisting in his gut. Lindsey. K-bar. Teal. "*Stramaledetto!*"

Lindsey had to get away from Todor and his stinky sweat. She moved to stand beside the incredibly tall Petia while Todor bragged on about his Kestonian nationality.

"The new order in Kestonia will soon amaze the world," Todor was saying. "And Vlados Zelasko will be hailed throughout history as the most powerful and effective leader the modern age has ever known."

Vlados Zelasko, the petty tyrant who had recently killed off his competition and taken over the little country of Kestonia, was known for strutting around in fancy suits, flashy jewelry and, of all things, a Gucci leather twin shoulder holster for his famous Beretta nine-millimeter handguns. He boasted that if half the population didn't want to see a leader dead, that leader was doing something wrong.

The North Korean, Yun, was nodding with enthusiasm. Foo Hai just stared at Todor with a look of indifference. Galina, the Russian woman, looked as if she wanted to exterminate Todor immediately. The psychics had all stepped back and

seemed a bit bored. Lindsey and Zuza eased themselves toward the mural.

"Waiting in this room of murderers is driving me nuts," she murmured to Zuza. "Do you think something's happened to Teal? Is that why Jeremy is stalling?"

Zuza shrugged. "I think not, but I don't know."

Lindsey forced her attention to the mural. Half of it was covered in thick, white dust, making the figures appear ghostly, but the part that had been cleaned revealed bright colors.

Jeremy's voice at her side made her flinch. "You enjoy the painting?" he asked. "It was walled in for protection during World War II, so it must be valuable."

"Let's get *on* with this," Todor boomed from across the room.

"Allow me to accompany you to your chair," Jeremy said as he took Lindsey's arm.

She was pleased that she successfully suppressed her instinct to snatch her arm from his touch. He led her and Zuza to the acrylic cubicle, to a pair of Gothic chairs nearest the servant's door.

A TV had been rolled in beside the cubicle and pairs of chairs were arranged in front of it at discreet distances apart. Foo Hai hadn't waited for his psychic Bing to catch up. He strode to the center chair and claimed it. Bing scurried up beside him. Todor looked as if he were about to order Foo Hai to yield the center seat, but Foo Hai, comfortably settled, ignored him. Todor instead dropped himself into the seat to Foo Hai's right with the wraith Petia drifting over like the Grim Reaper to join him.

Jeremy moved to center stage. "Genetics is the wave of the future, and the nation that controls human genetics controls the future. In a process that so far only works with the X chro-

mosome, thereby excluding genetic modification of males, I have developed the first generation of superwomen." He beamed and rocked on his heels, proud of his little opener, then he blabbered on a bit about Aldrich Peters' original process of genetic modification of embryos. "Of course, Peters never perfected the process. His first efforts suffered unfortunate imbalances and other side effects. The addition of my techniques corrected the problems beautifully, as you are about to witness. With Peters dead, I am now the only one who knows this complicated process. Enjoy." Jeremy started a DVD.

Lindsey recognized the first girl to appear on the screen as Lena. She was hiding behind a wooden structure, peering around the corner across what appeared to be a courtyard. She took a quick look behind her, which made it very obvious that she was, indeed, hiding from someone, and that perhaps she didn't know she was being taped. Across the courtyard, perhaps a hundred feet away, a wrought-iron gate stood partway open, except that it was blocked on Lena's side by a small, two-door Opel. To get through the gate a person would have to climb over the car's roof.

A man appeared who was walking close to the wall carrying an Uzi. He passed the car and kept walking and Lindsey had the impression he was a guard on duty. Lena shook her shoulders and shook out her hands. For several moments she seemed to be waiting, and then she bolted from behind her hiding place and raced for the gate. It had to be as obvious to everyone else as it was to Lindsey that Lena was going to scramble across the roof of the car to freedom.

When she reached the car she did not attempt to climb onto the roof. She grabbed the front bumper with both hands and shoved the Opel backward at least six feet.

Lindsey gasped and she heard several others respond similarly. The boy psychic, Yegor, said something that sounded like "Oh bald it," but which she took to be an expression like *wow* or *cool*. Lena Poole was only fifteen years old, slender, and probably not much more than five and a half feet tall, yet she had lifted and pushed the Opel with the strain Lindsey might have put into moving a card table.

Lena dropped the car's front end and raced through the gate only to stop suddenly, fall to the ground and convulse, obviously hit by a Taser before she could make good on her escape.

An electrical pulse charged across Lindsey's shoulders, a sympathetic physical response generated by her mind. She shivered, and felt her neck growing hot with rage. She pasted a smile on her face as the video continued.

Jeremy spoke up. "I show this next video so you can see the wide range of special powers you could produce in these genetically enhanced women."

The setting this time was indoors. A girl sat in a chair looking quite comfortable, not at all alarmed. Lindsey struggled to recognize her. She knew the face…. Then it came to her. This was Dawn O'Shaughnessy, one of Rainy's egg babies and one of a set of triplets. Dawn was at least twenty-four now. Lindsey knew little else about her. She must have been fourteen or fifteen when the video was made. She picked up a knife with a vicious, 7-inch, serrated blade—a KA-BAR—and slashed a deep cut on her forearm from the elbow to almost the wrist.

Blood rushed onto Dawn's skin and the table and Lindsey again heard gasps, a particularly loud one of dismay from Zuza. And then a total hush fell as before their eyes, the girl swiped a white towel across her arm to remove the blood and

then watched the wound's edges begin to seal together. Or grow back together. Or…Lindsey wasn't sure exactly what she was seeing, only that the bleeding stopped almost immediately and the wound closed.

"Is the time real?" asked the Asian psychic with the big black mole on his face.

"I assure you all that what you are seeing is real and in real time."

Lindsey could imagine how all these villains must be salivating, their minds now creating useful possibilities that would earn them money and power.

Suddenly they were back in the original courtyard, but this time the girl who was hiding, obviously thinking she might escape through that open gate, was Teal. When the guard passed by the car, Teal waited as Lena had done, and then she, too, dashed for what she thought might be freedom. But the speed at which she crossed the courtyard was so fast that Lindsey leaned forward as if to see closer. Teal easily leaped from the ground to the roof of the car and then to the ground on the other side.

But she, too, did not make her escape and was brought down by a Taser.

"That completes our demonstration," Jeremy said. His slick-looking henchman turned off the TV monitor as Jeremy stepped in front of it. "Sixteen more such genetic marvels exist, all between the ages of five and seventeen. They could be your 'broodmares,' so to speak, for ever more fantastic combinations."

Sixteen! Lindsey's heart stopped. There were sixteen girls? God in heaven. Would Jeremy kidnap and sell them all?

"These disks contain all the information you need to claim these amazing girls and begin your own program of altera-

tion," Jeremy blathered on. Lindsey drew in a deep breath as she yanked her reeling thoughts sharply into focus.

"Two disks offer five girls and the third disk offers six. Included in the purchase is the information needed to do the genetic procedures that will allow you to produce your own modified lines of superwomen using their already enhanced egg cells. Take that into consideration as you draw up your bids."

Sixteen girls. Samantha and Christine needed to know this immediately. This monster had apparently used the women in the fertility clinics, replaced their own ova with genetically modified eggs, and was now offering the girls for sale, some as young as five years old!

"When you purchase," Jeremy continued, "you may be assured that only you and I will possess this virtually price-less information, and I guarantee I will not sell it to others."

She didn't believe that he wouldn't try to sell again. She doubted that the others would believe him, either. They would, however, want to possess any information their com-petitors might acquire and be the first to have it. And she ab-solutely believed Jeremy possessed exactly what he was claiming. She knew all about Lab 33 and the extraordinary truth of the egg babies, but the others were demanding proof.

"Videos can easily be faked," Galina scoffed.

"This better not be all you've got here," Yun nearly shouted. He was skeptical but clearly excited at the prospect.

"Of course not." Jeremy's tone was a purr. "I give you Teal."

The servant's door opened. Slick Hair, holding her arm, escorted the seventeen-year-old into the room. Meekly, Teal stepped into the acrylic cell and sat in the chair as the entry port slid shut behind her.

Chapter 25

Teal looked angelic as she sat in the awful acrylic cubicle, head lowered a bit, eyes downcast so that her full black lashes fanned out prettily. Her lovely high cheek and brow bones caught the light, but her pallor enhanced the ethereal quality of her presence. Her long, blond-streaked chestnut hair was no longer pulled into the saucy ponytail she usually wore, but hung straight down behind her. She was dressed in the jeans and top she'd worn when she was captured, now dirty.

The urge to reach out to Teal threatened to overpower Lindsey. *Whatever it takes, sweetheart, we'll get you out of here.*

Teal slowly looked up and surveyed the crowd, stopping momentarily to look at Lindsey and Zuza. Lindsey longed to smile and wave the Athena wave at her, but she steeled herself, keeping her face impassive.

Jeremy harrumphed. "Not only does Teal possess astounding speed, she is able to sense, when close-up, aspects of

mood, emotion, personality and life events of nearly all individuals. With the assistance of the psychically talented aides you have with you, we will now perform a demonstration. I will give you time to think of an image. Any image you wish. You will draw that image. On the same paper you will also write out a description of your image. I will show these to Teal. She will immediately transmit the image to your assistant."

Jeremy hadn't mentioned Teal's ability to transmit images and feelings at great distances. Maybe Jeremy didn't know about that.

As Jeremy watched, Slick Hair passed a pad and pencil to Galina, Yun, Todor, Foo and Lindsey.

"Do I have to make it simple?" Todor asked.

"I can't draw," Galina protested.

Foo, Lindsey noted, remained silent and impassive. The longer she was in the room with him, the less she liked him and the more intimidating he seemed.

Jeremy shook his head. "You may make it as complex as you wish, Mr. Todor. The girl can convey to any receptive mind the finest of image details along with feelings. Imagine the potential of another generation bred by enhancement of her eggs," he continued. "Her daughters would be able to transmit in secret, undetected by any communications satellite, the most specific information you might wish to send or receive." He turned and smiled kindly at Galina. "Your drawing need not be accurate or beautiful. Use stick figures if you wish. But I encourage you to include at least one very specific item.

"Naturally, you must not reveal this image to your telepathic accomplices—which would defeat the purpose, of course. I ask that, for the time it takes you to compose your

drawings, that they be excused from the room." Again, the smug, self-pleased expression, as though he were as clever as a stand-up comic.

This man was intensely irritating, but he was right in that Lindsey must choose her image with extreme care. Brows, who moved away from the corner where he had been standing with arms crossed, signaled, and all of the psychics followed him out of the room.

Lindsey scoured her mind for the perfect image. "Can we include words?" she asked.

"Only if they are part of an object. The girl cannot convey sentences, per se, only images she sees and feelings."

So. Not words. The perfect image popped into Lindsey's mind's eye, a way to let Teal know that Lindsey was here and on her side. Teal's core group at the academy was named the Penthas, after the queen of the Amazon warriors at Troy, Penthesilea. The Penthas' logo was a woman riding bareback on a horse and wearing a quiver of arrows, her arms spread outward. The pose had reminded Lindsey of the classic scene of the boy riding on the beach in the old movie, *Black Stallion.* Since Jeremy knew about the Athena Academy only too well, Lindsey sketched a damn good image but omitted the arrows. The written image message she handed him: *A woman on horseback, arms stretched upward and outward.*

When all the sketches and written descriptions were complete, Jeremy collected them and, to Lindsey's dismay, he put all of them into one copper bowl and mixed them together. It looked as though Jeremy would hand the slips to Teal at random. The girl would have no way of knowing who had sketched the Pentha logo. The psychics returned to the room and their seats.

Jeremy drew one of the slips of paper and passed it to

Pietro, who pressed buttons on the acrylic cage and handed the note to Teal. She read it and closed her eyes. Almost immediately, the five psychics in the room began writing. When they stopped, each was asked in turn to read what they'd "seen."

Yun read what his petite Korean psychic had written: "An ancient Western god, half man and half goat. Very clear image."

Galina, the Russian woman, read what the boy had written: "The Greek Pan, very recognizable. A symbol that the gods were experimenters. They combined unlike life forms." Galina smiled, nodding enthusiastically.

Jeremy gestured to Foo Hai, who clearly didn't want to speak. Bing read his own words aloud. "The ancient fertility god of horn and cloven hoof and later prototype for the Western Satan, chosen, perhaps, as an image of new fertility in genetically altered beings. The clear image carries a sense of ideas, as well."

Whoa! Lindsey looked at Bing and back at Teal. This was astonishing. A sense of ideas embedded in the image? What would they make of her own image? Teal had sent so much more than just the simple image of Pan. The drawer's own thought processes, clearly Galina's, seemed to accompany the image. This was frightening. What if Teal inadvertently revealed Lindsey's true persona?

It was Petia's turn. Todor read Petia's written impression. "An image based on ancient superstitions. The goat man."

Zuza read hers last. "The god Pan. Fertility. Mixing life forms."

Lindsey felt relief that Zuza's reading echoed the others'. She'd actually been a bit nervous ever since Zuza had suggested that Lindsey and Marko were lovers.

Jeremy passed around the original image message Galina

had written, simply saying, "The ancient Greek god of fertility, Pan, half goat, half man." Then he said, "Teal apparently sent more than Galina's words. Is the idea of weaving modern fertility and genetics into the ancient image an accurate reflection of your thoughts?" he asked Galina.

"Quite," she replied.

Jeremy went on and on, but even without his used-car-salesman gushiness, the readings were genuine, and Teal had done her job beautifully. And she was holding up well. Clear-eyed and with erect posture, the girl was made of strong stuff.

The next symbol was generated by Yun. All five psychics saw the red star in a circle and identified it as a flag. Bing and Zuza recognized it as North Korean and felt intense patriotism attached to it.

Todor's image was of an instrument of torture, the iron maiden, which Bing pointed out was actually a hoax in Nuremberg. But the psychics all saw the casketlike device, lined inside with spikes, the head of a woman carved at the top. If the psychics understood that the image was chosen because Todor relished the use of torture, they kept it to themselves. It didn't require telepathy to know that that was true.

Foo Hai's image was of a dragon eating a spider. Yegor said, "The spider has long hairy legs that have hooks in the ends that dig into flesh." The way the psychics described the spider, it took all of Lindsey's self-control to keep from shuddering.

She hadn't imagined that the selection of an image would reveal so much about the person who chose it. Her simple horse and rider was last, and even as they listened, everyone would know the image was Lindsey's because everyone else had admitted the authenticity of the previous images. Would the psychics expose her? The urge to fidget set her foot to trotting in place, but she stopped it before anyone noticed.

Yun read Haneul's response to Teal's impressions of the horse and woman: "A woman is riding a black horse. Arms reaching outward. She is proud."

Lindsey hadn't said anything about the horse being black, but, of course, that's what she'd drawn.

Galina read Yegor's impressions. "I think a Native American woman is riding a horse. I see arrows rising from something strapped onto the woman. She will not hesitate to use them if threatened. She may be reaching for her weapon."

Thank you, Yegor, thank you.

Yegor jerked his head toward her, staring.

Yikes! Was he reading her mind?

Bing began reading what he'd written. "A woman of ancient times is riding on a horse. She believes in her cause, reaches across time, and inspires modern women. Her outward reach is symbolic of magnificence and power and the desire to change things or defend something. She may even be military."

This man was scary. He'd picked up not only Lindsey's thinking, but perhaps Teal's own emotional response to the image. Lindsey held herself rigid to keep from betraying her response to how dead-on this was.

Petia scowled as Todor read her impressions in an impatient voice: "A woman on horseback who believes men will let her have power."

Zuza spoke up immediately with her response. "A woman rides a black horse. She is fierce. She will do anything to succeed."

Lindsey allowed herself to take a deep breath and let it out slowly. It was clear that to a certain extent, the psychics put their own emotional spin on impressions. Maybe this fact would hide her true motives.

Todor spoke up. "How do we know the accuracy of these messages is because of this girl? Maybe it is more because of the gifted people we bring with us? This does not yet convince me."

"The psychics themselves have expressed the unusual clarity of the messages the girl sends," Jeremy said. "But she can also 'read' people well."

"Show us," Galina said.

Jeremy agreed.

"I don't trust your cage," Lindsey said. "Who knows what microphones and speakers the girl could be listening to in there? I know how supposed psychics perform. Take her out of the box!"

She'd started a minor rebellion, with everyone sharing her demand, and again, Jeremy consented. He and Pietro brought Teal out. Pietro stood between her and the bidders, who were to approach one at a time.

"She will tell you something about yourself that she could not otherwise know," Jeremy said.

Galina barged forward in order to go first, and Teal said to her, "You are writing a book you hope will be sold in the West and bring you money."

Galina stiffened, opened her mouth to speak, closed it, nodded and sat down.

"Who doesn't want to write a book and make money?" Todor said. "That could be a lucky guess. Try me." He stepped forward. "I bet you tell me I survived a bomb blast. Hah! Who can't see that?" Sweat dripped off the end of his nose.

"You also have scars on your back where your father, uncle and grandfather beat you harshly," Teal said.

For a moment, he kept his mouth shut, as if caught off guard, but then he frowned. "Could be another lucky guess.

Eastern Europeans all got big families who beat the kids."
He sat down.

Foo Hai stepped forward, and Teal studied him a moment.
"You barely survived your childhood in an orphanage and
managed to hide a tiny item, which is the only thing you have
that belonged to your original family." Teal let her gaze
wander over the man's face and hands. "The item is green. A
frog. Stone. Maybe jade."

Foo Hai returned to his seat, giving no hint whether what
she'd said was true or not. It was Lindsey's turn. As she approached Teal, she ached to grasp her tightly in a hug and then
turn and flee with her. Could Teal see that? What would the
girl reveal in front of all these bloody people?

"You aren't like the others," Teal said, loud enough for
all to hear.

Chapter 26

Jeremy glared at Lindsey. Slick Hair also straightened and stared at her, as did Foo Hai and Todor, all watching with eyes narrowed. Please don't expose me, Lindsey thought, willing her words to leap the space between her head and Teal's. With no other way of warning Teal, Lindsey stepped closer to Teal so that her back was now to all others watching except Jeremy, who stood to her extreme right. The potential for exposure was perilously high. Teal might have recognized the Pentha logo, but maybe not. Maybe she would know that Lindsey was from the Academy. Maybe not. Lindsey risked it. She winked at Teal with her left eye, praying that the bridge of her nose would hide the movement from Jeremy.

Teal frowned. Then she closed her eyes a moment, then opened them and "read" Lindsey. "You come from a wealthy family, but you still want more. Others here have some kind of vision, even though it may be cruel or desperate. A huge

desire for revenge, some weird loyalty, or a cause. You don't have any vision or cause. You love only money. Your heart is truly cold."

"Well, you're a nasty little bitch," Lindsey said. She turned abruptly, feigning anger, but inwardly cheering.

Everyone still watched her, frowns suggesting speculation. Had they bought it?

Teal had to have recognized Lindsey's true intentions, and, knowing them, helped hide them beautifully. But was she really acting? If only Lindsey could get a clear message to the girl that help was on the way.

She found the final two readings rather prosaic. Soon Jeremy had summed up the demonstration and seemed about ready to dismiss Teal when Foo Hai spoke for the first time all evening.

"This is not enough," he said in fluent, British-accented English. "You want millions from your highest bidder for this girl and the disks. The demonstration may be real or it may be a con. You say you have combined several enhanced abilities in her, but where is the proof? A demonstration of speed on TV? The Russian woman pointed out that videos are easily faked. It seems you have wasted our time, and people who waste our time…" He stopped to make sure Jeremy was paying attention. "…always regret it."

Jeremy paled. "We have other potentially very high bidders here tonight." He looked pointedly at Lindsey, then at Galina, and back to Foo Hai. "They aren't complaining. You are free to leave."

Todor said, "I also say show us more."

This was the moment to push for more information out of Jeremy. "You say you have sixteen other girls. Why are you showing us only one? Where are the others?"

Unanimously, the bidders all joined in demanding the answer.

"Where are they? In the U.S.? Would we have to kidnap them ourselves?"

Jeremy raised a hand to calm the furor. "Most do live in the United States. They do not live under high security. The disks you purchase will provide their names and locations. They live in suburban homes." He put a different DVD into the television. "I'll give a quick overview."

A series of pictures of girls four or five years old was shown on the screen. The faces and complexions were very different, yet there was something about them that made them seem related. All bright-eyed. Glossy-haired. Perfect teeth. Perfect features, perfectly proportioned.

"Average IQ of this group is 184," Jeremy said. "All are now older and look much different, of course. Their test copies are on the disks." He looked at Lindsey. "Imagine what wealthy people would pay to make sure their child not only had no birth defects, but was genetically enhanced in some manner to make them superior to all their peers."

Foo Hai looked at Lindsey, studying her openly, the first time he'd allowed himself to give even the impression that he was taking in everything he saw and heard.

Jeremy spoke to Galina, Todor and Yun. "Imagine what your intel ops and special forces could do if composed of such superwomen. And then using Lab 33 methods, imagine *their* progeny."

Foo Hai said, "I don't bid on this girl as also having the genes for great speed unless I see it myself. No video will be accepted."

"Let's see a live demonstration of the girl running," Todor said, and Lindsey joined Yun and Galina in repeating the demand. The more time she could spend with Teal, the more time she spent seeing the buildings and its grounds, the better.

Jeremy's protests were all based on logistics: ice, snow and cold, but eventually they all bundled up and went outside into the bitter chill of the night air. All the bidders were marched blindfolded toward some unknown destination. Lindsey longed to risk a peek at the exterior of the building, but heard the boots of someone move in close behind her.

From just ahead, she recognized the voice of Bing, muttering that the whole thing was "quite draconian."

"Shut up," Foo Hai said.

Lindsey caught a whiff, just behind her, of the stale cigarette smell of Slick Hair. A muffled metallic click and a sixth sense told her that he had a gun pointed at her—which, of course, no one could see blindfolded. Lindsey shivered. Zuza moved closer as they walked. Judging by the footfalls, it didn't sound as if any of the other bidders were followed closely by any of Jeremy's people. This might mean he thought she, of all the others, might try something. So, maybe they did suspect she was an agent. How she wished that Marko had somehow managed to follow her in spite of the GPS jamming.

The crunch of boots on gravel finally gave way to pavement, and they angled downhill around a bend until they'd reached a level area. Jeremy's place apparently sat on a low hill near flat land.

"You may now remove your blindfolds," Jeremy said and met no resistance.

Five vehicles faced the road at intervals between barren trees, motors running, headlights on, lighting the road for Teal. She wore a heavy sweatshirt much too large for her, and she was stretching and doing jumping jacks.

"She hasn't eaten much for the last few days…because of the flu," Jeremy said.

Teal stopped her motion and frowned at him but said nothing about being deliberately starved.

Lindsey subtly scanned her surroundings and the night sky. A dim glow on the horizon in the east suggested the ambient light from either a small town not too far away or perhaps from Prague some thirty minutes or so away. She also spotted Polaris and calculated that if Jeremy's place followed the curve of the road, it faced essentially south or southeast. The bark on the massive trees that lined both sides of the road looked smooth and almost silvery in this light, naked limbs glistening with ice.

When Todor shouted and all heads turned his direction, Lindsey stepped away from her position, snapped off a few twigs from the nearest branch and dropped them into her pocket. To cover her moves, she pulled a tissue from the same pocket and faked a sneeze, hoping that it would seem as though she'd stepped away out of politeness. Nevertheless, she saw good old Mr. Bushy Brows watching her from inside one of the cars.

A gunshot fired and Lindsey ducked.

Immediately, she felt stupid. The shot simply marked the beginning of Teal's run. Amazingly, the girl seemed turbocharged. Her wide strides were more like leaps, as the demo tape had shown, yet her legs moved so fast, the devil seemed right behind her. And probably was. As soon as a man in a suit clocked her, she slowed down, blocked at the end of the run by two more of Jeremy's henchmen. It was now obvious that Jeremy's operation wasn't simply Bushy Brows, Jeremy and Slick Hair.

Drivers, also in suits, sat in each of the five cars. And at least one of Jeremy's men escorted the bidder in each car, that was five, and the five drivers would also have to be his men

or they couldn't be trusted with the location. So Jeremy had at least ten men.

Teal was jogging now back toward Jeremy when she stumbled and fell onto one knee, as if dizzy. Doubtless she was faint from lack of food. Lindsey rushed to her, bent over and whispered, "Athena" as she pulled Teal up by the arm. Then she turned away, and said loudly, "She does run like the wind. I'd hate to see her hurt herself."

Lindsey had seen the light of hope in the girl's eyes, as if she'd glimpsed the cavalry riding toward the fort. *Please, please, let it be so.*

"This concludes our presentation," Jeremy said. He passed around printouts of minimum bids next to blank spaces for the bidder's offer. "Call the number on your printout with your bid by 10:00 a.m. You will be contacted by noon tomorrow if it has been accepted. Good evening."

Slick Hair hurried over, handing blindfolds to Foo Hai and Bing.

Just before Brows appeared, fumbling as he slipped the blindfold on Lindsey and Zuza again, Lindsey noticed that the bidding for each of the three disks started at ten million dollars. For Teal, listed as "Enhanced Live Female," the bid started at fifteen million.

Chapter 27

Blindfolded again, Lindsey decided the return drive to Prague was taking longer than the drive out. Brows had to be taking a different route. The car never picked up much speed, so they must not be traveling on throughways, just back roads and side streets, making it impossible to calculate their direction. She had no idea how she could find Jeremy's place again, only that she must.

Teal had to be recovered as fast as possible. Preferably in darkness, just before the light of dawn. And definitely before noon tomorrow when Jeremy would receive the bids and decide the winner. There would be no way to predict how soon after his decision Jeremy might hand the girl over to someone else if Lindsey's bid was topped. That meant 5:00 a.m. at the latest. Sam would be arriving soon, and Tito with an extraction team. But how to figure out the location for the raid?

She concentrated on putting together the clues of the locale, but what kept popping into her mind was the half-cleaned mural. At first she fought the interruption, but each time the image of the mural returned, she remembered something new. Maybe it was important. She'd loved how the revelers under the tree in the painting represented humanity: a mother nursing a baby, half-naked children, maidens with flower wreaths in their hair, a monk, matrons in shawls that covered their heads, men in nationalistic costume, old people smiling in contentment. All dramatically lit. Definitely not Renaissance or Baroque. Something almost modern about it. The goddess dimly visible in the tree—her headdress so distinctive. Something was trying to work its way to Lindsey's conscious mind.

She bit her lip, frustrated and angry as the car continued its slow progression. Tripping out on the mural just wasted time. If she had a few days, she could do some detective work and figure out the artist and then learn where this particular fresco had been painted. But they didn't have that luxury. They had until dawn. At least she had the tree twigs. Maybe that would lead to something.

What had Zuza said? *A tree will be important in solving this.*

Maybe Zuza was right. Lindsey couldn't wait to tell Sam and Marko—

Marko! Dear God, he must be frantic. A new sense of urgency pushed her. Aren't we there yet? she wanted to yell at Brows. Almost as if in response to her anger, she was thrown against the left rear door as the limo made a sharp turn. She'd barely righted herself when she was thrown against Zuza, who leaned to the right as they made what seemed almost a one-eighty turn. Then another turn and another. Then she heard the hollow, ringing roar of crossing a bridge.

She guessed they were crossing The Vltava River again. Several minutes later, Brows told her to remove her blindfold, and the limousine pulled up near a taxi stand, a different location than where they'd been picked up. They were just outside Old Town Square. The teenage boy stood there. He climbed in the front and tossed the purses to Brows. Brows all but threw the purses at her and Zuza and then shoved the two of them out the door. The driver sped off, tires screeching.

Other black cars flew by, heading south, the ones she'd seen at Teal's running demo. So, the other bidders had been let off somewhere nearby, as well. She and Zuza walked toward the line of taxis at the beautifully lit old square, still alive with milling people at 11:30 on a cold Friday night. Even at this distance, the ice sculptures glistened—pristine and beautiful.

"Wait a sec," she said to Zuza. She stepped back into an arched doorway, took out her cell phone, used a coin to open the back, and looked for bugs. She didn't find anything suspicious but decided not to risk a call to Marko at the safe house, just in case she'd missed something.

Zuza tugged her sleeve and gestured with her head to a black car that pulled up on the opposite side of the street beneath a streetlight. Its windows were tinted; Lindsey couldn't see faces inside, yet she was certain she caught the glint of gold on the driver's neck in the distinctive shape of Foo Hai's calligraphy pendant.

Not good! Lindsey thought as Zuza said, "We must hurry."

They bounded out of the doorway into a walk that was closer to a run, passing two of the dazzling ice sculptures before reaching the line of taxis. Lindsey gave the cabbie an address five doors down from the tobacco shop. Yesterday her taxi had proceeded southwest to reach the safe house. The man sped off, turned south but then east.

Panic welled. What the hell was he doing? He turned north on a one-way street, jabbering something in Czech. Zuza answered him, then translated. "He says the Ice Festival brings many tourists and traffic, so we are taking back roads. They say this all the time, but tonight, I think it is true."

He jabbered some more and Zuza added, "He says someone is following us."

Lindsey heard a loud popping and zings off the cab. Gunfire!

She and Zuza scrunched down. The rear of the car dropped and the sickening bounce of flat tires began. The cabbie pulled over and then another shot hit him. He called out and slumped over.

"Zuza! Get out! Duck and run toward that alley!"

Zuza leaped out and Lindsey followed her, bullets flying around them, the sound of their boots crunching in the snow. God, the poor cabbie. Her terror inched a notch higher when it looked like the narrow alley was a dead end with solid brick walls on either side. Second stories overhung the ground level. The only light came from two windows above in an alley so narrow people could almost shake hands with their neighbors from their upstairs windows.

Lindsey raced in front of Zuza. They ran in the shadow of the overhangs, hugging the walls, passing a couple of doors bolted shut, knocking down trash cans.

Lindsey glanced over her shoulder. Limned by the distant streetlights, dark shapes barreled toward them, one taller than the others. At least three. Maybe fifty feet away.

From behind Lindsey, Zuza called frantically, "Up ahead. Go left."

Two more shots zinged by as Zuza caught up and pulled Lindsey into a pedestrian passageway. They dashed into it.

The passageway took them back to the street. Zuza gasped and panted. The frigid night air sawed at Lindsey's windpipe. Slowed by their coats and boots, they wove through parked and passing cars as they dashed across the narrow street, not daring to ask for help. Anyone who stopped might also be shot. Lindsey didn't even dare to stop running long enough to pull out her cell phone.

"We hide in the old Jewish cemetery," Zuza called between great gulps of air. "I know a way in and a place they can't find us." She pointed toward an even less well-lit street and Lindsey led them. She didn't hear anything, but a glance behind revealed three shadows darting in and out of street-lamp glows, keeping pace. She could make them out clearly as a half-moon now stood high in the sky.

She and Zuza reached a walled-in park, only a tangle of barren treetops and a few evergreens visible from the street. They ran alongside a wall higher than their heads, past anti-quated buildings and then they turned a corner, now running parallel to the river. Just ahead a snow-thickened branch hung down over the wall.

"Here," Zuza said. She grabbed the branch, scrambled up the wall, straddled the top and stretched her hand down to help Lindsey.

As Lindsey hoisted herself over the top, shots rang out again. Zuza screamed. Lindsey crashed onto the snow on the inside of the wall and caught Zuza as Zuza rolled down from the top.

Zuza's coat had a horrible smoking hole in it. Breathing hard, her hands shaking, Lindsey pulled off one glove and opened the coat. In the freezing darkness, Zuza's blood looked like black oil as it flowed out of a hole, a wide exit wound on the right side of her chest near her collarbone.

Chapter 28

The top-hatted coachman halted the two horses at exactly fifteen minutes before midnight, right on schedule. From the horses' nostrils, exhaled breath created a gray cloud that rose in the late night air. The tour guide, robed in a hooded, monklike gown, launched into the crescendo of his Midnight Tour of Haunted Prague, speaking to the six black-clad tourists in his carriage.

"We have entered Josefov, possibly the most haunted of all places in Prague, the old Jewish quarter, actually the result of a pogrom throughout much of Prague's often tragic history. Be alert to the shade of Franz Kafka, who restlessly and angrily seeks out his former loyal friend and fellow artist through these streets. After all, the friend had the audacity not to destroy Kafka's work upon his death as promised. Now look what Kafka must endure—lasting fame. Those who have seen him say he's furious."

The guide did not tell them that in fact Kafka was buried elsewhere, in the New Jewish Cemetery, and the passengers commented and kidded about seeing Kafka just there or over there as they climbed down from the carriage. They followed the guide toward the side of the Pinkas Synagogue to "the cemetery, which was established in the fifteenth century."

Oddly, the tour guide thought he'd seen three or even four figures dressed in black scurry away at the end of the wall. The sight made his hackles rise. Had any of his customers noticed? He could swear that at least one of the dark wraiths had a mustache and thin goatee. The spirit of Flash Gordon's villain, the evil Ming? At least the figures seemed to be leaving.

He shook off the eerie feeling. Of course they had been men, not ghosts. They had to be. "Tonight," the guide intoned in his spookiest voice as he unlocked the iron gate, "on this special tour, we are going to experience something few people ever have seen—a haunted graveyard at midnight. This old Jewish cemetery has bodies buried as many as twelve layers deep, perhaps more than a hundred thousand restless spirits here."

The customers had grown quiet. The joking stopped as they moved down a central walkway. Moonlight and his lone flashlight shone on the stunningly eerie sight of a jumble of tombstones crowded together, most leaning or tilting like broken teeth, as if about to fall.

One of the tourists said, "Looks like the dead are pushing the ground up, trying to get out."

Other tourists shuddered.

Pointing with the beam of his flashlight, the guide said, "Rabbi Loew is buried here. The creator of the most famous of the Golem stories of the clay giant who came to life and killed those who persecuted—"

The guide stopped panning. The flashlight's beam returned to where it had been a fraction of a second earlier. Behind a bed-shaped tomb stood two women, one with blood all over her chest, leaning against the other whose hands were bloody.

Three tourists screamed.

Another said, "You chaps do stage the most delightfully bizarre things."

The guide couldn't seem to get his mouth closed or find his voice.

"Please help us," the pale pretty woman said.

Lindsey had thanked the good people in the carriage for taking Zuza and her to the nearest emergency care unit, which, as it turned out, was only a few blocks from the cemetery. The tour guide also called in seeking help for the cabbie, but he'd already been picked up. He'd been hit at the base of his skull, and Lindsey dreaded hearing about his condition. Killed or maimed for life because he'd stopped to pick her up. Unbearable. And Zuza had lost consciousness, in dire condition, as well, also because of helping Lindsey. She left Zuza in the care of the doctors, found a pay phone in the hallway, and dialed the safe house.

Marko hadn't returned.

Dread shot through her. She remained jittery, wired to the max. The whole demonstration with Jeremy, then the adrenaline racing through her veins during the chase, Zuza's getting shot, followed by their discovery in the graveyard by what had at first seemed to Lindsey like some posse from the Inquisition. She slumped against the wall by the phone. Bendrich explained that she had messages from a Sam and a Tito. Both had experienced delays and weren't sure when they'd arrive. Lindsey hung up and sank into a chair in the waiting area. Her

brain boiled, hyper as an MTV clip. No Samantha! Even worse, maybe no Tito! Seriously bad news. They needed to get Teal out before morning. Somehow Lindsey had to make it happen. And where in God's name was Marko?

An adrenaline letdown nearly overpowered her. She suddenly longed to curl up into a ball in her hotel room with the thermostat set to ninety. She felt completely alone…as Teal must have been feeling for days now. The girl's heroic instincts in not escaping when she had the chance were now endangering the lives of so many. And yet, they'd never have known about the sixteen other girls if not for brave, foolish Teal. There was such evil in what Jeremy and the bidders were doing. Those bidders…Foo Hai. At least one of her attackers had worn a calligraphy pendant like Foo Hai's. Why had they tried to kill her and Zuza?

Marko, I need you. Where are you?

Was he okay? Rats. It sure didn't help her focus to be worrying about him. After he'd lost contact with her, he probably decided there was no point in waiting around.

"Ha!" she said aloud. Some watchdog. Some help if he'd drifted off somewhere.

But what if something bad had happened to him? Annoying man. She didn't need the drag of having to watch out for anyone else, thank you very much, K-bar.

She looked up to see an elderly woman and younger man sitting together across from her chair, staring at her. Lindsey nodded; gravely, they nodded back.

Ah, her fatigue had been talking to her. She shook her head and pictured Marko following her out there in the middle of who knew where, not speaking the language… Marko was valiantly trying to help, and if he *was* in trouble, she needed to get on it immediately. She sat up and sucked in a deep

breath. Only something pretty serious would keep Marko from calling in, she decided. If something had really happened to him…

She thought of the looks that came over his handsome face when she was around him, a look of fascination intensely focused on her, of fun, of patience, of heroic willingness to help. Okay, she had to try to find him. It was 12:36. *Get it together and—*

"Lindsey?"

Marko was striding toward her. She flew at him. Their mouths locked together upon contact, arms clamping each other through heavy coats, his colder than hers. His lips warmed quickly next to hers. Applause sounded behind her.

Lindsey broke away and turned to see the old lady smiling gently and clapping. Lindsey waved back.

"I was sick that I'd lost you," Marko said.

Lindsey explained about Jeremy's interference device. "And, when I thought something had happened to you, Marko, I…" Uh-oh, she was turning sappy. She cleared her throat. "I knew how much I'd hate to lose a guy so good at first aid."

He grinned. "I only kept the damn Rolly on because I knew K-bar would hunt me down and carve me up if I lost you."

She made a face.

His expression went serious. "I never gave up, Linds, and when the signal finally came on again, well, I don't know where I was, but I followed it until it led me here."

Her throat tightened with all the feelings that stirred inside her, feelings they didn't have time for. She grabbed Marko's arm and headed for the exit. "Do you still have the car?"

"Barely. It works, though."

Barely? She knew at once that a bad story lay behind that one word. But not now. Time for his story later. "Then let's go."

Chapter 29

At the sight of a jagged hole in the rear windshield of Marko's rented car, Lindsey halted midstride; she really might have lost Marko. The spare tire, one of those small temporaries, looked pitiful.

"I froze my *culo* changing the tires," Marko explained. "The other rear tire I patched from a small emergency kit in the trunk. It's so cold, I doubt that the adhesive will stick much longer. Could blow anytime."

Lindsey climbed into the passenger's seat and they headed for the safe house. "Who did this, Marko?"

"Well, I know they looked Asian."

"Two of the bidding teams are Asian. One is, I think, North Korean and the other is...well, I don't know who they represent, but the bidder is one scary beast. I'd say Chinese."

Marko made a turn. "I fired back," he continued, "and they took off. I don't think they expected me to be armed. And

Linds, there was a chopper flying around *and* a car with someone who looked Eastern European, possibly a local. My gut says we were all looking for the same thing."

"These people are clearly dead set on getting their hands on that poor girl. I guess they'll do anything. I'm virtually certain that the men who attacked Zuza and me were with the man who calls himself Foo Hai. He probably led the attack."

"Perhaps he was helping to take out someone he thought might outbid him."

"That's been my guess, too. And I have more bad news."

Marko looked at her quickly, then back to the street.

"There are sixteen more girls scheduled to be future kidnap victims." She told Marko about the disks for sale that would provide the names and identities, locations and talents, of more exceptional girls like Teal.

When she'd filled him in on everything that happened at the demonstration, Marko said, "This just blows my mind. The science itself, and that these people want to become gods and don't give *l'oca* who gets hurt."

"Goddess, in the case of the Russian woman." Lindsey instantly thought again of the goddess in the painting, totally unlike Galina. The figure in the mural was a friendly, beautiful goddess. Wait a minute…" 1920s. Art nouveau. Alphonse Mucha!"

"Huh?"

"It's a Mucha! The mural in the room was painted by Alphonse Mucha. I'm sure of it. We might be able to figure out exactly where Jeremy's place is! The goddess's headdress was distinctive, but I couldn't remember right then exactly why. It was in the style of art nouveau—only done realistically! I'd bet you'd recognize all the posters he did in Paris at the turn of the century up though the twenties. He

practically invented art deco. But he also did more serious epic paintings and murals on commission that weren't as well known."

"I don't see how this is so helpful."

"Because if we can find a record of his commissioned works, we'll be able to find Jeremy's place."

"You can put hands on this information in the middle of the night?"

Lindsey slouched. "I don't know. It is our best lead, though. Oh, and I also have a twig from a tree lining the road near his place. An avenue of trees on both sides, all looking the same. I think we can go over satellite photos and maybe narrow things down."

Marko turned the car into the street with the tobacco shop just as the car bumped drastically in the right rear. A flat. Lindsey and Marko both groaned. They were only about four blocks from the safe house, so they pulled over and walked, Marko carrying the Rolly unit. The bitter cold stung Lindsey's face again as they hurried through the streets of Stare Mesto, Old Prague, now empty and quiet.

With time growing painfully short, Lindsey gulped black coffee and suppressed any urge to rest or sleep. People were hurt, maybe even dead. Monsters were on the move and Teal was still trapped among them. A long hot shower was what Lindsey craved above all creature comforts. Well, maybe even more, a hot shower with Marko. She settled for a change into her day clothing and another hit of coffee as she forced herself to plan for an extraction that had to happen—somehow.

Sam was suddenly unreachable, so Lindsey called Christine and Allison. She reached Christine, who was stunned to learn about the sixteen other girls.

Bendrich, now awakened, joined them and entered clearance codes that allowed Marko to work on satellite image photo-reconnaissance data. A CIA feed from satellite recon in the Prague area was, fortunately, a piece of technology the safe house did have. Marko sat fully engrossed in front of a computer screen. Lindsey caught herself staring at him. She was deeply in trouble about Marko.

She made a rough sketch of the curved road leading to the flat stretch with the trees and the probable orientation of the building, and then asked Bendrich if it was possible he could find a forensic botanist, not entirely sure there was such a thing.

"Oh, yes indeed," Bendrich said. "And she loves to be involved in big cases. She travels often, but if she is in Prague she'll surely come. The room she rents is very close by." He seemed pleased to have a specific task.

Allison called from Maryland where it was only a few minutes after 7:00 p.m. as opposed to just after 1:00 a.m. in Prague.

"Where's Sam?" Lindsey forced her voice to sound calm.

"There's a downpour of freezing rain in London that is slowing air traffic," Allison said. "The plane will leave as soon as the storm dies down. She should be there in three hours or so on a chartered jet."

"That means she won't be here until after 4:00 a.m. at the earliest! For what I plan, we need the cover of darkness. And in my view, predawn would be the last possible good moment to stage this thing."

"You know where Teal is held?"

"Well, no…not yet. But listen to this. You'd better sit down." Lindsey told her about the sixteen other girls scheduled for "sale."

"Dear God," Allison breathed.

In the instant of silence, Lindsey heard the rapid clack of Marko's fingers hitting computer keys, saw the flashes of light at his computer station as scenes changed on the screen. He was comparing day and night satellite images of the terrain around Prague.

Allison said, "No doubt all of the sixteen girls were born to mothers who looked to the Zuni Fertility Clinic for help. This is such awful news."

Lindsey went on to describe the bidders and how Marko was attacked and her own attack that ended at the cemetery with Zuza critically wounded and the cabbie near death.

This also hit Allison hard. "There was no way to anticipate this, Lindsey. It's a relief that your father sent this Marko Savin and that he's helping."

She thought of him getting lost and said nothing.

"So the North Koreans were there," Allison continued. "Not unusual. The Russians, sad but not terribly surprising, and, of course, the good old Kestonians. The one who was excessively sweating…"

"Todor."

"Something's bothering me about this Todor and his condition. I'm going to do some checking. Also the Chinese bidder you mentioned is quite puzzling."

"The only thing I know about that one is that he's here with at least two other thugs in addition to his psychic and that he seems independent of any government. He wears a gold calligraphy pendant. I'm sorry I couldn't memorize all of it, but I'll send a partial sketch shortly."

"Well, that would be a start. I'll run it all through databases. And I absolutely agree that we need to move ASAP, not only to get Teal out but now to stop Jeremy's potentially catas-

trophic little auction. You must get those disks, Lindsey. Even at great risk. You know that, right?"

This was Allison making clear that in the face of having sixteen more children in jeopardy, Lindsey might have to make some very, very hard choices as to who would live and who might die. "I fully understand, Allison. I will do what is required."

Lindsey told Allison about her theory that the mural was painted by the famous Czech artist Alphonse Mucha and that she needed a record of his commissioned murals.

"I'll get on it. Research is just my cup of tea. You work it from your end, too."

"I will. Allison…" Lindsey spoke softly. "Teal is truly amazing. She was poised and performed beautifully in the psychic demonstrations. And her running ability is breathtaking. I'm certain she understood that an Athena woman was there. I wish you could have seen the hope flash in her eyes. I'm not going to let her down, but I'm really a novice at extractions."

"I'll send you a tactical ops brief. When you receive it, you can use it as a guide to plan as much of the extraction as you can—the approach, the weapons, positions, if possible. Have you ever worked on a tactical team mission before?"

"No, I'm sort of a lone cowgirl, but K-bar is putting together a tactical squad for emergencies with his personal security company and is continually adding more to the NSI arsenal of less-lethal weapons, so I'm familiar with the gear and some of the concepts. Marko probably is, as well. I can fire and do combat reloading of less-lethal as well as standard weapons, and I'm trained in weapons safety, use of green laser optic targeting… A mix of skills. The friend I said was on the way, his people are fully equipped with cutting-edge gadgets and are experts. If they can get here before it's too late."

"Do I need to remind you that Athena cannot—must not—be implicated in this? You can't involve any local authorities who would demand answers to a lot of questions. Whatever happens, we don't know you."

Sheesh! How could Allison think Lindsey didn't know this? "No reminders necessary."

They rang off and she dialed Tito. "We're about ready to take off," he said. "The weather is not cooperating. We'll arrive as soon as we can, Lindsey. I'll keep you posted."

Chapter 30

In the safe house common work area, Lindsey watched Bendrich's body language as he spoke on the phone to someone at the emergency care center. He kept nodding.

"Ano...Prosim?...Prosim k sluzbam...ano."

Lindsey understood enough Czech by now to translate that last part perfectly. He'd essentially been saying, "Yes, Yes? Yes, and yes."

Bendrich hung up the phone. "Zuza and the cabbie are stabilized with blood transfusions and have been sent to a larger hospital, Motol. Both alive. Zuza conscious. Cabbie unconscious. They are both scheduled for surgery."

The elevator dinged and shortly afterward a buxom, attractive woman in her fifties stepped into the entry and then into the workroom. Her chin-length hair was mostly black, gone white around her face in beautiful streaks. Dita, the forensic botanist. She smiled, bleary-eyed but gracious. Lindsey

showed her the twig with a partial brown leaf still attached and explained how the trees had lined the road at the site in question. Dita ran it under warm water at the tiny kitchenette, essentially a sink, cupboard, microwave and coffeemaker.

Bendrich translated for Dita. "She says this is easy. Silver bark. Oblate cordate leaves. They are all *lipa* trees. Called 'linden' trees in English? *Ano.* The national tree of the Czech Republic!"

Dita added that the trees might even have names that reveal the family that originally planted them, like the famous five-hundred-year-old "Stuculipa" named after the Stuc family in Nebahovy. Dita and Bendrich chattered away some more and Bendrich translated, "The ancient goddess of love was supposed to visit the *lipa* trees, and then the Catholic Church later changed the story so that it was believed to be Mary in the trees. At one time people could be executed for chopping down a *lipa* tree. And there's some kind of *lipa* celebration during the summer solstice."

"I think the celebration with the goddess in the tree is what the mural illustrated," Lindsey said. "And the shape of the trunk and branches was very similar to the trees along the road. This is amazing!"

Dita jabbered again and Bendrich turned to Lindsey, a look of thoughtful surprise on his face. "She said your name is derived from linden trees."

Lindsey's jaw dropped a little. She thought of Zuza's prediction about a tree being important. Could she have actually meant Lindsey? Or the combination of living trees, the painted tree and Lindsey? Who knew? To Lindsey's way of thinking, information from psychics was interesting, but not reliable. Things could be interpreted so many different ways. Zuza certainly hadn't bargained on getting shot for her part in all this.

"You have an e-mail!" Marko called.

She silently wished Zuza and the cabbie well during their surgeries and then set Dita and Bendrich to work researching Mucha, linden trees, related place names and other possible links, like family names associated with linden trees. She then took the e-mail at a computer next to Marko's. Allison had sent her the extraction team guidelines for tactical ops.

The days of getting a few hotshots together to storm an objective "with all ya got" are history. Highly equipped professionals compose today's extraction teams, and they are well trained in using the wide array of weapons available, ranging from the less-lethal category to handguns to MGL-140s. Through hyper-conditioning in training, their personal reflexes and instincts are well integrated into equipment use, tactical maneuvers and teamwork. The objective isn't merely extraction, but the highest level of safety and protection possible....

No problem! She had to cram a six-week course into a few hours and then come up with a brilliant plan for a team that might not make it in time to hit a location she had no knowledge of. And how she'd love to lie down. Lindsey memorized hand signals, read on, and skimmed until the words went blurry. She stopped and rubbed her eyes.

When she opened her eyes again, a steaming cup of coffee sat on her desk, and Marko started massaging her shoulders and back.

"Mmmmm." It felt so good she could cry. Deeply, his thumbs pressed into her stiff and sore muscles. If only she dared let him work on her thighs and calves, now tight and jittery. This thought produced another image altogether,

however, so it was time for him to stop. She grabbed his hands, but he held on.

"Thanks, Marko," she said, keeping it light.

"I found thirteen possible sites from satellite recon," he said.

"Good. Let me have a look. I need a break from tactics." She swigged the coffee and stepped to Marko's area to look at the printouts, eliminating four of them. "These nine are good possibilities." She looked over at Bendrich and Dita. "How are you two doing?"

They looked up with frowns of frustration. "We have found a hundred and sixty street names with *lipa* as part of the name within the thirty-five kilometer radius of Prague," Bendrich said.

"Any in these locales?" She passed them the printouts and they began to make comparisons.

Lindsey had fallen asleep at the desk. She decided that she might better stay awake and keep a clear head if she changed location for a while. She headed into the little entry area by the elevator and plunked down onto the spartan sofa. The space was lit only by the light from the next room, which felt good on her eyes since they were burning from staring at the computer screen.

Marko followed her. He said, "I think I've wrung out all I can from the satellite stuff."

"And I'm feeling stumped. Until I know a specific location, I can't go much further."

She pulled a chair over, propped her head on her bundled coat, put her feet up on the chair and closed her eyes. Marko pulled another chair over for his feet, and his hand found hers. They rested that way in silence. She felt comfort flowing from him, and it felt good.

Her brain continued to spin tactical scenarios, maddening because they could only be for theoretical places and situa-

tions. Marko caressed her hand, helping her to relax. She'd been gripping him. She imagined snuggling up next to him with his arm around her and sighed at the loveliness of the idea. Maybe there could be such a time. Afterward.

"When I ran away at seventeen," Marko said, "just Teal's age, no one was upset. My mother helped me escape, in fact. Teal's parents are probably devastated. I want to help Teal get home. It is strange how important having a home has become to me."

Marko's thoughts were tender. He probably thought what he was saying was something a woman would want to hear. But she knew where the conversation was heading and Marko had her wrong. Like her ex-fiancée, Marko was finally itching to settle down. He'd want kids, loving them and making a home for them in the way no one ever did for him. He'd had little attention, and he wanted to make up for it.

Lindsey had had plenty of attention. Maybe too much. She loved the life she'd created and didn't want to abandon it for the responsibilities of being a caregiver and a child's source of security. She and Marko were in different places; they wanted different things. He was a wonderful, handsome, great guy, but, if she let this go on and grow, one or both of them would be hurt.

She pulled her hand out of his. "Unlike you, I was always in the crosshairs of my dad's watchful gaze," Lindsey said. "So, freedom and independence have become my goal, my dream. I love my work. I've learned not just to take risks, but to thrive on risk." She let the implications sink in: children shouldn't have a mother who was always taking risks, and so Lindsey shouldn't be a mother....

He'd remained silent a moment, then said, "But Lindsey, there is much more to you than—"

A phone rang in the workroom.

"—than this risk thing. Your freedom isn't—"

"Lindsey!" Bendrich called. "Allison is on the line."

She looked into Marko's eyes and kissed him on the cheek. "I hope you find your home and your homemaker, Marko." There was enough sadness in her voice to suggest that Lindsey didn't envision herself in the role.

There are certain looks that are never to be forgotten. Marko's frown in the darkened room as she turned and walked away from him was one that would haunt her. In those few seconds before she reached the phone, she knew he'd looked all the way through her and was telling her she was making a disastrous mistake.

Allison said, "Stefan just phoned."

Lindsey did a quick mental gear shift. "Another psychic impression from Teal?"

"Yes, Teal has eaten, apparently. Stefan said he felt an uncomfortable fullness during the connection to Teal along with images of bread, cheese and sausage. And more importantly, Teal is in the light and feels hopeful. Her abilities are getting stronger. While he can only see the room she's kept in, Teal is sending him metaphorical images, too. He sees her running toward a woman on a horse, if that makes any sense. But he said the spider is still there. He described it as watching her. Its web covers the ceiling of her room. He thought there was more to this spider image, but he couldn't tell if Teal herself knew what it was or if he just couldn't perceive it."

"Wow. Except for the…" Lindsey took a deep breath "…that spider, this is wonderful news." Lindsey told Allison more about the psychic demonstration and the image of Penthesilea on horseback. "So, it sounds like she knows Athenas are on their way. Any news about Sam?"

"She took off a little before 1:30 London time, so 2:30 your time. Arrival sometime after 5:30."

"That's cutting it close. Too close. Civil twilight begins at 6:34 here," Lindsey said, using the term she'd originally learned back in an Earth science class at Athena, and which referred to the sun's position at six degrees below the horizon, rising or setting. It indicated a transition beyond which objects couldn't be seen clearly, and she didn't want to be seen clearly. Nautical twilight was more to her liking with the sun twelve degrees below the horizon. It began at 6:30, and that was the cover they needed. "I want to be on-site by 6:00 to set up a secure base. Sunrise is an hour later, but it will be way too bright by then, especially with all the snow."

"Lindsey, has your extraction team arrived? You're not thinking like a cowgirl, are you? Do not attempt this rescue without the team. That is an order."

Lindsey thought about arguing, but since she didn't even know the location yet, she couldn't build up enough heat to protest. "It remains a moot point if we don't know where we're going. Did you find lists of Mucha's private commissions?"

"Not yet, but even though it's only an hour earlier in London than in Prague, I reached the Mucha Foundation in London—a minor miracle in itself. They are excited about the possibility of a new Mucha work and are looking for the records as we speak. What about you?"

Lindsey told Allison about the nine possible sites located from satellite imaging and about the linden trees, and then covered the phone to ask Bendrich if any of the street names appeared in the nine areas.

"Not one," Bendrich said somberly.

"I think we're narrowing it down," Lindsey said, although this was a definite stretch. She hung up. *Please, Tito. Come soon.*

The spider was watching. Its web covered the ceiling.

What exactly did that mean? Lindsey had thought when

she saw the spiderweb on Slick Hair's neck that Teal's spider images must refer to him. But a growing web, spread across a ceiling. That didn't sound like one man.

Teal had seemed to imbue her messages at the demonstration with so much more than the simple images written on paper, with impressions that were highly accurate. This spider thing couldn't be dismissed as a delusion caused by Teal's ordeal. Whatever she was referring to, it wasn't merely a small eight-legged creature.

Chapter 31

Lindsey checked the time. It was 3:23 a.m. Still no Tito, no site location, and therefore no concrete plan of attack. She had devised a backup plan. She would bid for Teal at noon, make the bid so high that it would be the winner without looking suspicious, and then, when Jeremy arranged for a trade, the team could strike.

Of course that plan was worst case. For starters, how could she be sure her bid would be chosen? Maybe they would have to—

Marko put his hands on her shoulders. "Who was it?"

"Allison. Teal is still alive and feeling more confident."

"Come out to the common room. Bendrich has laid out the gear you asked for that they have on hand."

"Terrific. Let's see what our options are."

In addition to a handgun for each of them, he'd laid out knives, flashlights and communicators. She felt a nasty twist

of disappointment in her gut. Handguns and knives were crude weapons, designed to kill. "I wish I was looking at a Taser. Or even a PepperBall launcher."

"But for a Taser to work," he replied with a grin, "you have to count on being less than twenty feet away and any closer than eleven feet and you might as well be using a handgun. If your objective is nonlethal, as you said you prefer, I like the pbl. An ops team doesn't always have time to customize the weapon to each situation. The PepperBall launchers let you be very aggressive in an assault, and they work. Jeremy's guards will be armed, so we can't give them time to turn and fire."

Marko sounded more knowledgeable than Lindsey had thought. "You've done special ops before?"

"Sure. Both in the FFL and for K-bar. I'm heading up the emergency tactical squads and their training for the company."

This was wonderful. "Marko! Why didn't you say so?"

"I didn't think you or your contact wanted me to be that involved."

"This is about getting the job done, not—"

The e-mail chime sounded and Lindsey broke off to return to her computer, Marko right behind her. The incoming message was to Lindsey from Allison at the NSA. The page showed Interpol's posting of something that had happened only an hour after the attack on Lindsey and Zuza. Two Russian citizens, identified as fifty-eight-year-old Tanya Belikov and her ward, thirteen-year-old Yakob Rozlitz, were attacked in a hotel suite. The boy was apparently left for dead by mistake and he managed to call for help. The call, in Russian, was recorded, and the last thing he said was "They came to make a deal…."

Lindsey gasped at the close-up photos that revealed

Galina's—Tanya's—black hair matted with blood that stained the white carpet around her. The boy lay dead by the phone table, the small hump of his back visible. She shuddered.

Bendrich stuck his head through the door and she gestured for him to come in, too. "The others also might want to see this."

Dita also joined them.

"I thought that perhaps it was Jeremy who attacked Zuza and me, that perhaps I'd somehow blown my cover, but this pretty much settles that it wasn't him. Jeremy would have no reason to attack Galina. She was a likely high bidder. I'd say the same bastards who shot Zuza also killed Galina. Just as you guessed, Marko. They're trying to eliminate their main competition. Given that glimpse I had of a pendant I thought looked like Foo Hai's, I'd say it's his work."

"Which means they thought you were a high bidder and that they still see you as a threat," Marko said.

Lindsey nodded. "But why kill the boy? He was one of the best psychic receivers at the demonstration, and so young!"

Bendrich studied the photos. "I'd guess that Galina died instantly from a clear shot to the head. The youngster has several shots. He was probably trying to escape." He shook his head.

All of them shared a look of disgust. To name the killers as evil monsters, though, was a waste of time—which grew ever more precious. Lindsey gave Marko the tactical file and began poring over all the information she could dig up on the artist, Mucha. Though Dita's work of identifying the twigs was officially done, she continued to assist Lindsey by pulling up on Bendrich's computer all of Mucha's work she could find. Bendrich arranged for an SUV capable of carrying an assault team of seven and the various equipment and weapons. Lindsey felt a surge of hope when she saw that one of

Mucha's epic paintings, called *Youth Oath Under the Slavic Linden,* was quite similar to the mural.

Further research produced four names of people in office when certain of Mucha's public works were commissioned. One was a public town hall mural for the mayor of Rokycana in 1933. She cross-referenced the other names to public records of real estate. None owned property in Marko's nine designated geographical sites.

At quarter to four, an e-mail came from the London Mucha Foundation, listing over forty patrons who commissioned private works, but which included no murals matching the one sought.

Lindsey felt like screaming.

And then at 3:52 a.m., Dita did scream *"Loto! Jako hra!"*

"What did she say?"

"I believe the best translation is, 'bingo!'" Bendrich said.

One of the names on London's list of patrons matched a name of Dita's very sketchy list of benefactors to the Czech Society Dedicated to the Preservation of Linden Trees. "Baron Barta Von Vlcek, Juniorsky."

Lindsey checked the London list. "The name from London was just Baron Barta Von Vlcek."

"The man's son. One way to say, *junior* in Czech is 'juniorsky.'"

"Seriously?"

Bendrich nodded. He immediately went to work on the Internet, and after a few minutes said, "The baron, senior, was a field marshal during WWI."

Lindsey's fingers flew in cross-referencing the name with the extensive real estate records Bendrich's search engines could access. She came up with three property listings for the Von Vlcek family during the years 1910-1939 and by 4:02,

figured out that one of the three *was* in one of Marko's nine possible geographic locations.

"All this doesn't prove we've found Jeremy's place, though, right?" Lindsey asked. She studied the satellite photo of the location.

Dita had found not only the parcel number of the place, but also its name. "Statek ze Vlcekulipa." She was beaming.

Bendrich said, "It would translate 'Chateau of Lindens planted by the Vlcek family.' The road name is Silnice Vlcek, which literally means Wolf Road. The Von Vlceks probably wanted to honor the linden heritage by commissioning the Mucha mural."

Lindsey was pacing now, virtually certain that they had their target. "Since it was walled off in the war and then forgotten, something must have happened to the owners. Alphonse Mucha was captured by Nazis in 1939. They let him go, though, and he died shortly afterward. Maybe the war prevented the mural from being recorded. Or maybe it wasn't quite finished. Most of it was covered in gray dust, so I couldn't really tell." She stopped pacing. "It's still hypothetical…."

Marko, Bendrich and Dita stared at her, waiting. There was no more time for research. She analyzed Marko's satellite view of the site yet again as he stood beside her, his hand resting on the small of her back as she bent slightly over the table. Fewer trees lined the road than she would have thought, but that could be due to her ground level perspective. She'd thought the gravelly drive connecting the building to the road curved more sharply. And there was a separate octagonal building in front of the chateau that she'd had no hint of, but that could be attributed to the blindfold….

She stood and squeezed the hand that had been touching her in an oh-so-possessive way. "Okay. We go with this."

Marko made a gung ho gesture with both fists.

Tito called in. Their ETA was 5:30.

"You should meet your extraction team colleagues at the airport," Bendrich said. "It's not too far out of the way to this chateau. If you wait for them to come here, you will lose half an hour."

Lindsey agreed, and Bendrich went to fetch and load the SUV with the gear and few weapons they had available at the safe house. Dita went to her apartment four blocks away to fetch Lindsey some ski pants, long johns, a thermal pullover and a parka. While she waited, she and Marko threw out ideas as they studied the photo of the chateau and its grounds.

By the time Lindsey had changed her clothes, Marko showed her his rough sketch of the plan so far. "We park here," he said, pointing, "get out and climb double-time to this point, which looks like it's a little above and behind the building, a good spot for a secure area. We leave the intelligence person, if the team has one, there with a grenade launcher, an MGL-140. Will he have brought one?"

"Tito absolutely will have one, Marko. Plus other equipment. Tasers and paintball launchers and who knows what else. Stuff for rappelling. He promised to come 'ready to take down the Death Star.'"

The main road ran east and west. The chateau sat well north of the road, its entrance facing south, and it was reached by a sweeping circular drive that looped up from the road. She studied the coordinates Marko had labeled: ground level of the northwest corner of the chateau was NW1, second floor at that end would be NW2. A basement in that area would be NWB, and so forth.

A modest-sized octagonal building stood separate from the chateau and in front of it, on the opposite side of the circular

drive. He'd labeled it OS for the south side octagon. Marko guessed it might have been and still might serve as a guardhouse and it was therefore to be a major objective.

A third building at a right angle off the east side was evidently a garage. He'd labeled it simply G. Two fountains appeared to sit in the front, one on either side of the entry door, although they were covered with snow and so fuzzy in the photo she couldn't be certain they were, in fact, fountains instead of statues or maybe huge planters.

When she felt she'd memorized the layout, she had Dita make copies of the sketch for Tito's team. Marko bundled up, as well, and at 5:12, they were just about to head to the airport when another e-mail from Allison came in for Lindsey:

In all the pressure to contact art researchers and coordinate the team's arrival, I almost forgot to check on the Kestonian who was sweating, Todor. Our experts think he may have taken a temperature-raising drug for purposes of site location through use of a heat-sensitive tracking and targeting device. Be prepared for anything. Good luck.

Chapter 32

At 5:23 a.m., Pietro Albioni sat bundled up in the darkness of his cold room in the chateau and aimed a small flashlight at the list of buyers for the girl and the CDs. He sat in darkness, wanting Jeremy to think he was sleeping. Pietro's brain had teemed with larval ideas ever since Foo Hai's parting comment at Old Town Square, ideas now beginning to hatch. Was Foo Hai the one to deal with, though?

Escorting Foo Hai and Bing back to Prague, Pietro had ridden behind the driver of the rented limo, his Beretta holstered just inside his suit jacket. Bing, the clever psychic, sat next to him, Foo Hai in front. The driver was one of eight head-bashers Pietro had hired for two days to help handle the bidders. Jeremy had insisted that Pietro serve as an escort along with the hirelings, and this infuriated Pietro until he realized that for once Jeremy was right. Foo Hai and Todor were the bidders most likely to pull something.

Hudak could take care of anything Todor might try, but it was up to Pietro to keep Foo Hai in line. He was one dangerous bastard. It took one to know one. Pietro would bet big money that Foo Hai was some kind of Chinese mafia. Less than ten minutes after leaving the seven-kilometer radius covered by Jeremy's jamming device, Foo Hai's backup men had found them and followed the limo. Very impressive, although it had made Pietro cross his arms, reach inside his jacket and keep his hand on the Beretta for the remainder of the trip into town.

Once parked in the square in Prague, Foo Hai stepped out from the front seat and shut the door. Bing and Pietro also climbed out, and Pietro strode around to the front passenger door. Foo Hai had stepped in front of the door, blocking Pietro's entry.

"You're still a wiseguy," Foo Hai had said, an edge of contempt in his voice. He slipped Pietro a business card. "Deal with me and I can make you your own man."

Foo Hai hadn't needed his little pipsqueak psychic to know that Pietro used to be in a Family. Foo Hai probably also knew that his offer would release dreams Pietro had tucked in the hiding places of his mind and set them slithering out over every old idea. Pietro didn't have to remain a victim, a muscleman for Jeremy or anyone.

Pietro grabbed his smokes and lighter and headed downstairs to the chateau's old wine cellar turned bomb shelter in WWII where the girl was kept. God, he hated the freaky little witch, always watching him with those damn spooky eyes. And damned if he could stare her down, not even if he smacked her a few times. She was tough on the outside, but he also could smell fear coming off her now and then.

He couldn't smoke anywhere in the main house. Jeremy

would wake up and whine about it. And just now, Pietro wanted Jeremy to sleep as long as possible. Candy-ass scientist trying to play with the big boys.

Pietro sat on a folding chair beside the stairwell where he didn't have a direct view of the girl's cell. A low-watt lightbulb burned in the hallway at all times. The stone walls around him harbored mold, fungus, bugs, rat holes and the grime of centuries. His cigarette smoke drifted upward, and a black spider dropped down from the cobwebby old rafters. He plucked the spider's line loose and held it, watching the thing turn and try to climb back up. Pietro let it fall onto the dark, ancient stone of the floor. Four hundred years of spider droppings alone probably made up the dull, fetid shellac covering. He covered the spider with his boot and ground it into a paste.

An overwhelming sense of satisfaction came over him. For a moment...

You're still a wiseguy....

Foo Hai had nailed it. Pietro had been a low-level Mafia soldier, and if things stayed the same, he might always be. Always doing work that enabled someone else to get rich off his risk and his pain and his smarts.

Just like Uncle Luigi.

Because Luigi really was his uncle, he hadn't whacked Pietro for trying to take over one of his cousin's operations— which Pietro could have run far better than his *babbo* cousin. Pietro had been "chased." Was dead to the family.

And now in the same rut, he was working, not for Jeremy, as Jeremy stupidly supposed, but for the one Jeremy only knew as A. The one who branded Pietro with her web. The one who'd learned what his uncle would have whacked him for, nephew or not. Pietro had been the one who named his cousin to the cops.

Somehow, A found out about it and had blackmailed Pietro into being her slave ever since. He was still a wiseguy, only instead of his uncle, his boss was an evil bitch, far worse than Luigi had ever been.

And for all the work he'd done on this current job, all the shit from Jeremy that he'd put up with, his cut of this latest fat deal was a mere twenty-five K. A for Arachne. A spider woman. She was as powerful, if not more so, than any Mafia—Italian, American, Russian or Chinese. There was no direct way to compare their power to hers, but she had contacts all over the world who did whatever she told them to do. Blackmail. Pietro was almost certain that was how she did it. She found out things. And the more things she found out, the more things there were to find.

If Pietro could deliver the little freak in the cell a few feet away, plus Jeremy's CDs, all sold to the right buyer, it would change everything. Pietro could be his own man. He'd have money to go where his uncle couldn't find him, where even Arachne couldn't find him. An island in Fiji. Or some little spot off South America. He'd buy his own goddamn island.

Pietro ground out his cigarette stub with his boot, as he'd done to the spider. He'd decided.

The real question still was, who was the right buyer? Foo Hai was just plain scary. Capable of a deal followed up with a knife in the back. The Kestonian was nuts, and didn't really have any money. Neither did Yun, the North Korean. Yun just didn't seem to want the package that much. The Russian woman and the Platt woman probably had the most money, but didn't seem like the types to risk a double cross. They might just back out of the whole deal, or even alert Jeremy. Pietro couldn't read women the way he could read men. Didn't want to deal with the bitches. None of the buyers

were quite right for what Pietro had in mind, but if he waited for perfection, he'd be as old as Luigi before getting anywhere. This was the moment. He pictured a tiny, jagged crack in the window of opportunity and brightened at his poetic thought.

The girl started coughing. She'd complained the first day about Pietro's smoking, and he had taken a full ashtray and dumped it on her. She was slowly learning to be less of a bitch.

5:34 a.m. He wanted more time, but if he was going to pull this thing off, he had to move now. Pietro made his choice. He'd just have to anticipate every possible way Foo Hai could sabotage him and be one step ahead.

Pietro called Foo Hai and made arrangements for the sale of Teal. Foo Hai need not bid against competitors. Pietro guaranteed Foo Hai delivery of Teal and the disks with information on the genetic procedures to produce modified embryos. The deal included fifteen million for Pietro alone in U.S. dollars, to be deposited in a Swiss account he'd kept secret since his Mafia days.

"I've made plenty of trades of goods for money," Pietro said. "And to be damn certain the bitch and the disks don't get away at some point in the transfer, I want to put a GPS on them."

"Why would they get lost?"

"Like I say, I've done this plenty of times. Things happen. I want to be able to find the girl and the disks. When you take possession, you can take the damn things off if you want. I can get my hands on Jeremy's bugs and tracking devices. Do you have the ability to find the girl and the disks if I give you the tracking codes?"

A silent pause—Foo Hai probably trying to figure out if there was some trick involved. There wasn't. It was simply good insurance, learned mostly from Pietro's experiences selling drugs,

but he figured the same principle would apply here. Any time things were in transit, something could go wrong.

"Of course, I have tracking equipment. Go ahead. Plant your bugs. But we have to move fast. How soon can you deliver?" Foo Hai asked.

Pietro needed an hour to plan and pull everything together and a half hour to drive to the city. "I can reach the Prague address by 7:15 a.m. Just after sunup."

"Too light. And we have a long drive. We're not waiting around. 6:45."

"You'd have had to wait until noon, even later to take possession, if I didn't deal with you."

"This change of plans only works for us on a much earlier time frame."

Pietro broke into a light sweat. Foo Hai was pushing him, deliberately undercutting Pietro's planning, rushing him, confusing him.

"7:00 is the best I can do. Final offer."

Foo Hai accepted and Pietro hung up.

It was now 5:37. Shit! He'd have to bust his balls. He stood, walked to her tiny room, and looked inside. "I got new plans for you."

Chapter 33

At 5:38, Sam's plane had arrived at the small, private airport, but not Tito's. Lindsey felt nauseated, her guts twisting slowly. Their best hope of taking Teal back was rapidly slipping away. Standing beside the SUV, she and Sam exchanged hugs. Marko shook Sam's gloved hand.

"Your team?" Sam asked as she looked around the empty space.

"Not yet here. Late. Due in at 5:30."

After a small silence, Lindsey said, "Do you agree, Marko, that we'd have very little chance to succeed if we attempt the extraction ourselves with the equipment we have and only the three of us?"

"Totally. Eye-to-eye. We could modify a bit. We'd still have the cover of darkness. But depending on how many goons Jeremy has kept around, this will be difficult to pull

off even if your team arrives. On the other hand, we have zero chance of success in daylight."

Lindsey slid into the driver's seat and restarted the SUV's engine. "We can't wait for daylight and we can't rely on winning the bid. We have to go now."

Her outlook was grim as they drove out of the parking lot.

"Wait, Linds!" Marko shouted. He'd been looking into his side-view mirror. He turned around and looked back. "There's a jet coming in."

Lindsey used Marko's cell phone to connect with Tito. The extraction team was there and ready to boogie.

Two women and two men lugged gear to the parking lot and dropped it beside the white SUV. They all looked like they meant business in their snowy-patterned camo overalls and parkas in shades of white, gray and light gray-brown.

Marko, Lindsey noted, automatically inventoried the weapons as Tito made introductions—first names only. Ferris, the team's information coordinator. Monique, a willowy brunette, expert in munitions and weapons. Tia, six foot two, looked to be half Asian, half African, their electrical systems specialist.

Lindsey introduced Marko. "My...associate, well trained in tactics. He'll brief you on the plan as we go." Marko shook hands heartily with the two men, Tito and Ferris.

Sam introduced herself quickly to Tito's team as people stacked gear in the SUV.

Lindsey did the driving, and they roared off in a direction southwest of Prague. Marko immediately began explaining the plan. When there were no questions, Marko said, "Okay, let's do a static run-through."

Very slowly, they all talked through each position and each tactical movement. Then they did a "fluid" step-by-step with

only short prompts from Marko. Then came the "dynamic" unprompted, rapid run-through. They repeated it. Were they able to, they would have done every move many times in real time and with a physical mock-up. This time, repetition with the map of the property in their hands would have to suffice.

"According to the SUV's GPS map, we're about seven minutes from target," Lindsey said.

She pulled over and jumped out, Marko relieving her at the wheel. As they drove ahead, Lindsey squirmed into the Kevlar vest, the boots, helmet and high-performance gloves they'd brought for her. Everyone else donned full gear, as well. Tia passed out individual audio units she called "earwigs," and everyone put them on. Tia and Sam ran a quick operational test of the devices that would keep them all in constant contact.

The first message through the earwig was Monique saying, "Who's T-1? Tito or Marko?"

Lindsey said, "Marko's plan is good as far as it goes, and we'll begin with it, but since we don't have a floor plan of the chateau or any idea where we'll meet resistance, or even where the girl is, the assault is highly dynamic. This is Tito's team. He should run it. Marko can be T-2."

They memorized everyone's alphanumeric designations. The intelligence officer, Ferris, was T-3. Lindsey was T-7, dead last in the chain of command. Fair enough. She clearly was the person here with least experience.

The SUV turned onto a road lined with barren trees on either side, sturdy silver-gray branches gleaming in the headlights. Her linden trees. Lindsey almost shouted for joy. This was the place. All their research had paid off. They'd gotten it right.

"Cut the headlights," she said to Marko. "This is *it*."

Chapter 34

With the SUV parked off the road between the lindens, team members unloaded and stuffed backpacks and gear belts. Lindsey was running on high speed and happy that someone else was in charge for the time being. She could just focus on getting to Teal and not have to worry as much about the whole team.

She watched Marko run in a crouch across a narrow, snow-covered field, occasionally sinking into snow almost up to his knee. In the gray dawn twilight, his dark green parka marked him as someone different in a way the team's uniform camo-patterned clothing would not. He became a shadow, charging the darkness like a moose. Lindsey's borrowed parka was white, fortunately, and her ski pants gray. Thank God for the boots Sam had brought. Lindsey wasn't comfortable with the close helmet worn inside the parka hood, but it was necessary.

A wooded area—blackened with a scattering of dense,

dark, evergreens—bordered the field. Marko became a mere blur as he moved along the tree line and up a little ridge. And then she couldn't see him at all, but he spoke inside her ear, as he did to the whole team.

"T-2," he said.

"T-1, responding," Tito replied.

"Secure area site seems okay," Marko said as clearly as if he stood right beside Lindsey. "High-gable, two-story building looks dark inside. Shabby. First-floor windows barred or shuttered. Entry from this side unlikely. Round tower, capped like a witch's hat with a spire rises up from the back. Looks like four stories. Center front of the chateau is a square tower like a castle. Three stories. Flat roof. Satellite photos didn't show it clearly. Wait, there's movement… Two men are up there, armed with rifles. Ground level of the tower has massive entry doors, flanked by two more guards…. Across wide driveway area, the O building. Light on. Its entry faces chateau… Someone's moving there, too. Armed."

O building. The octagonal building in front, Lindsey reminded herself.

"Roger," Tito answered. "Any other buildings?"

"Looks like a four-car garage east of the building. One story."

"Can you see the rear of the 'witch' tower?"

"Not from here," Marko answered, "but give me two minutes."

"Go."

Ferris, T-3, scurried over to the area they had decided would be their "secure" site first, carrying an MGL-140 and a bag along with his backpack. In the deep grayness, he looked like a fast-moving white ball, about to become a snowman. At twenty-second intervals, the rest of the team members also crossed to the site. Lindsey trudged double-

time through the newly trampled snow, ran along the tree line and joined the group. Sam arrived last. The team proceeded to set up the secure area according to Marko's plan.

Two canisters of extra rounds of red OC balls, Oleoresin Capsicum, the size of large jawbreakers stood out even in the grayness. They were extra rounds for the PepperBall launchers, and looked like giant timed-release medicine capsules. It was amazing how quickly the gear piled up. Their secure area site took on the appearance of a mini HQ. Lindsey helped the team build up a hasty snow wall to avoid being seen by the guards from the crenellated "castle" tower, now within ballistic range.

Tito turned to Lindsey. "You were inside the chateau?"

"Yes."

"You and Marko have worked together?"

"Yes."

"Teal has seen you?" Tito looked toward the eastern gray horizon, growing ever lighter.

"Yes." It was 6:16.

"We need to hurry," Tito said. "You there, T-2?"

"T-2 here," Marko answered. "'Witch' tower juts out from main building in back. Rear door is padlocked. Snow build-up indicates it's unused. Guard on a balcony, second floor."

"Other entries?"

Marko was silent a moment. "Not on rear north wall. I can't see the east wall, but if it's like the west wall, there is nothing. Unless it's under the snow."

"We don't have time for full recon. We go with what we know."

Marko explained a modified plan, choosing Tia as his accomplice.

Tito agreed. "New coordinate objective. Witch 2. Go."

Sam helped Tia with the necessary gear, and Tia loped off to join Marko. A twinge of jealousy stopped Lindsey for a moment: Why had Marko chosen Tia over Lindsey? Was he keeping his distance from her? She didn't like it, but had to let it go for now.

Marko waited for T-5, the exotic and stunning Amazon-like woman.

"Slip farther back into the trees, T-5," Marko said into his earwig speaker. "The guard looks through binocs into the woods every so often."

When Tia reached him, they moved through the woods together, absolutely silent in spite of zigzagging to stay concealed by evergreens. Lindsey, lacking the hours of training required to reach such silent perfection, might be pissed that he'd asked for Tia's help, but if Lindsey chewed him out later she'd also understand when he explained. Another great thing about Lindsey—for her the op was the point, success the goal, not personal stuff.

In back of the chateau, they turned toward one of the trees that stood maybe a hundred and sixty feet tall, like a giant Christmas pine, snow piled on its sagging branches. It stood only about thirty feet away from the second-floor balcony where a guard sipped from a steaming mug, staying close to what glowed like a camp heater.

Marko had also specifically asked for Tia because of her height. He knelt for her to climb up onto his shoulders, knees first, and then as she pulled herself onto him, she also carefully pulled up on pine boughs. An avalanche of snow tumbled from the branch, despite her care. Damage done, she stood, and Marko moved with her to their combined height of twelve and a half feet. They stood among the tree branches, frozen until Tia could see what the guard would do.

She whispered into her earwig. "He heard it. He's looking around."

A raucous call not ten feet away nearly made Marko leap out of his skin. Black wings flapped nearby. Tia gasped. A raven was leaving its nocturnal perch, croaking, unhappy about the intrusion. Crows soon joined in, and a small migration started of black rags flapping noisily in the grayness. Marko's pulse normalized.

"The guard is looking our way with his binoculars," Tia breathed.

Seconds ticked away.

"He put them down and is…not reaching for his weapon."

"Okay, proceed," Marko whispered back.

He'd clipped the PepperBall launcher onto his belt on one side, and on the other Tia's specially modified "less-lethal" twelve-gauge shotgun. The shotgun was fitted with a silencer and loaded with rubber bullets. The plan was to make the rescue but leave no dead bodies behind, nothing that might force Czech authorities into asking hard questions. K-bar had also adopted this policy for NSI. But just in case, all of them also carried very lethal handguns on their belts. Along with other goodies.

Slowly, so slowly, Marko passed the launcher upward, not disturbing a single snowflake. The thing looked like a kid's giant space-blaster squirt gun with a hopper full of red balls that some said looked like a gumball machine.

"Guard rubbing his hands by the heater," Tia whispered.

Marko felt her weight on his shoulders shift subtly and knew she was taking aim.

Pop!

The guard grunted loudly as if hawking up phlegm. Marko could see the harsh powder that rose up around the man, who coughed repeatedly.

Pop!

"Guard on his knees, voiceless, but…"

The guard produced a choked "okkk" sound.

"He's down!" she said softly into her earwig.

Marko turned, stepped away from the tree, and Tia jumped to the ground and handed him the launcher. They took off running toward the witch tower.

At the base of the tower, Tia pulled out her handgun and aimed it up at the struggling guard. "Don't move," she said clearly into her wrist unit. "Translate, E to C," she added.

"Neopovaz se podrazdit," said the speaker inside the device, but the man already seemed still, just sort of croaking in agony.

"First entry contact secure," Marko said into the earwig. A voice came from secure base. "T-2, T-5, put on goggles and half masks now, before approaching PepperBall area. T-6, over."

Marko pulled down safety goggles from inside his helmet and pulled up the lightweight mask from inside the knit collar of his turtleneck. Tia did the same. Tia pulled out the Natick retractable grappling hook from a pocket on the leg of her jumpsuit. Marko untied a lanyard holding fifteen feet of tubular nylon rope and attached one end of the rope to the grappling hook and the other end of the line to a climbing pulley on his belt. He hit a button and the hook sprang into a claw with three strong talons. He heaved the hook seven feet upward to the ledge where it caught instantly, and then tugged at the line for safety. The connection proved solid; he scaled up the wall and over the balustrade, then dropped the line down to Tia.

The guard was thrashing around, working his way blindly toward his Kalashnikov near the great wooden door to the tower's interior. If the guard pounded the door it would boom

like a drum. Marko kicked the weapon aside, pulled his own handgun out and held it on the man, whose cheek and forehead had purple-red welts on it the size of grapefruits. The guard squeezed his swollen eyes shut.

Tia scrambled up the rope and climbed onto the balcony, as well. She took the man's weapon, heaved it into a snow-covered shrub below, then took dead aim at the man with a device Marko hadn't ever seen before, let alone used. It looked like an extremely heavy, pointed flashlight.

As if Tia were Spider-Man, a white wad shot out and immediately enveloped the guard in a tough Kevlar Capture Net. She secured it in back. If the guy could talk, he'd probably say, *just shoot me and be done with it.*

Quickly retrieving the grappling hook and rope, Marko said to the man, "Some day soon, when you realize you're okay, you will thank me for this."

The guard began sputtering what sounded like someone trying to curse in Czech.

"*E anche tua madre!*" Marko replied.

Tia grinned at him flirtatiously and said, "Translate, I to E" into her wrist.

"And so is your mother," her wrist answered mechanically.

Marko smiled and threw the grappling hook to the next level. "T-2 to T-1," he said into the earwig *cosa.* "Witch 2, secure. Proceeding to Witch 4."

"Double-quick," Tito said back. "We're losing the cover of darkness. Hustle."

Marko checked his watch. 6:36. Still almost a half hour until dawn. They'd only used up ten minutes since Tia joined him.

He and Tia encountered no one on the second tower balcony—from which they could step off onto the steeply

angled roof that looked badly in need of patching. They scaled the roof quickly to the top level where a balustrade encircled the whole tower. The two guards there, now watching the front of the chateau, stood a mere twenty-five feet away and slightly below on the roof of the three-story "castle" tower. Smiling, Tia boffed his shoulder. We did it, she was saying.

0639 hours. The climb had only taken three minutes.

"T-2 to T-1. Witch 4, secure," Marko said. "In position to take castle tower."

"Copy that. All team, alert," Tito said. "Execute plan to storm front."

Chapter 35

Lindsey crouched with Sam, T-6, beside the southwest corner of the front of the chateau waiting for Tito's signal. Monique, T-4, was at her station on the east side of the chateau, near a midsize building that was clearly a garage. To the south, Tito waited by the nearest linden tree on the road beyond the octagonal building.

Lindsey wondered how close Teal had to be to pick up thoughts. She spoke to Teal in her mind. *Do you know we're here for you, Teal?*

Could this beautiful, smart, talented strong girl feel the presence of her rescuers? Lindsey tried mentally to tell Teal to be ready to roll. Their plan counted on the fact that Jeremy would never hurt Teal; she was too valuable a property. But now that Lindsey had found her, he must absolutely be prevented from sending Teal elsewhere. And then there were the disks—the lives of sixteen other girls

were also at stake. Jeremy must be taken alive and the disks recovered.

At Tito's alert, Lindsey rose, tense, ballistic stun shield ready on her left arm, her Beretta handgun ready but holstered. Her stun shield, a cutting-edge device invented by an Athena grad, could stop any bullet fired from greater than ten feet away and under ten feet, it could stop anything except armor-penetrating ammo. The plan was for her and Sam to immediately enter the house, where Jeremy and the others wouldn't be heavily dressed. So she held, instead of the Beretta, an Advanced M 20 Taser in her right hand, aimed at the chateau's entry. Sam carried their entry ram on her back.

Tito's command sounded. "Execute attack! Go!"

From the secure base, Ferris fired the grenade launcher twice. The first round hit with a stunning blast in the middle of the driveway area between the octagon building and front door. Almost immediately after, a second blast struck the drive in front of the garage. Tito shot a flash-bang through the window beside the chateau's door and followed up with a smoke bomb.

Balls of fire puffed up as high as the castle tower. Blasted snow melted into a shock wave of rain. Gravel shot out like shrapnel, pelting the chateau, O building and garage, and breaking off every icicle that hung from the pair of snow-covered fountains on either side of the door. Then from the south and east, Tito and Monique fired flash-bangs in rapid sequence, aiming near the doors to the chateau and O building, producing earsplitting noise and a terrifying fan of flame from a metallic powder that exploded harmlessly the instant it came into contact with oxygen. For Lindsey, and hopefully anyone inside, the overall effect was pretty spectacular. It looked as if a full-scale lethal assault were taking place.

* * *

At 6:40 a.m., and wearing his parka, Pietro slipped into Jeremy's den having already tied, gagged and bugged the girl. She was ready to be moved. Pietro needed only the disks. He had watched Jeremy placing things in his safe often enough to have memorized the combination.

A blast, like a dropped bomb, jolted him upright. Then another and another. Shock and panic stopped his heart a moment and sent its own blast of pure adrenaline. In overdrive, he frantically twirled the dial on the safe. Wrong turn. He started over again. Mother of God, another wrong turn. *Slow down!*

Jeremy burst into the room, wild-eyed, mouth agape.

He gasped when he saw Pietro. "What are *you* doing here?"

Shit! "I'm saving the disks. We're being raided."

Jeremy's face flushed from white to purple, his sarcasm venomous. "Reeeeealllly! Do you think so?" He whipped out a gun and pointed it directly at Pietro. "Get away from my safe."

What the hell was Jeremy to make of Pietro? Was Pietro responsible for what was clearly a major assault on the chateau? In this moment, Jeremy could not think, could not move.

"Bring the disks!" Pietro said, his face flushed. "Then we grab the girl and get the fuck out of here. Through the cellar door."

Jeremy brushed Pietro aside and started turning dials, keeping the gun trained on Pietro.

"That big bush by the side door to the garage," Pietro said. "We make a run for it. Then the garage."

The safe opened. Jeremy snatched up the fake disks and stuffed all of them in the pockets of his slacks. These fakes were CDs that appeared to be the real thing, but were, on careful inspection, useless and nonsensical. They were fabri-

cated from bits of truth, procedures, names and addresses, but fatally garbled and even he would have to study them a bit to discern the fraud. Jeremy had made them for the demonstration and just in case he needed to fool someone temporarily. Well, it looked as though that moment would soon be upon him.

Running ahead of Pietro, he dashed for the kitchen. He would grab his jacket, then the girl. As they reached the bottom of the stairs to the cellar he felt Pietro bump into him hard, almost as though on purpose.

"Keep the fuck away from me," Jeremy said. "I don't know whether to kill you now or later."

Great, just fantastic! Pietro thought, waiting for the sound of gunfire as he pulled his hand away from Jeremy's coat pocket. Was this Foo Hai double-crossing a double-crosser? You could never trust anyone.

As Lindsey sprinted along the chateau wall toward the front tower entry, she heard excruciating yelps from the tower roof above. Marko was up there. A part of her brain registered worry that he might be the one suffering pain, though logic told her he'd most likely inflicted it. She and Sam were halfway to the "castle" tower door.

A mechanical voice spoke over a bullhorn in Czech, coming from Tito's direction. It was Tito's message translated by his wrist translator and electronically magnified. The intimidating effect was to make it sound like a robot was leading an invasion. She told the guards that they had a chance to surrender peacefully now or be attacked on the count of three.

"Jeden...dva...tn..."

One man yelled something in Czech as he fled the octago-

nal house, one hand raised, the other throwing down a Kalashnikov. Another man followed him out of the octagon,
also leaving behind his automatic weapon.

Apparently seeing the capitulation, two more guards
stepped out of the front of the chateau, coughing and rubbing
their eyes, seemingly ready to surrender, as well. Because
neither was wearing a heavy jacket, Lindsey kept the Beretta
holstered and trained her Taser on one. Sam did the same,
holding a Taser on the other man.

At the same instant, Monique emerged from beside the
garage, her handgun trained on the heavily clad guards at O
building. Tito ran up the driveway, carrying an assault rifle.
One of the door guards—Lindsey's man—who'd been in the
act of setting his weapon down slowly, suddenly whirled
toward Tito.

Lindsey fired the Taser. Two darts, probes attached to
wires, shot 50,000 volts into the man's back. He jolted straight
up and fell over, squeezing off a few rounds harmlessly into
the snow as he fell. The Taser's takedown power was
supposed to be more effective than a handgun, and Lindsey
believed it. To reload, she immediately removed the spent air
cartridge and snapped in another.

Sam said, "Cover my man," and she ran to the fallen
guard, kicked the Kalashnikov away, pulled out a strange
weapon Lindsey had never seen before, aimed and fired at
the man, instantly encasing him in a net. He began moving
a little and moaning.

Staring wide-eyed at the amazing net, Lindsey aimed her
Taser at the other guard. Having secured one guard, Sam
reloaded her gizmo and similarly secured the other guard.

Tito shouldered his rifle. Lindsey heard him say in English,
"Anyone else want to try anything?" Tito then raised the

bullhorn clipped to his waist. The translated robot voice posed the same question in Czech. The two remaining men shook their heads.

Next Tito said, "Front guard takedown complete. T-4, secure the prisoners. T-2 and T-5. Your status?"

"Secure and coming atcha," Lindsey heard Marko say.

Thank God, Marko was okay. A sense of relief like a physical wave surprised her. She looked up and almost directly above her, Tia and Marko were rappelling down the tower wall, Tia with a Kalashnikov slung over her shoulder, obviously taken from a guard.

The house was quiet. Lindsey thought, ominously quiet. Seven guards were down. Counting Slick Hair and Jeremy, at least four armed men were probably inside. The team must keep up their momentum. She guessed that from the time of the first firing of the grenades, not more than two minutes had passed.

The chateau door stood open so Sam ditched the entry ram—having it on her back would only hinder her movements. Stun shields at the ready, side by side, Lindsey and Sam rushed the door.

Chapter 36

Lindsey faced a guard running down the stairway. He stopped at the base, about ten feet from her, a slick-looking Glock waving back and forth between her and Sam.

The man fired two deafening shots. A bullet zinged off Sam's shield and another hit Lindsey's shield where it stuck. She fired the Taser. The man lurched and fell before he could fire a third round, and Sam leaped in and snatched his weapon. Rapid footfalls. Someone was running from a side room. Lindsey crouched and turned her shield just as the approaching man fired at her. Mr. Eyebrows. The bullet hit the shield at an angle and ricocheted. Her ears ached with the noise.

She rearmed her Taser with another cartridge. Apparently seeing that the bullet didn't penetrate the shield, Brows kept running and jumped her, only to land directly on the shield, shocking himself and knocking them both to the floor. His eyebrows froze in a look of astonished pain. Flushed with

satisfaction, Lindsey wiggled out from under him and sprang to her feet.

Sam fired capture nets over the two men as the rest of the team rushed inside, absent Ferris, who was holding down the secure site, and Monique, whose job was to make sure no vehicles left the garage.

With Sam beside her, Lindsey sprinted to the back of the stairway, looking for stairs that led to the basement. Lindsey had asked Marko specifically about the basement. All of Teal's images to Stefan had seemed to scream "basement" or "cellar."

"The kitchen," Lindsey said to Sam. They dashed back past the foot of the stairs. Tito and Tia were leaping two steps at a time upward, their task to search the second floor where the demonstration had been held in case Jeremy had kept Teal captive nearby. Marko's job was to comb the first floor.

Lindsey found a narrow wooden spiral staircase leading downward from the back of the kitchen. Their footfalls sounding way too loud in her ears, Lindsey moved swiftly down with Sam at her back. She expected to find one big room. Instead, a hallway lit by a single bulb extended straight in front of her and then divided.

"Split," Sam said. She took off to Lindsey's left and disappeared into the first room off the hallway. Lindsey turned right and checked the first small room there. Nothing but dust-covered storage boxes.

She moved back into the hallway and heard footsteps from behind. She quickly backtracked to the stairway. Halfway down the central hallway leading to the other side of the basement, Jeremy pushed a bound Teal in front of him as Pietro followed them both.

Lindsey charged down the hallway toward the three

figures. "T-7 to T-6—girl spotted," she said, her pitch elevated and her speech rushed. "Back me up."

Jeremy and Slick Hair whirled toward her, and Slick, who was holding a gun on Teal, fired a shot that tore through Lindsey's parka's right arm. She didn't feel anything. Maybe he'd missed.

She tackled him around the waist and they spun in a half circle, her back crashing into the wall. Another shot from Slick went wild.

"Kill her, kill her," Jeremy shouted.

Lindsey pushed Slick, and the two of them crashed into Teal, who fell to the floor. Jeremy grabbed Lindsey around the neck from behind and pulled her away from Slick. A barrage of gunfire from the other end of the hallway deafened her. She rammed her elbow into Jeremy's gut, he released her, and she threw herself on top of Teal as the firing continued.

She heard Jeremy and Slick's footsteps scrambling away from her down the hall, fleeing from Sam's gunfire. They couldn't know that Sam had strict orders not to kill anyone.

"T-7 to T-1," Lindsey said into her earwig mic. "We have Teal!"

The whole team responded through their mics with a quick cheer.

"Are you wounded?" Sam asked Lindsey as she sank to one knee.

"I'm okay." Tape across her mouth, Teal moaned, but her eyes shone with relief.

Sam rose and turned to chase the two men when they heard Ferris say, "This is T-3. Stealth movement outside between SE-1 and G. At least two figures."

Tito said, "T-2, begin pursuit. There must have been

another exit we couldn't see on the recon photo. T-5 and T-7, meet me at the front of the house."

Marko was in the kitchen, a room on the chateau's east side, when Ferris reported movement of at least two men outside and Tito gave the order for Marko to pursue. At the kitchen window, Marko looked outside. Jeremy and another man—most likely the one Lindsey called Slick Hair—were hunkered beside an enormous bush next to the garage.

A small door appeared to lead from the kitchen to the garage. He headed for the door.

Sam hesitated for a moment as if unsure whether to chase the men or follow Tito's directions.

Lindsey scrambled to her feet. "Go," she said to Sam. "I'm right behind."

Sam turned and raced toward the front of the house. Lindsey pulled Teal into a sitting position. She turned off her communicator. "Athenas are here for you, sweetie." She pulled a knife strapped to her ankle and cut the duct tape binding Teal's wrists. More tape covered Teal's mouth. No time to do the painful job of removing that. "You're safe. I want you to sit here, okay. Don't you move until I come back for you. Okay?"

"Mmmm mmmm," Teal muttered, nodding.

Flicking her communicator on, Lindsey raced back up the stairs. Again, she heard Tito. "T-6, do you have GPS units on you?"

"Yes, and magnet dart gun," Sam replied.

"Good," Tito said. "A reminder! All team—do not fire standard weapons directly at any escaping car. The captive guards and team members will be in target area. Remember— no bodies can be left behind! This must be clean."

In the entry hall Lindsey met up with Sam, Tito and Tia. Tito hand-signaled Tia and said, "T-5, assume diversion position outside. Repeat diversion as needed."

Tia dashed out the front door. "On me," Tito commanded, looking at Lindsey and Sam. The two of them followed him out the front door. Tito indicated with a hand signal that Lindsey should take up a position near the main garage door opening. Lindsey did as ordered, but felt a rush of fear. The site had no cover for her except her stun shield.

Tito and Sam dashed across the curved drive and ducked down beside the easternmost of the two fountains. The two snow-cloaked blips on the satellite photo had proved to be large matched fountains.

Tito continued, "T-1 and T-6 are now at O. T-3, standing by with MGL."

Gunfire sounded inside the garage. Lindsey dropped into a squat, her shield extended in front of her, her heart thundering in her ears. The old wood doors burst open, and the tires of a limo screeched as the car shot forward. Through her earwig, Lindsey heard the sound of Marko struggling, swearing in Italian and then a loud *oof.*

What's happening?

Tito rose and began firing magnetic GPS darts at the fleeing limo. Monique fired flash-bangs and smoke grenades to try to blind and confuse the driver, Slick—the only person Lindsey could see in the car. Hell fire! Did he have Jeremy? Did he have the disks?

"T-2, here," Marko said, panting. "Prime target secure. Secondary target alone in car." Lindsey leaped up. Slick made a surprise U-turn, spewing snow and gravel as he drove out the other end of the driveway.

"All team, stop that limo, BAMP!" Tito's voice said in the earwig.

BAMP. "By any means possible." An explosion sounded, and then the ack-ack-ack of at least two Mk-48-O models, momentarily deafening Lindsey. But to no avail. Slick's car was fast disappearing down the lane of trees.

"Hold fire," Tito said.

The sudden silence seemed to ring in Lindsey's ears.

Lindsey checked her watch. 6:54, still ten minutes before sunrise.

She ran into the garage. Marko was flex-cuffing Jeremy, who now endured a nasty, bleeding cut at the corner of his mouth.

"Teal is still in the basement," Lindsey said. "I'm going to her."

"I'll meet you in the kitchen," Marko replied.

Lindsey found Teal still sitting on the floor, her back to the dank wall. She was trying to peel the duct tape from her mouth. Lindsey helped her stand up, and Teal grabbed Lindsey in a breath-stealing hug, long and fierce. Lindsey felt tears welling and blinked them back. "Come with me to a better place. I'll get the tape off."

Marko had flex-cuffed Jeremy's hands behind his back and taken him into the chateau's kitchen. Lindsey and Teal joined them. Without a word being spoken, Marko stepped over to Lindsey, pulled her close, and pressed her head to his shoulder. He didn't need to use words. They simply stood that way a long moment. She let herself relax into the feeling of being safe—and cared for.

Then, with the help of Tia's first-aid kit, Lindsey gingerly eased the tape from Teal's lips. Other team members were rounding up gear and captives—all recovering from their

stuns and PepperBall ordeals. Before they left, the team would bind the men with everyday, common rope, they would clean the site of ammo and anything else incriminating, and when they were well away, they would inform the authorities where the men could be found.

Jeremy kept muttering and swearing. He'd handed over the disks he'd been attempting to take with him as he fled. "I goddamn well knew you were Athena. I knew it," he muttered again.

"Stop moaning, Jeremy," Marko said. "Where is your office?" He pushed Jeremy out of the kitchen. Bringing Teal and the first-aid kit, Lindsey followed them.

In Jeremy's office, Marko shoved Jeremy into an armchair and took the seat at Jeremy's computer, which was still turned on. "You may think you're a brilliant scientist, but you're canal scum, a common criminal."

Marko inserted a disk, opened a file that was in English, and started reading it. Lindsey watched over his shoulder. She had no way of evaluating whether Jeremy's procedures were correct or not. At least it wasn't simply garbage. It looked like sophisticated formulas and procedures. Marko put in a new disk. Jeremy stood up and Marko didn't protest when Jeremy also started looking at the screen.

Teal took Lindsey's hand. "Thank you, Lindsey. Thank you so much," she said.

Lindsey squeezed back.

"My parents?"

"Someone from the Academy will contact them soon. When we're safely out of this country and in a secure location."

"I have so much to tell you about what I think is really going on here, but…" Her stomach growled. "…do you have any food? I'm so hungry."

The earnest look in the girl's lovely eyes made Lindsey want to ransack the house. She was about to say no, but she checked the first-aid kit, found several nutrition bars and handed them to Teal, who tore one open and bit off half.

Tito's voice over the earwig said to Tia, who was with Monique, now back with Ferris at the safe site, "T-5, did the GPS magnets stick to the limo?"

"Yes. Three of 'em. I'm tracking them now. The man's heading toward Prague."

"T-2, are the items legit? Are they what we're looking for?"

Marko answered quickly. "I'm checking now. There's a lot here."

"Stop scrolling," Teal said to Marko. She leaned closer to the screen, frowning at the names. "Nikki Bustillo and Jessica Whittaker are girls at the Academy."

"Okay," Sam said through the earwig. "I heard that. Good enough for me. We have finished cleaning up." She chuckled. "Some folks are *not* happy. Let's exit."

Marko ejected the disk, placed it in its labeled case and grabbed the other four cases. For a microsecond Marko looked at Lindsey in a way that was soft with caring and with optimism that the ordeal was almost over. He rose and turned off the computer.

The first sun rays appeared in the east as Lindsey hurried out of the chateau with Teal. Marko jerked Jeremy along.

"I need my medicine," Jeremy whined.

"Shut up, asshole!" Marko said.

Lindsey and Teal had run less than halfway across the field to the safe area when Ferris's voice suddenly yelled into her earwig. "Incoming chopper! Assume combat alert!"

Chapter 37

Running with Teal at her side, Lindsey looked at the girl in sudden horror. Someone in that chopper was coming to take Teal. Lindsey couldn't think how she knew this, but she was certain. Though her ears were still ringing from all the gunshots, she could hear the approach of the chopper through the earwig. Ferris asked permission to fire the MGL.

"Negative," Tito said. "Continue to maintain low profile. We don't know who these guys are yet."

Lindsey looked back at Marko. He'd fallen too far behind as he struggled with and prodded Jeremy to move. Lindsey looked ahead toward the safe area. She and Teal wouldn't make the two hundred-and-some yards before the chopper was on them. The tree line was closer. She steered Teal toward it. They could work their way to the safe area by winding among the bare, ice-laden trees and snowy evergreens.

"All team," Tito said, "hide and wait. Only if things turn hostile do we use lethal force."

Lindsey and Teal reached the trees and squatted under the low, drooping branches of a towering conifer to look for Marko. Grateful for the precise movements afforded by the rappelling gloves, Lindsey popped another cartridge in her Taser and pulled out her Beretta, as well.

She watched Marko yank Jeremy down next to the tree nearest the southwest corner of the chateau. And then the chopper loomed overhead, hovering while its pilot obviously considered the landing site. The pilot ignored the wide open field between O building and the road, a clear site that would have made anyone disembarking an easy target.

Instead it began descending over a spot that would put it in the center of a triangle formed by the coordinate points of Lindsey, Marko and the secure area. Letters on the side of the dark green military-type chopper appeared to be in Cyrillic.

"T-1 to T-3," Tito said, "can you make the chopper?"

"It's an H1-17 out of the Czech Republic. It could be Czech cops," Ferris said.

"If only," Tito said. "Can you guarantee that?"

"No. Only that it's Czech. Don't know who is in it."

Tito added, "T-2, does this look like the chopper you saw last night?"

Marko answered, "Possibly. Same size and shape. Similar sound. But it was too dark for me to confirm absolutely."

Teal tugged at Lindsey's parka sleeve. "I don't think it's the police. There are very bad, evil feelings pouring out from the men in there."

A look of bleakness darkened Teal's eyes. Her face rippled into a frown. She was shivering in only a sweatshirt, jeans and tennis shoes. Lindsey stripped off her parka and put it on Teal

and gave Teal the knit gloves on loan from the botanist. Lindsey's adrenaline was running high, and the special gear she was carrying would help keep her plenty warm, though a part of her wondered how she could have even a drop of adrenaline left.

The chopper landed, its position slightly closer to Lindsey than to Marko or their secure area. "The girl thinks our visitors aren't cops," Lindsey said into her earwig as the side door of the chopper burst open, facing the chateau. The new arrivals were protected from everyone's line of fire except Marko's— and he only had a handgun and a PepperBall launcher, nothing that could stop the armed men pouring out of the chopper door.

Six invaders moved out in silence and scattered, hunched over and running like vermin toward the building and along the walls. They all wore uniform gray parkas. The chopper kept its rotor turning while two men headed for the back of the chateau. Three others headed toward the front and would pass not thirty feet from Marko and Jeremy. One stayed near the chopper. All of them carried shields and AKM-47s.

The man guarding the outside of the chopper kept staring into the woods, almost as if he could see Lindsey and Teal, although at a hundred feet away, he surely couldn't see into the snowy branches of the massive fir tree. "Don't move," she whispered to Teal.

And then she saw why the man seemed to be staring right at them. The early rays of the morning sun had risen to an angle that cast Lindsey's and Teal's deep footprints in the snow into sudden dark blue shadows, creating a path as clear as elephant tracks leading directly to them. Nonchalantly, he turned and walked toward the front of the chopper and then further on out toward the front of the chateau, as if he hadn't noticed a thing. But surely he must have.

The two guards moving along the chateau's rear wall disappeared around the far northwest corner. Lindsey relayed this to the team.

The chopper guard kept scanning the area in front of the chateau, and Lindsey could see his profile, lips moving rapidly. With his parka hood up, it was impossible to tell if he had an earwig, but he certainly could. She started thinking of all the signs of the struggle she'd been too intensely involved in to consider before: the smell of smoke, OC gas and explosives still in the air, craters the size of kiddie pools from the grenades, the many foot trails in the snow out front. Marko's and Jeremy's trail would jackknife back toward their meager hiding place at the tree. Marko surely had to know how vulnerable he and Jeremy were.

"This is T-1," Tito said. "The three men that entered the chateau have exited the building after looking around. They may have talked to the men we secured in the basement. The other two who disappeared in back of the chateau are now unaccounted for. If these guys aren't cops and are also after our package, we gotta hope they think they're too late. Otherwise, the Neutron Dance is about to begin."

Please keep this simple. Let it be cops. But they sure weren't wearing cop uniforms. Or Czech military uniforms.

"T-1 to T-3. If these bandits make one wrong move, take out the chopper."

"Copy," Ferris answered.

"All team. The three in front are splitting up. One is heading to the garage, one…stepping off the drive area and into the snow toward the west fountain, the other toward the east fountain."

What the hell were these guys doing?

Her attention snapped back to the man guarding the

chopper. He jerked and she heard him speak. A split second later he dropped to the ground facing Marko's tree and began firing his automatic at Marko and Jeremy. A steady barrage of weapon fire began in the front of the chateau, as well, magnified by all the earwigs also picking up the sound.

"Shit!" Marko said over the noise. "We're taking fire from two points. We are pinned! Can't hold out against two-point attack…shit!"

Lindsey heard a babble of sound, Ferris swearing mostly. Someone, probably Tia or Monique, was firing the Mk-48 at the chopper. The chopper pilot returned their fire.

Lindsey could also hear Jeremy's intermittent voice in the staccato microseconds between bullets, hysterically swearing and accusing Marko and the Athena women of total incompetence.

What happened to the MGL-140? Marko was in extreme danger. She knew what needed doing, but the team must avoid hitting each other in crossfire. "This is T-7. Permission to take out chopper guard."

Tito's voice came on next. "Hold, T-7. T-3, where are the grenades?"

"Launcher's frozen!" Ferris said. "I'm working on it."

"Damn!" Tito said. "Okay, T-7. T-3, T-4, T-5, hold fire. T-7, proceed."

"T-7, copy," Lindsey answered. To Teal she said, "Stay right here," and then she bolted out from the tree line running in a crouch, stun shield hanging on her left elbow, Taser in her left hand, Beretta in her right, aiming both at her target.

At thirty-some feet away from him, she saw him turn, in what seemed like uncanny timing. Too far for the Taser to work. It was shoot him or be mowed down. She fired the Beretta before the guard turned completely around, and hit

him somewhere in the chest. He continued firing into the side wall of the chateau as he fell, not entirely disabled.

Closer now, she shot him in the right shoulder with the Taser. He spasmed and released the automatic. She dashed toward it and picked it up just as more automatic weapon fire sounded behind her. She dropped into the snow instantly, shield in front of her like a barricade.

Behind her?

Someone was firing from exactly where she'd left Teal.

God oh God oh God, please no....

The helicopter, only forty feet away, lifted, blasting her with snow. It circled and headed for the tree line. In her earwig, the sound of steady gunfire from automatic weapons still sounded from the front of the chateau, somehow distinguishable over the noise of the chopper and the painful ringing in her ears. No chatter, though; Tito and Sam must be completely engaged in defending themselves and Marko.

"This is T-7," Lindsey said, forcing herself to move beyond the sick fear she was feeling for Teal. She was about to tell Ferris, Tia and Monique to fire with everything they had at the chopper, but when she risked a peek over the shield, she watched with a sinking feeling as the copter landed near the fir tree where Teal waited. *I should never have left her.*

"This is T-3. MGL ready, fixed on chopper. Go or no go? Your call, T-7."

Another hail of fire and Lindsey ducked down. She quickly popped up again and saw a shadowy figure dragging Teal from the giant fir and toward the chopper while a second man kept firing at Lindsey. This couldn't be happening. Where had they come from?

But, of course, something in her had known the instant the chopper guard had turned to fire at her. The whole front op-

eration at the chateau was a decoy to distract the Athena team from the two men who had disappeared, and, on cue from the chopper guard, who obviously *had* noted two sets of footprints in the snow, doubled back through the woods and found Teal.

Lindsey could see Teal struggling. The spunky girl jabbed her captor with something whitish, maybe an icicle. He released her and fell down. The man firing at Lindsey instantly stopped, turned and gun-butted Teal. She fell, and he scooped her up and carried her toward the chopper, his injured partner struggling to follow.

"*Help!*" Teal screamed.

"This is T-3, ready to take chopper out. Respond, T-7."

Lindsey gasped. "No! Hold your fire, T-3. They have the girl on the chopper."

Its blades thrusting snow in every direction, the chopper rose up and then flew over the chateau. Teal's face was pressed against the small side window. A splotch of red stood out against the white of the borrowed parka. She put her hand against the glass as if trying to reach out to Lindsey. And then she was gone.

I lost her…lost her…it was my fault….

Monique and Tia rushed down to secure the wounded chopper guard with unremarkable plastic ties. The idea of facing Monique and Tia and Sam—having to face anyone— seemed unbearable.

Heartsick, Lindsey headed toward Marko and Jeremy to see them rising, unscathed, from the snowy mound around the tree that had helped protect them in all the chaos of gunfire— which had finally gone silent.

Her ears ached with the high-pitched ringing and felt like

they were stuffed with packing popcorn. Everyone else apparently had the same problem because they were all shouting into the earwigs.

"That guy at the fountain fought like a crazed demon." The voice sounded like Tito's.

"I can't believe they're just leaving their dead and wounded." This was Sam's voice.

"All team," Tito said. "Clean up everything that's ours. Leave the rest. Whoever these shits are, they can try their own explaining to the Czech authorities. Not our problem. T-7, you're closest. Help T-6 *appropriate* the remaining car in the garage. Double-quick." This meant Lindsey and Sam should hot-wire the car if necessary. "The SUV was crowded coming out. Now we have another man with us, too. We don't have to be crowded. Let's take two cars back to the airport and then get the hell out of the country."

Glad to focus on something other than how miserable she felt, Lindsey ran toward the garage as Tito ordered Marko to load Jeremy into the nearest vehicle, the one in the garage. As she ran, Lindsey saw Marko trip. Jeremy turned and ran, hands still cuffed behind him. What an idiot. Marko quickly tackled him. In the earwig, she heard Marko say, "Try that again and you'll feel the effects of this stun shield. You won't like it."

Passing the fountain, she glanced at a dead man lying faceup and was shocked to recognize him. A bullet had bored into his left cheek and exited behind him, judging by the red pool of blood in the snow. The eyes in the face long scarred from an explosion stared up at nothing. Todor. He'd been so sure he was a part of greatness in the making. *Maybe you'll get a posthumous ribbon, you damn fool.*

"All team. We proceed to airport ASAP. T-2, you ride with

T-3 so you can upload the disks and report that we've lost the girl as we ride."

"We have a big problem." This was Ferris's voice. "Chopper fire knocked out the secure satellite-direct computer. Upload is no go."

Chapter 38

While Lindsey waited in one car outside the tobacco shop with Monique, Marko and Jeremy, Sam and the rest of Tito's team waited in the SUV. Tito and Ferris had gone inside to use the computer to send Allison the disastrous news about Teal and to upload Jeremy's disks.

Now, as they caravanned toward the airport, Lindsey wanted to go off somewhere, anywhere, to be by herself. Losing Teal was a crushing weight. A search of Jeremy had produced the key to the vehicle Lindsey rode in, making it unnecessary to break the lock and hot-wire the car. Monique was driving, and Marko sat in back with Lindsey, Jeremy between them.

She reminded herself that Allison and Christine now had the disks, that the op had at least saved sixteen other girls from Teal's fate and saved the world from Jeremy's cruel genetic manipulations. Having him sitting here beside her gave her the willies. And the image of Teal looking down at her from

the chopper haunted her. A teenage girl shouldn't have experiences that warranted such a bleak expression. *How could I have fallen for that decoy?*

"I need my medication," Jeremy said. "I'm really not feeling well."

"Some good news at last," Marko said. "I hope you're in so much pain your guts twist. In fact, I'd like an excuse to make your pain worse."

"Boorish imbecile," Jeremy muttered.

"This damn traffic!" Monique said. "I missed the green light. We're cut off from Tito and the others. Do you remember the way to the airport?"

"Yeah," Lindsey said, "if you take a left up ahead, you can bypass some of this mess."

Monique turned off the main drag, drove a few blocks and turned again to proceed on a parallel course through the quaint streets of the city's older parts. On the console, one of the secure cell phones rang. Monique handed Lindsey the receiver.

Sam said, "What's going on? Where are you?"

"Bad traffic. But we're coming."

"I have more bad news. Allison just called me and said the disks are bogus."

"Bogus! Are they sure? How can they possibly know so quickly?"

"Inconsistencies and nonsensical data were found on all four disks by the people who are thoroughly familiar with the Lab 33 procedures."

Lindsey glared at Jeremy. "We already know the disks are bogus. I bet Tito is going to take you apart limb from limb. This team won't leave this country without them."

Jeremy looked as amazed as Lindsey felt and said, "They can't be fake. I…Pietro…"

"Fake?" Marko said, echoing Jeremy.

"It seems the disks Jeremy had on him are worthless."

Another blow. No Teal. No disks. Only this repulsive creature sitting next to her. *Think! Think!* A failure so great was simply not acceptable. "We need to have another *chat* with our captive," Lindsey said, leaning over to look at both Jeremy and Marko meaningfully. "We may be delayed," she said to Sam. "We'll meet up with you at the airport. I'll keep you posted." Lindsey ended the call.

A gleam came into Marko's eyes. "Do I get to mangle this piece of canal scum?"

Lindsey nodded slowly, squinting at Jeremy, who studied the bindings on his wrists. He didn't look particularly crest-fallen, not like a man who'd been robbed of something incredibly valuable. Another idea occurred to her. If Pietro had somehow double-crossed Jeremy, then Pietro might have the genuine disks. "Monique, have you checked the location of the car you tagged?"

"Ah, no. I didn't know the man inside was a priority any longer. You want me to check?"

"Yeah."

Monique multitasked, driving and pushing buttons on her GPS tracker. Suddenly she swore. "According to the GPS tracker, the car I tagged is about two cars behind us!"

Jeremy gasped. "How can that be?"

The street narrowed, traffic decreased. Ancient buildings cast shadows everywhere despite the brightness of morning sun reflecting off snowy roofs.

"I see the car in my side mirror," Monique said. "The guy who got away at the chateau...what's his name?"

"Pietro," Jeremy said.

"A gun!" Monique blurted. "Get down!"

Lindsey ducked down, along with Marko and Jeremy.

"He's passed one of the cars behind us…now he's passing the next guy. Hang on!" Monique swerved into a sudden right. Probably thinking to fool the driver behind her, she swerved into a hard right again and hit the gas.

Lindsey was thrown against the door and Jeremy leaned into her. Repulsed, she shoved him away.

"What the *hell?*" Monique shrieked and slammed on the brakes.

Lindsey peeked over the top of the seat to see a very familiar black limo, the one that last night had chased her and Zuza. As if the limo driver had known where they were headed, it pulled into the oncoming traffic, blocking Monique's ability to pass. Lindsey twisted and looked behind. The car with Slick—Pietro—bore down at high speed. She caught a fleeting glimpse of the passenger behind the driver, the profile of a big man. It could only be…

"Pietro and Foo Hai are behind us. They are together," she yelled. "Those are Foo Hai's henchmen in the limo."

"Run for it!" Monique yelled, sliding across the console to throw open the front passenger door. She bolted out, squatted, and immediately drew silenced gunfire, the only indication of firing being the pinging sounds of the bullets against the car's metal.

Marko, also on the passenger side, leaped out and dragged Jeremy out by the handcuffs and they crouched behind the open rear door. Lindsey slid toward them and Marko pulled her out, too.

"That way!" Lindsey called and pointed to an alley behind them.

Scrambling together like flushed rabbits, they ducked into the first cross alleyway they came to, and then ran along the

back of a public building. Lindsey pointed to a stairwell descending below ground level. At the bottom a door stood ajar.

Their pursuers rounded the corner, firing, Foo Hai in the lead. If Pietro had Jeremy's genuine disks, why were these guys here? It had to be that Jeremy was lying to everyone. He had given Lindsey fake disks, but Pietro didn't have the real disks, either.

Lindsey dashed down the stairs with the other three following. Monique cried out suddenly. Lindsey looked back. "I'm okay." She motioned that Lindsey should keep going.

Inside the building, Lindsey slammed the door behind them. A janitor appeared, yelled at them and pointed to the door.

"He's saying the museum hasn't opened yet," Jeremy said, eyes darting as he scanned the room.

"Don't even think of bolting," Marko said.

"You can't let them get me," Jeremy wailed. He seemed to be hyperventilating. "Foo Hai will torture me."

It suddenly occurred to Lindsey that Jeremy was a thorough coward. He was losing it. So, given her own impression of Foo Hai as one extremely dangerous predator, she wasn't at all surprised that Jeremy would be deathly afraid of the dark, silent Asian.

Monique staggered and then fell. "My leg…"

A growing red patch was spreading on the thigh of her snow-camo pants below a round half-inch hole. The shocked janitor started speaking frantically in Czech.

Pounding noises came from the door. Their pursuers were kicking it.

Wide-eyed, the janitor pointed toward the other end of the room and spoke rapidly.

Weakly, Monique said, "I can't make it. You have to go."

The door rattled with the assault from outside.

"I'm okay here," Monique said. "Go!"

Marko scooped her up and carried her to a partial hiding place, a small chamber behind a display of some kind of contraption. He set her down gently. Dear God! The contraption was an ancient torture device. Lindsey glanced about and was stunned to see medieval weapons and, just beyond, skulls grinning at her.

The spitfire of silenced guns sounded outside and bullets pelted the door.

Chapter 39

"That way!" Jeremy pointed to a sign above a door in the opposite wall that Lindsey imagined probably said Exit. He ran toward the door.

The janitor called something after him.

"We'll come back as soon as we can," Lindsey said to Monique and then hurried after Marko, who was chasing Jeremy.

This museum was bizarre. Human skulls were used decoratively with other human bones in design structures. It looked like an ossuary for interior decorators. She dashed past an armchair-sized bell made entirely of skulls and bones and hanging next to a chandelier constructed from the same grisly building blocks. Beside the exit door hung a shield with bones forming a coat of arms.

How sick is this?

Gunshots, even though fired through a silencer, sounded

louder than before. Foo Hai was in the building. In horror, Lindsey saw reflected in one of the fish-eye security mirrors positioned at the corners of the room the janitor with his hands raised. Foo Hai shot the man in the throat, then pointed down at the floor where Monique lay and fired again.

F-ing bastard! Lindsey's cheeks burned with fury and helpless frustration.

Jeremy pushed the bar handle down. An alarm clanged. Lindsey and Marko rushed through the doorway following him. One of four messages on the door was in English and a fragment registered as she passed. *STOP. This exit is for extreme emergency only. This museum cannot be responsible for…*

The door shut silently. Aided by only a single dim orange mercury light above the museum door behind them, they scurried along in near darkness under a curved corrugated ceiling surrounded by storage crates. Ten feet from the door, a pipe railing was all that prevented someone from walking off an edge into blackness below. She couldn't see if the drop was five feet, fifty feet, or bottomless.

Five feet beyond the beginning of the rail another dim orange light revealed looming structures vaguely resembling an underground parking garage, except that the spaces between the levels were far too low. The place looked like it might be a condemned mausoleum. The frigid air smelled of dankness and decay. They scrambled down one flight of narrow stairs.

"Where the hell are we?" Marko pulled out a small but high-beam flashlight from his pocket. The orange light was now exceedingly faint.

"Look for the tunnel…" Jeremy said, hyperventilating as he tried to speak. "The janitor said…" *Gasp* "…something about this being…" *Gasp* "…an old bomb shelter and there's…" *Gasp* "…a tunnel through the old ruins. An exit."

That poor hapless janitor. Probably dead. *And Monique!* But they must race on. More stairs descended on either side of a dark chasm.

"Right or left?" she asked.

Jeremy's gasp was almost a sob. "I don't *know.* How could things have gone so badly?" He was panting. "I planned everything so carefully."

Lindsey hated agreeing with Jeremy on anything, but he was right. She could make out old yellow warning tape stretched in front of them with a message in Czech. Probably, *danger* repeated over and over.

She led left and they moved quickly but carefully along the tape, which simply ended, trailing an unhelpful sash over the edge of the chasm. Marko jerked the tape off the rail, crumpled it, and stuffed it in his pocket.

"Souvenir?" Lindsey asked.

"Maybe Foo Hai and his men will run off the edge," Marko said.

Jeremy nodded frantically. "That would be good. Yes, very good." He now seemed close to babbling. "That greasy Italian lowlife criminal has betrayed me. I just knew I shouldn't trust him. I knew. I knew."

Here the greenish glow of bioluminescent spores and mushrooms spread along the base of the multilayered mausoleum-like structure on the other side of the ditch. There must be a lot of rotting wood, Lindsey decided. This place looked like it was a cave-in waiting to happen. Less than twenty feet above her head she could see barely discernible features of an old bridge or aqueduct. Was this now supporting a modern street or parking lot? The thought was not reassuring.

In the distance ahead, a single drop of water dripped into

what sounded like a pool in an echoing tunnel. They moved as fast as the scary dimness allowed toward the sound. Another dim, flickering orange light revealed a low Roman-esque archway.

"That way." Lindsey stepped forward, but as she put her weight down, she slipped and crunched through an icy surface into black, vile-smelling water that found its way through her boot to her foot. The odors around the frigid puddle intensi-fied into smells of mold. And a swampy methane smell. A spi-derweb brushed her cheek, and she shivered and clenched her teeth to swallow back a scream.

"Move closer to the wall." Marko flashed his tight beam of light along ancient stone with nooks and crannies that probably harbored slithery things. She heard the squeaking of rats from somewhere distressingly nearby. The beam traveled up and across ancient wood and cross-timbers as if they'd entered a basement several centuries old—which they probably had. Bendrich had said that old Prague was built on layers of ruins people hadn't bothered to deconstruct. Marko especially would have to duck to pass under the old, sagging, creaking beams.

"I think I'm going to faint," Jeremy gasped.

Lindsey shared the feeling, but would bite off and eat her tongue before she would admit it. Where was that archway? It had disappeared. Her only guide was the occasional drop of water, its sound magnified in the echo of what had to be the tunnel the guard had mentioned.

The sound of the alarm from inside the museum above grew loud. Lindsey, Jeremy and Marko all stopped and looked behind them. The emergency door had opened, maybe the length of a city block away, casting a quick flash of weak light on the layers of past civilizations and on the silhouettes of Foo

Hai, his henchmen and Pietro, their mutterings muffled but audible.

Lindsey hardly breathed as she, Marko and Jeremy crept toward where she thought she had seen the archway. A gun fired and the bullet zinged off a stone behind them and then another.

"Sweet Madonna! How could they have known so quickly that we chose this direction?" Marko whispered. "How could they have found us at all?"

Mercifully the archway appeared again, revealed by a strangely iridescent, blue-purple glowing ball that shifted... and then was gone.

Every hair on Lindsey's head stood up.

"What the hell was that?" Marko asked.

"I think..." Jeremy panted. "I mean, I thought...that Pietro might have put a bug on my car." Jeremy evidently hadn't seen the strange light. "But now..." *Gasp.* "I think it's me. In my jacket pocket." He pulled out something that looked like a vitamin capsule.

Marko slammed Jeremy against the stone wall, snatched the unit and pitched it like a bowling ball along the ground behind them. It immediately drew fire.

Bullets must have hit something that released a gassy methane odor, because the air ignited with a boom. Behind her, stone and brick rained down. The floor was suddenly moving as terrified rats scurried toward who knew where.

A wooden beam above Marko creaked and broke. Rocks tumbled from the walls beside her. Water gushed from somewhere, smelling a thousand years old. An ancient cistern? Here and there, pockets of flame burned greenish.

Marko was nowhere in sight. And no Jeremy, either. Lindsey crouched, hand over her nose to keep out still-de-

scending dust, climbed up a step and peeked over the top of rubble now blocking the way back to the museum entrance.

His back against the remains of the stone wall, Jeremy stood on the other side, a look of sheer terror holding his eyes wide open. A stocky Asian man jumped over a beam that pinned down another man and ran up to an apparently paralyzed Jeremy, gun-butted him and dragged him backward.

In the light of the green fires, Lindsey recognized the spiderweb tattoo on Pietro's neck as he struggled against the weight of the beam pressing down on him. Blood, that in this dim light looked black, ran from his mouth. Pietro was in big trouble. Probably a crushed spleen. He wasn't going to be walking out of here on his own…if at all.

"Hey! Foo Hai! Help me out here! You owe me!" he called out.

Foo Hai stepped out of the shadows, smiled, raised a gun, aimed it at Pietro's chest and fired. Pietro died with a look of rage pasted on his face.

Foo Hai signaled two men to move the beam blocking their way, and as they did so, Foo Hai shoved Pietro into the chasm with his foot. Pietro dropped in, followed quickly by the sound of a splash.

"Marko?" she whispered. She turned, backed down from the rubble mound and stared into the dimness. "Marko?"

A groan issued from the chasm. The rock avalanche that separated her from Foo Hai and Jeremy had taken Marko over the ledge. Water continued to pour into the trench or whatever it was. She crawled to the edge and called down. "Marko? Are you okay?"

"Nnnnn…help me…"

He couldn't be more than five or six feet below her, but things were crawling up out of the crevice. Spiders. Dozens

of them. One climbed onto her sleeve. She jumped up and flicked it off to see three climbing up her leg. She flapped at them, kicked in a blind frenzy that left her shaking and sickened, sweating and clammy. "Oh my God, oh my God, oh my God."

She turned toward the archway and ran. Blindly, heart beating wildly. She tripped on something and fell. She scrambled to her feet and thought, *What am I doing?*

She couldn't leave anyone here, and especially not Marko. She turned back, made her feet move. She'd failed at everything she'd set out to do on this trip. Teal gone, and now, coward that she was, she had come close to abandoning Marko.

Foo Hai had probably killed Monique and the janitor and he now had Jeremy and would soon unleash Jeremy's brand of evil into the world. *Oh, Teal, I'm so sorry...* What would the Kestonians do with Teal? And Marko....

She teetered at the edge of the dark chasm, her heart pounding so hard in her chest, it seemed about to burst. Pain gripped her insides and she doubled over and groaned, fighting the need to vomit, shaking uncontrollably, unable to take a step or even think.

Chapter 40

"Lindsey!"

Marko's voice sounded strong, and it reached Lindsey like a lifeline.

"I'm here…I'm coming," she answered.

She would rather be dead than have things end this way. Nothing, not Foo Hai, not the spiders, nothing could be worse. Hating herself for her cowardice, and still shaking, she crawled to the ledge, scrunching small, hairy things underneath her as she moved. She could hear water still rushing into the dark void.

By the light of the nearest rubble fire, Lindsey saw something that could help. A stout plank. The remnants of some ancient footbridge, maybe. Perhaps a foot and a half wide, six inches thick and eight feet long, the plank spanned the crevice where it narrowed, just a few feet away from Marko. Like the whole damn place, the plank was alive with spiders. Webs hung from it like curtains. She crawled to it, dragged it over

to her side, knocked off some of the webs and tiny scurrying bodies and dragged it back toward Marko.

She extended one end of the plank down to him and heard it hit water. He started sloshing around. "Will it help?"

"It's a beautiful board," he said. "Got to dig myself out a bit. A mother-bitch of a hunk of stonework has my ankle pinned. Where's Jeremy?"

"Foo Hai has him." Swatting spiders and fighting nausea, she told Marko what had happened. While he grunted, strained and cussed in Italian, she noticed what looked to be a light far off to her right. Maybe the exit.

"Hold the noise down," she said. "I don't think they can escape back the way we all came in. They will eventually climb past this rubble to come here. That will take them some time. I see a light. But we may not have much time. I keep hearing more rocks fall into this crevice—whatever it is."

"Antique shit hole."

She actually giggled, partly amused and partly out of nervousness. "Yeah, this place is toxic. Green mushrooms don't grow in places that are optimal for humans." She recalled a science class in which the professor said that Scandinavians used to mark their way through the forests using smears of glow-in-the-dark spores. Hmmm…

In the distance, another boom let loose and a bright, fiery green glow spread through this hideous underworld then snuffed out. Doubtless another pocket of gas exploding. Maybe Foo Hai's efforts to find a way out had triggered it. "We need to exit, Marko. Fast."

Think! How could they get out, get away? How could she recapture Jeremy? Jeremy must have the genuine data on the Lab 33 procedures and the sixteen modified girls hidden safely somewhere.

Marko groaned again. "The water's up to my neck. It's so cold I can hardly move, but it keeps the pain from…. Aaaughhh!" Marko splashed wildly, angled the plank, hoisted himself up and caught Lindsey's arm. He was waterlogged and heavy, but he clambered up onto the ledge. He lay there shivering. She threw herself on top of him, embraced him, shaking even more violently than he was. "Thank you, God," she whispered. "Are you okay? Can you wiggle your feet?"

Marko moved his right foot and then as he moved the left one he winced. But then he grinned at her. "I will work around it."

At that moment, Lindsey knew something, a precious something that she could only tuck into her heart since the timing was so rotten. Yet this new certainty stopped her shaking. She would do anything, give her life, to get him out of this place.

"I have only one bullet left. You?" she asked.

"Wet gun. Ammo long gone."

"Hold on to me while I lean over the edge and retrieve that 'beautiful' board. I have an idea."

"One of those American so-crazy-it-just-might-work ideas?"

"Yeah. One of those," she said. Foo Hai must be feeling as desperate to escape this cold hell as Lindsey was. A quick recon revealed that the light farther on indeed entered from an exit. But they needed Jeremy. The opening was passable, but she and Marko—who, though limping badly, uttered not one word of complaint—set blocks in front of the opening so that no light shone in. The way out would not draw attention.

She began to smear little dabs of dimly glowing spores to mark where she laid the plank across the chasm. No one could pass by here and not see this little glowing trail and footbridge.

She hoped it looked as if locals might sometimes use the

plank. Surely, Foo Hai would reason, there would not be a plank across the chasm unless it led to somewhere, and that somewhere would most likely have an exit. He would have to at least try it.

The plank actually dead-ended. There was no exit on this side. They took up ambush positions, Marko on top of a beam that overlooked the path and Lindsey squatting down behind a half-fallen stone wall. Lindsey had secured the Danger tape to the end of the plank and entirely covered the tape with peaty dirt. The other end of the tape she held in her hand.

With glowing fingers, she waited and watched and listened. After an excruciating three or four minutes, she heard whispers. No more than thirty feet away. The men were past the rockfall now and should soon reach the plank. The still-burning fire above revealed two Asians, followed by Jeremy, followed by Foo Hai.

They stopped. Argued. A flunky came across first. Jeremy kept saying that he refused to cross the plank, but Foo Hai aimed a big Glock at him and, of course, he did. Next came the second flunky, and then Foo Hai. The minute he was across, Lindsey yanked on the Danger tape, drawing the plank to her and off the crevice. The four men, stunned, turned toward the chasm and stared.

Marko, a stone the size of a grapefruit in his hand, dropped onto one of the Asians. The lackeys were his responsibility. Lindsey stood and aimed the Beretta at Foo Hai and commanded, "Drop your—!"

But before she could finish the sentence, he was firing. She heard Jeremy scream as she placed a neat shot between Foo Hai's eyes.

Foo Hai fell. Marko had bashed the first blackguard immediately into unconsciousness. He was rolling, struggling

with the second thug, then bashed him into unconsciousness, as well. Jeremy had fallen onto the floor and kept screaming.

"Shut up, Jeremy," she shouted.

He obeyed, but he lay bleeding and moaning.

From behind, Marko gave her the biggest, strongest bear hug she would probably ever feel. He pulled back and winked. "Do we really need to bother with Jeremy? He's obviously going to die here. I say we leave him."

"You can't leave me," Jeremy shrieked.

"Why shouldn't we?" Lindsey asked, staring down at Jeremy in disgust. "I think Marko is right. You deserve to be left in this dark hole to bleed to death."

She stepped away from Jeremy. "Let's go." She bent to the plank and placed it back across the dark chasm.

"You can't leave me."

"Sure we can," Marko said, sounding quite happy.

Lindsey stepped onto the plank. Jeremy howled. "No. Wait. Take me to a doctor. I will give you the information. All of it."

Jeremy, who had been clutching his wounded leg, fumbled to make the leg bend and then fumbled with the heel of his shoe. It pivoted open and he took out what Lindsey immediately recognized as a flash drive.

She returned to stand over him. "You lied before. How can we know this isn't just another trick? I'm telling you, Jeremy, that if you don't convince me you're telling the truth, we'll take your flash drive and then leave you here."

Jeremy's hands, covered with blood, were back on his wound. Lindsey wasn't sure now whether the wound was superficial, as she originally thought, or if he in fact might be seriously hurt. "I suggest you talk quickly."

"I swear, this is what you want. Names. Identities. Talents.

Locations. All the genetic procedures. Would I have left this behind? No!"

"How did you set up the kidnapping? To tell you the truth, Jeremy, you don't seem like a particularly capable criminal."

"It wasn't me, not really. There is someone. A blackmailer. Someone who knows all about Aldrich and his lab. After the lab went down, I contacted this person, at first pretending to be Aldrich. I thought I might develop the same kind of mutually beneficial relationship with him. I was stupid. I thought their relationship had been profitable and amicable. But this bastard has been blackmailing me ever since. He put me in contact with the Colombians."

Excited, sure that he was telling the truth and that this was information that Christine and Allison didn't know, Lindsey leaned close to Jeremy. "What's his name?"

"I don't know his name. He only identifies himself as A."

Another lie. Lindsey scoffed and stood. "Let's leave him."

"Please, no! I swear on my life I do not know his name. I have never met him. He signs e-mails and faxes only with the letter A and there is always a spider image or spiderweb on them."

Did she believe this? Jeremy was panicked, afraid he was dying, and he'd given up the flash drive, which Lindsey did believe held the genuine information. That he didn't even know who was blackmailing him actually had the ring of truth.

"I buy it, Linds," Marko said, confirming her judgment.

She nodded. Marko used two plastic handcuffs to make a tourniquet. Toting Jeremy in a fireman's carry, Marko lugged the twisted scientist across the plank, then, supporting Jeremy between them, they made their way to the tunnel opening. She called Sam to pick them up. She figured Tito and his team would be on their way out of the country and Sam and Jeremy would be on a military plane back to the States within the hour.

Chapter 41

At 11:05 a.m., Lindsey leaned on the corridor wall while Marko used the key card to her hotel room and opened the door. He held it for her. Just pulling herself from the wall required extreme effort, but she managed it and walked inside, beyond exhausted, too wired to relax, shaky with adrenaline letdown, sore in a hundred places, weak, so hungry she probably couldn't eat, as thirsty as if she'd been in a desert, and worst of all, still feeling like a worthless failure over losing Teal. K-bar's deep voice boomed in her memory, "We'll have to talk about what you could have done differently."

Marko followed her in and let the door close. "Want to talk?" he asked. "Or do you want to be alone?"

Alone? God, no. *I want to sit on your lap and have you rock me to sleep.* But she was a sullen wretch and probably looked like hell. Why would anyone want to be with her? Es-

pecially after going through the same ordeal. Marko had sprained his ankle and said he had bruises in eighty places. If he didn't want to stay, though, he wouldn't have let that door close.

"I don't want to be alone."

He stepped in, eyes fixed on her, reading her. Bless him. He had to feel like more of a mess than she did—at least physically. He brushed her cheek with the back of his hand, a grimy, dirt-encrusted hand that matched hers.

"Want a drink?" she asked.

"Sounds great." He took off his parka and dropped it on the floor.

She stripped off her borrowed parka, tossing it on the chair at the window. She grabbed a water bottle off a table and sank into the chair. "Make mine strong. Double scotch."

As she gulped water, the image of Teal's face in the helicopter's window flashed into Lindsey's mind yet again. Anguish immediately struck her heart. Teal's being snatched away again was simply too hard to bear. She extinguished the image by focusing on Marko's profile as he stood at the bar.

Her duties were not yet over, however, and she used a secure cell phone, freshly supplied by Bendrich, and punched in Allison's number. Allison knew already from Sam that they had lost Teal again. Mercifully, Lindsey wasn't required to go over the sickening, embarrassing, sad details of her failure. "I wanted to talk with you personally," she said to Allison, "about the issue of Jeremy's blackmailer, this mysterious A."

"Sam briefed me. I've talked it over with key insiders, including Christine. The connection to A is an astonishing and profoundly important discovery, Lindsey. Since the takedown of Lab 33, we've known about this woman who is called a

number of names, but is mostly known as Arachne. Just as she did with Jeremy, if she identifies herself at all she uses the letter A, and all communications from her that we've been able to get our hands on concluded with the spiderweb Jeremy described."

"A is a woman?" She felt surprise at first, but then a strange, inexplicable sense of correctness.

"Yes. She seems bent on bringing down the Academy. Most details about her are closely held, but I can tell you that even though we don't know yet who she is, let alone how to stop her, what you've found out confirms that she has something to do with Lab 33 and that her influence continues to spread."

Exhaustion was hitting hard now. Lindsey said goodbye. Marko handed her the drink. She took one good slug, then said, "I'm going to shower and then I have to lie down. Stay…if you'd like." The thought of Marko leaving evoked a panic that clutched her threat. "I want you here with me."

He gave her a gentle smile and plunked himself with a sigh onto the edge of her bed. Carrying the drink with her, she headed for the shower. When she finished and came out, smelling like a fresh apricot, Marko rose and headed for his own cleanup. She lay down on top of the bed, expecting that they would talk after he was clean and comfortable.

Lindsey woke suddenly, totally disoriented. Was it day? Night? Where was she?

"*Cara mia,* you are so damn beautiful."

Marko, who had apparently been watching her sleep, stroked a finger across her forehead.

Prague. Warm room with a fire in her lovely ceramic stove. Teal still missing. Lindsey's fault. She felt tears welling. They spilled warmly onto her cheeks.

"Don't cry, *cara mia.*"

Marko kissed her. Softly at first, but then he gently inserted his tongue into her mouth, as if he might gently invade her body in another way, and began to explore. At first sadness held her back, but his passion, the tenderness of his hands as they caressed her neck and shoulders, proved irresistible. Life-affirming.

She wrapped her arms around his naked torso and responded, wildly returning the kiss and groaning. She needed this release. Wanted it. Had craved melding with Marko for days.

His hand slid over a breast and his lips soon kissed where his palm had caressed. She moaned again and sighed his name. "Marko."

He kissed her other breast that ached for the touch of his lips. "Oh, yes."

With one hand he spread her legs slightly and then he used the lightest of touches to stroke the inside of her thigh.

The wonderful burning deep in her belly flared and she ran her fingers into his hair and pulled. "You want me?" Marko asked.

"Yes. Yes."

"Not too soon. You'll like the waiting for it."

His kisses moved slowly down her belly, kissing, licking. Pushing slightly on his head, both hands now in his hair, she encouraged him to go lower.

When he finally spread her legs even further, she felt any sense of him and herself slipping away. There was only the delicious, intimate licking. "Uuugh," she moaned. "Ohhh."

She was on the verge of exploding right then but he sat up over her, opened and rolled on a condom that had been lying on the sheet beside them. For a moment the magic became reality again and she knew he'd planned this. And that was good, too.

She helped him inside and the slow rhythm of lovemaking began until his body grew slick and the speed of their movements together increased. She was losing herself. Losing…

The climax took her and she sensed he'd come, too.

The next time Lindsey woke, Marko lay beside her, one arm resting across her belly. She moved, intending to slip away to the bathroom a moment before returning to him. She didn't want to wake him. He surely needed rest.

But at her first slight movement, he awoke immediately. He grinned at her. She grinned back, and they kissed.

"Want to go again?" he asked.

"You?"

"I will if you will."

Her stomach growled. They laughed out loud. She said, "Don't you want to sleep?"

"No. I have never felt more alive." He sat up in the bed beside her. "I'm totally awake." He seemed to be glowing with happiness. She could tell—Marko was projecting into the future, thinking that maybe Lindsey could be the one.

She turned her head away from him. "I keep going over things I might have done, should have done, to keep them from taking Teal. K-bar would have a thousand complaints."

He took her chin and made her look at him. "You know, I just thought you might be doing that. There wasn't a thing you could have done differently, Linds."

"Maybe."

Again her stomach growled. He rolled over her and onto his feet. "We need food. You need to have your thoughts distracted. Let's dress and go out."

"What time is it?"

Marko bent over the small clock on the bedside stand. "7:30."

He was right. Getting out of the room would be distracting, and she was wide-awake. They dressed warmly and left the hotel.

As they had done with their ice displays in Old Town, ice festival participants had set up brightly lit statues the entire length of the boulevard leading to the National Museum. She and Marko crossed the street, dodging still-active traffic. "I bought a wurst that was damn good," Marko said. "Maybe we can find the guy again."

They passed a beautiful and intriguing sculpture depicting "The Firebird and Ivan in the Garden of Golden Apples." Spotlights of flickering gold and red tones made the gorgeous ice phoenix seem to be truly on fire. Marko especially liked the next sculpture depicting a "rusalka," a pre-Christian lusty female forest spirit with abundant wild hair curlicuing around huge naked breasts. Her head was thrown back in laughter.

When they passed a tender scene of "The Lady in White" teaching young Bethushka, a child who is supposed to be spinning flax, to dance, Marko said, "You would make a wonderful mother, Linds."

She let the comment pass.

Her cell phone rang. They had found the vendor Marko was seeking. "Have him put lots of mustard on mine," she said, and then answered the phone. The caller's number she knew belonged to Christine Evans.

"We want to keep you posted, Lindsey. Teal has sent images and feelings to Stefan. She seems strong and determined again. Images were of a man with a terribly ugly, scarred face, and then of the inside of a plane or helicopter—and on the control panel is a Kestonian flag. She knows we

will be looking for her now. And this must be her way to ask for our help."

"Put me on follow-up. I'm ready to go after her. Right now."

Marko, holding wursts in both fists, said, "Tell her I'll go with you."

"My colleague, Marko Savin, is with me. He's also ready to roll."

"I'll keep you, and Marko, in mind for backup. But getting into Kestonia is going to be extremely tricky, and I have a perfect Athena grad who should be able to do so without suspicion. But be assured, we are on it here, and either I or Allison will keep you posted."

After Lindsey snapped the phone shut, Marko handed her her wurst and grinning, said, "I'll go anywhere with you."

"Christine said they are sending someone else." Lindsey couldn't keep her despair out of her voice.

"Linds. *Cara mia.* What's wrong?"

"Nothing." She bit into the wurst, her mouth watering with the taste of mustard and spices. They moved away from the vendor, strolling slowly among the crowd past the sculptures. They passed a violin player and accordionist playing a sweet tune, entertaining to make a few euros from tips.

"You sound…so sad."

"The Kestonians have Teal! And now Allison has refused to put me onto the trail. I failed. And I'm a…" She couldn't bear to say "coward" out loud. "I almost wasn't able to pull myself together to figure out a way to help you."

"But you did. I heard you gagging with fear. I felt your shakes. But I don't think it's what you think it is. It's just your body's way of telling you that you're forcing yourself."

"I shouldn't have to force myself, goddamn it!"

He stopped walking and captured her gaze. "But look at

what you—we—*have* accomplished. Sixteen young girls are safe because of what you did. And Loschetter's instructions for making these extraordinary girls was kept out of really bad hands."

"I'm a fraud, Marko. I was scared spitless in that hellacious underground place."

"Who wasn't? You are human, not a robot. But you know what, Linds, I think you *are* a bit of a fraud."

She hadn't expected him to agree, not really. She felt a prick of anger.

After the briefest pause, Marko went on. "It's not that you lack courage, though, which is what you seem to be thinking. You have plenty of courage. You saved me twice this morning. Those guys with the automatics would have nailed me if you hadn't stopped the one by the chopper. You figured a way to pull me out of the ditch. You took on Foo Hai. You had a huge fear, and you beat it. But I think you fight your true nature."

"Which is?"

"You're an artist, Linds. I've been asking myself over and over, why does she do this stuff? You aren't like me. A sort of adrenaline freak. All this crazy daredevil stuff isn't your first choice. If you could be totally honest with yourself, you might quit it."

"What nonsense are you talking?"

"I think the far-out risk-taking goes way back. To prove to K-bar that you are as tough as any son he could have had."

She started to spit out some kind of angry protest, but he smiled at her, a gentle smile. A smile that also seemed to be saying, I accept you as you really are.

So instead of yelling at him, she thought a moment about her relationship to her father, to the tough K-bar she knew her

father to be. There was truth in Marko's comments. She could admit that. "When I saw all those spiders, for a few minutes I was four years old again," Lindsey said. "We were camping at night and my parents told me not to move and set me down on a rock and went to get firewood. I was so scared I started shaking. A spider crawled onto me, and I screamed my lungs out. My father came racing back and looked disgusted. 'No daughter of mine is afraid of such things,' he said. I've just always had this terror of spiders."

"You sure pushed past that down in the third level of Hades."

"Yeah." Lindsey smiled, suddenly self-conscious. "I did. I guess I've always felt that I was unlovable unless I was an all-out thrill freak."

"You don't need to be a daredevil. You don't need to prove anything to anybody. You proved that you could do whatever it takes long ago. And you sure as hell are no coward."

"You don't understand. It's not just that I get…scared. I love the thrills. I love the excitement. I've, well, it's not like I haven't thought about…I just don't think I could give it up now. I'm hooked, too."

"I think I *do* understand. And who says you have to give up all thrills and excitement? We could still ski and skydive and scuba. Hell, we can go climb mountains together. Dozens of things for adventure. There are lots of thrills and excitement that don't involve risking your life by confronting people who might try to kill you."

"Marko—"

"How about taking the risk to be more honest about who you are? Dare to be you. The wonderful artist that you are is good enough for anyone—even K-bar."

The fiddler and the accordion player stopped close by, playing now for her and Marko. They were playing the French

love song, "Plaisir d'Amour." She thought of its first lines, "The joys of love are but a moment long."

Longing welled up, nearly choking her. She loved Marko. She'd known it beyond a doubt when she helped him out of that crevice. She suspected that he might love her. And it seemed that he understood her maybe better than she understood herself. She'd been on a very long daredevil journey. Maybe it *was* time, now, to step onto a different road. She knew that someday she wanted a deeper life of family and commitment. She wanted that joy of love that the songs all sang about, even if only for a short time. Was it really possible to have it both ways? Excitement and responsibility?

"What do you think, Linds? Am I right?" Marko put a euro in the tin cup their serenaders held out.

She took Marko's arm and then another bite of the scrumptious wurst as they began to walk together again. "Yeah. You are."

Why not make some changes? She could follow her heart, fully and completely.

She could start by eliminating the extreme, high-risk stuff she did just to prove she could. Just thinking about letting that part of her life go felt right. Felt easy. She did have commitments, though. She would take dangerous Athena assignments, but only when the stakes would justify risking her life—the life of someone who was loved and needed.

They'd circled back around to the ice sculpture of the wild and lusty "rusalka," her head thrown back in laughter.

"So," he said, "here's something to think about risking. Admit that you love me. I dare you."

Even though K-bar admired Marko, he would protest—at

least at first, but she'd outlast him, wear him down. Lindsey tilted her chin up, matching the same confident angle as the rusalka, smiled at Marko and drew him closer. *Challenge accepted.*

* * * * *

*Don't miss the next exciting chapter
in Athena Force CHARADE
by Kate Donovan
available October 2007.*

Silhouette®

Romantic
SUSPENSE

Sparked by Danger, Fueled by Passion.

When evidence is found that Mallory Dawes intends to sell the personal financial information of government employees to "the Russian," OMEGA engages undercover agent Cutter Smith. Tailing her all the way to France, Cutter is fighting a growing attraction to Mallory while at the same time having to determine her connection to "the Russian." Is Mallory really the mouse in this game of cat and mouse?

Look for

Stranded with a Spy

by *USA TODAY* bestselling author

Merline Lovelace

October 2007.

Also available October wherever you buy books:

BULLETPROOF MARRIAGE *(Mission: Impassioned)*
by Karen Whiddon

A HERO'S REDEMPTION *(Haven)* by Suzanne McMinn

TOUCHED BY FIRE by Elizabeth Sinclair

Visit Silhouette Books at www.eHarlequin.com   SRS27553

Silhouette Desire

There was only one man for the job—
an impossible-to-resist maverick
she knew she didn't dare fall for.

MAVERICK
(#1827)

BY *NEW YORK TIMES* BESTSELLING AUTHOR
JOAN HOHL

"Will You Do It for One Million Dollars?"

Any other time, Tanner Wolfe would have balked at being
hired by a woman. Yet Brianna Stewart was desperate to
engage the infamous bounty hunter. The price was just
high enough to gain Tanner's interest…Brianna's beauty
definitely strong enough to keep it. But he wasn't about
to allow her to tag along on his mission. He worked
alone. Always had. Always would. However, he'd never
confronted a more determined client than Brianna. She
wasn't taking no for an answer—not about anything.

Perhaps a million-dollar bounty was not the only thing
this maverick was about to gain….

Look for MAVERICK

Available October 2007 wherever you buy books.

HARLEQUIN®

Mediterranean
NIGHTS™

Sail aboard the luxurious Alexandra's Dream and experience glamour, romance, mystery and revenge!

Coming in October 2007...

AN AFFAIR TO REMEMBER

by

Karen Kendall

When Captain Nikolas Pappas first fell in love with Helena Stamos, he was a penniless deckhand and she was the daughter of a shipping magnate. But he's never forgiven himself for the way he left her—and fifteen years later, he's determined to win her back.

Though the attraction is still there, Helena is hesitant to get involved. Nick left her once...what's to stop him from doing it again?

REQUEST YOUR FREE BOOKS!

2 FREE NOVELS PLUS 2 FREE GIFTS!

Silhouette® Romantic

SUSPENSE

Sparked by Danger, Fueled by Passion!

YES! Please send me 2 FREE Silhouette® Romantic Suspense novels and my 2 FREE gifts. After receiving them, if I don't wish to receive any more books, I can return the shipping statement marked "cancel." If I don't cancel, I will receive 4 brand-new novels every month and be billed just $4.24 per book in the U.S., or $4.99 per book in Canada, plus 25¢ shipping and handling per book plus applicable taxes, if any*. That's a savings of at least 15% off the cover price! I understand that accepting the 2 free books and gifts places me under no obligation to buy anything. I can always return a shipment and cancel at any time. Even if I never buy another book from Silhouette, the two free books and gifts are mine to keep forever.

240 SDN EEX6   340 SDN EEYJ

Name	(PLEASE PRINT)

Address	Apt. #

City	State/Prov.	Zip/Postal Code

Signature (if under 18, a parent or guardian must sign)

Mail to the Silhouette Reader Service™:
IN U.S.A.: P.O. Box 1867, Buffalo, NY 14240-1867
IN CANADA: P.O. Box 609, Fort Erie, Ontario L2A 5X3

Not valid to current Silhouette Intimate Moments subscribers.

Want to try two free books from another line?
Call 1-800-873-8635 or visit www.morefreebooks.com.

* Terms and prices subject to change without notice. NY residents add applicable sales tax. Canadian residents will be charged applicable provincial taxes and GST. This offer is limited to one order per household. All orders subject to approval. Credit or debit balances in a customer's account(s) may be offset by any other outstanding balance owed by or to the customer. Please allow 4 to 6 weeks for delivery.

Your Privacy: Silhouette is committed to protecting your privacy. Our Privacy Policy is available online at www.eHarlequin.com or upon request from the Reader Service. From time to time we make our lists of customers available to reputable firms who may have a product or service of interest to you. If you would prefer we not share your name and address, please check here. ☐

SRS07

nocturne™

Look for
NIGHT MISCHIEF

by

NINA BRUHNS

Lady Dawn Maybank's worst nightmare
is realized when she accidentally conjures
a demon of vengeance, Galen McManus. What
she doesn't realize is that Galen plans to teach
her a lesson in love—one she'll never forget....

DARK
ENCHANTMENTS

Available October wherever you buy books.

Don't miss the last installment of Dark Enchantments,
SAVING DESTINY by Pat White, available November.

HARLEQUIN® Romance®

New York Times bestselling author

DIANA PALMER

Handsome, eligible ranch owner Stuart York knew Ivy Conley was too young for him, so he closed his heart to her and sent her away—despite the fireworks between them. Now, years later, Ivy is determined not to be treated like a little girl anymore…but for some reason, Stuart is always fighting her battles for her. And safe in Stuart's arms makes Ivy feel like a woman…his woman.

Winter Roses

Available November.

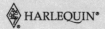

EVERLASTING LOVE™

Every great love has a story to tell™

An uplifting story of love and survival that spans generations.

Hayden MacNulty and Brian Conway both lived on Briar Hill Road their whole lives. As children they were destined to meet, but as a couple Hayden and Brian have much to overcome before romance ultimately flourishes.

Look for

The House on Briar Hill Road

by award-winning author
Holly Jacobs

Available October wherever you buy books.

ATHENA FORCE

Heart-pounding romance and thrilling adventure.

A new 12 book continuity begins this August with *Line of Sight* by Rachel Caine.

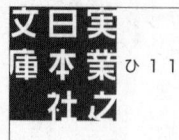
はく　ぎん
白銀ジャック

2010年10月15日　初版第一刷発行
2010年10月25日　初版第三刷発行

著　者　　ひがしの けい ご
　　　　　東野圭吾

発行者　　増田義和
発行所　　株式会社実業之日本社
　　　　　〒104-8233　東京都中央区銀座 1-3-9
　　　　　電話 [編集]03(3562)2051 [販売]03(3535)4441
　　　　　ホームページ　http://www.j-n.co.jp/
印刷所　　大日本印刷株式会社
製本所　　大日本印刷株式会社

フォーマットデザイン　鈴木正道（Suzuki Design）

初出誌
月刊ジェイ・ノベル2008年10月号～2010年9月号

＊本作品はフィクションであり、実在の個人および団体とは、一切関係ありません。（編集部）